THE DAEDALUS
INCIDENT

THE DAEDALUS INCIDENT

Michael J. Martinez

NIGHT SHADE BOOKS
SAN FRANCISCO

Night Shade books may be purchased in bulk at special discounts for sales promotion, corporate gifts, fund-raising, or educational purposes. Special editions can also be created to specifications. For details, contact the Special Sales Department, Night Shade Books, 307 West 36th Street, 11th Floor, New York, NY 10018 or info@skyhorsepublishing.com.

Night Shade Books™ is a trademark of Skyhorse Publishing, Inc.™, a Delaware corporation.

Visit our website at www.nightshadebooks.com.

10 9 8 7 6 5 4 3 2 1

Library of Congress Cataloging-in-Publication Data is available on file.

ISBN: 978-1-59780-472-1

Cover Illustration by Sparth
Cover Art and Design by Victoria Maderna and Federico Piatti
Interior layout and design by Amy Popovich

Printed in the United States of America

For Kate, for her love, support and faith in me
And for Anna, for teaching me joy and wonder each day

DATE: 1 Aug 2132
TO: POTUS, POTEC, UKPM, UKMOD, USSECDEF, SECGEN NATO, CINC NATO
FROM: VADM Gerlich, CINC JSC
BC: BG Diaz USAF, LCDR Jain UKRN, P4 Durand JSC
CLASSIFICATION: TOP SECRET-GAMMA
RE: The *Daedalus* Incident

The following represents the sum total of our knowledge regarding the incident on Mars that took place between 24-28 July 2132. You have been individually briefed on these matters, but I urge you to read and view the following closely, and please remember we continue to develop new data. I further urge you to follow security protocols to the fullest extent in handling this information, as the implications and repercussions remain incalculable.

Based on this information, I recommend the creation of a task force to further study these events and, if necessary, defend against future incidents in Sol space. This task force should focus on both Mars and, to the extent possible, Saturn. A holoconference has been scheduled for 2 Aug 2132 at 0900 EDT to further discuss these matters. The quantum cryptography key for the link will be sent separately.

I cannot stress enough the importance of decisive action in the days and weeks ahead to address this historic incident. I look forward to speaking to you tomorrow.

VADM Hans Gerlich, GN
CINC JSC

CHAPTER 1

July 24, 2132

Mars is supposed to be dead, just a big hunk of cold rock hanging in space.

Right now, though, Mars seemed very much alive—and pissed.

Lt. Shaila Jain dashed across a subterranean cavern, dodging boulders the size of shipping crates as the floor bucked beneath her. Maybe Mars wasn't supposed to have earthquakes like this, but it sure felt she was smack dab in the middle of one.

Shaila had a decade of experience in the Royal Navy and the U.S./E.U. Joint Space Command, but earthquakes on Mars were definitely new. Nonetheless, her training was enough to get her ass moving. She grabbed her companion, Dr. Stephane Durand, and shoved him toward the center of the lava tube—an immense, circular cavern just underneath the red-rock slopes of Australis Montes. Shaila hoped the center of the cavern would be far enough away from the crumbling walls, so long as the ceiling held.

"Where's Kaczynski?" Shaila asked through her comm, her voice echoing slightly inside her pressure suit.

"He was by the wall," Stephane said, his French-accented voice quavering. "I do not see him."

"Shit. Get under the skylight," she said, again shoving the young planetary geologist toward the ropes that snaked downward from the opening in the lava tube some fifty meters above. "That ought to be safe, right?"

Stephane staggered toward the ropes, dodging falling rocks as best he could. "I don't know. This is all wrong!"

"Figure it out later," Shaila said, pushing him ahead. "Jain to Kaczynski, come in, Ed."

Nothing.

They reached the ropes and skidded to the ground. Shaila hoped the pressure suits could handle such rough-and-tumble use, but it seemed more important to get under the opening above them—the only area in the cavern that didn't seem to be raining rubble. The quickened pace of her breathing was the loudest sound in her ears, echoing around in her helmet and accompanied by the staccato of rockfall vibrating through her suit.

Shaila ventured a look back to where she last saw Kaczynski, but his suit lights were nowhere to be seen. She thought she could make out a large pile of rocks in the shadows where he stood just thirty seconds ago, but the light from the pinkish sky above did little to illuminate more than a fraction of the immense, kilometers-long cave, and her helmet lamps didn't add much more.

She flipped a switch on her suit gauntlet. "Jain to McAuliffe, priority one. Come in, McAuliffe, emergency priority one."

The radio crackled before McAuliffe Base replied. "McAuliffe to Jain, Adams here. What's up, chief?" It was 2nd Lt. Rory Adams, U.S. Army, the ops officer on duty.

Even in the middle of a crisis—or perhaps because of it—Shaila bristled at the informality. "We are in an earthquake, repeat, we are experiencing an earthquake. Kaczynski is missing. Send the crash team to this position. Over."

A few moments of silence. "Say again, Lieutenant? You're in an earthquake?"

"Dammit, Adams. This is not a drill! Scramble the emergency response team NOW! Reply, confirm and get it done! Over!"

"Right, ma'am," the young lieutenant replied shakily. "Confirming your emergency. Scrambling crash team, ETA to your location 15 minutes. Over."

"Jain out," she grumbled, stabbing at the switch on her gauntlet again. "Still with me, Steve?"

"I am," Stephane said tentatively. "Sensor readings are very strange. I cannot find the source of this quake." Shaila was surprised to see him waving his sensor pack over his head, taking readings of the cavern even as it threatened to flatten them both.

"Get down!" Shaila said, pulling his arm back toward the floor. "How long is this going to last?"

"It should have ended already. This feels big."

A rust-red boulder the size of a small car crashed down two meters away, sending a wave of reverberation through their pressure suits. "No kidding," Shaila said. "Kaczynski, come in. Kaczynski, we are not reading you, over."

Still nothing. Shaila ventured another look around, only to see broken rock covering at least half of the visible cavern floor. Their suit lights, covered with red dust, no longer allowed them to see the walls of the cavern clearly. The cave felt like it was closing in on them, threatening a final crescendo of plummeting rock that would make them a permanent part of Mars' long and ancient history.

And then, just as suddenly as it started, the tremors stopped. A few final rocks skittered down the piles of rubble in the cavern before silence reigned once more.

"Reading normal again," Stephane said after a few moments. "No seismic activity."

Shaila climbed up on all fours and pushed herself to her knees, carefully breathing in and out to clear her mind and check for any immediate injury. "You sure?"

"No, I am not sure," Stephane said as he clambered ungracefully to his feet, hands trembling as he tried to adjust his sensor pack. "I have no idea what just happened, or why. There has not been this kind of activity on Mars for a million years. Was Kaczynski taking core samples?"

Shaila slowly got to her feet, testing each joint as she did so. "Don't know. First things first, though." She did a quick visual scan of her suit, finding no visible tears and all systems normal. She did the same for Stephane; he had only been on Mars for six weeks, and the pressure suit was still both a novelty and a burden to him. Seeing his suit remained in one piece, Shaila grabbed his helmet and swung his attention toward her. "All right, Steve. Let me see you."

He looked confused, his attention already back on the walls and ceiling of the lava tube. "What for?"

Shaila saw his green eyes were focused, and there were no bruises or blood anywhere on his face or head. "Making sure you've got your wits about you.

Do I look all right?"

At this, the Frenchman smiled. "I have always thought so."

"Stow it." Shaila grimaced slightly and gave his helmet a good rap with her gauntlet. In his short time on base, Stephane's reputation as a flirt was already well established. At least he bounced back quickly. "Let's find Kaczynski."

That task was far more daunting. In their frantic dash for the skylight, they had covered a good eighty meters very quickly, aided by the low Martian gravity. Their lights only managed about twenty meters or so of illumination, while the lava tube itself was fifty meters in circumference, slightly flattened at the bottom and top from the billion-year-old lava flow that had carved it.

They split up, each of them walking back up the cave along one wall, sensor packs at the ready. Unfortunately, the mining sensors were limited in both scope and range—they had to satisfy themselves with heat readings, and even then they were good only to about thirty meters.

Shaila walked carefully over the rubble, brushing away rocks with her boot so she could firmly plant her foot on the floor with each step. After about fifty meters of slow progress, her sensor pack's readings went from blue to red. "Got him. Heat signature twenty-five meters ahead," she reported. "Up against that wall there...let's see.

"Oh, shit."

She hadn't been imagining that pile of rubble after all. The heat reading—presumably Kaczynski's, unless Mars had other, far stranger surprises in store today—was coming from the same heap of rocks. Shaila immediately took off for the pile, leaping across the stone-strewn floor.

"Be careful, Shay!" Stephane said. "I do not know how stable this area is now!"

She did her best to arrest her speed, but was barely able to slow down before plowing into the rock pile. "Take a look at this. You think we can move this rubble safely?"

Stephane came up behind her, picking his way slowly across the cavern floor. "If we are careful. If you come across something large, let me know. Otherwise, dig from the top as best you can, or push it backward away from us."

Together, they started moving debris. Despite the lower gravity, it was still hard work—the rubble pile was nearly three meters high, and some of the rocks required the two of them to heave-ho together. But they made steady progress, and the pile disappeared even as their white pressure suits took on a dirty reddish tint.

"I see white!" Stephane said excitedly.

Shaila followed his pointed finger and saw a bit of pressure suit peeking out from under the rock. "OK, let's take this slow. Get him uncovered as best you can." She flipped her comm over to the base channel again. "Jain to McAuliffe, confirm we have a man down. Repeat, Kaczynski is down. What's the ETA on medical?"

"McAuliffe to Jain," Adams responded. "I have medical en route to your position. Should be there in five minutes, over."

"Roger that," she said as she dug. "Alert Billiton it's one of theirs. Jain out." Kaczynski worked for Billiton Minmetals, the second-largest mining company on Earth. Billiton had been mining on Mars for nearly a decade, paying JSC for the use of McAuliffe Base as a staging ground as they explored—and exploited—the planet's resources.

Carefully digging with their gloved hands, lifting rocks rather than shoving them, the two astronauts finally found the outline of Kaczynski's unconscious form, his limbs splayed out. Shaila methodically checked his suit. Unlike the JSC pressure suits, which were bulky relics of days gone by, the Billiton suits had all the bells and whistles—integrated heads-up displays in the visors, modular sensor units implanted in the frame, tiny holoprojectors to display data embedded in the gauntlets and chest. Damn lot of good it did Kaczynski now, though, since the electronics were shot. At least his helmet appeared to be intact. She ran her hands over his entire body, looking for signs of rupture in the tough composite fabric of the suit.

There. A small tear, about six centimeters wide, on the lower left torso. The rocks must have created the rip, and then covered it up to keep his suit pressure from dropping too rapidly. But she could now see a light breeze emanating from the tear where Kaczynski's air was escaping. She dug into the carryall pouch at her side and pulled out a roll of silvery tape.

"What is that?" Stephane asked.

"Duct tape," she replied, a slight smile on her face. "Don't leave Earth without it." Shaila always thought basic JSC training should include a lecture on the proud history of duct tape in space. She pulled off a piece and slapped it onto the rip, then spun off a few more strips to make sure the seal would hold. "I want to get it around him to seal it off better, but I don't want to move him without the crash team here."

Shaila checked the rest of Kaczynski's suit as best she could, but found no more ruptures. She hooked her suit's oxygen tank to his suit for about a minute to give him more air and pressure. At least he still seemed to be breathing.

Meanwhile, Stephane had resumed surveying the cave. "This is incredible," he said, eyes intent on his sensor pack. "There are no fissures, no signs of stress fractures anywhere. I cannot even find where most of this rockfall came from."

"Could Kaczynski have caused this?" Shaila asked. She wondered if Kaczynski had been on one of his infamous drinking binges the night before. Bootleg liquor was the number one commodity on McAuliffe, perhaps even more valuable than the deuterium-laced "heavy water" mined from the Martian ice caps.

"I doubt it. It may be possible, but this was a very large quake. This little sensor here is limited, but I am sure the rockfall is everywhere in this cave. Look around."

Shaila poked her head up around the rock pile. While the memory of the cave prior to the tremor wasn't exactly burned into her head, the walls and ceiling still seemed as they were before. She could still see the geologic strata neatly outlined along the cave wall—the same strata that had both Stephane and Kaczynski excited when they first arrived. The ceiling likewise seemed to be intact, without any major indentations or cracks. It seemed, overall, there was simply *more* rock in the cave, as if the gods had taken a big sack of stone and poured it into the lava tube.

"So what do you think?" she asked Stephane.

He threw up his hands, which struck Shaila as a very Gallic gesture. "I have no idea. We were in an earthquake that should not have been, and now there are rocks that should not be here."

Before she could respond, Shaila's comm crackled again. "Levin to Jain, come in. We're at the skylight." Dr. Doug Levin was McAuliffe's chief medical officer, and his voice was pure Brooklyn.

"Jain here, doc. Kaczynski was buried under a rockfall. He lost some pressure in his suit, but nothing too bad. I'm worried about moving him."

"Roger. I'm coming down with a body board."

"You sure about that, doc? Steve and I can get him strapped down if you want," Shaila said. She knew Doug Levin met the bare minimum of JSC's fitness standards.

The portly doctor was already making his way down the rope. "Be nice to me, girlie," Levin said. "At least the gravity's low. I'll bounce, right?"

"Just make sure we're only coming back with one casualty, not two," she said.

Levin managed to make it to the cavern floor without incident and only a handful of expletives. The board was lowered down a moment later by the other members of the rescue team. The doctor wobbled his way over to Kaczynski and slowly bent down to examine him, medical sensors in hand. "Hard to tell with the suit on, but he doesn't seem too bad. No spinal injuries at least," Levin finally said. "Nice job taping him up. Let's get him strapped in."

Levin and Shaila gently lifted Kaczynski out of the rubble and onto the board. She used more duct tape to secure him tightly, and gave his torso a few more loops to make sure the leak wouldn't get worse. Stephane volunteered to help Levin carry Kaczynski back to the ropes.

Shaila went to follow them, but something in the rubble caught her eye. She turned back to where Kaczynski had fallen and saw another fleck of white. Fearing another, larger tear in Kaczynski's suit, she quickly bent down to brush the rocks away.

There was nothing there.

Yet, unbidden, she heard her own voice in her head, somehow distinct from her normal train of thought: *You know, that could be where I found it.*

Scowling, she ran her hands through the rocks and dirt once more, but came away empty handed.

"Jain, get over here. I need your help rigging this board up," Levin said over the comm.

Shaila ran her hands through the dirt one more time before responding. "Yeah, all right. I'm coming." She stood up, reflexively brushed her gauntlets clean, and headed back to the skylight.

She could've sworn she saw something. Oddly enough, it looked like paper.

"I need to get out of this cave," she muttered to no one in particular.

CHAPTER 2

February 18, 1779

Father,
    You have often asked me about my life in service to His Majesty's Navy, and I have endeavoured to tell you as much as I can, but often detail escapes me in the telling. So it is upon the occasion of my first assignment as second lieutenant that I have decided to keep a journal of my time aboard HMS Daedalus *and make it a present to you when next I return.*

Daedalus is quite typical of frigates in His Majesty's Navy, boasting 32 guns and a crew of some two hundred souls. She is an older ship, but with fine lines and quick handling regardless. I hear tell of engineers and alchemists who would alter the design of our Void-going vessels, but ever since the Spaniard Pinzon ventured off Earth for the first time in 1493, it seems such talk has resulted in little. Be it sea or Void, Daedalus *handles true, and to my eyes, needs no alteration.*

As I write this, we are mere weeks out of Portsmouth, on a course for Jupiter that takes us quite near Mercury, where the Sunward Trading Company has a rather extensive mining operation. From there, we shall move past the Sun, skirt Mars and traverse the Rocky Main en route to our assignment. Upon our arrival in the Jovian system, we shall aid in the blockade of New York, so that the Ganymedean rebels shan't receive aid from their fellows or, worse, the damnable French.

"Mr. Weatherby! You're wanted on the quarterdeck!"

Lt. Thomas Weatherby turned and looked to the door of the wardroom, where Midshipman Forester—still evidently lacking in the finer points of decorum—had called for him. He thought of reprimanding the boy for his breach, but he was gone as quickly as he had arrived.

The young lieutenant closed his journal and quickly shoved it into his open sea chest, shutting the latter with a slam and grabbing his hat on the way out of the wardroom. Hurrying through the gun deck toward the stairs, he barely acknowledged the salutes from the crew as he buttoned his coat and brushed lint off his uniform. They could be under attack by the entire French fleet, but Capt. Sir William Morrow still expected his officers to maintain a high standard of appearance and composure, even under duress. Especially under duress.

Weatherby climbed out onto the main deck and saw the ribbon of yellow motes stretching into the Void from the ship's stern—they had arrived at Mercury at last. He turned to search for the little planet, but had to look away quickly—the Sun was not only more than six times larger than it appeared on Earth, but six times as bright. While this was his first voyage to Mercury, he nonetheless cursed himself for being so careless. He instead focused on the leeward side of the ship, away from the glare and onto the inky blackness around the ship, punctuated by millions of tiny stars.

One of those stars would be Earth, where they had sailed from Portsmouth just four weeks ago. Mercury was but a stopover en route to Jupiter, where *Daedalus* was to join the fleet there and crush the insurrection of the British colonies on Ganymede. It was a good assignment, Weatherby knew, with a chance at both glory and prize money. What's more, it was safer than most, for the Ganymedean Navy, such as it was, hardly deserved the name, and had few ships to match even an older frigate like *Daedalus*.

The young officer quickly mounted the stairs to the quarterdeck. "Lt. Weatherby, reporting as ordered, sir," he said, crisply saluting the captain as he approached. The commander of *Daedalus* cut a fine figure on the lee side of the quarterdeck, standing beside the clockwork orrery that tracked the position of the Known Worlds. Morrow's weathered face, lined by both wind and wisdom, held dark, discerning eyes that seemed to take in everything before him at once. His black hair, graying at the temples, was tied back in a simple tail, and his uniform appeared quite ready for a Royal inspection.

Morrow cocked his head slightly toward the young lieutenant, but his gaze was fixed outward, about three points off the larboard side. "We still cannot make out their colors. Quite a problem when you don't know whom to shoot at. You have good eyes. Can you make them out?"

Weatherby pulled out his glass and looked ahead. Now that his eyes had adjusted, he could see Mercury off in the distance—a barren, pock-marked sphere suspended in the Void. Much closer, however, he picked out a merchantman, her planesails unfurled at either side, her ruddersail suspended a full eighty feet below her keel. Along her larboard side, puffs of smoke erupted from a second vessel, most likely a large frigate or small ship of the line.

"No, sir, I cannot see their colors," Weatherby said. "The merchantman is certainly outgunned. The frigate looks to be a French make."

"Very well. Stay on your glass," Morrow said. He turned to his first lieutenant, George Plumb, who had already reported. "Mr. Plumb, we may as well be prepared. Beat to quarters, if you please."

"Beat to quarters!" shouted Plumb, a large man with a stone face and gravelly voice. Immediately, the marine on watch below grabbed a drum and began to beat out a martial rhythm, while one of the young midship-men started ringing the ship's bell, just aft of the mainmast.

A torrent of ill-shaven, groggy and half-dressed men burst onto deck from below, roused prematurely from their slumber by the prospect of battle. The smaller, more nimble seamen started scurrying up the rigging toward the sails, while Maj. Harold Denning began sending his marines aloft, so they could rain deadly shot upon any enemy officers that might present themselves as targets.

Meanwhile, the larger, burlier crewmen pulled the wheeled guns back from the railings of the main deck, while others used giant brushes to swab out the insides and prepare them for firing. Sacks of powder were placed inside, followed by alchemically-treated cannon shot, then wad-ding to keep everything in place. That done, the guns were run out again, with ropes and pulleys doing the job, while the main gunner for each weapon primed his gun with more powder and prepared to fire.

Within less than three minutes, *Daedalus* was fit for battle, each of her 32 guns ready to spew forth iron shot and alchemical essences of destruc-tion upon whatever target was deemed a threat.

Meanwhile, Weatherby tried to determine what that target might be, if any. While the Sun's brightness masked many of the stars, it perfectly illuminated the two vessels in combat, as well as the golden stream of the sun-currents behind them. Those currents would make for a quick escape, whisking a ship toward the outer planets at incredible speeds—if only the merchantman could reach them in time.

"Ganymedean flag on the frigate, sir!" Weatherby finally shouted. "Dutch on the merchantman."

Morrow frowned. "I thought the Dutch were well disposed to the Ganymedean rebels," he said. "Thank you, Mr. Weatherby. You may join your division. We have no official quarrel with the Dutch, but we certainly have one with our wayward colonies. We shall engage the Ganny."

Weatherby folded his glass, saluted, and clambered down the stairway to the gun deck. As second lieutenant, he was in charge of the starboard division, and he quickly inspected the readiness of his men and their guns. A slack line here, a misplaced powder charge there, but Weatherby found his men had responded well, especially given the early hour. He looked to the ship's bo'sun, James—an older seaman whose time aboard ship likely surpassed his days on land—and this worthy returned his lieutenant's gaze with a nod. They were ready.

"Ganny privateer, is it?" asked one of the men before him, the burly gunner Smythe, his eyes alight at the prospect of battle—or perhaps simply prize money.

"Mind your gun, Smythe," Weatherby said steadily. "We'll know soon enough."

Weatherby turned to see Third Lt. John Foster approaching. "Our first battle then," said the young man, who was a year shy of Weatherby's age. He was newly minted a lieutenant, and like Weatherby, had yet to see action aboard *Daedalus*. Foster extended his hand. "Good luck, Tom."

Weatherby managed a small smile. Foster was a good shipmate, if a little too sentimental at times like these. "And to you, John," he managed, shaking his fellow officer's hand. He then quickly turned back to his division, firmly putting his mind toward the task at hand.

Daedalus approached the two vessels under full sail, looking like a cross between a shark and a blowfish. In addition to her three masts of sails, used on terrestrial seas as well as the Void, she boasted a large planesail on each side, sticking out like the fins on a whale. These helped the ship move larboard and starboard and, more importantly, up and down against the planetary plane and giving them three dimensions of motion. Underneath, the ruddersail stuck out nearly a hundred feet from under the vessel, helping catch the solar winds and sun-currents to provide further direction.

Weatherby eyed the starboard-side planesail closely, hoping his recent drills amongst the men there would bear fruit. The sail would have to be quickly brought in before a broadside could be fired, lest the *Daedalus* shoot off her own sails and leave her without the ability to ascend or descend.

"What's all this commotion then?" came a voice from behind him.

Weatherby turned to see Dr. Joseph Ashton, the ship's alchemist and surgeon, tottering up to him. The elderly scientist might not have been the most nimble sailor, but his facility with the Great Work kept the *Daedalus* sailing between the Known Worlds. It was he who managed the sail treatments that allowed them to catch the solar winds, as well as the lodestones in the hold which provided air and gravity for all aboard. Ashton also provided curatives for the wounded and alchemical shot for the guns.

"Ganymedean ship engaging a Dutch merchantman, Doctor," Weatherby replied. "We're after the Ganny, of course."

"Hmph. Yes. Rightly so, damned rebels," Ashton said. "'Free and independent states,' indeed!" The alchemist clapped Weatherby on the shoulder and made his way toward his station below decks, where he would stand ready to care for any wounded that might result from the engagement.

Weatherby looked through the gun port and saw Morrow would be engaging the frigate off the starboard side. That would serve to position *Daedalus* between the Ganymedean and the merchantman, perhaps allowing the latter to make a run for the sun-currents and make a rapid escape. It would also put Weatherby's division at the forefront of the engagement, firing the first shots and taking the brunt of the frigate's response.

Faint booms echoed across the blackness, and Weatherby saw green fire erupt from the Ganymedean's guns as she fired upon the merchantman. Morrow was right; it made little sense for the rebel to fire on the Dutch, as the latter nation was far better disposed to the errant Jovian colonies than the Crown; the Dutch, it seemed, wanted little else than to put a crimp in England's burgeoning Known Worlds trade.

"Ready on the guns!" Plumb barked from the quarterdeck, snapping Weatherby's attention back to the task at hand. The men of the starboard division primed their weapons and prepared to fire before Weatherby could echo the order. The young lieutenant was well pleased with their effort and hoped Plumb or Morrow noticed their efficiency in the coming action. The son of shopkeepers in London, Weatherby had long imagined more for himself than groveling before customers, though he would never say such before his hard-working, genial parents. A distant relation had secured him a spot as a midshipman when he was twelve. Now, at nineteen, Weatherby had embarked upon his first assignment as second lieutenant, and he hoped for a quick promotion to first lieutenant, or even post-captain, in a few years. From there, he occasionally allowed himself to dream of commanding a first-rate, of brocade upon his shoulders—but he tamped down on these fantasies quickly. While young, he had at least enough wisdom to know he had much to learn in the interim.

"The Ganny's turning!" came the call from the crow's nest, high upon the mainmast, the sailor's voice filtering down below. "I count forty-two guns!"

Grim news it was, as the *Daedalus* was well outgunned by the larger ship. Nonetheless, Morrow appeared undeterred. "Three points upward on the planes!" Plumb called down, relaying the captain's orders. The *Daedalus* quickly rose higher into the Void, above the level at which the Ganymedean sailed. Morrow had opted to try an angled shot in the hopes of raining a broadside—a fusillade of cannon fire from the entire starboard battery—down upon the rebel frigate's unprotected main deck. Hopefully, that could occur before the Ganny's guns could punch through the *Daedalus'* lower hull.

Weatherby looked up through the cargo hatch toward the quarterdeck, where Morrow stood, a statue of calm except for his eyes, which darted about and beyond the ship, taking in everything and feeding the calculus of battle in his mind. Next to him, Plumb was a barely leashed hound, barking orders and seemingly ready to pounce on anyone not following them to the letter, ensuring the ship would be ready for whatever Morrow would have in mind.

"The merchantman's making for the current!" Foster called from the larboard side. In the distance, Weatherby could see the yellow trail of the sun-current snaking past, away from the Sun and toward the other planets. Should the merchantman reach the current quickly enough, she would be miles away in mere moments, carried off at impossible speeds by the power of the Sun itself. While good news for the merchantman, it would mean *Daedalus* would have to capture the larger Ganny in order to determine what had transpired between them.

And the Ganymedean was closing fast, having abandoned the merchant-man in order to turn and engage the English vessel. Weatherby could see her planes unfurled as well, trying to compensate for *Daedalus'* trajectory, but it would be a lost cause. *Daedalus* would indeed approach from above, and a quick maneuver on the planes would bring her guns to bear squarely above the Ganny's deck.

"Secure body lines!" Weatherby shouted. Immediately, the men began tying ropes around their waists; the other ends were affixed to metal loops driven into the hull. The ship's gravity, administered by alchemically treated lodestones in the hold, often didn't compensate quickly enough when the ship maneuvered radically, and the lines prevented anyone from being lost overboard.

The Ganny approached quickly—the engagement would be rapid in-deed. Unlike battle at sea, where wind and tide forced opponents to creep together slowly, the sun-currents swept ships together as though they were mounted knights of old. They would have one chance at a blistering broadside before the two ships passed—and with luck, only one would be able to come around for a second pass.

Weatherby felt excitement and ambition dwindle into a familiar fear. Though this was not his first battle, either at sea or in the Void, it was his first in command of so large a division, and his first against a larger vessel. The other engagements to his credit were barely worthy of being called battles, lopsided as they were in favor of the Royal Navy. "Steady, men!" he called, though it was as much for his own nerves as theirs. Nonethe-less, his voice rang out cleanly, and the men tensed and prepared for the coming onslaught.

"Down five points on the starboard plane!" Plumb shouted, immediately echoed by Weatherby. Four men heaved upon the appropriate lever, and the large planesail on the side of the ship angled downward so that it was perpendicular to the ship—right under the guns. The maneuver not only tilted the ship toward the other frigate, but brought the plane parallel to the line of the ship, freeing the guns to fire above it unimpeded. They would not have to draw in the sail after all.

Weatherby saw the other ship starting to angle upward as well, trying to bring its guns to bear. He frowned—they would get some shots off under the waterline. There would be repairs to be made before *Daedalus* could splash her keel down upon the oceans of any world.

"Starboard division—FIRE!"

Morrow shouted the command himself, which was quickly echoed by every officer and midshipman aboard. The *Daedalus'* guns replied immediately, sending a towering crash of green-glowing cannon shot toward the enemy ship. The guns jerked backward from the recoil and were met by the well-drilled crewmen, who stood ready to swab out the bore and reload.

Suddenly, the ship lurched, and Weatherby was sent flying back into the thick trunk of the mainmast. He could hear cannon shot bursting upward through the deck behind him, and his vision was quickly clouded by a spray of wooden shards erupting from the wooden planking. He slumped to the deck, his back to the mast, just in time to see one of his cannons being shot apart by another blast, the gun itself hurtling up through the cargo hatch and out into the Void—along with two of the gun's crew, their lines failing them. The rest were burned horribly by the alchemical shot, and blood and screams soon mixed with the wooden shrapnel in the air.

The cries of the wounded helped Weatherby focus his mind once more as he shook off the daze and ache and attempted to regain his feet. Yet he could not gain ground, and quickly feared that his head had been struck much harder than he realized.

And then he looked down. He was floating a foot above the main deck.

Likewise, a handful of the men near Weatherby—and one 1½-ton cannon—were no longer safely aboard either. Debris swirled in the air around him.

"Captain! We've lost a lodestone!" Weatherby called. He then turned to his men. "Lash that gun to the deck!"

Similar shouts came from all over the ship, detailing the damage inflicted by the Ganymedean, which by this point had limped away and appeared to be coming about in a wide arc, making for the sun-current. Morrow ordered pursuit, but it quickly became apparent that the *Daedalus* had been the less fortunate. There were several holes in her hull, some of which shot cleanly through the lower decks and out the main deck. At least one other lodestone was lost near the forecastle. While the gravity was erratic now, that was less troublesome than the prospect of losing air—a ship needed its lodestones to not only keep everyone on deck, but to retain the air necessary to breathe on long voyages between the Known Worlds.

Most importantly, the Ganny had managed to shoot the *Daedalus'* rudder-sail completely away—making the capture of the Ganymedean an impossible task, as a ship's sea rudder was wholly unsuited for navigating the sun-currents between worlds.

Yet *Daedalus* had acquitted herself admirably, causing the other vessel severe damage amidships. Lookouts reported that the rebel ship suffered a damaged mainmast and a number of guns lost. Little wonder she was making for the sun-current instead of coming around for another shot, Weatherby thought. Perhaps this would, at the very least, convince the Ganymedeans to stay in the Jovian system instead of targeting Crown assets such as Mercury.

"Stand down!" Plumb called. "Repair crews to stations!" Weatherby repeated the order with disappointment, but knew the captain was wise in not attempting pursuit. Besides, there were his men to attend to. Starks and Adler, two of his best gunners, were already out of sight and lost to the Void; there was nothing to be done for them. Flung far from the ship, they would soon succumb to lack of air, and drown on nothingness. Were they further out from the Sun, they might have died of the horrid chill of the Void first, but 'round Mercury, not even this small blessing would be theirs.

Yet there were four others severely wounded, with sickly charred burns and bloodied limbs, and these were men who may be saved. Putting the unfortunates lost to the Void out of mind, Weatherby quickly called for the orderlies, fighting back the bile in his throat as he knelt beside the worst casualty.

"Where is Ashton?" Weatherby demanded of one of the crew who came to render aid.

The man merely shook his head sadly. As the fog of battle cleared from his head, Weatherby could see the gaping holes in the deck beneath his feet, and feared that little aid would be forthcoming from the ship's alchemist.

Thankfully, officers carried a handful of curatives on their persons at all times, and Weatherby managed to stop three of his men from bleeding out. The fourth, sadly, breathed his last before Weatherby could get to him.

With his men stable and the orderlies bandaging their burns, Weatherby picked his way up to the main deck to report, stepping around a small gathering of marines; Maj. Denning was among those who had fallen in the engagement, and they knelt in prayer over his corpse. Yet once Weatherby arrived upon the quarterdeck, he found Morrow was elsewhere; James directed him toward the cockpit, where the captain had gone to check on Ashton.

Weatherby rushed back down below toward the belly of the ship, hoping Ashton somehow managed to survive the battle. When he entered, he was aghast at conditions therein, and crushed at how misplaced his hopes had been.

There was a massive hole in the lower half of the starboard wall, where one of the Ganymedean's shots had penetrated, strewing charred and blasted wood throughout. Floorboards and walls still smoldered where fires and acids from the lab were released. And in the middle of the room, Morrow and an orderly were kneeling over the battered and bloody body of Dr. Ashton, attempting to administer curatives in the dim lantern light.

Weatherby attempted to walk into the room, but tripped—upon Ashton's severed leg, which had been thrown from his body. Unable to keep his stomach calm at this, Weatherby quickly rushed toward a hole in the hull, rent by alchemical shot, and made it there in time so that his hurried breakfast did not stain the deck as it came forth.

When he turned back around, he saw Morrow and the orderly, still kneeling before the rest of Ashton's body, but with resigned looks upon their faces. "It's no use at all," Morrow said. "He's dead." The captain looked up to see Weatherby staring in horror; Weatherby knew full well that the captain had taken note of his lack of composure. "Mr. Weatherby, please ask Mr. Plumb to change course. We'll have to put in at Elizabeth Mercuris to make repairs.

"And we'll need to find a new alchemist, sad to say," he added.

Weatherby nodded and saluted, then rushed away above decks, grateful for Morrow's discretion. He knew the captain would be less forgiving if there had been more crewmen about, however, and he resolved to steel himself more thoroughly next time.

As Weatherby delivered Morrow's orders and began overseeing repairs, his thoughts drifted to the kindly Ashton—the old puffer had called Weatherby his fellow "bookworm"—and, more importantly, what he meant to *Daedalus*. Other than the captain himself, a ship's alchemist was the most important person aboard ship. He conducted the occult operations necessary to keep the ship aloft in the Void, made air and gravity possible and, on small ships like *Daedalus*, also acted as ship's surgeon. While officers sometimes made a study of the Great Work, their knowledge was typically quite limited compared to those who devoted their entire lives to the Art of Transformation.

I despair of finding an alchemist worth his Salt at the Elizabeth Mercuris mining colony, now mere hours away. There is little in the way of order there, let alone learning, and from what my shipmates have told me, the stories told in the London taverns are true, in that it is an altogether rough and ill-fortuned place. Yet the ores mined there, used in alchemical shot and shipbuilding alike, are critical to England's supremacy in the Void. So the Royal Navy keeps Elizabeth Mercuris afloat above that sun-blasted rock of a planet—and because of that, I doubt they have an alchemist to spare, as it is no mean feat to keep a wooden outpost hanging in the Void above that woebegone cinder of a world.

And while we might press men into service there to replace those lost, I am certain no one of alchemical learning would find themselves in such a place without ill tidings having befallen them, despite the outpost's importance to England. So even if there be an alchemist available to us, what sort of man would he be?

But we have little alternative, Father. Without someone to tend to the ship's lodestones and sails, we would be adrift in the Void, perhaps forever lost to

Earth, England and home. So I must hope that Elizabeth Mercuris may give us something of a miracle—in the form of a suitable alchemist.

July 24, 2132

"OK, let me get this straight. There's never been a recorded earthquake on Mars. Or…Mars-quake. Whatever," said Col. Maria Diaz, U.S.A.F., commander of McAuliffe Base. "So logically, what you experienced can't actually be a quake, right?"

Shaila looked straight ahead, in her best "at-ease" pose, staying out of the conversation while idly regarding the holopicture of Diaz, posing with her old F-334 Lighting VII fighter in some jungle somewhere, hanging on the wall behind the colonel's desk. Stephane, meanwhile, was growing more and more flustered as he tried to explain what happened in the lava tube—or, more precisely, explain why there was no explanation.

"I have been in earthquakes, Colonel," he said. "I was in San Francisco in '27. I know what they feel like. This was to me a seismic event equal to an earthquake."

Diaz leaned back in her chair, stretching out her compact, muscular frame. "I'm not doubting what you experienced, Dr. Durand. What I'm saying is that we generally agree, you and me, that it couldn't have been a *real* earthquake, right?"

"There has never been a recorded earthquake on Mars, no. And we are certain that while Mars has tectonic plates and the like, it has been geologically dormant for a million years. This should not have been an earthquake in the traditional sense, but it is, technically, possible. And there may be other causes that might result in the same effect. I cannot imagine the mining operations were responsible, but I suppose that if we go through the data—"

"Fine. Here's my problem, Doctor," Diaz interrupted, leaning forward and brushing a strand of black-gray hair from her face. "In about five minutes, Harry Yu is going to come barging through my door demanding to know what happened and whether it's going to impact his mining ops. What do you recommend I tell him?"

Harry Yu was the vice-president in charge of Martian exploitation operations for Billiton Minmetals. Unlike his predecessors, Harry actually moved out to Mars for the job—a move most JSC astronauts felt was solely to make their lives miserable. Yet he turned a marginally profitable enterprise into a steady money maker, and while the miners didn't exactly love the guy, they did like the paychecks he produced.

Stephane sighed. "The lava tube was in an area not set aside for mining yet. Most of the company's operations should be far enough away. Right now, I do not see any danger to the miners. However," he added, just as Diaz was about to respond, "they should be very, very careful. I recommend putting in more sensors, more finely tuned to seismic activity, so that if there is something larger going on, they may have some warning. Meanwhile, I will comb through the data their sensors generate to be sure."

"Nice ass covering," Diaz said, jotting down Stephane's recommendation. "Jain, how's Ed doing?"

"Last I heard he was bugging Levin for a drink, ma'am," Shaila said. "Broken leg, a few busted ribs. Should be up and about by morning."

"Too bad we can't ship him home, the cranky bastard," Diaz said, the ghost of a smile flickering across her face. "You able to question him yet?"

"Not yet, ma'am."

"Well, give him my official get-well-soon when you do. Meantime, Durand, I want you in the lab to gather as much data as possible and write me a preliminary report to send to Houston and the suits at Billiton. Jain, talk to Kaczynski, then clear your schedule for tomorrow. Unless Steve can come up with something new in the lab, you're taking him back to the lava tube in the morning. You're both relieved of all other duty until this thing is solved. If Billiton can't mine here, we're all out of a job. Dismissed."

Stephane and Shaila turned to go. "Hang on, Jain," Diaz said. Shaila nodded to Stephane, then turned to face her commander as the geologist left the office.

"You think he's up for this?" Diaz asked once Stephane was gone.

"Steve?" Shaila said with a slight smile. "He's smart enough. I think he's genuinely curious about it. Just gotta keep him motivated—and away from the floating poker games."

Diaz nodded. "All right. Make sure he stays on track." She then handed Shaila a datapad. "Latest from Houston on your request," she said simply.

"Sorry."

Shaila took the little tablet, already knowing what it would say. Sure enough, her application to be the pilot for the *Armstrong's* next mission to Jupiter was denied. She read it through a few times, but there was very little in the official-ese to give her any hope. It was a real shame; *Armstrong* was a new ship, with all the bells and whistles a pilot could hope for.

She handed the pad back. "Thanks, ma'am."

"Hang in there. I think JSC's finally ready to get a Saturn mission put together in the next few years. Could be huge."

"If I can't get another survey mission to Jupiter, I doubt I'll get Saturn," Jain said, trying to sound level-headed and practical. "Not after what happened on *Atlantis*."

"*Atlantis* wasn't your fault. Don't let anyone tell you otherwise." Diaz said. "What about the XO position here? It's still open. You've been acting number-two now for a month. I'll put in a good word for you. Probably mean a promotion, too."

Shaila smiled. "Thanks. That means a lot. But I'm a pilot, ma'am." She nodded toward the picture over Diaz' shoulder. "You know what it's like. I want to be out there."

"I know, believe me. Like I said, hang in there. Maybe check out some of the other JSC postings, do a Venus survey or something."

"Thanks, ma'am. I will," she said, a hint of determination breaking through her voice, though mostly for show. She doubted she'd even get to do a Mercury trip—not that there was anything there worth visiting. Her dream of returning to long-duration space flight had just taken a big hit.

Diaz and Shaila regarded each other for a brief moment. "All right," Diaz finally said. "Go figure out that earthquake. Dismissed."

Shaila walked out of the office and into McAuliffe's command center. Thankfully, the two officers on duty in the cramped space were busy looking at the multitude of monitors before them, not at the look on Shaila's face. She paused, took a deep breath, and then headed down the stairs toward the medical berth.

The command center, along with Diaz' office and a conference room, sat atop a three-level dome, the base's original structure dating back to 2079. The second level consisted of the galley, mess hall and other multipurpose rooms that, originally, served as crew quarters. Beneath that was the Hub—a gigantic warehouse-sized room that now served as the main EVA staging area. From the Hub, six corridors—new additions funded by Billiton—stretched out away from the dome. Four of these housed Billiton's mining operations, the fifth served as day-rooms for JSC officers, and the sixth contained various laboratories and the medical berth, with the base reactor housed at the very end—away from everything else, just in case.

As Shaila made her way down to medical, she didn't make her usual mental scan of the condition of the hallways. The once gleaming white walls were dull and slightly dirty, and the electricity would occasionally flicker randomly in places. McAuliffe held up well for a 53-year-old base, but it couldn't help but show its age. Engineering would be thankful for Shaila's lack of attention today—ever since she became acting executive officer, she had them frantically combing the base making repairs, large and small.

She moved through the mess hall and down into the Hub, perpetually bustling with miners coming in and out of the airlocks and JSC personnel scurrying about with their duties. Shaila didn't even bother issuing her usual glare at the Billiton miners. Women were rare enough at McAuliffe, and Shaila's mostly Indian ancestry—dusky skin combining with the curves granted by a hint of Anglo-Saxon blood—was quite kind to her, in the miners' estimation. It was mostly harmless; they usually stared just a little too long at her standard-issue red coverall—why someone thought *more* red was needed on Mars eluded Shaila—and a harsh look in return would put their eyes back on whatever they were doing.

This time, though, their looks were more questioning. Word traveled fast, and one of their own was laid up in the medical berth after a cave-in. Unlike most of the JSC crew, the miners had a very personal, very financial stake in the base's success. And she was slightly more sympathetic to those stares.

Putting the miners out of her mind, Shaila walked into the cramped medical berth to find Stephane already talking with Kaczynski, who was in a perfectly foul mood. A few feet away, Harry Yu was leaning up against a cabinet, arms folded, scowling.

"I'm telling you, kid, there's no goddamn way a four-meter-long, five-centimeter-diameter core sample from a laser drill is going to bring the fucking roof down!" Kaczynski yelled.

"I believe you, I believe you!" Stephane said, hands up in supplication. "I do not doubt you did everything right. But something had to trigger that quake. I need to find it."

"Yes, you do," Harry said. He ran a hand over his perfectly coiffed black hair, which matched his perfectly pressed grey coverall. His normal intensity, fueled by caffeine and spreadsheets, was amplified by nerves and frustration. "And none of this, repeat none of this, can jeopardize my ops here."

Stephane opened his mouth to reply, but Shaila walked over and put a hand on his shoulder. "Take it easy, boys. How you feeling, Ed?"

"Like I've been through a meat grinder," the old digger grumped, his permanent scowl deeper than usual. "I've been digging longer than you've been alive, and I've never seen anything like that. Not on Earth, not on the Moon, and definitely not here."

"You and me both," Shaila said. "You were taking a core sample at the time?"

"Just finished it up when it hit," Kaczynski said. "And yes, I tested the strata before I bored. Everything came back stable. Too bad, too. I think there's some decent platinum and uranium down there, maybe even a nice vein of gold."

Shaila smiled. The big money on Mars was deuterium, a hydrogen isotope distilled from the "heavy" water found at the ice caps for use in fusion reactors. That was a big part of why Billiton agreed to help keep McAuliffe running ten years ago, since the base was only 50 kilometers from the southern cap in winter. But the company was also interested in the wide variety of other mineral wealth Mars had to offer, especially during the year-long Martian summer.

That's why they were in that lava tube in the first place. Kaczynski had requested a survey, and Durand—the JSC geologist assigned to the base—had to go with him, along with someone from JSC's operations department. It had simply been Shaila's turn to draw that duty.

"I don't think anybody's heading back down there any time soon, Ed. Not until we figured out what caused it," Shaila said.

"Not good enough," Harry interjected. "Who's running the investigation?"

"Me and Steve," Shaila said. "That a problem?"

"Don't you have anybody else?" Harry asked.

"Why? The base executive officer and our resident planetologist not good enough for you, Harry?" While she'd never concede it, Harry did have a point—while she and Stephane were the best qualified JSC personnel on site to investigate the quakes, it was only because there were just 17 JSC astronauts on base. And if Houston wanted to send out a full survey team, it would take at least four weeks to arrive.

"I want my own investigation," Harry said. "If Ed's right, we need to be down in that cave exploiting it."

Shaila regarded the executive sternly. "You know damn well that JSC takes the lead on all potential hazards. You can chip in, but this is our show."

Harry stood straight and headed for the door. "Fine. We'll chip in. But we only have a couple of weeks until our latest dig is tapped, so this gets figured out stat." He nodded to Kaczynski and swooped out the door, looking terribly busy.

"Charmer, isn't he," Shaila said.

"Total bastard, but he writes the checks," Kaczynski grinned. "I agree with him, though. Once I'm healed up, I want to get back down there."

"Only after I have explored every inch of that lava tube," Stephane said.

"One step at a time, Steve. First we see what the data says. I'm not exactly thrilled about going back into a potentially unstable cave."

Kaczynski snorted. "It's fine, believe me. One of the best looking lava tubes I've seen anywhere. No goddamn reason it should've done that."

"And yet it did," Stephane countered. "I wonder if there was a stratum of some sort of crystalline lattice behind the wall you drilled into. That could have caused a wave? A cascade? Something like that."

Kaczynski shook his head with a grin. "You're the one with the Ph.D., kid, but I ain't never seen anything like you're saying."

Stephane shrugged. "It is the only theory I have right now. Otherwise, we are left with an earthquake that should not have happened." He jabbed a few buttons on his datapad. "I should go to the lab. I have a report to write for the colonel."

"Go on ahead. I'll join you there in a bit," Shaila said.

Stephane winked and headed for the door. "It's a date, *chere*."

Kaczynski wiggled his eyebrows at Shaila once the geologist left. "You could do worse, you know."

Shaila smirked and shook her head. "French playboys aren't my type," she said. "Anything else you can think of on this?"

"Eh, you'll probably think it's bullshit," Kaczynski said.

"Try me."

"All right, what the hell," he said. "Right before the quake hit, I saw this blue flash for a second there, out of the corner of my eye. I thought it was some sort of refraction off the laser, maybe, but that was turned off. Maybe some light hitting a smooth part of the core sample. Anyway, no idea what it was, but you asked."

"Blue flash, huh? You sure you didn't hit the bottle before you came out with us?" Shaila asked with a smile.

"You poured it all down the can last week, Lieutenant," Kaczynski groused. And he was right—Shaila had found a rather large stash of contraband "Scotch" on her last inspection. That was strictly against JSC operating procedures, of course, so it went down the septic system. Well, most of it. Shaila felt that contemplating one's dwindling career from a backwater mining outpost on Mars warranted a drink now and then.

"All right, all right. Blue flash. We'll check it out. Colonel says to get better fast," Shaila said.

She walked out of the medical berth and headed for the lab, thoughts of career and love—or lack thereof—shunted aside in favor of the puzzle of the Martian earthquake. The quake would at least be easier to solve.

CHAPTER 3

February 20, 1779

F*ather,*

It seems fortune is with us, for there is indeed an alchemist available to us on Elizabeth Mercuris. This is most timely, for we have found that Deacon, the late Dr. Ashton's alchemist's mate, is no match for the occult workings needed to tether the Essences of Earth and Air to our lodestones. The man tried, of course, but the result of his efforts was an area below decks in which everything not bolted down crashed suddenly into the ceiling.

The commandant of the Royal Navy shipyard here has recommended one Andrew Finch to us. He is already in the employ of His Majesty, having been detailed to the workings necessary to keep the outpost—one of England's most lucrative and important holdings, dating to the time of Charles I—afloat over the dark side of Mercury. Of course, we immediately assumed that this Dr. Finch was someone the shipyard commander would be happy to be rid of, but we cannot afford to be choosy in this matter. Thus, Captain Morrow ordered me to go collect our new alchemist, which was a most interesting experience.

Weatherby quickly hurried along the wooden footpaths of the Elizabeth Mercuris outpost. Looking down, he couldn't help but note the appalling gaps in the walkway, with nothing but black Void and the rocky, hard surface of Mercury below. When he first sighted the settlement the previous day, as *Daedalus* came up alongside, he couldn't help but think how precarious it looked, hanging above the heat-blasted world, hidden from the burning Sun by Mercury's bulk.

28

Yes, Elizabeth Mercuris was a wonderful feat of engineering—an entire town, made of dozens of old ships lashed together with rope and planking, held above the planet by hundreds of carefully deployed sails and lodestones. From that distance, it seemed quaintly cobbled-together and altogether marvelous, belying its reputation as a run-down shanty-town of miners and those who would give them the rudiments of comfort. Even the hodge-podge of sails poking forth in every direction seemed inventive and charming.

But as Weatherby walked through the outpost, it now appeared that only a bare handful of rusty nails and worn rope kept the entire assemblage from crashing down upon the surface of Mercury or floating off into the Void. In addition to the gaps in the walkway, ranging from a few inches to a hole two feet wide, the "buildings" on either side were covered in scavenged planking and poorly constructed add-ons, so that only the barest hint of the ships they once were remained.

To the inhabitants of Elizabeth Mercuris, however, this must seem like paradise compared to the surface. There, miners labored in either bone-chilling cold or oppressive heat, depending upon where their tunnels were situated, to bring up valuable ores from inside the rocky husk of a world. Unlike the Void, there was air upon Mercury, but it was a dusty, sooty stew that demanded kerchiefs to be worn around the miners' faces. Ingenious mechanical contrivances, powered by rope, pulley and the muscle of many men, brought the minerals from the depths of Mercury to towering wooden platforms, where ships could safely dock and thus ferry the goods to the outpost above. There, in addition to the foremen and traders, the other denizens of Elizabeth Mercuris eagerly served the miners; there seemed to be a drinking establishment every ten paces and a house of ill repute every twenty.

A squadron of red-jacketed soldiers trotted past as Weatherby neared his destination. They seemed to be in an awful hurry, and the young Navy man assumed they were on their way to break up the latest tavern brawl or some such. Around the next corner, another group hustled past, led by a worried-looking officer not much older than Weatherby himself.

For a moment, he wondered if there was some sort of riot going on. Perhaps there was a sudden deficit of libations.

Weatherby finally arrived at the boarding house where Dr. Finch was said to have taken a room. What was once a proud sloop fifty years ago was now generously called a lodging. The gunports were turned into windows, though few had glass within them. A door was hewn from the side, and various chimneys and holes were cut into the hull, the purpose of some of which remained elusive. Taking a deep breath, Weatherby entered.

The parlor consisted of a very small room, a desk, and an ancient crone of a woman sitting there. "Aye? Needs a room?" she barked preemptively without looking up.

"No, ma'am, thank you," Weatherby said, doffing his hat. "I'm here to inquire about Dr. Andrew Finch. I am to understand he lodges here?"

The woman opened a ledger on the rough-hewn desk. "Finch…Finch… aye! That blighter owes me eight shillings!" She eyed Weatherby warily. "You'll not be taking him before he's paid up, I'll tell you that!"

Weatherby frowned. "I assure you, madam, he will make good on his charges before he leaves. Pray, what room?"

The woman directed him up a flight of rickety stairs and down a hall toward what was once the stern of the vessel. If anything, the ceilings were lower than that of *Daedalus*, and the once-ship was in a worse state of repair inside than out. Finally, he came to a door and rapped upon it. "Dr. Finch?"

There was no reply. A second knock and a second request garnered only a low moan, the kind of groan that a man in some distress or stupor might make. Weatherby tried the door but found it locked. "Dr. Finch, I am Lt. Thomas Weatherby of His Majesty's Ship *Daedalus*. You are required to report for duty," he called out.

"Go away," came a sullen, tired voice from inside.

This was going to be considerably more difficult than Weatherby had wished, and his stomach began to feel slightly ill—whether from nerves or foul odor remained to be seen. Orders being orders, however, and noting that the door shared the same general disrepair as the rest of the lodging, Weatherby put his shoulder to it and shoved.

The door gave way easily, but struck something hard not two feet inside and stopped. It opened barely enough for Weatherby to squeeze his way through, which he did, only to discover a large crate blocking the way. He shoved the crate further aside and entered the room.

He was immediately appalled—and frightened for the future of his ship.

The room was in complete disarray, with books and papers strewn haphazardly across the chamber's lone table and chair, as well as most of the floor. Another crate was along one of the walls, and upon it was a neatly tailored Royal Navy uniform that had been casually flung aside. The bed was a crudely wrought affair, the linens in desperate need of washing.

The man upon the bed was similarly composed. He was in his night-clothes, his long dark hair disheveled and unkempt. He held a water-pipe to his lips, and Weatherby could see it was attached to a smallish device upon the floor that reminded him of a hookah from India. A most noxious fume permeated the room, with the hookah the apparent cause. Weatherby quickly surmised that it was some sort of plant, probably Venusian in nature, designed to addle the mind and senses. It seemed to be working quite admirably.

The man on the bed lolled his head toward Weatherby and looked up at him. "Who the hell are you?" he slurred quietly.

Weatherby straightened up and adopted his most stern demeanor. "I am Lt. Thomas Weatherby of His Majesty's Ship *Daedalus*, as I have already announced, and I am here to collect one Dr. Andrew Finch. I pray God you are not that man, for you, sir, are most unbecoming of an alchemist in the Royal Navy."

The man upon the bed smiled, and rather stupidly at that. "Ah, good. My chariot awaits, then, and I shall be off this decrepit wooden piss-pot. Be a good lad and collect my things while I attend to my toilet, will you?"

Weatherby had expected a variety of responses, but this one had eluded his imagination. How much leeway should he offer to such a man in this state? And what would Morrow say should Weatherby fail to return with him?

Such questions were most assuredly not on the Admiralty Board's lieuten-ants' exam.

Weatherby opted for controlled wrath, hoping it would mask his nerves. "I am not your valet, Finch. I am a representative of His Majesty's Navy, and you will put down that infernal device, get yourself out of bed and get yourself together. And you will address me as 'Mr. Weatherby' or 'sir.'"

"Actually," Finch said, swinging his legs off the bed and pushing himself up to a sitting position, "I think it is *you* who should address *me* as sir. You see, my father is the Earl of Winchilsea. So he is to be addressed as His Lordship, while I..." Finch's voice trailed off a moment. "Well, I dare say I warrant at least a sir…or something…don't you think?"

Weatherby had no inkling of Finch's aristocratic lineage. Thankfully, the Royal Navy put rank before birthright, and Finch's actual ranking aboard *Daedalus* was generally on par with the officers of the wardroom. Given the circumstances, Weatherby felt justified in grabbing Finch by his gown and hauling him to his feet.

"You will listen to me most carefully, Dr. Finch," Weatherby said, tamping down his nerves and summoning as much cold fury as he could. "You are in service to the Royal Navy, and you will do well to remember your place. Now, I will give you five minutes to assemble your effects and make yourself presentable. If you fail to do so, I will have you thrown in the brig for insubordination and laxity of duty. The inevitable court martial likely will result in a short but difficult prison term on Europa. Do I make myself perfectly clear?"

Finch could only nod, a terrified look on his face that put Weatherby's own fears at ease somewhat. Weatherby let go of the man's clothes and stalked back out the door, closing it behind him and pulling out his pocketwatch to mark the time. A shout down the stairs brought the ill-tempered matron to Finch's door, whereupon Weatherby prevailed upon her to bring some coffee. It cost him a half-crown for her to comply, but that at least settled Finch's debt in the bargain.

Five minutes and fourteen seconds later, a mug of foul-smelling coffee in hand, Weatherby prepared to do battle once more. Too soft, and Morrow might criticize him for bringing such a wastrel aboard. Too harsh, and Finch could very well create problems for him. Feeling ill-prepared and altogether too inexperienced, Weatherby took a deep breath and reentered the squalid little chamber.

To his very great surprise, Finch was actually dressed in his uniform, though it remained askew, and was hastily throwing books, papers and unidentifiable chemical apparatuses into the crates. Despite this marked improvement in dress and surroundings, Finch looked altogether horrible—glassy-eyed and sweating, his thin face all too pale for someone residing so close to the Sun. Weatherby thought the man would keel over at any moment, but he continued to work steadily, and even apologized for keeping the officer waiting. Weatherby allowed him the few extra minutes, feeling that a good effort was worth at least that much.

Finally, Finch stood before Weatherby in something approximating attention. Weatherby checked his uniform fastidiously, commenting on a loose neckerchief and fixing a button here or there. Despite his pallor and overall ill-cast look, Finch at least resembled an officer.

Weatherby regarded him a moment longer, gauging how best to proceed. If Finch were simply a crewman or a midshipman under Weatherby's command, his next move would be obvious. Finch's posting and lineage complicated things somewhat.

Or perhaps not. *In for a pence...*

Weatherby reached back and slapped the doctor in the face.

Finch cried out in pain, forgetting his meager attempts at decorum. "Damn you! What in blazes was that for?"

"To help you find your wits, man," Weatherby said coldly, feeling a touch more confident. "I will not have you appear before Captain Morrow in such a state. You have your coffee here. Drink it up before we are off. I will send some of the men for your effects."

"Yes, fine, but I assure you Mister...Weatherby, is it? I assure you that such handling is completely unnecessary," Finch said as he reached for the coffee.

"And I assure you, Dr. Finch, it is. Whatever lax discipline you enjoyed here, you will adhere to Royal Navy standards and become an officer worthy of that uniform. Fail to do so, and I will beat your poisons out of you one by one. Is that understood?"

Finch stared hard for a moment, while Weatherby tried to keep his nervousness out of his eyes. It was a bold gambit, but one his superiors had often recommended when dealing with new recruits. There would be time for bonhomie later.

The doctor relented. "Quite so," he said simply, gulping down his coffee with a grimace. "Shall we, then?"

The two quickly strode out of the hovel—with the matron giving Finch one final, withering stare—and made for the *Daedalus*, moored at the Navy shipyard on the other side of the outpost. Weatherby kept a close eye on Finch; despite his modest improvement in dress and demeanor, the doctor seemed somewhat unsure of his feet as he followed along, and a thin sheen of sweat began to cover his pallid countenance.

Yet when they turned a corner in the middle of the outpost, Finch's face managed to get paler still. Before them was the troop of soldiers Weatherby had earlier spied, standing guard in front of what likely passed for an upper-class home on Elizabeth Mercuris. It likely was once the windowed aft section of a first-rate warship, commissioned before the reign of William and Mary.

Finch made a surprisingly rapid beeline for one of the soldiers. "What has happened here?" he demanded. "Is Dr. McDonnell all right?"

The soldier demurred, nodding toward the entry of the home. Without further ado, Finch stepped inside, leaving a confused and annoyed Weatherby to follow quickly in his wake.

"Doctor," Weatherby protested, "we must report to Captain Morrow in all haste. Otherwise, I daresay…"

Weatherby's sentence was left hanging as he spied the interior of the home, which was ransacked to a near total degree. Furniture was overturned, while books and papers were spilled out across every available surface. A number of soldiers and official-seeming personages had just made way for two men carrying a stretcher—with a dead man upon it, the dagger which caused his demise still protruding from his chest.

A wail erupted from a corner of the room. There sat a young woman, in the garb of a house servant, her blonde hair disheveled and her face—pretty in the simple way of the lower classes—profusely streaked with tears. A gentlewoman sitting next to her on the low sofa pulled the girl's face away from the scene, holding her close and whispering comfort to her.

"My God! It's Roger!" cried Finch. "What happened?"

A rather portly, older man, dressed in faded finery and a slightly askew wig, approached them. "'Tis murder, Finch, and far more than that!" The gentleman looked over to Weatherby. "You're from the *Daedalus*, yes?"

"Lt. Weatherby, at your service," he replied, stunned, still looking at the corpse as it was removed from the home. "And unfortunately, I must take Dr. Finch here—"

"I hope you are indeed at my service, for I may have need of you and your ship," the gentleman interrupted. "These are fell events indeed!"

Finch drew his own gaze away from the body as it left sight. "Governor, what of his work? Tell me it is still intact!"

"I am afraid not," the gentleman replied. "'Tis gone, all of it. Notes, materials, everything!"

Finch pressed a hand to his head and leaned up against the wall. "I told him to pay mind to his security," he bemoaned. "He was as stubborn a Scotsman as there ever was."

Weatherby cleared his throat. "Finch, terrible as this is, we have duties to attend to."

Finch shot him a hard look. "None so great as unraveling this," the alchemist said disdainfully. "You've no notion of this matter."

"I suppose I don't, but 'tis not our issue, Finch, and you'll mind your place," Weatherby snapped before turning to the gentleman. "So…Governor, is it?"

The gentleman turned and drew himself up to his full height, still several inches shorter than the young officer. "Sir Alastair Worthington, governor-general of Elizabeth Mercuris."

Weatherby immediately felt uncomfortable as he continued. "Of course. My apologies, Governor. You have my condolences for your loss here, but Dr. Finch and I—"

"Loss?" Worthington snapped. "This is no mere murder, boy! Roger McDonnell was our foremost alchemist, and a researcher into the mystical properties of Mercury's ores. And most recently, he told me in confidence that he may have discovered a method for reliably producing Mercurium."

Finch pulled himself upright once more, eyes alert. "So it's true. He found it!"

"So it would seem," Worthington replied. "We cannot know for sure, but if he has, and it is now in the hands of a party willing to murder for it, this cannot bode well for England. Not at all!"

Weatherby looked at one man, then the other, then finally took Finch by the arm. "Governor, again I must apologize, but Dr. Finch here has just been transferred to the *Daedalus*, and we are already late reporting."

"Transferred? Like hell he has!" Worthington sputtered. "Do you even know what Mercurium is?"

Weatherby merely frowned at the governor, prompting Finch to elucidate. "It is nothing less than the alchemical essence of the planet itself, a material that could hold the key to many occult mysteries, and with numerous practical uses besides. It is cousin to the Philosopher's Stone itself in terms of power!"

"And who has it now?" Worthington cried, his belly shaking with his indignation. "The Spanish? The damnable French?"

"And what of our navy?" Finch added, eying the young officer most critically.

That struck a chord in Weatherby, prompting him to release Finch's arm as he contemplated the potential enormity of what may have transpired. Captain Morrow had standing orders that the officer of the watch beat to quarters when sighting any ship, even an apparently friendly vessel—better to be ready for naught than unready at the wrong time. The same calculus applied here, he felt.

"I think," Weatherby said finally, "we should adjourn to the *Daedalus*. Captain Morrow should hear of this matter, and quickly."

July 25, 2132

Shaila finished reading Stephane's preliminary report and put the datapad down on the mess hall table between them. "Nice job," she said, reaching for her third cup of coffee this morning. "I mean, it doesn't actually *say* anything, but it's well written. Lots of nice, big words."

Stephane leaned back in his chair and ran a hand through his dirty blond hair. "I know, Shay, I know. We have nothing."

The two of them had spent six hours in the lab the previous evening poring over sensor data from across McAuliffe's area of operations (AOO). There were more than five hundred AOO sensors spaced out across three hundred square kilometers of territory, each sensor set atop a ten-meter high pole that also carried communications gear. The sensors picked up fluctuations in radiation, temperature—anything that could impact mining ops. That also included seismic activity; Mars wasn't prone to earthquakes, but the ops could trigger a rockslide or collapse that could literally have repercussions elsewhere.

And within that comprehensive sensor blanket, exactly three sensors picked up the barest hint of seismic activity. Stephane believed the quake could have reached a 6.5 on the Richter scale within the cavern, but the three nearest AOO sensors, each roughly a kilometer away, barely registered a minute tremor.

Aside from that, the only other thing they managed to wheedle out of the data was a half-second communications outage which occurred two seconds before the sensors detected any seismic activity. The outage covered all incoming and outgoing transmissions in the area, including the signals every sensor sent back to the base computers, on-planet audio and video signals, and even the narrow-beam laser array that kept McAuliffe in constant contact with Earth via the six MarsSat satellites in orbit around the red planet.

Coincidence? Possibly, but Stephane chose to include it in the report. After that, there wasn't much more he could do, mostly due to lack of in-depth geologic data. So that's where Stephane and Shaila left things before heading to the sleeping centrifuges for the night. Living on Mars took a toll on the body, but sleeping in capsules hooked up to giant centrifuges allowed McAuliffe personnel to at least sleep in Earth gravity. That, along with twice-daily exercise and a regimen of pharmaceuticals, helped stem the effects of low-G living.

Stephane had offered to continue their "research" in Shaila's sleep pod— one of his typically outrageous flirtations. She, of course, declined, though with a bit less annoyance than usual; he had turned out to be a pretty smart guy after all, now that he had something to do. Besides, sharing a pod was out of the question anyway—the last couple that tried it unbalanced the entire centrifuge, prompting a week's worth of repair work.

"So I guess we're heading back there," Shaila said between bites of tofu scramble. The McAuliffe mess was decent enough for most meals, but seemed to have issues with breakfast. "I'm still not thrilled about going back in that cave, you know."

Stephane shrugged. "There is no sign this will happen again. Of course, there was no sign before, but we must chance it. Otherwise, we will never know what happened, or if it will happen again."

"All right. What do you need to bring?"

He called up a new file on his datapad and slid it back to her. "It is all here."

Shaila scanned the list, which took up two pages. "Jesus, Steve. That's a hell of a lot of equipment. Audio/video? Radiation sensors? Seismic units? We don't even *have* a portable GPR imager."

"Billiton does," he replied. Ground-penetrating radar imaging was standard fare for geologic study. "I've already talked to Yuna Hiyashi this morning. She's willing to lend us the imager, but she wants to come out to the site with us."

Shaila groaned into her coffee. Dr. Yuna Hiyashi was a pioneering astronaut from the glory days of JSC. First woman on Venus, first *person* on Europa. She spent the better part of 40 years in space—so much so that her body could no longer handle Earth's gravity. When she retired eight years ago, Billiton hired her as a consultant at McAuliffe, a great public relations move given that she once commanded the base earlier in her storied career.

Retirement didn't seem to suit Yuna well, however. She puttered about the base, engaging in scattershot experiments ranging from terraforming to geologic history—with little to show for it. And her intense curiosity meant she stuck her nose into just about anything going on. She was your typical old-lady neighbor with too much time and not enough to do—albeit an old lady who retired as the civilian equivalent of a two-star general and lived on Mars.

"Steve, you can't just invite random people to go on an EVA like that," Shaila said, trying to summon up patience. "Especially Yuna. Harry's bad enough, but now Billiton is going to be really all up in your business because she's going to be reporting to them. Not to mention the fact that she'll have you chasing random ideas all over the place."

"I know, I know," Stephane said. "But we could use the extra set of hands, and eyes. She has seen a lot of things in her time. And I need that imager. I need to see what is under that rock, and this is the safest way to do it. Besides, I think she could use the distraction. She does not have a normal life any more."

"Yeah, well, trust me. Astronauts don't get to have normal lives," Shaila said. "Stay out here long enough, you'll see."

"No, thank you. After Mars, I plan to get a nice little university job somewhere. Somewhere with nice trees and grass outside and big wooden desks I can sit behind and talk all day." Stephane looked up and waved to someone behind Shaila. "And there she is now."

Shaila turned and saw Yuna walking over to them, breakfast tray in hand. She was a thin reed of a woman, her white hair kept back in a simple ponytail, her smooth features giving away nothing about her age.

Shaila gave Stephane a hard glare. "You still should have cleared this with me."

"I am sorry, *ma cherie*. I am not used to all of these JSC rules yet." His smile, however, told her otherwise.

Before Shaila could rip him a new one, Yuna had taken a seat next to them. "Good morning!" she chirped. "I have your GPR imager loaded into Rover Two. And Shaila Jain! Why haven't I seen you in my yoga classes lately?"

"Sorry, Yuna, just been busy is all," Shaila replied crossly. "I know Steve brought you into this, but I'd appreciate it if you'd let JSC make an official report to Billiton before you fill them in on things."

Yuna smiled. "Don't you worry. I was JSC since before you were born. Billiton doesn't even give me anything to do around here. Besides, who doesn't like a bit of mystery?" Her grin was contagious, and Shaila even felt her frown twitch upward a few millimeters. "The Billiton wing was buzzing this morning. They're pretty up in arms about this. We'll probably see them already out there."

"Super," Shaila said. "I just hope they stay the hell out of the way."

As Yuna and Stephane exchanged pleasantries and nattered on about fault lines and strata and such, Shaila reviewed his shopping list one more time. She'd have to clear out every last bit of equipment in storage, and the junior officers would probably see their own little pet projects delayed for a while. But Diaz told her to solve this, so solve it she would.

An hour later, they were suited up, outside and readying Rover Two for their return to the cave. "I couldn't lay hands on anything else besides the GPR imager," Yuna reported. "I imagine Harry had them pull all the sensor gear for the other mining sites."

Shaila looked over to Billiton's depot, about 150 meters from McAuliffe proper. The ore haulers were out, as usual, ferrying deuterium and ores between the mining sites and the smelting and loading bays here. But Billiton's own personnel carriers—super-sized pickup trucks with bench seating in the back—were gone as well.

"I just hope it's manageable out there," Shaila muttered, climbing in and revving the rover's engine. "Hard enough as is without Harry getting antsy about things."

Twenty minutes of rolling Martian terrain later, they arrived at the cave, located atop a gently sloping ridge that leveled off onto a wide plateau. Yesterday, before going down into the lava tube, Shaila had thought how desolate and bleak it looked.

Now, however, it was frenetic.

As she pulled the rover to a standstill, she could see at least a dozen people milling about the skylight leading down to the cave, and three of them were busy erecting a scaffold around the skylight itself, probably to support some kind of lift system. The surface was blanketed with sensor modules, creating an array at least 250 meters wide, while a few technicians were taking soil samples and other readings.

Jumping off the rover, Shaila headed toward the Billiton personnel, leaving a trail of red dust clouds in her wake. "Who's in charge here?" she demanded over the Billiton comm channel.

"You are, Lieutenant," Harry responded. She looked around and saw him hop-shuffle over. Naturally, he wore the very latest in pressure suit tech. His gear was more form-fitting and far less cumbersome, and had all the bells and whistles; she could even see the lights of his heads-up display dancing across his helmet visor. "We're just chipping in."

"You call this chipping in?" she said. "You're running your own damn investigation here!"

"We're providing you with data you wouldn't otherwise have," Harry said, holding out his palm. A small holoimage sprouted from his hand, showing a local map of sensor arrays. Shaila pulled out her datapad and saw that Harry already sent her links to every sensor around her—including a sensor they managed to suspend from the skylight inside the cave. "And nobody went in there yet," Harry added. "We waited for you."

Shaila frowned at the datapad. "So why the burst of generosity, Harry?"

"It's not generous," he said simply, dismissing the holoimage simply by closing his hand. "It's common sense. I don't want quakes on Mars. We've been steadily profitable for ten straight quarters now. It's not ending on my watch. So you get our help."

"And you breathing down my neck," she shot back.

"Goes without saying," Harry said. "We need this dig." With that, the executive shuffled off toward his crew, leaving Shaila staring mutely at all the useful data scrolling across the datapad, wishing she had access to the shit-hot tech Billiton gave its executives. After a minute, she began barking orders.

Normally, it was hard enough for Shaila to get the Billiton people to follow base rules when it came to loitering in the Hub or cleaning up after their late-night mess hall parties. But here, the techs jumped at her every command. They quickly unloaded the GPR imager, checked out all the equipment—and even peppered her with unaccustomed "yes, ma'ams."

There had to be something in the cave that Kaczynski didn't mention for Harry to be this forthcoming and generous, Shaila figured as she prepared to re-enter the cavern. Otherwise, he wouldn't play nice with JSC to get back in there. On the flip side, the unprecedented cooperation implied that Harry would be quite ready to blame JSC, and Shaila in particular, if the investigation didn't go well.

Finally, after sending Yuna and Stephane into the cave to set up equipment, Shaila hooked her suit to the rope-and-pulley contraption the mining company rigged up and began to lower herself in. Thirty seconds and five meters of bedrock later, she got her first glimpse of the cavern, lit by the pale pink sunlight streaming in from above and the lamp lights below. To her surprise, it looked…*different.*

She was reminded of visits to her parents' house in Birmingham, England, between off-world assignments. There would always be little changes—a new piece of furniture here, some rearrangement there—that usually added up to a larger sense of difference. That's kind of what she was getting here.

Yes, her first visit to the cave was frenetic, to say the least. But still, some of the rubble seemed oddly out of place. Shaila could've sworn the pile of rock that buried Kaczynski was bigger than it appeared now. And wasn't there a smaller pile off to the right? Shaila looked around carefully, trying to recreate the harried, blurry scene of the previous day in her head. It wasn't working very well.

Her observations were cut off abruptly as the rope started to vibrate. She looked up reflexively, only to see small rocks and dust starting to fall from the ceiling.

Out of the corner of her eye, it seemed there was a quick flash of…blue. "Oh, shit."

A second later, Shaila started swinging wildly, thirty-five meters from the ground, as large rocks started to fall in earnest all around her. She struggled to grab the rope with both hands as the cavern whirled around her.

Suddenly her vision blurred, and she let go of the rope a moment. Vertigo, she thought. But then an image flashed before her eyes—some kind of structure, standing impossibly tall in the Martian sunlight, a rust-red plain stretching before it, mountains tall behind it.

It was gone a moment later.

Then she felt the rope go slack. And the floor of the cave suddenly rushed up to greet her head.

CHAPTER 4

February 20, 1779

Placing a number of men, all convinced of their place and importance, inside a small room is perhaps not the best way to find accord, Weatherby thought as he watched Governor Worthington argue his case, as it were, before Captain Morrow. It hadn't helped that the governor had essentially tried to order *Daedalus* to investigate the murder; while he had the power in theory, its use was fraught with political concerns. So he was reduced to arguing before the captain in order to obtain his cooperation. And, as it turned out, Mr. Plumb made for a fine counterpoint.

"With all respect, gov'nor, there's no way a ship of His Majesty's Navy can go haring off to find a single murderer when there's a bloody war going on 'round Jupiter!" Plumb said firmly while Morrow, his eyes half-lidded, observed with detachment. Next to him was seated Worthington, and next to the governor was the distraught housemaid, who was introduced as Miss Anne Baker, the deceased's only domestic servant and companion.

"This is no mere murder, sir!" Worthington roared in response, slapping Morrow's table with his hand and sending waves through his corpulent body as he shook with indignation. "You've no idea what the implications of this action may be!"

"And you do?" Plumb thundered back.

"I do, sir," Finch said from where he stood wedged between Weatherby and Foster. "And it is my opinion as this ship's alchemist—for that is what I am now, is it not?—that the loss of the Mercurium in this murder is a loss

43

of far greater proportions than you realize!"

Weatherby took Finch's measure once more, and as he talked, found him possessing more backbone than he had first considered. While still pale and sweating, the look in the young alchemist's eye was steely, his jaw was set, and his focus was clear. His sense of decorum, however…

"You keep it quiet, Finch," Plumb growled. "You'll give your opinion when your superior officers ask for it. And besides," he added, turning to Morrow, "'tis not the first time some bloody alchemist has sent honest sailors off on some wild goose chase."

At first blush, Weatherby could not agree more, as he had often believed alchemists to be inscrutable at best, and either charlatans or fell arcanists at worst. And yet, the governor had mentioned something about the Navy whilst still in Dr. McDonnell's rooms. "Excuse me, Mr. Plumb, gentlemen?" Weatherby ventured. "Perhaps Governor Worthington would be so kind as to relate this tale from the very beginning, so that we might better weigh our options."

This prompted a small smile from Morrow. "A fine idea, Mr. Weatherby. Governor, if you would?"

Frowning, Worthington nonetheless sat down and began relating the particulars of what occurred, as he had come to understand them. Last evening, Dr. McDonnell was at home in his study, reading, when there was a knock at his door. The housemaid, Miss Baker, answered to find three men there—a gentleman of some sort, with fine dress, and two others attired most poorly. The gentleman asked for an audience with McDonnell, who agreed to see them despite the hour. As one of the very few reputable alchemists at the outpost, his modest home—once a small merchantman—often received visitors at all hours. Miss Baker showed the men into McDonnell's study and then retired to her chamber.

At this point, Worthington asked the girl to continue the story. She nodded quickly, gathering herself, and plunged ahead in a quiet but steady voice. "I could not hear all that was said, but I could tell after a short while that Dr. McDonnell was getting quite angry, and that one of the other men—the gentleman, I presume—was likewise becoming upset. I heard shouting. Something about Mercurium, about not giving it away. The gentleman seemed to be desperate, said something of a 'great working.'

"Finally, I heard Dr. McDonnell shout, 'Get out, all of you!' I heard an awful scuffle then, and the voice of my master crying out briefly," the girl continued as she started to tremble. "Then there was naught but silence. I hid in my cupboard, I'm ashamed to say. I was too frightened to move, and I must have fainted within it. When I awoke not a few hours ago, I…"

At this, Miss Baker again broke down completely, sobbing. Weatherby instinctively moved to console her by offering his kerchief and pouring her a glass of water from the ewer on the table. The girl smiled up at him, which he returned as sympathetically as he could muster without appearing too untoward. Morrow called Midshipman Forester into the room and had him escort the girl outside for air, and the governor resumed the story after she departed.

"The poor man was stabbed, once, in the heart," Worthington said. "I'm told it killed him quickly, which is a blessing, I suppose. And the room was ransacked."

"A tragedy," Plumb said, though his mien did not seem particularly sympathetic. "But I still don't see how we're to be involved in this when we've already orders to go fight 'round Jupiter."

Worthington glared at Plumb, but addressed the captain. "Sir William, I must agree that the murder is, sad to say, rather beside the point. Dr. McDonnell's killer should be brought to justice, but the more important matter here is the Mercurium."

The ship's new alchemist stepped forward. "I agree with the governor, Captain," Finch said. "Roger's death pales in comparison to the groundbreaking work he had accomplished, a work now in hands not our own."

"What'd I tell you, Finch?" Plumb said, his voice raised.

Before he could continue, however, the captain silenced his first lieutenant with a gesture. "George, please," he said quietly before addressing his newest crewman. "All right, Dr. Finch. I think it's high time we come to some understanding of this Mercurium. Explain what it is, if you would."

Finch cleared his throat and looked nervously at the others; Plumb already had a keen effect upon him. "I shall try, sir, though Dr. McDonnell was quite hesitant to discuss his work, except in the broadest of terms, due to its sensitivity. In any event, Mercurium—theoretically—is a liquid metal alloy distilled solely from the ores of Mercury. Of course, the primary component is the liquid metal mercury, or quicksilver as it is known, but a wide variety of other metals are also necessary, and some of these are exceedingly difficult to obtain.

"Now, the existence of Mercurium had been, until recently, simply theorized. Alchemists believe that each planet among the Known Worlds possesses an alchemical essence; the famed Philosopher's Stone is widely considered to be Earth's essence. But it was McDonnell's goal to see it through, and when last I spoke with him some weeks ago, he was confident of his eventual success."

"And what would it do?" Morrow asked. "Do we not hear of new discoveries every day now?"

"Well, like the Philosopher's Stone, the applications would be numerous," Finch said, his voice steady even as his fists clenched. "Mercury itself governs the spheres of rapidity, communication and healing, and McDonnell felt there would be many practical uses for it. Given his work on behalf of the Company, it could possibly become the foundation of a new treatment for sails and hulls, endowing English ships with greater speed and dexterity."

"And with this Mercurium in the hands of an unknown party, and its means of production as well, it could shift the balance of power in the Void away from England," Worthington said, once again slapping the table for effect.

Finch turned to the governor. "We are absolutely sure, then, that the Mercurium is gone? Was there anything else taken?"

"Actually, yes. Miss Baker has been most helpful in that regard," Worthington said. "I had no idea she could even read, and yet she was well informed and quite knowledgeable. She identified a number of items, including a handful of treatises on the alchemical and medicinal value of Venusian plant life, and another on the mysterious Xan peoples of Saturn. Of course, all the doctor's stores of Mercurium are gone, as well as his notebooks on the processes involved in creating it. As you can imagine, the Sunward Trading Company is quite up in arms about the whole matter. They had funded his research through the years, and seemed finally ready to capitalize upon it when this happens!"

"What of the girl, then?" Morrow asked quietly. "How is it that a simple housemaid would be so well acquainted with the deceased's work? Might she be an accomplice, or even the guilty party?"

Weatherby was stunned to hear such an accusation, but had to remind himself that this was not England, nor even Earth itself. At home, women upheld their responsibilities to hearth and home, and some had proven to be canny in the ways of business and the arts as well. This outpost seemed to be another matter entirely.

"Anne Baker is no murderer, Captain, I can assure you," Worthington said. "McDonnell took her in a year ago, straightened her out quite nicely. And she comported herself quite well under our examinations."

"I'd have to agree, sir," Plumb said quietly. "Women are not murderers. And it's a low man indeed to kill a woman outright, so it's not a surprise she's still alive. If anything, I'd say those that did this would've left Mercury immediately. Any ship that went off between the murder and now is suspect. I doubt we'd catch her at this point."

"Perhaps you might," Worthington said. "We have conducted a complete search of the outpost, and Miss Baker could not identify any of the killers among our residents. And only one ship has left since the event—the *Groene Draeck*, a Dutch merchantman, sailed that very evening, before the murder became common knowledge. One of her crew was heard in the taverns saying he was next bound for Venus."

Weatherby gasped—was the ship under attack by the Ganymedean the one that carried the killer? He opened his mouth to speak, but caught a glare from Morrow, and quickly demurred. Instead, in part to cover his lapse, he said: "Perhaps this talk of Venus was a ruse, designed to cast us off the trail. Why would one advertise one's next destination?"

"Aye, and what if these bastards used this Mercurium on their own ship? They could be halfway to Jupiter by now!" Plumb added.

Morrow looked to Worthington. "It may be that they're bound for Venus, but even that world is quite large, and held by the Spanish no less. And if they are not there, then there's no telling where they might have gone."

"You must try," Worthington said. "I must report this to both the Navy and the Company, and it should go over well for both of us if I can say that you've at least stopped in at Venus en route to Jupiter in order to make inquiries. And I promise you, Sir William, I would not ask if the need weren't great."

Morrow appeared to consider this. Weatherby knew the calculations well; Venus was indeed positioned well for a course to Jupiter, so that they might lose less than a week if they detoured. And they were but a day behind the merchantman, strange alchemy or not. Plus no captain wanted to find himself on the wrong side of a colonial governor—even from a colony so small as this one.

"We cannot linger there, Governor," Morrow said, sounding slightly defeated. "Our duty to England in the Jovian system must take precedence, until the Admiralty itself tells me otherwise. But we will stop, and hopefully luck will be on our side. Is that amenable to you, sir?"

Worthington agreed, and was soon taking his leave of the officers, his broad smile quite annoying to the tired, battle-weary officers. Before the governor left, however, Finch asked him: "Governor, what will become of Miss Baker herself? I should think that with her employer dead, she may have a hard time of it."

Worthington snorted. "True enough, I suppose. But how is that your concern?"

"She is the only person alive to have seen the faces of the murderer and his accomplices," Finch said, turning to the captain. "Sir, with that knowledge, as well as her insight into the deceased's work, I would suggest she join us as we make our enquiries upon Venus. If we cannot find the killers, then we may at least take her to Earth, or Ganymede. She may yet help us recreate the formulae necessary to duplicate Dr. McDonnell's work."

Weatherby gave Finch a slight smile and a nod at this, which he returned wanly, while Morrow considered the doctor's proposal. "I do not like the thought of a woman aboard," the captain finally said. "However, you have a good point, Doctor. She may speed our investigation considerably, and we may offer her a kindness that requires little in the way of effort on our part. You will, of course, surrender the alchemical lab for her use and make berth in the wardroom."

Finch frowned, caught in a trap of generosity. "Of course, sir."

"Mr. Plumb," Morrow said. "Arrange a watch among the officers, the mids and the doctor, and ensure that a sentry is posted at the door to her quarters. Miss Baker is to be under guard at all times, either locked in her quarters or accompanied on deck by a fully armed officer. A lone woman aboard a ship with two hundred and fifty men deserves no less consideration that that."

That was a point upon which all present could readily agree, and it was upon that note the discussion concluded. However, Morrow asked Weatherby to tarry a moment. He remained, standing as tall has he could before the captain until everyone else had left. "Sir?"

"What is your opinion of Dr. Finch?" the captain asked when they were alone.

Weatherby would rather have been asked to sleep in the bilges. "I am sure he is quite knowledgeable in matters of alchemy and physic, sir," he said tentatively. It seemed plausible enough—Finch sounded the part when he spoke. He had a great many books as well.

Morrow gave a faint smile. "Come, Weatherby. We have no cause for unnecessary discretion here. I ask because I want to know your mind."

Weatherby cleared his throat. The day was quickly being filled with decisions of politic. "Very well, sir. I find him to be a drug-addled wastrel of a man, and I fear for the lives of our crew should he be required to actually perform any kind of alchemical or medicinal duties under duress. Sir."

"Your opinion, once drawn from you, is most certainly unstinting," Morrow said with amusement. "But you are quite correct. The port commander tells me Dr. Finch is a hard case. But he is also brilliant. His studies at Oxford were exemplary, and I am told he left his teachers confused and embarrassed by his rapid advancement in the occult and scientific arts. However, he is most undisciplined, as you have no doubt seen. I know his father, who has always despaired of Andrew's ways. I have already posted a letter to His Lordship promising to help turn Dr. Finch into a proper officer."

Weatherby simply nodded, his worst fears about the evils of the aristocracy confirmed.

"I am assigning Finch to you, Weatherby," Morrow continued. "What you lack in formal education, you more than make up for in a keen mind and natural awareness, so do not let the mysteries of alchemy daunt you. You are, after all, a prodigious reader, I'm told. You will make sure Dr. Finch performs his duties, and discipline him when he does not."

"Yes, sir," Weatherby said, hoping his reply sufficiently masked his extreme discomfort with the notion.

"Don't worry, Lieutenant. I shan't ever give you an assignment I do not think you can perform," Morrow said. "Your record is exemplary, but it is in these special cases that we truly attain new heights. Finch is a challenge, but it will go very well for you if you are able to turn him about. After all, as you advance in the service, you may be required to command far more noble, and more difficult, men than he."

Weatherby nodded in understanding. "Thank you, sir. I will not disappoint, and neither will Dr. Finch."

"I will inform Finch of your supervision," Morrow said. "In addition, with the unfortunate death of Major Denning, we are without an officer to oversee the marines. Mr. Plumb will take over that duty, and I am assigning you to run the midshipmen's classes that he would normally teach."

"Of course, sir," Weatherby replied. At least teaching the mids would be easier than minding Finch.

"Good man. Dismissed."

Weatherby managed to catch up with Finch as the latter man made his way back across the main deck; apparently, his lack of sailing experience was such that he needed directions to his lab in the forecastle. "A moment, Doctor?"

Finch turned. "Only if you don't intend to hit me again," he said with a wan smile.

Weatherby flushed uncomfortably at that. "Not at all, Doctor. I was impressed with the way you acquitted yourself in our gathering. I was merely curious as to any theories you may have in mind." Weatherby had already determined that if he were to indeed supervise an alchemist, he had best educate himself as best he could.

"Oh, I think it's quite early to have theories, Lieutenant. But I will go have a smoke and consult some of my texts. A bit of research should help."

"Research indeed, but you will have to go without your smoke," Weatherby said, trying not to sound apologetic. "I'm having your hookah locked up with the grog for the duration of our mission."

Finch wheeled about and gave Weatherby a frustrated look. "Really, Mr. Weatherby. Is there neither time nor space to call my own?"

"No, actually, there is not," the young officer responded, straightening up and fixing Finch with his best officer's glare. "We may be beset by the French or Ganymedeans at any time. You will do us no good if your vices render you incapacitated at a critical moment."

Finch sighed and looked down at the decking, apparently allowing Weatherby's words to sink in. "I had no idea the deprivations under which you suffer aboard ship," he said quietly. "I do believe I shall have words with my father when next I see him."

"You may do as you wish, of course," Weatherby said sternly. "However, you will perform your duties in the interim, lest the captain have words with him as well. I will expect a report on your research, Doctor."

Weatherby turned and headed back to the quarterdeck, leaving Finch to his duties—and little else, hopefully.

July 25, 2132

As she hurtled toward the cavern floor, Shaila Jain could only think that this, of all possible outcomes, was not the way she wanted to go out.

Any further thoughts on the subject were halted as abruptly as her fall. She cried out as the rope snapped taut, feeling her body rattle inside her pressure suit and her stomach threaten to release its contents.

Shaila opened her eyes to find that she was now dangling some ten meters above the surface of the cave, having fallen at least twenty-five meters in a split second.

Rocks continued to crash down around her, the rumble of the quake permeating her pressure suit and creating a vibrating echo all around her. She tried to look around, but the rope was tangled around her arms and her suit, making it impossible for her to see anything except the cavern floor beneath her. Thankfully, it wasn't getting any closer to her.

On the other hand, the rope's motor was dead, leaving her hanging, literally, and hoping a massive rock wouldn't fall on her, or that she wouldn't vomit inside her suit. If she had to choose, the former would've been preferable.

"Durand, report!" she managed to bark out.

"Quake!" he said simply, his voice cracking.

"No shit. Take cover!"

"We're coming up right below you," Yuna said just as she and Stephane appeared directly under her, seeking out the relative safety of the skylight as rocks continued to tumble down from the walls and ceiling of the lava tube.

A stab of worry hit Shaila. "You sure you want to be under me? This rope isn't secure."

"Better you than a rock, Shaila," Yuna said, her voice remaining cool under the circumstances. And Shaila had to admit, the old-timer had a point.

Shaila felt something large and heavy strike her right foot—the reinforced boot took much of the blow, but the impact also sent her spinning wildly on the rope. She saw the sensor the Billiton folks had suspended in the cave crash to the floor and break into several large metal and glass shards.

"Shit!" Shaila cried as the room swirled and spun around her. She could see both Yuna and Stephane reaching up toward her as they flashed past her field of vision, but she knew it was pure folly. "Get your asses down!" she ordered.

She then closed her eyes once more and hoped she'd get to open them again. If nothing else, it helped with the nausea.

Finally, after what seemed like an hour but was probably no more than 30 seconds, the thrumming sound of the quake stopped. Shaila ventured a look around, only to see that she was still spinning around in the air like a glorified circus act.

"All hands, report," she said curtly.

"We're all right down here," Yuna said. "Shaken up, that's all."

From the surface, Harry chimed in through a short burst of static. "We're OK out here. No injuries."

Shaila released the breath she had been holding. "Good. Keep your people away from the skylight, Harry. Now let's see if I can get my ass down from here."

It took some doing, but Shaila slowly managed to untangle herself from the rope so that she was at least hanging vertically once more. She gently lowered herself down the rope until she was hanging on only by one hand. From there it was a three-meter drop—a mere hop in Martian gravity.

A moment later, she was on the cavern floor, a cloud of red-brown dust at her feet. Both Stephane and Yuna looked relieved—and slightly stunned by everything that just happened. The thought of the structure that she saw in her head came back again, but she dismissed it quickly. Business first. "All right, suit checks," Shaila said. "Everyone in one piece? That also goes for you and your people, Harry."

The reports came back; one Billiton tech had a readout malfunction on his pressure suit, but the suit itself seemed intact. Everyone else, above and below the surface, was fine. This time.

"All right. So apparently, we come down here, it's an earthquake," Shaila said.

"Maybe, but we cannot say for sure," Stephane cautioned. "We searched for Kaczynski after the last quake, and there were no more tremors during that. But it seems there may have been a tremor since then, with all the rock that has seemed to move around. And really, how could we three destabilize a cave of this size?"

"Fine, we're just having godawful luck," Shaila said. "Let's get everything in place and get the hell out of here, OK?"

Despite the severity of the tremor—at least as severe, if not more so, than the one the previous day, according to Stephane—there seemed to be only slightly more rubble in the cave. If anything, the piles of existing rubble seemed bigger, especially toward the center of the cave.

Their equipment survived nearly intact, with only a pair of lights and one sensor suite destroyed by falling rock. The rest of the gear was in its containers or still topside. They immediately got to work unpacking and placing the sensors. Unlike the handheld sensor packs, each of these sensor suites was far more advanced, with longer range and greater finesse in detection. Each suite was a bulky one-meter cube, with stubby little feet on the bottom and a light-and-camera mast sticking up another meter.

The three of them spread out to place the sensors throughout the cavern. Ultimately, they ended up with a sensor suite of some kind or another every fifty meters or so, cloaking about a kilometer's length of the cave in electronic monitoring.

"Can we start it up?" Stephane said as he walked back from the edge of the sensor array.

"Not yet," Shaila said, crouching down over the main sensor control. "I've got to get it programmed first. Why don't you go and play with your new toy?"

"I have it all set up for you," Yuna added. "Well, I think I do. I've never actually used a GPR imager before."

Stephane bounded over to the device, which looked oddly like an old-fashioned baby carriage with off-road tires and a computer screen and keyboard where the baby should be. A few minutes of twiddling and tapping later, Stephane was happily rolling the device across the floor of the cavern.

"This is magnificent," he said. "I'm getting far more data than I thought. What a wonderful imager!"

"So happy for you," Shaila deadpanned. "Does that mean you know what happened?"

"Oh, no. No idea. The data makes no sense, of course."

Shaila looked over at the geologist, who was still pushing the imager around with a look of enthusiasm on his face. "Say again?"

"I see the usual mix of basalt, clinopyroxenes, iron. The strata are tightly compacted. The matrixes around this cavern are all very stable." Stephane paused a moment to check a reading. "Kaczynski was right. A core sample could not have caused this. What is more, I do not see any fault lines, fissures—barely a crack." Stephane rolled over one of the smaller rocks that had fallen during the tremors. "See here? If this rock had fallen from the ceiling or the wall, it should have some stress fissures in its matrix. Yet the imager says it is solid."

"I'm no geologist, but it sounds like you're saying there was no earthquake here," Yuna said. "Or at least those rocks didn't come from an earthquake."

Stephane shrugged, his eyes still glued to the imager's readout. "I am saying nothing. I am hoping that I can find something I can explain before I run out of cave."

"For what it's worth," Yuna said, "this simply *looks* unusual to me." She was using a holocamera to record their efforts, and was focusing closely on the walls and floors of the cave.

"How?" Stephane asked.

"Well, I've seen my fair share of Mars, you know," she said. "And I've been in a few lava tubes and caves, some old canyons too. And the way these rocks are piled up, it just doesn't make sense. It's hard to explain."

Shaila tapped the last few commands into the sensor array readout. "Well, we're good to go. Sensors coming on line…now."

Shaila pressed the keypad and watched the diagnostic screen run through its final checks. One by one, each sensor in the tube came to life, bringing audio/video, seismic, electromagnetic and radiation sensors to bear on the mystery. The array was linked to the datapads they all carried, as well as the central computer back at McAuliffe. There were multiple fail-safes—Shaila was big on redundancy when it came to computers. No matter what happened, the data would be stored somewhere, somehow.

She looked up to see the lamps atop each of the sensor suites lighting up, one by one, better illuminating the cave. Seeing the lava tube's full immensity, and its inky depths still far off, made her feel like she was in the gullet of some giant Martian worm. Shaking her head, she turned back to her readout.

"And we're on," she said, standing up straight and working the kink out of her back. "If there's anything here, we'll find it."

"Thank you," Stephane said. Even over the comm, his response sounded genuinely grateful. If only he wasn't such a...

Shaila's datapad beeped. "That was fast," she said. The sensors had picked up a radiation signature that she didn't recognize.

Her heart skipped a beat, but quickly she saw that it was non-ionized radiation. That was good—it was the ionized radiation that would kill you. Non-ionized radiation was pretty much everything else, from radio waves to light and heat sources. Shaila wasn't a physicist, but it seemed to her that this particular radiation should be somewhere on the visual light spectrum. Whether the light was the only radiation or just a byproduct of some other activity remained to be seen.

It was also weak, which was another good sign. But the sensors couldn't pin down a source; it seemed to permeate the entire cavern.

"Yuna, you ever see anything like this?" Shaila said, sending the rad signature data to the older woman's datapad.

Yuna studied the signature for several long moments, pressing buttons on her datapad. "Seems familiar, but I can't place it."

"Well, the cavern's full of it," Shaila said. "Doesn't seem dangerous, but doesn't seem normal, that's for sure. I wonder—"

A couple of small pebbles rolled by Shaila's boot, derailing her train of thought. It took a moment for her to figure out why.

"Steve, you picking up any seismic activity?" Shaila asked.

Stephane stopped pushing the imager around and pulled out his datapad. "I do not see any. Why?"

A couple more pebbles rolled slowly past her. "I'm seeing movement here."

"What kind?" he asked.

"Just some rubble, nothing big. But if these are moving, wouldn't there be more?" Shaila saw a few more roll past her, almost languidly, while others—both larger and smaller—remained still.

"The rock piles may be settling," Stephane said. "Though we would see that on the sensors. Hang on. I am coming over. I—wait. I see them here too."

Shaila stood and moved to the center of the cavern, where Stephane had joined Yuna. They watched as a handful of rocks—some barely a centimeter in diameter, some nearing ten centimeters—continued to roll northward into the darker part of the cave.

"Seismic activity is rising," Stephane said, his voice stuttering slightly. "It is not a spike. A very small rise, sustained."

Shaila looked at her feet again just in time to see two rocks—one just a pebble, another the size of her fist—roll past her boot, leaving several other bits of rubble behind. "Guys, what's the slope here?" she asked.

Stephane pressed a few buttons. "The cave slopes up that way," he said, pointing in the direction of the northern, dark end of the cave. "The rocks are rolling...uphill."

They stared for several long moments, processing the scene before them. Shaila was the first to react, and only because she felt something strike the back of her boot.

She turned and saw a larger rock, one the size of a basketball, start rolling again as she lifted her foot up.

"They're getting bigger," Yuna said quietly as she panned the holocam to follow the rock up the tunnel.

"Yeah," Shaila said, willing herself to think clearly. She checked the read-outs from the equipment they had set up; everything was still functioning normally. And both the low-level seismic activity and ambient radiation were creeping higher. "Harry, get some more ropes down here. Now. We're leaving," she said.

Nobody argued with her.

CHAPTER 5

March 1, 1779

In order to make the time necessary to investigate upon the Green Planet, Captain Morrow opted to have the crew complete repairs from our ill-fated engagement en route, rather than at the Elizabeth Mercuris dockyards. Thus, our work is doubled, but at least we are away from that abysmal place. It is cheerfully debaucherous on the surface of things, but the sadness and desperation of many of its denizens was all too apparent beneath.

The men pressed on Mercury to replace our fallen comrades have taken to their tasks surprisingly well, given they were rousted from their homes and taken aboard with little notice. Even the landsman has been seen laughing with his new mates, and has taken to learning his duty with, if not fervor, then a certain pragmatism. I imagine life aboard ship in the Royal Navy, with steady pay and a chance at prize money, is more attractive than life aboard an oaken scaffold above a hot coal of a world.

Our voyage through the Void is not unlike travel upon the seas of Earth, or any other world. The sun-currents that link the planets carry us along quickly, whilst our sails catch the light-motes of the solar wind, further hastening our journey. But for all this, we may as well be upon the ocean itself. There are eddies and wakes within the currents, and occasionally we shall encounter solar storms that, instead of water, rain down glittering motes. It would be pretty, save for the winds that would threaten to shunt us out into the broader Void, if not for a steady hand upon the wheel. Were the Sun not shining brightly through the night watch, we might actually mistake ourselves for being in the Channel itself.

It is but two weeks from Mercury to Venus, including the time we might spend upon the Green Planet's seas; the worlds are close together here, whereas the transit from Mars to Jupiter is far longer, depending on the currents. We do hope to make a rapid descent to Venus and complete our inquiries quickly, for none of us besides our new alchemist, Dr. Finch, have taken to our new mission with fervor.

That passion for the lost Mercurium seems to be fueling Dr. Finch in lieu of his preferred vices. The doctor had a rough time of it for the first few days of our journey, and I had thought it a touch of Void-sickness. Yet seeing the rapidity of his improvement since, I cannot help but wonder if the loss of his hookah was more to blame. He looks well enough now, though, and has performed his duties with competence—and only minimal reticence.

Our other newcomer, Miss Baker, has no duties, but is rather a duty to the rest of us. However, I do not consider accompanying her as such, for I find myself looking forward to my watch with her each day…

"Do you happen to know, Mr. Weatherby, the alchemical formula for the solution applied to the sails that allow us to catch the Sun's winds?" Miss Baker asked as they walked along the main deck after the midday meal.

Weatherby smiled. Every watch he stood accompanying Miss Baker reminded him of his lieutenant's test at the Admiralty. She was curious to the point of being intellectually voracious, asking questions about the operations of the ship, travel in the Void and the life of an officer in the Royal Navy. Yesterday, he had practically given the midshipmen's lecture on the flow of currents from the Sun to each planet, and how the ship uses its ruddersail and planesails to navigate them. Indeed, he had finally invited her to listen in on the midshipmen's class he ran, so that, if nothing else, he would not be forced to repeat himself.

"I'm afraid, Miss Baker, that Dr. Finch could give you a better answer than I," Weatherby said, regarding the sails. "The formula need only be applied a few times each year, and its creation and composition is generally left to the ship's alchemist, or to any alchemists in port."

She nodded, her gaze still fixed upon the square-rigged sails upon the mainmast. "I would imagine some alchemical Essence of Air is involved, though some extract of Jovian gases would do the job nicely. I will ask Dr. Finch, then. I cannot imagine how the early explorers managed to reach the Moon, let alone other planets, without modern means."

"Dr. Finch tells me you have some knowledge of the Great Work yourself," Weatherby said. "Does that stem from your service to Dr. McDonnell?"

Miss Baker looked down, a brief flicker of pain in her eyes, and Weatherby immediately regretted bringing up her deceased employer. She was truly a dedicated servant, and Weatherby felt sure McDonnell had been an outstanding employer.

"Dr. McDonnell was most kind to me," she finally said. "Yes, I kept his laboratory and library organized, but he also saw fit, in his spare time, to educate me on the rudimentaries of alchemy." She noted the surprise on Weatherby's face and smiled. "Come now, Mr. Weatherby, it is not entirely unknown for women to have some faculty with the Art, now is it?"

Weatherby knew, of course, that she was quite literate, for she was particularly delighted to learn of Weatherby's predilection for reading, and had already drawn from him the promise of borrowing some of his small collection of books aboard. "Well, no, there have been some," he allowed as he guided her past a group of crewmen scrubbing the deck. "But it is my understanding that solitary alchemists such as Dr. McDonnell guard their secrets jealously."

"'Tis true enough, though if all alchemists kept their knowledge so closely, there would be no future generations of alchemists, would there?"

Weatherby readily conceded the point with a smile, and the two resumed their stroll. Her questions continued, whether they were on the formulation of alchemical shot, the history of the Royal Navy beyond the Earth, how long it would take to visit Saturn and its unseen, mysterious alien denizens—were they actually to permit visitors, of course—and even the slave trade of the diminutive Venusian lizard-men at their next destination.

While answering as best he could, Weatherby also kept an eye on the men as they walked across the deck. Two days out from Mercury, a seaman by the name of Matthew Weaver wiggled his eyebrows at Miss Baker in a most unseemly manner, and was caught in the act by Midshipman O'Brian. The mid, all of thirteen years old, bravely stood up to the much older seaman; Weaver later received six lashes for his trouble. Order was restored, O'Brian garnered new respect from the crew despite his age, and Miss Baker had gone untroubled since.

"Mr. Weatherby," came a voice from behind. He turned to find the bo'sun, James, saluting him. "Dr. Finch says he's ready to tend the lodestones, sir."

Weatherby had been looking forward to this. "Very good, James. Please inform the doctor I am on my way. Mr. Forester!" Weatherby had seen the older mid passing by. "Would you be so kind as to relieve me and accompany Miss Baker on deck for a short time? I have business with Dr. Finch."

"Could I not see the operation upon the lodestones?" Miss Baker asked. "I would be most keen to understand the working involved."

Weatherby thought a moment. "Perhaps another time, Miss Baker. This is Dr. Finch's first time performing this duty, and I need have my full attention upon him."

Weatherby took his leave and proceeded below decks, trying to put the echo of her face out of his memory. She was, of course, part of his duty. More importantly, despite her intellect and charm, she was but a household maid. Weatherby knew his future in the Royal Navy depended as much on improving his social standing as it did on his skills as an officer. Weatherby had sworn to make his mark in the service, and would be undeterred in his goals. Even if presented with someone like Miss Baker.

Or Finch, for that matter. Weatherby had thought it prudent to keep the alchemist as busy as humanly possible. Thus, in addition to replenishing the ship's sail treatments, alchemical shot and curative stores, Weatherby ordered the doctor to likewise attend the daily classes given by the officers for the benefit of the midshipmen. Weatherby felt it wise to give Finch at least a working knowledge of seamanship if he were to be an officer aboard ship. And it amused him to see the tall, lanky man tucked in between five boys, some of whom had yet to begin shaving, and a housemaid who, he was gratified to note, hung upon his every word.

Weatherby rendezvoused with Finch at the stairwell to the hold. From there, they made their way downward toward the bilges, where the ship's lodestones were kept. While it was easy enough to sail between Earth and the Moon without such innovations, long voyages between the planets became much more difficult without them. Both air and gravity dissipated the further from a planet one voyaged. In the early 1500s, Spanish alchemists discovered that the mystic properties of common lodestones, once properly treated, could allow a vessel to retain air and gravity almost indefinitely—so long as the stones were regularly rejuvenated with the appropriate workings.

"My God, what is that smell?" Finch said when they ventured below the hold and into the cramped bilges, which were no greater than four feet in height. "I should have hoped never to smell such filth!"

"It is seawater, Doctor, likely combined with rats and their leavings, and possibly some small amount of the men's waste as well," Weatherby replied, giving an honest assessment of a typical ship's bilges.

"And I am to come down here regularly?" Finch asked with incredulity.

Weatherby could not help but smile. "That is one of your assigned duties, Doctor. If you do not, we shall lose our air entirely, and perhaps even drift off the very decks of the ship!"

"Surely one of the men can be assigned this task with proper guidance from me," Finch said as his bright-polished shoes dipped tentatively into the murk of the bilges.

"Not according to the manual in your hand, Doctor," Weatherby said. "These workings are far too vital to be left to anyone other than a learned alchemist like yourself, and it is most important that it be done properly."

Finch grimaced back at him. "How do you live like this, in this rotting wooden pestilence?"

"I don't live here, Doctor, and I assure you, I will visit far less than you!" Weatherby laughed with a certain satisfaction. "Now off to your working, so that we may both go above decks at our earliest opportunity."

Despite his daily barrage of questions to Finch and his own reading, Weatherby could only follow the barest hints of the rituals which Finch enacted. He knew the liquids in Finch's possession contained quintessence drawn from both plant life and stone, though the exact ingredients eluded his memory. The plant life somehow fed the air, while the weight of the stone symbolized the weight of each man aboard, keeping them firmly on the deck. The recitations were in the form of prayers; Weatherby wondered just how much devotion Finch might have to the Almighty, but he also knew from his own research that the prayers served as mnemonic tools to help the alchemist remember the procedures.

"Are you sure you're doing it in the proper order?" Weatherby asked at one point. "I had thought the angelic recognitions came prior."

Finch fixed him with a disdainful glare. "Been reading up, have you?"

"Of course," Weatherby replied, trying not to take offense.

"I suppose that's admirable, but do leave the details to me," Finch said. "Much of the workings in the official manuals are woefully inefficient."

"So you do not fear that your changes will unravel the working?" Weatherby asked. "Our air and gravity are at stake, Doctor."

Finch proceeded on to the next lodestone. "Quite sure. It takes far more than an omitted phrase to undo a working."

"And what would it take?" Weatherby asked, warming up to the subject.

Finch sighed, seeming tired of the conversation already, as he picked his way through the muck. "To everything there is an opposite," he said, seemingly from rote. "What can be done can also be undone, typically by working in reverse."

Sensing his displeasure, Weatherby allowed Finch to continue working in silence. There were six stones in all, from bow to stern, and it took Finch at least thirty minutes to attend to them all. When he was done, his breeches were caked with filth up to his thighs, and his arms to his elbows as well.

"I feel disgusting," Finch said. "And this is to be done regularly?"

"The exact timing, as you well know, depends on our position in the Void and the movement of the planets," Weatherby said, remembering his perusal of the task the night before. "That is, of course, yours to determine. But I urge you to calculate well, as I much prefer the stench of this air to having none at all."

Finch shook his arms and legs as they ascended the stairs to the hold once more. "I dare say this experience may prompt a new avenue of research."

"Oh?"

"Indeed," Finch said. "I shall make it nothing short of an all-consuming goal to find a way to extend this working so that it may be performed far less frequently."

"You would do the service a great good if you were to do so," Weatherby said, "though I know your reasons are quite self-serving."

"Most alchemical innovations are self-serving, Mr. Weatherby," Finch said as they made their way back above decks. "I am quite certain the Count St. Germain did not fashion the Philosopher's Stone in order to cure mankind's poverty—merely his own."

Weatherby left Finch to clean up and went above decks to relieve Mr. Forester and resume his watch over Miss Baker. As he walked along the main deck, he saw one of the able seamen of his own division, young Jim Rooney, sketching some of his fellows as they labored on the ropes. Rooney was not on duty, and he kept well out of the way, but Weatherby was curious as to his work.

"What have you there, Rooney?"

The young man held up his paper, and Weatherby instantly recognized the faces of the men in his division. "Just something to pass the time, sir, idle hands being the devil's own work."

"Remarkable likenesses," Weatherby commented. He had endeavored to get to know his new charges as well as he could, while still maintaining the necessary remove that would allow him to command them dispassionately. He gave Rooney a small smile and a nod and began to walk off. Then an idea formed in his head. "Rooney," he said, turning back. "Can you make a sketch of anyone?"

"Well, sir, I've a bit of trouble with the women, sir. I gets a bit distracted when I try it. But aye, give me a face and I'll draw it like life itself."

"And what if you hadn't a face, but a description instead?"

The young man pondered this. "Like, if you told me what someone looked like, and I worked it up as you said it? I don't know, sir. Never tried."

"On your feet, man. Come with me." Weatherby stalked off and made for Forester and Miss Baker, who were peering over the side of the quarterdeck.

"Thank you, Forester. You're relieved," Weatherby said. "Miss Baker, this is our Jim Rooney, whom I've seen is a quite talented artist." Rooney blushed heavily and bowed, while Miss Baker smiled at him uncertainly.

Weatherby laid out his plan, and soon both Rooney and Miss Baker grew quite excited. The lieutenant sequestered them in the wardroom as they worked—under marine guard, of course. Two hours later, he had what he had hoped for—a sketch of each of the three men Miss Baker had admitted to her master's rooms the night of his murder.

Shortly after that, all three stood before Captain Morrow with great anticipation as he looked over the sketches. "You believe these to be accurate likenesses, Miss Baker?" the captain asked.

"Yes, Captain, I do. As very close to perfect as can be done, I believe."

Morrow gave Rooney a hard look, and Weatherby began to wonder if they would be in trouble for shirking their duties. He had thought the idea was sound, but had yet to determine how hard a captain Morrow might be.

He needn't have worried. "Mr. Weatherby, please inform the steward that Rooney here is to receive a double ration of grog for the next three days—one for each of these drawings. Dismissed, Rooney."

The young seaman's face blossomed into a wide grin as he saluted and took his leave.

"This solves a problem that had vexed me of late, Mr. Weatherby, and that was how to allow Miss Baker here to identify the culprits while trying to protect her in port. Some of the Venusian towns are difficult for proper Englishmen to navigate, and Puerto Verde is the worst sort of pirate's nest," Morrow said. "With any luck this shall make our investigations all the more rapid, and we may appease that bombastic Worthington as well. Neatly done, Mr. Weatherby, neatly done indeed."

Weatherby's chest swelled with pride as he escorted Miss Baker back to the quarterdeck. To have impressed his new captain within the first few weeks of service was no small thing for a freshly minted second lieutenant.

It was almost enough to allow him to forget the absence of Miss Baker's genial company that day.

Almost.

July 25, 2132

The first thing Shaila did when she emerged from the skylight above the lava tube was to slap an immediate quarantine on the area. Given that there were less than a hundred souls stationed at McAuliffe—all of whom wore location beacons on their pressure suits when outside—it was easy enough to keep tabs on anybody who got too close to the cave. With two quakes recorded, it might have been coincidence that both occurred while people were in the cave, but Shaila wasn't keen on taking chances.

Shaila ordered all Billiton personnel to stay at least a kilometer away from the cave, which was at least 15 kilometers from the nearest mining site anyway. Once Shaila had shown Harry the sensor video of the moving rocks, any protest he may have lodged was quickly silenced. She also ordered him to increase his operational safety level, which included new sensor screens of all the ops sites, and to report any unusual seismic or radiation activity.

Reporting rocks rolling uphill went without saying.

Stephane and Yuna spent the ride back poring over the data the sensors continued to churn out. The rise in radiation and seismic activity was very modest, but still climbing slightly—no more than a hundredth of a percent every ten minutes or so. If things kept going the way they were, the lava tube would be a collapsed pile of glowing-blue rubble in three days.

Of course, less than 24 hours ago, there was nothing going on in that cave. *That we know of,* Shaila reminded herself. The uncertainty gnawed at her and, frankly, scared the hell out of her. And that…vision?…or whatever landed in her head back there, it was bothering her, probably more so than she'd care to admit. Mars was supposed to be lifeless. Boring. Shaila didn't realize just how much she had come to rely on that. Or how complacent she had gotten.

As she pulled the rover up to the base, she figured her days of complacency were done. Even though most of the Billiton people were still checking things out at the dig sites, it was obvious that word traveled fast—the few miners and JSC personnel outside the base stared as she herded Stephane and Yuna toward the airlocks.

But nothing prepared her for what she saw when the familiar hiss-whoosh of the airlock gave way to the base entrance…and she walked right into the middle of a holovision shoot.

A burly man with a professional holocamera rig and a bright klieg light was filming a tall, lanky, silver-haired man as he pointed around the Hub and talked into the camera.

"Christ," Shaila said, yanking her helmet off. "I bloody well forgot he was shooting in here today. Damn him."

Him was Dr. Evan Greene, host of the critically acclaimed holoshow *SpaceScience.* Greene, with producer and cameraman in tow, had arrived three days ago to do a piece on McAuliffe and the Billiton mining ops. As always, JSC granted him all-access, all the time. She figured that would probably include the cave-in, given that it was the biggest news within the nearest 100 million kilometers.

Greene was as big a celebrity one could be for someone with a Ph.D. in astrophysics. His show was on in 52 countries on Earth and was regularly fed to all JCS commands in the Solar System. In it, he breathlessly described the wonders of space and in the intricacies of exploration, usually by putting himself smack-dab in the middle of where people were trying to work. Yet apparently, the viewers at home ate it up; it was the highest rated science program of all time. The show's Web site even offered posters for sale featuring the handsome Dr. Greene, perfect for pinning up in some geek-girl's room back home.

Shaila quickly strode away from the shoot, aiming for the equipment lockers on the other side of the Hub and hoping Greene wouldn't notice her. Stephane, however, seemed far more enamored of the pop scientist. "I am to be interviewed in two days," Stephane said. "It should be fun, yes?"

"Oh, heaps," Shaila said, tossing her helmet into a locker. Then a warning light flickered in her head and she quickly turned on Stephane. "You do *not* say a word about this cave-in to him, whatsoever. We clear?"

"Well, yes, but he will ask about it, no?" Stephane wore a perfect deer-in-headlights look in the face of Shaila's grimace and pointed finger.

"Not. A. Word. Steve," she repeated. "He beams this stuff back to Earth and we'll be second-guessed from here to hell and back."

"Shaila," Yuna said gently, putting a maternal hand on Stephane's shoulder, "you realize that Col. Diaz has already sent all our data back to Houston already. And Billiton is in close contact with their home office, too."

Shaila wrestled out of the top half of her suit. "I know. Don't care. This thing needs to be solved and wrapped up with a bow before the public finds out about it. Unless you two managed to solve this thing on the ride back."

"Ummm…not yet," Stephane said. He struggled with his own suit until Shaila, seeing his futile attempts, reached over, undid the pressure seals and yanked the top half of the suit over his head for him. "Thanks for that," he said.

"No problem," she replied, tsking. "When this thing is over, you're gonna go in for remedial training, though." They shared a brief smile. Stephane was turning out to be far more competent than she had first thought. What was more, when he dropped the playboy shtick, he was actually pleasant to be around.

"Lt. Jain! A moment, please!"

She looked up to see Greene, his shoot complete, hop-skipping over to her in the low gravity. "Shit," she muttered before putting on her best faux smile. "Dr. Greene. What can I do for you?"

The scientist fixed her with his own grin, full of brightly polished teeth and holovision charm. "I was hoping I could borrow you for a few minutes to talk about the cave-ins. I hear some strange stuff happened out there, but the information's pretty conflicting right now."

"No can do, Doctor," Shaila said, stepping out of the rest of her suit. "I'm due in command in about 15 minutes to brief Col. Diaz. And we're still gathering facts ourselves."

A bright flare of light made Shaila jump—but it was merely the holocamera light shining on her. Two hundred million kilometers from Earth, and she was in the middle of a paparazzi scrum? "I totally respect that, but I'm hearing some pretty interesting stuff from the folks who were out there with you," Greene said.

"Doctor, please," she said, her smile disappearing in the face of the rolling holocam. "We're not going to talk about this until we have some answers. That goes for Dr. Durand, myself and all of JSC."

"Are you heading up to command now? I'd love to get a shot." Greene started motioning his cameraman to take up a better angle.

Shaila straightened up. "Doctor, we have jobs to do."

"Lieutenant, I have JSC all-access. That includes this," Greene parried. "I'll be well out of your way."

"Dr. Greene, when Col. Diaz herself invites you into a private briefing, then you can come along. But right now, I would...strongly suggest...that you let us do our jobs and figure this thing out," Shaila said, trying to keep herself from lashing out. "We're under enough pressure from everyone else without worrying about the home viewers. OK?"

That actually took the smile off Greene's face. "OK," he said, nodding gravely. "Just let me know when you're ready to talk about it."

Surprised at how quickly Greene relented, Shaila managed a curt nod. "All right, then. Thank you."

Greene smiled once more, then turned and headed off down the Billiton corridor, his crew in tow. Shaila knew he had a reputation for not backing down; on Venus, he famously insisted on four different angles on a survey crew's work, which involved three JSC astronauts sweating out declining oxygen levels and rising suit temperatures for over an hour, despite the mission commander's protests.

For now, at least, she didn't have to worry about him. Briefing Diaz, however, was another matter. It took a half hour just to recap their adventures in the cave, followed by the colonel quizzing them on their theories. Shaila, of course, was way out of her league, while Stephane went on about possible deposits of radioactive or magnetized ores beneath the surface. But they were just that: theories. And the live video feed from the sensors still showed rocks rolling uphill into the darkness.

Shaila peered closely at the video feed. "They're moving out of range," she said. "We need more lights at that end of the cave. Maybe another camera."

"Unless there's another quake, of course," Yuna said. "I'm not sure we ought to be going down there again. Shaila was almost killed."

Shaila shot the older woman a look. "Please. I'm fine."

"Oh, I know you are, Shaila," Yuna said with a smile. "You remind me of me forty years ago. Ready to brave the great unknown! But even so, I do think we should move a little more cautiously."

"Agreed," Diaz said. "Nobody's going back down there today, at the very least. That thing rattles again, we'll know about it anyway. So what's your next step?"

"I want to get better images out of that cave," Shaila said immediately. "And I want to see where those rocks are going."

"So do I," Diaz said. "So how do we get there without risking bodies again?"

Stephane cleared his throat. "We work with Billiton," he said tentatively. "I think they have a robotic probe."

"Not bad, Durand," Diaz said. "Yuna, can you liaise with Billiton, see what you can get out of them?"

Yuna grinned. "I'll pull whatever strings I have."

"Good. Now, meantime, we have a mystery rad signature and higher EM levels. Any progress?"

Shaila shrugged. "I ran another search before I came in here. The signature doesn't show up in the database."

"Odd," Diaz frowned. "Well, I want that signature loaded up onto every sensor we got on Mars, inside and outside. If it pops up elsewhere, I want to know about it. Same with any unusual EM readings. Anything else?"

The three astronauts merely shrugged uncomfortably.

"All right," Diaz said, standing. "Right about now, everybody on this base knows we got rocks rolling uphill in a cave that's had at least two earthquakes in as many days. They're gonna get antsy, scared or both. And need I remind you, they outnumber us more than three to one. So we keep this investigation close to the vest, and we give them answers, not theories. I'm going to go tell Harry the same thing right now.

"Between Houston, Billiton, and Evan Greene, we're gonna have enough people crawling up our ass on this one. So let's put our heads down and get it done. Now—"

Diaz was cut off by a blaring claxon. A moment later, Adams' voice came over the base intercom. "Crash team assemble. We have two miners down. Repeat, crash team to EVA staging. Two miners down."

Diaz jumped out of her seat and dashed into the command center, Shaila right behind her. "Report, Adams," Diaz barked.

The young officer didn't bother looking up. "Billiton reports two surveyors down in some sort of rover crash, roughly 1.5 clicks from that cave."

"How do you crash a rover on Mars?" Shaila asked. "It's not like there's traffic!"

Adams finally looked up at his superior officers. "They say they ran it into a ditch and, um, well, they said it wasn't there before."

Diaz and Shaila looked at each other for a moment in disbelief. "Get out there," the colonel finally ordered. "Take Durand and Yuna with you."

Stephane scowled at the entryway to the command center. "They told me six months on Mars would be fun. Liars."

Shaila grabbed his arm and literally pulled him down the stairs, Yuna quickly following behind.

CHAPTER 6

March 5, 1779

Father,

We are upon the seas of Venus, where ships of His Majesty's Navy are rare, as England's holdings here are few indeed. The massive Spanish presence upon the Green Planet is the legacy of De Soto, Cortez and Pizarro, among many others. So we must tread carefully. Whilst we are not at war with the Spanish, our relations with them are not entirely cordial, either.

We make for Puerto Verde, the largest port on the planet. Here, the Spanish export sugar cane, the strange Venusian tobacco plants and the bounty of both harvest and mines. They also engage in a hearty slave trade as well, as the small Venusian lizard-people, while strong and hale enough, cannot match mankind's advances in weaponry.

As we prepare to row one of our boats onto shore, I find myself envious of the duties of our men. They have but a handful of serious tasks aboard ship, whether they be topsmen or gunners. They learn through repetition and rote, through methods passed down by generations of seamen before them. They are the wheels of our great machine, and I am proud to lead such fine men.

As an officer, however, there are times when one is called upon to do far more than sail a ship, and our time upon Venus will be one such occasion…

Weatherby walked uncertainly over the cobblestoned streets of Puerto Verde, his shoes sending pangs of ache into his feet with each step. It did not help matters one whit that the clothes he now wore were thickly woven and embroidered, for the close, humid Venusian air was unforgiving.

It had been Finch's idea, naturally, that they pose as gentlemen adventurers during their investigations on Venus. Morrow had initially suggested they be disguised as common seamen in order to inquire about the *Groene Draeck*, but it was fairly evident that Finch was wholly unsuited to the task. Weatherby had considered leaving him aboard the *Daedalus*, but there were already precious few aboard who spoke Spanish, and among Finch's talents was a facility for languages.

They alit upon the seas of Venus two days prior, swooping in from the southern pole and riding the aurorae—that mystical gathering of sun-current and alchemical essence—down onto the waters with a surprisingly gentle crest. From there, it was a relatively simple matter of sailing toward the port whilst staying undetected for as long as possible. Venus' clouds, fog and humid gloom served as an effective camouflage in that regard.

Daedalus weighed anchor well north of the town, discharging the search parties ashore for a more subtle entrance into the Spanish holding. Lts. Plumb and Foster did indeed adopt the guise of sailors, while it fell to Weatherby to become an aristocratic gentleman alongside Finch. The clothes he now wore were borrowed from the doctor, and Weatherby had to order Finch to stop demanding promises they be returned intact.

Plumb and Foster, each accompanied by a Spanish speaker from among the crew, kept to the docks and warehouses in their search. Weatherby and Finch, meanwhile, climbed up the cobbled streets toward the better section of town. "Better" was a relative term, of course, for Weatherby was sure he had never seen such a hive of wretched excess and sinful villainy in his life. And having just come from Elizabeth Mercuris, this was a bold statement indeed.

Yet this was not the simple excess of the British mining outpost. No, the Spanish, laden with gold and slaves from the Venusian mountains, took their debauchery to a more sublime height. Even the lowliest sailors put on their finest garb, such as it was, to go into port. There were no bordellos that Weatherby could see. Instead, it seemed every so-called lady upon the streets was more than welcoming to any proposition, whether she wore a scullery maid's dress or the finery of a noblewoman.

And yes, public drunkenness was common; it seemed almost fashionable to be drunk at midday, and those so indisposed had an air of sodden satisfaction about them. Of course, despite the clouds and humidity, Puerto

Verde was indeed quite green and verdant, and there was a certain lush warmth to the place that appeared to lull its inhabitants into a state of happy stupor.

Then there were the slave markets, one of which they had to pass through en route to the town's better inns. There, the diminutive Venusian lizard-people were chained to the wall by the dozens, and kept in large metal cages by scores. The Spanish, who first colonized Venus in the 1500s, had quickly developed a burgeoning trade in Venusian slave labor, for these primitives were easily subdued by the superior stature and technology of Men. In mere decades, the various tribes among the Venusians—and there were many such clans stretching across the green planet's three continents—had taken to warring amongst each other simply to provide the losing side to the slavers. The Spanish, understandably, were quite content with this arrangement.

The Venusians that Weatherby and Finch spied were barely a yard tall, all long gangly limbs covered in tiny green and blue scales, with cats' eyes and beak-like snouts and a plethora of frills and horns upon their heads that looked quite similar to ladies' fans. As the two *Daedalus* officers walked past, the creatures' odd croaking voices begged for release in various Venusian dialects as well as a few human tongues besides. Weatherby wondered where they would end up—on Earth? The horrible Spanish gold mines on the moons of Mars? Perhaps the Ganymedean plantation farms or the blistering iron mines of Io?

Thankfully, Weatherby's aching feet and heat-stoked exhaustion took his mind off such distasteful thoughts. By the time the duo reached the first of what would be many taverns and inns, Weatherby was drenched in sweat, and Finch looked at his loaned clothing with barely veiled dismay. They both hoped they would find their quarry quickly. Morrow had consulted the ship's orrery and determined they could stay but three days. Weatherby was sure he would melt completely away before then; no doubt Finch would consider his outfit lost entirely at that point.

While it was moderately cooler in the taverns, their investigations took time. Finch was quite adept with his Spanish, and Weatherby could see that, despite his vices, the doctor had a natural affinity for personal interactions that, at times, escaped the young lieutenant. He surmised this was a byproduct of his aristocratic upbringing, and said as much to the doctor in between establishments.

"Oh, I wouldn't say that," Finch said as they walked to the fourth tavern of the afternoon. "I have known many so-called noblemen who regularly make themselves fools with but the slightest utterance. It is intelligence and confidence, Mr. Weatherby, which make a man personable, though this must be well balanced, as too much of either makes him most tedious indeed."

Weatherby had a good laugh at this quip, though he wondered whether the humid air, combined with an afternoon of frequenting taverns, contributed to his finding humor in it. Weatherby had policed both their intakes assiduously, but they still had a part to play, and the roles included buying, and consuming, drinks. He had forgotten to ask whether Finch could produce a bit of alchemy that would lessen the effects of alcohol, and in hindsight was not surprised that the doctor hadn't volunteered one himself.

This fourth establishment, called Casa Moncada, was much like the others, built of clay brick and tiled roofing in the Spanish style. The courtyard was all but abandoned in the afternoon heat—even hidden by the constant cloud cover, the Sun still warmed Venus considerably—and Weatherby wondered if they would soon run up against the traditional siesta. It seemed the Spanish needed the nap after a long morning of debauchery.

Inside, the tavern remained crowded, the bricks providing cool shelter against the large disk of the sun. Long tables held a broad array of Puerto Verde's inhabitants, from prosperous merchants and shippers to lowly sailors and scalawags, all joined together in proper drunken camaraderie. There were women of all stripes as well, from seemingly proper ladies (who ought not to be in such a place to begin with) to obvious prostitutes with their petticoats and décolletage exposed to an alarming degree. The din of loud conversation and raucous laughter permeated the room, overcoming the valiant efforts of a guitarist in the corner, busy plucking out a sprightly tune.

By now, their approach had become routine. Weatherby and Finch settled in at the most crowded table, exchanging pleasantries with those around them. Finch had concocted a story about the two of them seeking passage to the Jovian moons as part of a lucrative business arrangement involving Ionian sulfur-iron. Eventually, the name *Groene Draeck* would come up and, ultimately, the sketches Rooney drew would be produced. Thus far, their efforts had resulted in nothing but spent coin and a hint of tipsy dizziness.

Here too, at Casa Moncada, there was little in the way of progress. Nobody had heard of the *Groene Draeck*, and the sketches were passed about the table to no avail. Thankfully, the drink here was of a higher quality than in the other establishments, and there was something approaching edible food as well, for which Weatherby found himself immensely grateful

It was near sunset when Weatherby was about to give up on Casa Moncada. However, a man sat down next to Finch and asked, in Liverpool-accented English, to see the sketches. He was dressed as something of an explorer, with sturdy leather boots and the kind of loose linen clothing that withstood the heat well. His beard was shaggy and his demeanor was rough, but there was intelligence in his eyes as he scanned the drawings.

"I've not seen the gentleman in the fancy clothes, I'll tell you that. I'd have known it if I had," he told them. "But this one," he added, holding up the image of one of the two ruffians, "was in just this morning, looking for a guide."

Weatherby leaned in close. "A guide? To where?"

The man smiled. "Well, sir, I'm not sure I should say. I've no reason to cause trouble. You're not working for some constabulary, are ye?"

Finch smiled winningly and deftly produced a few coins, sliding them across the table toward the newcomer. "I assure you, my friend, we are nothing of the sort. We simply heard that these men had an excellent ship for hire."

"Well, he said nothing of a ship, though I wager he'd need one. This fellow here, he says he's hoping to trade with the Va'hakri tribe. They've a trading post that's a good ways down the coast, about a half day by ship, and a hike through dangerous jungle after that."

Weatherby looked questioningly at Finch, who said, "The Va'hakri are considered the lore-keepers of the Venusian people. They stand apart from the usual inter-tribal bickering of the rest of their kind, and are typically the ones who handle any dealings with Men."

"Aye, any guide worth his salt knows this," the other man said. "Not a month goes by that one of us isn't off down that way. Not surprising at all to have someone come in asking."

Weatherby pondered a moment. "I do not recall seeing any kind of native settlement on our charts. But then, this is primarily a Spanish holding to begin with."

The other man smiled broadly and stroked his dirty beard. "Aye, it is, lad. And you're not a couple of gentlemen traders either, I'll wager."

Finch glared at Weatherby briefly for his ill-advised comment before sliding a full crown toward the stranger. "Forgive my companion, sir. He is young and most loquacious when he shouldn't be."

"Oh, I don't care," the man grinned as he pocketed the coin. "But seeing as I missed a chance this morning with the other fellow, I'd be willing to show you down to the Va'hakri village if ye wish."

Weatherby nodded. "I think that would be most welcome, sir. May I have your name, and your word as a loyal subject of King George that our dealings be kept private?"

"The name is Bacon, and I've been no subject of king nor nation for many a year. But ye have my word. It's not the first time my silence been bought. And they've got the tide and a head start, so best we go back to your ship before long."

The three rose from their drinks. "You're distressingly transparent, Mr. Weatherby," Finch muttered.

"At least the job is done. We're well upon the trail," Weatherby said, somewhat embarrassed. "Come, Mr. Bacon. You're quite right—we must be on our way quickly."

July 25, 2132

The rover hadn't simply crashed into a ditch—it had fallen into a rocky ravine two meters wide. About a half kilometer away, the access road snaked back to McAuliffe, and the lava tube was on the other side. It was as if a giant trench had been dug into the Martian crust between the two.

"This is at least 200 meters long," Stephane reported over the comm, looking at his sensor pack. "And just like the cave, there are no pressure cracks in the matrix. Aside from the fact there is no erosion, this looks as though it has always been here."

Shaila listened to her breathing inside the pressure suit—inhale, exhale, slowly and carefully—and looked on as the emergency crash team carried the miners away from the rover's wreckage on stretchers. The whole situation was getting stranger by the minute. The injuries were relatively minor—a few broken bones and concussions—and their suits remained blessedly intact. "And this trench wasn't here before," she said to Stephane. It wasn't a question.

The planetologist clumsily holstered his sensor and pulled out a datapad, nearly dropping it in his gauntleted hands before managing to call up satellite maps of the area. "No, this is new. We have good resolution here, and this is not on our images."

Shaila nodded, though inside her thoughts were roiling. Mars was breaking every law of geophysics and they had no idea why. "This related to the quakes in the cave?"

"I have no evidence yet, one way or another, but yes, that would make sense," Stephane said. "If any of this were going to make sense."

"What about our permanent sensors? Any trace on there?"

Stephane tapped again on his datapad. "About the same as the earthquake in the cave. A few minute readings on a handful of sensors, but nothing that would trigger the alarms."

"Fuck," she said suddenly, feeling the desire to stop standing there and move about. "Have the base get us some new satellite imagery of this entire area and run a comparison. This is getting too weird."

Before Stephane could respond, Shaila was already shuffling off toward the trench. Harry Yu was standing at the precipice, overseeing the rescue efforts of his people. She keyed into his suit frequency. "Get anything out of them?" she asked.

"The miners? Not really. They were driving back from the site when they just fell into this." He sounded unusually sedate and cautious to Shaila. Perhaps this stuff was getting to him, too.

"Any sense of when it showed up?" She pointed to a set of rover tracks about 10 meters away. "I think those were our tracks when we went back to base earlier. If they weren't, there'd be another rover down there."

Harry shrugged within his suit. "No idea. Probably some kind of side effect from the quake."

"We're going to have to expand the quarantine area around this thing," Shaila said, half to herself. "At least five clicks, maybe ten."

That got Harry's attention. "For how long?" he asked.

"For the duration, I imagine."

Harry turned to look her square in the visor. "Jain, there's a shit-ton of gold and uranium in there. The sensor data backs it up, and it's our job to go and get it."

"No matter how many bodies pile up?" Shaila asked, focusing her nervous energy on him. "What happens when this whole area collapses and your guys are busy digging holes?"

"Listen, Jain," he said, his voice returning to an approximation of calm. "I'll send you the data. It's huge down there. Really huge. This could secure funding for McAuliffe for the next twenty years, all by itself."

Shaila just shook her head as she watched the crash team pull the stretchers out of the ravine—a *new* ravine. On Mars. "Honestly, I couldn't care less, Harry. You bring people in here, and you'll endanger their lives—and ours too if we have to go and save their sorry asses. So don't you go telling your bosses and Houston that we're being unreasonable about this."

"Doesn't have to be that way, Jain."

Shaila turned to back to Harry to find him wearing a slight smile and an inscrutable look on his face. "And how is that, exactly?" she asked.

Harry grabbed her wrist and punched a few keys on her gauntlet. They were now talking on a private channel. "Look. Our ops here are profitable, but barely. It's a huge amount of resource for a handful of basis points. This cave could change that in a matter of weeks. We need to get down there, no matter what. And I'd appreciate it if you could make that happen as soon as you can."

Shaila glanced at him sidelong. "I bet you would."

The mining exec shrugged. "The company pays a pretty nice discovery bonus. You were part of the discovery team. You and Kaczynski. Even Durand, if you want."

"I'm JSC, Harry," Shaila warned. "So's Steve. You know that's against the rules."

"If we can get down there in the next day or two, I'd make sure you were in on it regardless. Something to think about. It'd be a pretty good chunk of change. Plus, I'll leave you out of the report if we're able to get down there and get that ore out." He pressed a button on his own gauntlet, severing the private link. "Durand told me you need one of our robotic probes," he continued. "Tell him he can pick it up out of storage whenever."

"Fine," Shaila said, still not quite believing what she just heard. "Meantime, you and yours are ten clicks away from that cave—anywhere along the length of it—until we sort it out. Got it?"

With a nod, Harry walked off, leaving Shaila staring at the ravine. The past 24 hours was quickly filling up with firsts, which now included her first official bribe offer.

The ride back to base was, thankfully, far more uneventful. Stephane and Yuna immediately made for the labs in order to huddle over the latest data, leaving Shaila to give the colonel a woefully incomplete report. Diaz took it in stride, thankfully, and seemed content to wait for the science geeks to come up with answers. Shaila omitted the part about Harry's bribe, however—her thoughts were jumbled enough as it stood, and she wanted to get her head straight. Plus, she was hungry. So she decided to head up to the mess hall, hoping to grab some food, sit quietly in a corner, make a to-do list—and then think about whether she really wanted to even be in JSC anymore.

She never got the chance.

"Stop with the excuses!" boomed a gruff, angry voice from the mess hall, prompting Shaila to vault down the stairwell from the command center in a single leap.

When she rounded the corner and entered the mess hall, she was greeted with the sight of Lt. Enrico Finelli, an Italian air force officer seconded to JSC, flying across one of the dining tables on his back. On the other end were three miners, all muscles, stubble and indignation.

"Stand down!" Shaila barked, striding toward the miners.

"Bullshit!" growled one of the miners, a hard case named Mike Alvarez who was one of McAuliffe's most notorious boozers. "We need answers, and you guys aren't telling us shit!"

"So you gonna beat it out of us?" she retorted. "You're *this* close to getting busted back to Earth, Alvarez."

The miner strode toward her with the look of a very unsatisfied man, and one who'd been spending part of the evening hitting the bottle besides. Shaila stopped and adjusted her stance minutely. She hadn't come to blows with anyone on base during her tenure there, but this was a first she could easily handle.

"Mikey, let it go," one of the other miners said. Shaila couldn't place his name, couldn't care less. Her focus was oddly soothing after everything that had happened.

"Shut it," Alvarez growled. "I lost a day's wage today, probably more tomorrow, and someone's gotta pay for that."

He took his swing, and Shaila couldn't help but smile.

It was a big, meaty right cross, full of drunken frustration. For Shaila, it was child's play to simply step back out of the way. "And now you're going home," she quipped.

As she expected, Alvarez' left came back the other way as he moved forward in pursuit. This she stepped into, jabbing her left knuckles into his trachea while grabbing his forearm with her right. Another spin for leverage, and Alvarez was flipped end over end, his back slamming into the table where Finelli had slid past a few moments before.

Low Martian gravity combined well with combat training.

"Anyone else?" Shaila shouted, perhaps a touch too forcefully, as Alvarez coughed and clutched as his throat.

The other two miners stared at her mutely. The response came from behind her.

"Get him out of here," Kaczynski grumbled at his colleagues. Shaila whirled around, only to find the old digger with his hands up, palms open. "Easy, tiger."

She allowed herself to relax and glance over at Finelli, who was picking himself up off the floor and sporting a trickle of blood at the corner of his mouth. "You OK, 'Rico?"

"Yes, Lieutenant," he said, face turning red as he approached. "They thought I wasn't telling them what's going on."

She clapped him on the shoulder. "Go see Levin about your face. It's OK. Ed and I are gonna have a little chat."

Finelli filed out of the mess hall behind Alvarez, who had a miner on either side supporting him. To his credit, the Italian didn't hesitate following them; of course, the other two knew that Alvarez was on the next ship home, and probably out of a job with Billiton altogether, and they didn't want to be next.

"Not good, Ed," Shaila remarked as she took a seat at the table. "Your people are losing their shit."

Kaczynski, still hobbled by his injuries the day before, eased himself down across from her. "You blame them? First I get laid up, now we got two more down because of some ditch that came out of nowhere. These guys spent the day shoring up tunnels, laying more sensors and not making any money. Tomorrow, this keeps up, more of the same, right?"

Shaila shrugged. "Don't know yet. I know Harry's going to press to keep digging no matter what, though."

"Like he gives a shit about us," he snorted. "We're bottom of the barrel here, and we're gonna be the ones grabbing our ankles in the end."

"Really, Ed? I didn't know you swung that way," Shaila said with a smirk, trying to defuse the situation.

It didn't work. "Don't start with me, *Lieutenant*. This shit's gotta get *fixed*. We need to be out there digging, but if it can't be fixed, then you gotta get us off this rock. We've got families. And nobody's telling us a goddamn thing."

Shaila had to admit the point. The miners were contractors—Billiton charged them for the round-trip from Earth, as well as room and board. They had to earn it back from mining. Yes, most of them walked away with a nice fat paycheck at the end, but a bad dig or a delay in ops could really hurt them.

"I read you, Ed. I really do," she said finally. "We really are working on this, both Houston and Billiton. It's barely been 24 hours, and I need you guys to understand this'll take time. Yeah, you have to stay ten clicks from that cave, but that still leaves a lot of Mars left to dig. We just needed you to take a day and make sure your shit's in one sock, that's all. So long as you stay away from that cave, I figure you'll be back digging tomorrow.

"Yeah, sure, but what's this shit about rocks rolling up hill?" Kaczynski asked, leaning in toward her with a hushed voice. "That's the most fucked up thing I've ever heard of, and I tell ya, that can't be good for business."

"I know," she said. "Really, we're working on it. You can go and dig tomorrow. Should be fine."

"Better be," Kaczynski said, standing up and making for the door. "We need to be digging, but we need to be alive to count the money. Fix this shit."

"Roger that," Shaila said, trying to sound authoritative and reassuring at the same time. She figured she probably failed on both counts, but she stood and gave the table a little nod as she went to get her dinner. She loaded up her tray with something resembling pasta, then headed up to the command center, careful not to spill red sauce—calling it marinara would've been generous—all over herself.

"Evening, ma'am." The watch officer on duty, Ensign Pete Washington, U.S. Navy, was manning the second shift—worse than the overnight, really, because he had to miss out on what little socializing McAuliffe Base had to offer. Shaila was thus duly surprised at his chipper grin.

"Heya, Washington. Just a sensor add-on before I rack out," she said, taking a seat next to him and putting her tray on the console. She started typing, pausing only to inhale dinner, and within twenty minutes, the base sensors were updated with the mysterious rad signature.

"Heard you got caught in an earthquake?" Washington said as Shaila packed up to go. "I thought Mars wasn't supposed to have earthquakes."

Shaila was getting pretty tired of answering questions. Then again, it stood to reason that the JSC kids would be just as nervous as the miners. "Yeah, well, tell it to Mars," Shaila replied.

"What about the mining ops?" the young man asked.

"Don't know," she said, piling the detritus of her dinner on her tray. "It's isolated, and pretty far out from the sites. We'll see."

She grabbed the tray and said her goodnights to Washington, but barely managed to get out the door before she heard the ops monitors ping.

"Ummm…ma'am?" Washington said.

"Yeah?"

"We're getting a hit on that signature you downloaded."

Shaila covered the distance back to the ops station in a single jump. "Show me."

The young American pointed at his screen, where a map of the base showed a distinct blotch.

Right in the middle of the base's fusion reactor room.

"That signature is coming from the reactor?" Shaila asked in disbelief.

"Yes, ma'am. Looks like it." Washington's fingers flew over his keyboard. "I can't pin it down exactly, though. Could be outside the reactor, too."

"Shit." Shaila jabbed a button to open the base-wide comm system. "Alert Level Two. Repeat, Alert Level Two. All JSC personnel report for duty immediately. All civilian personnel to their staging areas for possible evac. This is not a drill."

She switched channels as the base alarm system started blaring. "Ops to engineering. Start emergency diagnostics and prepare for immediate reactor shutdown. We may have a leak."

It took less than a minute before the command center started to fill up. Washington was joined by two other ops officers to help start the alert checklists, while an engineer immediately went to work on the sensors. Shaila watched with a certain amount of pride; they were taking this one in stride, doing their jobs, handling it well.

Diaz walked in, managing to look crisp and in-control despite the chaos around her. That didn't make her any happier, though. "Report," she said curtly.

"The radiation signature we detected in the lava tube is present inside the reactor room," Shaila said.

Diaz' demeanor changed immediately. "Where's engineering?"

"Checking on leaks and prepping emergency shutdown, just in case."

"Did you track down what the hell this radiation *is*?"

"It looks non-ionized, but it's more than just visible light. Nothing more yet." Shaila grew uncomfortable suddenly, wondering if her reaction had been overboard.

"Let's see the signature again," Diaz said. Shaila gave her a datapad with the information on it. "This looks familiar somehow. Can't place it. Anybody grab a look besides you?"

"Yuna did. She didn't know, either."

"All right. You did the right thing for now. If it's outside, then we probably don't want it inside," Diaz said. "Tell engineering to go for immediate shutdown. Put us on battery power."

Shaila turned to issue the order, only to see Evan Greene standing at the entrance to the command center, his producer behind him with a holocam—one that was up and running. "What the hell are you doing here?" Shaila demanded.

Greene walked right past her. "Colonel, let me see the radiation signature you were talking about."

Diaz regarded the pop scientist harshly for a second, before thrusting the datapad at him. He looked for a moment, then started laughing.

"Care to tell me what's so funny, Dr. Greene?" Diaz said, ice in her voice.

"I'm sorry, Colonel, but in about 30 seconds, your engineering staff will be calling to ask whether this is some kind of joke." Greene handed the datapad back. "You don't need to shut down the reactor."

CHAPTER 7

March 6, 1779

F*ather,*
*   I fear we have been thrown into a most dangerous intrigue. I write*
this knowing that I have survived great peril, whereas others have not. It
is with a most serious and humble mind that I record what has transpired of
late. I fear there is now much more to our quest than the mere apprehension of
a murderer...

The green murky waters of Venus' Pinzon Sea lapped against the hull of
the *Daedalus* as she weighed anchor a quarter mile away from the bay and
beachhead leading to the Va'hakri village. A small spit of land, jutting out
from the coastline and covered in tall palm-like trees, kept the Royal Navy
ship hidden from the bay beyond, just in case the murderers' business had
kept them there.

Weatherby kept his glass trained upon the coast before him as his men
rowed their small boat toward shore. A second boat was to their starboard
side, carrying Mr. Plumb, their new guide Mr. Bacon and more sailors and
marines. Their goal was the beachhead, but they would take a very different
route.

Looking back, Weatherby already had a difficult time making out *Dae-*
dalus in the dark, foggy distance. The air on Venus seemed as thick as the
water, and the water thicker than stew. But Mr. Bacon seemed to know his
way, thankfully, and Weatherby's boat followed Plumb's safely to shore. It
didn't surprise Weatherby, given his bumbling, that Bacon had found him-

self right at home upon a ship of His Majesty's Navy. At least he had proven to be a competent guide, guiding the ship through the shoals and reefs to the Va'hakri village, some twelve hours south of Puerto Verde. To Captain Morrow's happy surprise, Bacon hadn't even demanded too exorbitant a fee.

Morrow was quite surprised to learn the potential whereabouts of their quarry, as making a deal with the Spanish authorities made far more sense than braving the jungles to meet with the Venusians. Finch, for his part, was at a loss as well, as the Venusians' alchemy did not appear to have need of Mercurium; they were too primitive to have ever wandered off-world. Many scholars suspected the numerous ruins found upon the planet's surface were the legacy of the insular Saturn-dwellers known as the Xan, or even the fabled race of Martians from ages past, rather than that of an ancient, more advanced Venusian civilization. In any event, the goals of these murderers remained as clouded as the Venusian skies.

Weatherby guided his rowers to a spot on the shore next to Plumb's boat, and he disembarked his men as quickly and quietly as circumstance would allow. It was an hour before dawn, give or take, and despite the darkness, Plumb insisted on inspecting his troops prior to embarking on the trek into the wilderness. All was as it should be, of course, and while Weatherby might have found it laudable to be so thorough in any other instance, time was a factor. Finally, Plumb ordered young Rooney—one of the most nimble men aboard—to scout ahead while the rest began an orderly march to the promontory which shielded the bay and beach from the currents. Everyone kept pace, though Finch remained a laggard to a degree, huffing under his pack as he progressed into the Venusian jungle; the doctor had been brought along for his medical knowledge, in case a firefight erupted, and also for the signal rocket he carried, so that they might alert *Daedalus* should their quarry be found.

It was a straightforward plan—an assault on the beach, with *Daedalus* ready to assist if need be—when hatched in the warm comfort of Morrow's cabin. Now that Weatherby was on shore, with the strange Venusian plant life seeming to latch on to his shoes as he walked and the humid air once again drowning him in sweat, the short distance to the bay might as well have been a voyage to the fabled ring-cities of Saturn.

Weatherby was surrounded by flora of all shapes and sizes, from towering trees to creeping vines. Even in the darkness, there seemed to be dozens of shades of green around him, punctuated by some of the most vibrant flowers he'd ever laid eyes upon. And the life around him seemed very much alive—he swore he could see some of the vines moving of their own accord…toward him. The rest of the crew ashore had taken to slashing at the plants with their cutlasses before Plumb ordered them to desist. The only two of their party not discomfited by the aggressive undergrowth were Finch, who had to be reminded he was not to stop to take samples, and Mr. Bacon, who of course was likely quite familiar with the surprisingly aggressive Venusian flora.

Plumb held his hand up as a rustling sound was heard ahead. It was Rooney.

"Ship moored ahead in the bay, Mr. Plumb. She's a frigate, forty guns, maybe more. Couldn't make the name, sir, but she's not the *Groene Draeck*—one word, and smaller."

Weatherby and Plumb exchanged looks; it was all too easy to forget that most of the crew was quite illiterate. "Does she appear ready to make sail?" Weatherby asked.

"Aye," Rooney said. "There's three boats on the beach, and one was preparing to cast off as I watched."

Weatherby smiled. "Then we have them!"

"We still don't know who we have," Plumb countered. "It's not the ship we're looking for, after all."

"But sir," Weatherby said, "what other ship might it be? It is exactly where Mr. Bacon said it would be, and he did identify one of the drawings."

Plumb fixed the younger man with a stare that could crack stone. "So you wish to start shooting, do you? What if they're English merchants, then?"

Weatherby felt himself shrink under the first lieutenant's gaze. He had always been told, in his training as a midshipman, that he should respectfully stand his ground should he feel a wiser course was available, though he found it took all his courage to do so under Plumb's weathering glare. "Perhaps, sir, you might allow me to scout forward with Rooney?"

"Fine, but you better be damned sure before we attack, Mr. Weatherby," Plumb warned.

Taking his leave silently, Weatherby followed the young sailor through the undergrowth, trying his best to ignore the luminescent insects and slithering things under the verdant leaves. After five minutes of walking and sweating, the two came to a small bluff overlooking the cove. There, two small boats were being loaded, a third already upon the water. The men loading the boats looked to be in sorry shape, dressed in naught but castoff rags and looking ill-shaven and ill-intentioned. They were also heavily armed, with swords, pistols and muskets each.

Weatherby pulled out his glass and looked toward the waiting ship. It was a heavy frigate, some 44 guns—more than a match for *Daedalus* under most conditions. It also looked to be of French make, and Weatherby suspected it to be the one he had first seen over Mercury. Perhaps the "merchantman" simply had its gunports closed and painted over as part of a ruse. Finally, Weatherby shifted his glass toward the stern of the ship, where her name could be seen plainly—perhaps even freshly painted—beneath a blood-red flag.

Chance.

"Good God," Weatherby breathed.

"What is it, sir?" hissed Rooney, crouched at his officer's side.

Before he could answer, Weatherby was distracted by shouts from the beach. He turned his glass back to the cover to see a huge man shouting at the others there. This one, most obviously in charge, was tall and broad, with a massive black beard and a voice that brooked no dissent. He was dressed in a glut of finery, all of it mismatched and ostentatious. He wore the hat of an English admiral, but the snippets of language Weatherby could hear sounded French.

"Unless my eyes are mistaken, that is the *Chance,* and the blowhard ashore may be Jean-Jacques LeMaire," Weatherby whispered.

Everyone who had taken to sea or Void knew of LeMaire and *Chance.* LeMaire was the most notorious pirate, and the *Chance* the most famous pirate ship, to sail the Void. Many things were said of LeMaire: that he had taken a third-rate ship-of-the-line in a one-on-one engagement despite being outgunned by a factor of three; that he had a base on one of the larger boulder-islands of the Rocky Main; that he always left one man alive on any ship he plundered, so as to spread his infamy.

It was the stuff of scandal sheets and tavern tales throughout the Known Worlds. And he was a mere fifty yards away. Weatherby tugged at Rooney's sleeve and quickly made his way back to the rest of the group.

And there, he found Plumb, sitting upon a fallen log, looking as dour as when he had left. "Mr. Plumb!" Weatherby shouted, as best as one could shout whilst whispering. "The ship out there is the *Chance*!"

Shocked out of his gloom, Plumb turned to regard Weatherby with amazement. "You're joking," Plumb said.

"Not at all, sir. And I believe LeMaire himself is on the shore!"

Plumb stood from his perch, his cold stare returning. "You'd best be right, Mr. Weatherby," Plumb said, offering the sentence somewhere between concern and threat.

Nonetheless, Plumb began to plan the attack. He would lead one group south, hiding in the foliage until the alleged pirates were between them and the water. Weatherby would take up a position just north of the beach. "When I give the word, fire upon the shore and we may catch them between us," Plumb said. "And Finch, as soon as we engage, fire that rocket aloft to alert *Daedalus*. While they still have men upon the shore, we may catch them by the heel!"

The group split in two and spread out. Plumb led his men through the undergrowth and around, ultimately facing the pink-sanded beach, the bay and the unknown vessel beyond, while Weatherby took up the flanking position looking south across the beach from the promontory. Soon, twenty muskets were pointed at a small group of men as they prepared to embark within two small boats. The third was well en route to the waiting ship.

The assault came quickly. "FIRE!" Plumb shouted. Weatherby gave the order as well, and soon Finch's rocket was three hundred feet in the air, glowing with the light of the Sun and illuminating the quick carnage that erupted upon the sand. Of the twenty men left on the beach, eight fell upon the first volley between the two groups.

Sadly, the man who might be LeMaire was not among them. Weatherby saw him quickly clamber into a boat, pulling another man along with him. Those already aboard started rowing quickly as LeMaire drew pistols and returned fire.

The other men on the beach weren't as quick to act, torn as they were between the decision to fight or flee. Some ran for the other boat, while their fellows pulled their pistols and shot blindly into the trees, aiming mostly at Plumb's group, which was closer. Meanwhile, Weatherby could see the first boat—the one that had already departed—had reached the *Chance*. Under the dim pre-dawn light, he could even see a very well-dressed gentleman ascending the ladder. It was impossible to tell whether it was their suspect, though this seemed likely.

Plumb's men suddenly charged from their cover, swords and bayonets at the ready. Weatherby immediately ordered his own charge and was soon dashing across the sand, sword in hand. Those left standing on shore were outnumbered by more than two to one, and quickly realized the folly of their position; their weapons were cast down to the sand before either group arrived.

"Open fire on the boat!" Weatherby ordered, purely out of instinct, even though it was Plumb's duty to give that command. Nonetheless, the men immediately knelt in the sand, reloaded and fired. Weatherby could see two men go down on the boat—again, the black-bearded leader appeared unharmed—but the little dinghy kept moving steadily toward the *Chance*.

And that was when *Daedalus* appeared from around the promontory at full sail, quickly wheeling to larboard in order to offer a broadside against the *Chance*'s stern; surely Morrow could see the identity of the famed pirate vessel by this time, and had opted to engage.

However, it appeared *Chance* earned her reputation fully, in every sense. She was lucky to be positioned well upon the currents, so as soon as the remaining boat was abreast of her, those aboard cut the anchor chain entirely. The result was that the stern of the ship began to turn toward land—not only pointing the ship in the right direction, but allowing her to easily offer her own guns to *Daedalus* as well.

The shots resounded across the beach, as each vessel fired upon the other. It was impossible for Weatherby to tell whether either had been damaged, given the smoke that immediately obscured the battle from view. But he soon saw *Chance* moving away from the cloud at full sail. Meanwhile, *Daedalus*—having survived the exchange with little damage—was nonetheless tacking toward shore, away from her quarry. Even at that distance, Weatherby could see the helmsman spinning the wheel furiously, with Lt. Foster assisting, in order to come about in time—but there was nothing for it. By the time *Daedalus* had her bow pointing away from shore, *Chance* was at full sail, and the winds were in her favor.

Chance's maneuver was uncommonly canny. By cutting the anchor chain, the pirates had protected their vulnerable stern, shielded their incoming fellows from the onslaught, put themselves in position to return fire *and* immediately captured the winds coming off the land to speed them off to sea. Even if *Daedalus* had opted to tack away from shore during the attack, *Chance* would have kept the advantage.

"Damn them!" Plumb roared as he saw the brilliance of the move. "*Daedalus* shan't reach them in time!"

"Why not?" Finch asked. The officers and half the crew looked at him as if he were mad. "I'm sorry, but I'm still rather new at all this," he added with a shrug.

Weatherby explained the situation as briefly as possible while the marines rounded up the surviving *Chance* crew. Meanwhile, *Daedalus* remained undaunted, unfurling more canvas in an attempt to overcome the fleeing pirate. It was a good 300 miles to the southern aurorae, the nearest means of ascent into the Void. Yet *Chance* had opted to flee to the north, with the prevailing wind, which struck Weatherby as a short-term expediency at best. Perhaps *Daedalus* could catch her after all....

And then, beyond all reckoning, they saw the *Chance* start to rise from the green Venusian seas.

"What in blazes?" Weatherby muttered, stopping in his tracks as he watched.

The *Chance*'s keel slowly rose from the water, and they could see its crew immediately begin to unfurl her planesails. Weatherby could not be entirely sure, but he thought he spied the familiar motes of sun-currents around the pirate's keel—quite impossible so far from the aurorae.

And yet there it was, a sight that defied all notions of sailing and alchemy both. The *Chance* rose majestically into the skies, leaving *Daedalus* in its wake.

"That can't be," Plumb muttered, staring off into the distance as the pirate ship faded into the foggy skies.

"Doctor?" Weatherby asked quietly.

Finch stared wide-eyed at the sight. "I could not tell you, Lieutenant. It is a working beyond anything I've seen." He turned to Weatherby, an odd smile on his face. "We're into something here, I'll tell you that."

In stunned silence, those on the beach watched *Daedalus* tack in sheets and weigh anchor. Weatherby was sure he knew the calculus in Morrow's mind—there were still men ashore, captives to be had and a Venusian village to investigate. There was no sense in undertaking an effort already doomed to failure, as they would have to make sail for the poles to pursue *Chance*—and she would be long gone before they even lifted off from the sea.

Finally, the *Daedalus* officers turned their attention to their new captives. There were eight still standing, another eight dead or wounded. Finch tended to these as best he could, though Plumb cautioned him not to use too many curatives, as they were still upon a foreign and potentially hostile shore. Weatherby attempted to question the captives, first in English, and then in his rudimentary, halting French, but they sat tight-lipped, staring off toward the water and their escaping comrades, knowing full well that their surrender meant prolonging their lives but a little. Piracy was a hanging offense, and they would soon all have a noose around their necks.

Meanwhile, Bacon was looking down the trail that, presumably, led to the Venusian village. "It's kicked up something fierce," he reported when Weatherby joined him. "Must've been at least twenty men that went down that trail. Can't imagine the Va'hakri could've withstood that many."

Weatherby nodded grimly. While his knowledge of the Venusians was limited indeed, he knew their tools of warfare were limited to spears and bows, though a few tribes were known to utilize particularly virulent poisons, drawn from the alchemically rich plant life around them. Twenty men, twice the size of a typical Venusian and armed with muskets, pistols and swords, would make short work of an entire tribe, poisons notwithstanding.

"Signal from *Daedalus*," Plumb said to Weatherby as he walked up to the trailhead. "We're to proceed to the Venusian village. I've detailed six men under Forester to stand guard over the prisoners. Gather the rest, Mr. Weatherby. We'll out what these bastards are up to."

As the men prepared to venture into the interior of the Venusian jungle, Finch sidled up to Weatherby. "I admit, I remain perplexed."

"How so, Doctor?" Weatherby asked. "Aside from the fact that they reached the Void without benefit of the aurorae?"

Finch shrugged. "For most, that would be enough, would it not? That's a fine prize, indeed. But they came here, and risked capture. Thus, it stands to reason that there's an even greater working afoot. Otherwise, they would take the Mercurium—and their new formula for ascending the Void—and sell it to the highest bidder. So what then is their true purpose?"

Weatherby eyed the trail leading into the foliage. "I pray the answers are in that jungle."

July 25, 2132

Thirty seconds after Diaz grabbed Greene by the arm and shuttled him into her office, engineering had called the command center, wondering what the fuss was all about. No, they didn't see it as a joke. But neither did they understand why this particular bit of radiation had threatened to put off their sleep cycles, either.

In Diaz' absence, Shaila ordered engineering to continue a full diagnostic check of the reactor, but not to take it offline quite yet. They didn't seem worried, even though she was. And Greene's cameraman and producer were still filming, which didn't help one bit.

Shaila's mood brightened when Stephane sauntered into the command center, Yuna in tow. "How can I sleep with all these alarms?" he said with a disarming grin.

Shaila walked over to him, taking him and Yuna by the arm and pulling them away from the holocam. "It was the rad signature we found in the cave," she said quietly. "It was all over the reactor room."

"Is it dangerous?" Stephane asked, suddenly looking rather worried.

"Nobody in engineering seems to think so. We're running checks now, and Diaz is in with Greene. He seems to know what it is."

Stephane's response was cut off by Harry Yu, who stalked into the command center looking like he was ready to hit someone. "Anyone mind telling me why I have sixty miners in pressure suits ready to evac?" he barked to no one in particular.

Shaila approached him with a nod to the cameras. "You mind? We're getting this under control here."

Harry looked the cameraman over quickly before fixing his gaze on Shaila. "This is *not* under control, Jain. My guys are pissed off enough as is, and now you're talking evac and this-is-not-a-drill? Do you know what sixty pissed-off diggers looks like?"

Shaila opened her mouth to respond, only to see Diaz reemerge from her office, looking irritated. "Stand down from alert status," Diaz told Shaila. "Engineering can finish up their checks and go to bed. You, Durand and Hiyashi—in my office. Dr. Greene here has volunteered to give us a little science lesson. Harry, feel free to tag along."

Shaila followed everyone into the commander's office, where she and Stephane stood along the wall while the others sat huddled around Diaz' desk.

"All right," Diaz said, taking her seat behind the desk. "Everybody listen carefully to Dr. Greene here and learn from this little disaster, shall we?" She nodded to Greene, who downloaded the radiation signature from the sensor pack to the desk's holodisplay.

"This is the rad signature for Cherenkov radiation," Greene said in his best holovision voice. "First and foremost, it's harmless. It's actually a fancy name for a specific kind of light.

"Cherenkov radiation is light emitted by charged particles that move through a medium in which the speed of light is actually slower than the speed of the particles. Think of light moving through water; the density of the water not only bends the light, but slows it down. Of course, the vast majority of atoms passing through water molecules aren't charged.

"Now, let's say you produce a charged particle and put it through that light-slowing medium—say, particles produced in a reactor that are then sent through the heavy water surrounding the fuel cells. The charged particles are still traveling at the speed of light, and when they zip through the water coolant, they produce radiation that shows up at the blue end of the visual spectrum. The glow you see in your reactor chamber is actually Cherenkov radiation."

"And that's why engineering detected that signature in the reactor area," Shaila said glumly. "It's supposed to be there."

"Exactly," Greene continued. "Now, if you didn't get a read on this signature before, it was probably a good idea for them to check to be sure that nothing got out of the containment chamber, because that would indeed mean some kind of leak. But then again, if Cherenkov radiation were to somehow escape, a whole bunch of nastier radiation would escape with it, setting off the automatic alarms."

Stephane cleared his throat. "Doctor, does Cherenkov radiation happen naturally outside of fusion reactors?"

"Any time you have a charged particle moving through a medium that slows light, yes, you can get Cherenkov radiation. We've had satellites in Earth orbit for over a century looking for it in deep space, and we've caught a few glimmers—mostly ionized particles going through an area of dense gases or some kind of dark matter. Sometimes, you'll get a Cherenkov effect when cosmic rays whip through the atmosphere, too. At least on Earth—I haven't heard of it on Mars, but I suppose it's possible."

Shaila chimed in as she put the pieces together in her head. "OK, but what if you had evidence of this radiation without actually detecting charged particles?"

Greene looked at her quizzically. "I'm not sure I follow. What exactly did you have in mind?"

"I'm afraid, Doctor, that I'll have to get clearance from Houston on that one," Diaz said quickly. "And besides, you got your special EVA coming up to compensate you for your time, and for your creative editing of this evening's events."

"That's true," Greene smiled. "I look forward to working with you, Lt. Jain."

Shaila shot Diaz a look, but the commander studiously looked down at her hands while Yuna took over the questioning. "Is there anything else you can tell us about this Cherenkov radiation, sir? Anything you can think of?"

"Nothing much, really. Mostly having to do with particle physics and some quantum mechanics, and unless you've got a hundred-kilometer particle collider around here, you don't need to worry about that. Charged particles moving through a light-slowing medium are rare enough as is. My guess is you've got a sensor screw-up related to the reactor."

The group around the table was silent for a moment before Diaz spoke up again. "Thank you for helping us clear this up, Doctor, and of course I appreciate your discretion with regard to all this. I'll have Lt. Jain get in touch with you tomorrow morning to set up your EVA."

"Always a pleasure, Colonel. Happy to help." With another grin at Shaila, Greene took his cue and left the conference room.

"Shut it, Jain," Diaz said as Shaila started to speak. "We'll discuss Greene later. Meantime, you can tell us how we apparently missed one of the most common forms of radiation known to man."

Shaila stood a little taller, trying not to feel like a dressed-down cadet. "Ma'am. This Cherenkov radiation was what we picked up inside the lava tube right before the quake destroyed the sensor array. When I saw the same signature coming from the reactor room, I sounded the alert."

"This is common radiation, yes?" Stephane asked. "You searched the database for it?"

"Yeah," Shaila said, catching on. "And the search turned up nothing."

"Do it again," Diaz ordered.

Shaila pulled out her datapad, plugged the radiation signature into the search engine, and waited a moment.

"What the hell?" she muttered.

The search came back with a definition: Cherenkov radiation. The computer even provided her with a helpful précis that neatly mirrored Greene's explanation.

Shaila looked up. Diaz was staring at her with a tired consternation, while Yuna and Stephane had concern and, goddamn it, pity on their faces.

"I swear, this is not the result I got when I did the search before," Shaila protested.

Diaz seemed to weigh responses in her head a moment before settling on one. "Simple mistake, probably," she said quietly. "It happens."

"No, ma'am, this is not the result I got before!"

"Jain, enough," Diaz said. "You probably plugged it in wrong the first time. Whatever, crisis averted, let's move on."

"Bullshit," Harry said. "Crisis is not fucking averted, Maria. Jain here had my guys stop digging for an entire day, and then pulls this crap? You want a riot on your hands? You know these guys aren't boy scouts!"

Diaz turned to the executive, lips pressed tight. "I've reviewed their records, Harry, and believe me, it took some reading. Now's not the time for a critique of Billiton's hiring practices."

Harry turned red in the face, a vein on his forehead threatening to pop clear of his skull. "I want someone else leading this investigation," he said, leaning over the colonel's desk. "She can't even manage a database search. She can't handle it."

Diaz came right back at him. "Well, that's too bad, because she's the most qualified person here to do it. And you're gonna cooperate with her and Dr. Durand and Dr. Hiyashi to see this thing through. You got me?"

The look on Diaz' face prompted Harry to straighten up again. "Don't make me lodge a formal complaint, Maria."

"Do what you want. Even if Houston launches a team out here tomorrow, they're at least four weeks out. By then, either everything's back to normal or Mars is split in two. Bitching about it won't help, but knock yourself out." Diaz leaned back in her chair with a satisfied smirk on her face.

Harry wheeled around and made for the exit. "Yuna, I want regular updates on this. Don't let this get out of hand again," he called out before the door slammed behind him. Shaila shook her head angrily. Figure he'd try to bribe her then, a few hours later, try to undermine her. Bastard.

Diaz broke the ensuing silence. "All right. Durand, Hiyashi: Figure out why this damn cave is emitting the same radiation as our reactor, and whether it's a danger to anyone. Make sure the 'bot you got is keyed on this signature. It goes down the hole first thing in the morning. And double check that new ravine for signs of it as well. Dismissed."

Stephane and Yuna filed out, leaving Shaila to face her commanding officer. Diaz didn't mince words.

"In exchange for some creative holo editing, you're taking the 'bot to the cave tomorrow, and you're taking Greene with you," Diaz said. "He wants to holo it, and he's promised not to air anything until we have our solution in hand. And as the leader of this little enterprise, you're going to get your head on straight and give me that solution. Clear?"

Shaila's protest raged against the inside of her skull: *My head* is *on straight!* She tamped it down quickly, however. "Aye, ma'am. If I may?"

"What?"

"*Atlantis.*"

At this, Diaz finally let her anger visibly slide off her face and body. "He's been told not to ask about it, or the deal's off."

Shaila nodded, trying to keep her composure. "Thank you, ma'am."

"Shit happens, Jain. I'm going to write this off as an unscheduled drill, and I'll get Harry to play ball. But you gotta get this done for me. I'm running out of plays, and if Houston has to come out here and clean up our mess, we're all screwed."

Shaila nodded. "Aye, ma'am. Thank you, ma'am."

A moment later, Shaila was striding through the command center and down the stairs, her hands shaking uncontrollably. She knew—just plain old *knew*—that she didn't screw up a simple database search. She had run similar searches a million times before. She had run *that* search three or four times. And didn't Yuna run a search while they were in the cave?

Shaila was so into her own head that she nearly plowed straight into Stephane, who had waited for her outside the mess hall. "Are you OK?" he asked, his face showing genuine concern.

Shaila's voice was as dead as the planet and darker than the cave at night. "I'm fine. Excuse me." She wheeled past him and took the stairs into the Hub, four at a time.

CHAPTER 8

March 6, 1779

The men of the *Daedalus* moved through the Venusian jungle as quietly as possible. The body of an important Va'hakri warrior—identified as such by Bacon due to the cloak of blue feathers and barbed spear adorning the corpse—was discovered just five minutes' walk from the beach, confirming that the men of the *Chance* likely left naught but carnage in their wake. The Royal Navy men did not want to be seen as the second wave of attackers, and pointedly kept swords sheathed and muskets shouldered during the inland trek.

The sounds of the Venusian jungle were disturbing, full of strange twitters and buzzing, with the occasional, far-off grunt of some animal or a rapid rustling of nearby plants. Furthermore, the humid, fetid air left most of them gasping as the hour-long journey neared its end.

The next of the corpses appeared with the hazy light of day through the trees, and soon the *Daedalus* men were finding dead Va'hakri every fifty paces or so, then twenty, then ten. Grips were tightened around muskets, cutlasses loosed in sheathes, nerves and jitters heightened as alertness increased. Yet Weatherby wondered if there would be anything at all left to the village when they arrived. There was a prodigious number of bodies at this point; he counted at least thirty dead Venusians by the time Bacon announced the village was near.

"Finch!" Plumb called out from the lead, causing nearly the entire company of men to jump. "I see quarried stone here! What is this?"

Plumb waited—somewhat impatiently, Weatherby thought—next to the ruins of a short wall as he and Finch approached. Despite being overgrown with vines and other, stranger plants, Weatherby could see the outline of a structure of some sort, eroded by age. "I thought these little buggers didn't cut stone like this," Plumb said by way of greeting.

"They don't, sir," Finch huffed as he tried to catch his breath, then bending down to examine the stone carefully. "It's far too old and worn to be recent work. I've heard some scholars suggest that the few ruins found upon Venus may be the remnants of outposts from either the Xan or the ancient Martians who disappeared long ago."

Plumb cast a wary eye at the stone. "Just so long as they're not around now," he said as he began to walk again.

"Doubtful," Finch responded as he and Weatherby followed. "Mars is a wasteland now, and the Xan do not venture past Saturn, except to their outpost on Callisto."

"Aye, and we can't venture there," Plumb said disdainfully. "I never liked those Xan. Too damn mysterious, they are. Telling us where we can and can't go."

"Yes, well, they're far more advanced than we, sir. And to be fair, they treat us better than we treat the Venusians," Finch responded. Weatherby turned around to see Finch smiling at the first lieutenant, apparently enjoying the opportunity to challenge his views.

The gradual lightening of the clouds above was punctuated by the glow of fire ahead. It quickly became evident that this was more than a mere bonfire, and Plumb wisely counseled steadiness as they stepped into a clearing.

The entire village was ablaze.

There were roughly a dozen structures ringing the clearing, and another larger one in the center, all in various stages of destruction by flame. The bodies of several dozen Va'hakri were strewn about; some were burned, but it appeared most had fallen to blade or shot. As the group walked slowly forward, Weatherby blanched as he saw that the criminals who had attacked the village—certainly the men of the *Chance*—cared not as to whether women or children were harmed or killed.

Behind the village, shadowing it from the rising sun, were the vine-covered ruins of an ancient pyramid, the stones cracked and worn, yet piled more than three hundred feet high, in six different terraces. The top seemed to have held some kind of structure apart from this at some point, but all that could be discerned now was a pile of rubble of a different sort from the pyramid itself. The ghosts of carvings could be seen upon the stones as the group drew closer to the village, but these were only vaguely present. Some seemed to depict man-like beings, but detail was erased long ago, it seemed, and all sense of scale in the images was lost to the ravages of time.

A few groans and croaks, laced with pain and agony, competed with the crackling of flames as the only sounds to be heard. They came from a bare handful of Va'hakri still alive; Weatherby saw no more than eight left, and most seemed at least bloodied, if not hobbled to some degree. They were tending to those with greater wounds, mourning their dead, and crying out to the cloudy skies above.

Then one of them saw the group of men in the clearing, pointed, and screamed. Almost as one, the Venusians took up their spears again and charged, their high-pitched croaking rasps prompting many of the men to take a few steps back despite their better numbers and arms.

One of the men—it was Smythe, of Weatherby's division—immediately raised his musket to respond, but Plumb quickly reached out, grabbed the barrel of the gun and pointed it toward the ground. "Stand fast, man," he said, then turned to the rest. "Throw down your arms, quickly, all of you!"

With only a moment's hesitation—not to be disparaged in the least under the circumstances—the men put their muskets to the ground and exposed themselves to the onslaught. Thankfully, the Va'hakri took note of this, and the charge across the clearing transformed from a full run to a cautious approach, with their spears still pointed in the proper direction. Weatherby could see a few of the Venusians gesturing to him and some of the others, then fingering the few ornaments on their bodies as they croaked back and forth to one another; the reptilians saw and understood that, at the very least, this group of men was better dressed.

Finally, the two groups stood a mere ten feet apart and stared at each other for several long moments. Plumb finally broke the silence, turning to Finch while still keeping his eyes upon the angry Venusians. "Doctor, you wouldn't know any words of Venusian, would you?"

Finch cleared his throat; he looked shaken and sallow. "A bare few, but I shall try." The doctor pulled a small vial from his pocket and dabbed a bit of the liquid therein on his tongue. He then stepped forward, between Plumb and Weatherby, and began to speak in their odd croaking language: "Kahlak mu'u thal. Gareshn'ak Va'hakri'an uru nakha."

At the very least, Finch's attempt at communication did not prompt an immediate attack. A flurry of words erupted among the Va'hakri, with Finch responding as best he was able when queries were directed at him. The spears still pointed at the men, but those holding them were, at the very least, less tense. The largest of the Va'hakri, wearing a number of beaded items upon his head-frills and a short cape of blue feathers, began talking animatedly with Finch, gesturing angrily with his spear between the bodies of his fellows and the Royal Navy men.

"He is not entirely sure if we represent a threat, but will allow us to be judged by their…elder, I suppose, is the word. Priest, perhaps," Finch reported after a few moments.

Before Finch could continue, an ancient, wizened Venusian appeared from a small gap in the base of the pyramid. This worthy appeared to have substantial rank amongst his people, for his headdress and cape contained a rainbow's worth of colored feathers, and he was well draped in beads and stones as well. His reptilian eyes had bags beneath them, and his beak seemed dulled by years of use.

This elder began a slow croaking chant as he saw the dead Venusians, who were now being tended to by their brethren in the center of the village. As the dead were laid gently upon the ground, their limbs laid out in repose, the elder moved from one to the next, placing his hand upon the brow of each of the fallen. Each time he did so, Weatherby could see a large gemstone around the elder's neck glow brightly. The young officer turned to Finch, who looked on with amazement.

"What are they doing?" Weatherby whispered.

Finch actually smiled. "Apparently, it is some ritual that has to do with joining the deceased with their ancestors. At first, I thought it simply a trite custom, rubbish really, but now I see it may be otherwise."

"How so?"

The doctor pointed to the elder. "Note how he dips his fingers into his pouch before he touches each of the dead. I wager there is some alchemical solution therein, and it could conceivably allow him access to the dead Venusians' memories. And if he's able to store these memories in the stone…. well, I dare say the Venusians may be far more advanced in the mystic arts than we've given them credit for!"

Weatherby watched, more reverently now, as the elder finished harvesting the memories of the fallen. Once finished, a number of the other Venusians present began to prepare the bodies for some sort of funerary rite, washing the bodies and adorning them with various flowers and leaves.

Whilst this was happening, the elder finally turned his attention toward the humans and their Va'hakri escorts. And it appeared he was not happy. The elder began gesturing wildly at the Va'hakri warrior who had held back from attacking. The warrior responded with seeming supplication, at one point kneeling before the elder and placing his spear upon the ground repeatedly.

"Doctor?" Weatherby whispered.

Finch, eyes narrowed as he followed the conversation, leaned in toward Weatherby. "I dare say we've impressed the young warrior there, as he's arguing our case fairly well," the doctor said. "Unfortunately, the elder is apparently quite fed up with humanity as a whole. He's going on about broken agreements and dishonor, and there's some sentiment amongst the other tribes that an example needs to be made."

"I assume we're to be the example," Weatherby said, his calm belying the sudden stab of nervousness that rushed into his heart. He had no wish to quarrel with these unfortunate creatures, but self-preservation would certainly win out.

"That is certainly a possibility," Finch said. "Our friend the warrior, there, is actually a fine advocate. He's noted our willingness to lay down our arms and remain respectful during their memory harvest—their words, apparently—and our generally honorable behavior. The elder recognizes these acts, but still believes we would be of greater use to his people if…" Finch paused here. "Well, suffice to say, we wouldn't survive what they have planned for us."

At this, Plumb grew frustrated. "This isn't going to work," the first lieutenant grumbled. "Men, prepare yourselves. If they move toward us, attack at will and retreat to the ship."

Finch wheeled upon him. "Sir, with due respect, this is a delicate situation. These people have seen an entire village massacred, and I believe only our continued honorable behavior has kept us alive to this point. Allow me to at least plead our case!"

Plumb opened his mouth, apparently quite ready to give Finch a solid dressing down, but then thought better of it. "You've one chance, Finch. Otherwise, we're getting out of here, one way or another."

"Even if it's in a coffin?" Finch muttered. He then stepped forward toward the warrior and the elder. Immediately, dozens of spears and arrows were pointed at him, but he walked slowly, his hands raised and open. When he reached the warrior's side, he went to his knees and prostrated himself as he had seen the warrior do earlier, prompting a snort of disdain from Plumb. Even Weatherby was taken aback at this—yes, there was something of nobility in the Venusians' simple rites, but did diplomacy involve bowing and scraping before rank savages?

Yet Finch's words, unintelligible to the rest of the men, seemed to have a softening effect on the Venusians. Spears were slowly lowered once more, arrows carefully stowed for the time being. The elder listened intently to Finch, then ultimately nodded. Finch turned and waved Plumb and Weatherby over. "I've managed to gain something of an audience for you," he said to the two officers. "Please, try not to show disrespect, gentlemen."

Plumb folded his arms and stood proudly before the elder half his size. "We've come to find out what's happened here," he said, slowly and a touch louder than necessary. "We do not wish you harm."

Finch began to translate, but the elder held up his hand. "I know your words," the creature croaked in passable English. "But I do not know your minds. Great evil has been made on the Va'hakri tribe this night. If you are of this evil, we will kill you, even if we must die as well."

To his credit, Plumb did his level best to assure the elder that they were not responsible for the atrocity, and pointed to their laying down of arms as proof. He also added that some of those responsible had been captured. This last point seemed to assuage the creature, and after a brief discussion, the Venusian spears were finally laid to rest. The old one slumped down upon the ground and began to weep, croaking again in seeming mourning. The croaks were soon echoed by the other Venusians present around the pyramid.

Oddly touched by this display, Weatherby knelt down on one knee to meet the elder's gaze. "Can you tell us what has occurred?"

The frail little reptilian looked up at the young man with tearful eyes. "I am the elder of our tribe. We are the teachers of our kind. We keep the words and stories. And because we learn, we dealt with you and your people when you first came here, many long days ago," the elder said. "When these men came last night to our village, this was normal. Many come from your stone villages seeking our plants or our defeated enemies to buy."

Weatherby was startled that this creature might facilitate the enslavement of his own people, but he said nothing as the elder continued.

"The leader of this group was different. We saw he wore fine things. He spoke our words well. But if he knew our ways, why would he ask for the va'hakla?"

"Va'hakla?" Plumb repeated, looking over to Finch.

"A very rare flower, considered sacred by the Venusian people," Finch said quietly. "The alchemical properties are said to be immense, particularly within the schools of healing and plant life, but there are very, very few flowers that are outside the control of the tribes."

The elder's tearful yellow eyes regarded Finch closely, with a hint of suspicion. "You know something of the va'hakla. It is a gift to us from the world. My people not die if it was still here. It cures us, brings us life."

Finch nodded. "Yes it does, sir. And those few of us on Earth who have experimented with it have found numerous other uses as well. But again, when a flower blooms only once every 224 days, and there are so few plants to begin with, it becomes all the more precious." He turned to his shipmates. "A fraction of an ounce can command hundreds of pounds sterling."

"We grow the va'hakla," the elder said. "We tend its roots, we trim its leaves. We harvest its flowers for the good of all the people. We share much of our world with you. But the va'hakla is for our people. It is not yours. He asked for it. We said no. He kept asking. He offered us other things. He offered gold, guns. We said no. He became angry." The ancient lizard-creature paused a moment, eyes welling up. "He spoke something in words we did not know. And then they began to kill us."

The elder started crying again, but Plumb knelt down next to Weatherby and spoke regardless. "And your flower? Did he take it?"

This actually prompted more sobs. "All gone. All flowers. Gone. He took the flowers. He burned the plants. No more."

"Who?" Weatherby asked urgently. "We must find him. Did he tell you his name?"

The elder straightened at this. "Yes, he said he was great among your people, a healer and wonder-worker. An alchemist. He calls himself…Ka-lee-oh-sto." The creature stumbled over the unfamiliar name.

Behind the two lieutenants, Finch breathed in quickly.

"You know this person?" Weatherby asked him.

"The name is Cagliostro," Finch said. "He is an Italian mystic and, it is said, one of the finest alchemists in the Known Worlds."

"Might he be responsible?" Plumb asked.

"I dare say so," Finch responded, "for I have heard naught but ill of him. His faculty with the Great Work is said to be mighty indeed, but his character is that of a liar and a thief. If the stories I have heard are true, he cares not for civility or morality, only the power that the highest truths of alchemy can provide him."

Plumb shook his head sadly, suddenly looking quite tired. "Then we've bigger problems on our hands," he said. "We must return to *Daedalus* and report."

Weatherby saw the remaining Venusians begin to dig holes around the perimeter of the pyramid. Through the undergrowth, he could see a number of salvaged stones, crudely etched with sigils. A handful of other lizard-people were making new etchings on to fresh stones.

The Venusians were beginning to bury their dead.

It seemed appropriate, somehow, to allow them some privacy in this, so the men from the *Daedalus* took this as an appropriate time to take their leave, though in doing so, Mr. Bacon was nowhere to be found. "He probably thought we were to be skinned alive," Plumb said dismissively, "or didn't want to be associated with this mess should he truck with other Venusians later on."

They were escorted back to the beach by the remaining warriors of the Va'hakri village, who did not seem to mind the growing heat and humidity, even though it left the men staggering and panting before the trek was complete. When they arrived on the beach, they were surprised to find Captain Morrow had come ashore.

"We were considering a search party," Morrow said, failing to keep his consternation from his voice. Weatherby saw his crisp uniform and ramrod posture and wondered whether the captain would even allow himself to perspire. "I do hope you spent your time productively."

Plumb's report, however, assuaged the captain of time well spent, and

Weatherby was surprised to hear commendable words about himself and Finch from the first lieutenant. Morrow was heartened to see that they had made friendly contact with the Venusians, for, as it turned out, he had some plans for them—and for their captives from the *Chance*.

A few minutes later, the officers of the *Daedalus* lined up on the beach as Captain Morrow formally presented himself to the Va'hakri warrior and the few remaining members of the tribe, with Finch's linguistic assistance. Morrow spoke words of condolence, and swore justice on the perpetrators and friendship between His Majesty King George III and the Va'hakri people. Through this, of course, the Va'hakri looked confused and, truth be told, slightly bored.

Then Morrow made an offer.

"These men have committed grievous crimes against your people," Morrow said, nodding toward the bound pirates who remained prisoner on the beach since they were taken captive. "Their lives are forfeit should we bring them to justice on Earth. However, their crimes against you are far greater."

The warrior nodded, a quizzical look in his reptilian eye, as Finch translated, then responded with a series of croaks and grunts. "He agrees that the men are evil and should be killed for destroying their village and taking their sacred flower," Finch reported. "But he says they are your people, and yours to deal with."

Morrow stood up taller. "No, sir. I hereby remand them to your custody, so that you may carry out justice as you see fit."

Finch turned from the captain with a slight smile and translated. The reptilian looked surprised, but nodded quickly at Morrow, then let forth a staccato barrage of chirps, croaks and grunts to his fellow Venusians. The surviving Va'hakri whooped and shook their spears—and the captives from the *Chance* paled considerably.

"You can't do that!" one of them yelled, his Irish brogue coming through. "They'll skin us alive, they will!"

Any further attempts at pleading for clemency were overrun by the swarming Va'hakri warriors, who immediately grabbed the prisoners and began dragging them away toward the village, the smoke from which was still visible in the sky above the jungle. Weatherby closed his eyes against the sight, but could not close his ears against their screams.

"Jupiter!" the Irishman called as he was pulled into the dense trees. "They make for Jupiter! Save me and I'll take ye there!" A few moments later, the screams had faded into the distance, and the *Daedalans* prepared to return to the ship.

"'Tis a rough justice, sir," Plumb said, though the first lieutenant didn't seem to be harboring any question about Morrow's decision; it was more an observation.

Morrow frowned. "Most certainly. But it sounded as though the Venusians were quite ready to make war upon mankind anyway. If these pirates serve as their example, then so be it, and relations between the tribes and our fellow men may yet be salvaged."

A half-hour later, they reassembled in Morrow's cabin to plot their next course of action. Whilst they were indeed scheduled to make for the Jovian system, Morrow was quite alarmed at the *Chance*'s newfound ability to make the Void from anywhere upon a planet's seas. The tactical gains by any party possessing such a secret of the Great Work would be nigh insurmountable, and Morrow was keen on hearing Finch's learned opinion of the matter.

Yet Finch had little to add. "We witnessed a stunning display of high alchemy in their escape, sir," the alchemist said, looking at his feet awkwardly. "And yet they seem to seek more. The va'hakla plant is said to have prodigious properties, and yet I cannot fathom how the va'hakla plant and Mercurium might be used together. Indeed, they would seem to cancel each other out, as they are from different worlds and governed by different houses of the zodiac and differing humours besides. If Cagliostro is indeed planning a great working of some kind with these two materials, I cannot see what it would be. They are both quite rare, and both still very theoretical in their uses. Whatever he is planning, it is on a scale I've not even heard of."

"So who can help us?" Morrow asked. "What of your teachers, Doctor?"

Finch smiled slightly. "In alchemical circles, Captain, we have a saying: Those who cannot Work, teach. Without boasting, I am more a master of the Great Work than they, and if this problem escapes me, I hold no hope for even the chair at Oxford. The greatest alchemists do not deign to teach publicly, but are often private individuals, like the late Dr. McDonnell."

The captain turned to Miss Baker, who was invited to join them due to her familiarity with the late Dr. McDonnell's work. "Did your late master have any correspondence with other alchemists? Perhaps one might be able to answer our questions and, in doing so, help thwart this criminal."

"There is but one that comes to my mind, sir," she said quietly, "but I wonder whether he will be disposed to help us, for I am sorry to say that he is no friend of His Majesty."

Morrow raised an eyebrow. "Is he French, then?"

"No, sir, although his latest letter came from Paris, where he is assigned as a commissioner of the Ganymedean cause."

"Surely," Plumb said with recognition, "such a man won't help us. Even if we were to gain audience, he's a revolutionary of the worst sort. He'll laugh us back to the Channel." At this, Weatherby and Foster looked at each other and shrugged, though it seemed most of the others in the room knew of the man in question.

Morrow seemed to consider Plumb's words, but said: "I met him once, years ago, before the war broke out. Whatever his politics, I found him to be most kind, genial and upright. His charity on Ganymede is well known, and his scientific and alchemical knowledge is impressive. What say you, Doctor?"

"The man's reputation is impeccable, both in character and in knowledge of the Great Work," Finch replied. "And of the handful of alchemists I would consider capable of aiding us, he is the only one we might easily track down. His personal interest in the matter can only help as well. And if I may, I would stress that such powerful and rare materials in the hands of someone of Cagliostro's reputation should be seen as a dire threat. He may yet sell his secrets to an enemy power, or his purpose may be even more disturbing."

Morrow nodded at Finch, taking it in for a moment. "Mr. Weatherby, what is our distance to Earth? And to Jupiter?" he finally asked.

"The planets are well aligned, sir. We could make the Channel in less than three weeks," he responded, thankful he remembered to check the orrery prior to coming to the cabin. "Jupiter would be three months from here. However, I believe that if we tarry on Earth a few weeks, her path would take us within a mere five weeks of Jupiter."

"And thus we may detour and save a few weeks in the process," Morrow said as he rose from his chair. "It's your watch, Mr. Weatherby. We shall make for Earth, and the Channel. While Mr. Plumb takes *Daedalus* into Portsmouth to report, we shall attempt to visit Paris, God help us.

Dismissed."

Weatherby caught up with Finch outside the great cabin. "Doctor, who is this alchemist to whom you referred?"

Finch smiled. "Why, Mr. Weatherby, do you not read the London papers?"

"Apparently not closely enough," Weatherby grumbled. He was much more interested in news of battles and war than politics. "Who is he?"

"Benjamin Franklin," Finch replied, "certainly the most skilled alchemist to ever come out of the colonies. It's really quite a shame he's thrown in his lot with the rebels. They've sent him to France to negotiate for aid on their behalf."

And so now we are on to Earth, and to France. I admit, I've had little truck with alchemists, and find their ways most peculiar. Yes, of course, every ship in His Majesty's Navy has an alchemist on board, and those of third-rate or higher often have two: one to maintain the ship and another to act as surgeon. Yet despite my interactions with these—and my recent oversight of Dr. Finch—I am lost quickly where the greater mysteries of alchemy are concerned.

In my limited experience, there seems to be two types of workers in the Great Art. There are those who treat it as simply another science to master, much like the mathematics used in navigation or shipbuilding. And there are those who seem more akin to mystics than men of Reason. I would number Dr. Finch a rarity in that he seems to be an amalgamation of the two, when he is inclined to give an opinion.

This Cagliostro seems to be of the mystical bent, and a wonder-worker of his caliber, I am told, could do much with the powerful items he now possesses. With Dr. Finch at a loss as to his aims, I am truly concerned that we have taken a truly dangerous quest. Why in Heaven would men meddle in such matters to begin with?

And, furthermore, to have our hopes hinge on the knowledge of a traitor to the Crown? There may be worse fates, but none come to me at the moment. Is this what we must resort to?

July 26, 2132

The staring was really getting to Shaila.

It started the previous night, with her JSC colleagues and subordinates at the sleeping centrifuges. They looked to her—chief ops officer, acting number two—with the obvious questions in their eyes. Why the reactor alert? What's going on? She refused to meet their gazes, sealing herself in her pod as she looked forward to the heavy press of increased gravity lulling her to sleep.

It resumed in the morning, from the moment she got out of the pod, through her morning shower routine, and all the way through the entire JSC wing. It wasn't entirely bad—they were looking to her for answers, much like any junior officer would when regarding a senior officer. But given that her answer to last night's fiasco would be "I fucked up," and the larger answers regarding the cave and ravine weren't there, Shaila opted for silence.

It got worse in the Hub, where the overnight smelting shift was coming off duty and the morning diggers were getting ready to head out. That was at least thirty pairs of eyes, all fixed on her. Conversation stopped, fingers were pointed—literally in a few cases. The questioning stares were supplemented and obscured with harsher overtones: fear, anger, doubt, derision. She was sending Alvarez home, after all, and most of them didn't care to mull over the fact that she was the one who was physically attacked first.

She had hoped to see Stephane at breakfast, as usual, but a quick scan of her inbox told her that he and Yuna would be in the lab this morning, and would rendezvous with her at the cave. From the timestamp on his message, it was quite possible he was up all night trying to figure out what was going on, but all he could say thus far was that the ravine hadn't changed since yesterday afternoon, which was a positive sign.

Despite Stephane's not-quite-perfect English, his e-mail had a very distinct tone to Shaila's eyes: strictly business. Of course, he could still be pissed, or he could just be giving her space. What's worse, she found herself caring which it might be, which only irked her further. Sure, he was charming, and was one of the few people on base who could make her laugh regularly. But still…he was a dilettante, nothing more, even if he was shaping up to be a pretty good geologist.

Over a particularly bland tofu scramble, Shaila quickly finished scanning her morning messages—status reports, shift-change requests, a note from her mother in Birmingham, all unanswered for now. She dumped her tray and headed over to the lab where Stephane and Yuna had set up shop.

He wasn't there, and neither was Yuna. Evan Greene was, however. "Morning, Lieutenant. Durand and Hiyashi told me to tell you they were heading to the cave," Greene said as he slowly panned a portable holocam around a six-wheeled robotic probe, the one Harry had offered.

"Looks just like the old *Opportunity*," Shaila said, trying to make small talk. And to be fair, it really did indeed look like the early 21st century rover, now gathering dust some 2,500 kilometers to the north of McAuliffe.

The little six-wheeled robot on the table was roughly a meter long and a half-meter wide, with various probes and cameras tucked into its chassis. The six wheels were individually articulated, to make it easier for the 'bot to scoot through rocky terrain—perfect for the lava tube. It also had two strong lifting arms, for moving and storing rock samples.

"Well, it's lighter," Greene said. "Only about 65 kilos, and runs on battery instead of solar—kind of important for a mining probe."

"Why didn't they just take this with them?" Shaila said.

Greene gave one of his gleaming smiles. "Because I wanted to get holo of it getting loaded up, the trip to the cave—all of it."

"Right. Of course." Shaila said. "Whenever you're ready."

"Just about. We're going call out each of the features of this probe on the holovid—graphics, description, the works," Greene said.

"Lovely," Shaila said, grabbing a work cart from the storage area of the lab.

To his credit, Greene offered to help load the 'bot onto a transfer cart, but in the Martian gravity, it wasn't really necessary. Besides, Shaila was determined to accept as little help as possible from him. Together, they rolled the probe down the JSC-only corridor and into the Hub, where the ops officer on duty—Adams this time—had their pressure suits ready to go and their rover on standby.

"Thanks for agreeing to do this," Greene beamed as he prepared to suit up. "I'm excited about our little trek."

She grabbed her suit and pulled it over to the bench next to his. "Just following orders, Dr. Greene. You need a hand with that?"

He deftly pulled the top half of the suit over his chest and expertly flipped the seals closed. "I've logged 200 hours of EVA time, Lieutenant. Earth-orbit spacewalks, Europan ice, you name it."

Shaila shrugged into her own suit. "Fair enough, doc. Let's get out of here, then," Shaila said, sealing her helmet. Out of habit, she checked Greene's suit as well; it was in perfect order. "Comm channel three, radio check, over," she said absently, the routine engraved in her brain. "Sorry, I mean, we'll be on channel—"

"Comm channel three, I hear you five-by-five, over," Greene responded.

Maybe he really did know what he was doing, Shaila thought. "So what are you, former military?" she asked as they entered the airlock.

"JSC Civilian Corps," he replied before a deafening whoosh marked the evacuation of breathable air from the chamber. "It never really took."

"Why not?"

"Look around, Lieutenant," Greene said as they exited the airlock. Personnel transports packed with miners headed off down the access road, while a massive hauler filled with ice rolled past. "I wanted to do science, not play corporate contractor."

The two headed toward one of the rovers parked outside. "Everyone has bills to pay," Shaila replied. "That's why I'm chauffeuring you around."

Rover Three looked somewhat like a late 20th century pickup truck, with a flat bed in the back for loading gear. Shaila placed the 'bot in the back, securing it with cargo straps under the watchful gaze of Greene's holocam. He even panned around as she closed the tailgate and got in up front. She resisted the very childish—and very tempting—impulse to flip him the bird. Instead, she revved the motor and took off down the access road toward the cave.

It wasn't a silent ride, but it wasn't overly uncomfortable either. Greene piped up occasionally with questions about the geography they passed, as well as the mining operations. He expressed grudging admiration for Billiton Minmetals' efficiency—they launched a couple thousand metric tons of deuterium, uranium and other valuables back to Earth each month. Shaila deferred much of the mining questions to Harry Yu's people, but found herself warming up to the conversation when topic turned back to the unique features of the Martian landscape.

"Hey, Lieutenant, can you do me a favor?" Greene asked.

"Aren't I doing you one already?" Shaila asked.

She heard the scientist chuckle. "All right, fine. Another favor. That ridge over there, does it overlook the base?"

Shaila already knew where this was going. "Yeah, and one of the launch pads for the ore-hauler pods. Lemme guess."

"Five minutes," Greene promised. "I just need a few shots."

Shaila wheeled the rover off the access road and toward the ridge. "You got three."

She eased the rover to a stop about ten meters from the edge of the ridge. Beyond it, she could see one of the Billiton launch pads in the background, and McAuliffe itself behind that. She had to admit, it was kind of pretty in a space-geek kind of way, and Greene was impressed enough to quickly hop out of the rover and start setting up his tripod.

As Greene began recording, Shaila pulled out her datapad and went through her e-mail again. Stephane and Yuna were at the cave and ready; she told them she'd be a few minutes late due to Greene's detour. And Diaz forwarded a reply from Houston with regard to, well—everything.

"Currently, we have no theories with regard to seismic anomalies, electromagnetic anomalies or Cherenkov radiation presence," the mission liaison officer-on-duty wrote. "Working group established; will advise. Continue investigation. Allow mining operations so long as seismic anomalies are confined to current affected area."

It was just what Shaila expected: *We don't know. Status quo for now until you either solve it or everything really goes to hell. At which point, we'll blame you.* She made that last bit up, but she wouldn't be surprised if that's how it panned out.

"Lieutenant, can you come here a second?" Greene said over the comm. Shaila looked up to see him about 15 meters away, fiddling with his holocorder.

"Sure," she replied, climbing out of the rover. As she walk-skipped over, she saw him picking up the tripod and moving it back and forth, left and right. "What are you doing?"

"I've got something here I've never seen before," he said. "Maybe you know what it is."

Shaila was immediately on guard. "Mars isn't supposed have anomalies, you know." Houston's archaic terminology seemed to be contagious.

"Seems to have plenty, lately," Greene said, pointing to the small flip-screen on the holocam. The middle of the screen was obscured by a line of fuzzy static.

Shaila looked at him quizzically. "Bad imaging chip?"

"No. Keep looking at it." Greene picked up the tripod and moved it back and forth. The line moved toward the top of the screen as he moved the camera toward him, then back down as he held it further out. In the course of about eight centimeters of movement in either direction, it disappeared entirely.

"Huh," Shaila said, unimpressed. "Wonder what that is."

"Holocams don't get static, Lieutenant," Greene said. "Pixilated, sure, but not static."

He had a good point. And the stationary nature of the effect meant that it wasn't Greene's equipment, but something there that was affecting it. "Doc, can I see the camera?"

Greene stepped back from the tripod and waved her toward it. She did the same thing he did, moving it back and forth. Sure enough, there was a fixed point of interference—a spot on the ground, seemingly, that created the line on the screen.

"All right, so Mars has an anomaly every now and then," she said.

"No kidding. This equipment is rad-hardened, so I'm at a loss."

Shaila jumped back to the rover to fetch a sensor pack. It was standard issue on every rover, and while it didn't have all the geological settings the surveying sensors had, it had a better range. Thankfully, once she got back to the camera, the little sensor didn't disappoint.

"I'll be damned," she muttered.

"Trace electromagnetic field readings?" Greene said. Shaila turned to see him looking over her shoulder.

"Apparently," she said, her voice neutral. "Wonder why."

Greene picked up the camera again, this time moving it sideways a half-meter in each direction. "It's a line," he said. "A very narrow band of EM radiation."

Shaila's mind flooded with possibilities: a fissure in the Martian crust with a pocket of magnetic material below? Some kind of electrostatic effect between the base's AOO sensors? She moved the sensor around the invisible line as best she could. "It's not extending upward. Seems to be under the ground," she said. She turned to look at the holovision host. "You're the physicist. What do you think?"

Greene arched an eyebrow and grinned slightly. "Sure you don't want to just report it to Houston and keep me out of the loop, Lieutenant?"

"You already know about it," she parried. "Might as well get some use out of you while you're here."

Greene started walking off with the tripod, keeping an eye on the flip-screen to keep the static in view. "All I know is that highly focused EM fields like this aren't found in nature. And most electronics radiate EM omnidirectionally, in a sphere."

"I know what omnidirectional means," Shaila groused, following Greene as he walked. "Where are you going?"

"End of the line, I suppose," he said. "If it's not natural, and it's not omnidirectional, then it's in a line for a reason. Why else would you place a perfectly straight line of EM energy in the middle of nowhere?" She could practically hear the grin in his voice. Scientists and their curiosity....

The line continued across the ridge, then down into a gully. As they picked their way down the rock face, they saw the line on the screen grow larger; Greene theorized that as they descended, they were getting closer to the line of EM that, for now, still apparently resided under the Martian surface.

"How far under, do you think?" Shaila asked.

"Dunno," Greene replied. "But it would have to be pretty focused and very powerful to have this kind of effect on the holocam. Like I said, it's rad-hardened. Either this is a whopper of an EM, or the EM is a byproduct of something else that your sensor isn't picking up."

Shaila suddenly had a thought. "So why aren't our suits affected?" Shaila asked. "I mean, they're rad-hard, too. But if it's affecting the camera...."

"Good question. I have no idea. Could just be that the EM that the camera normally gives off is somehow interacting with whatever's underground in just the right way to produce this effect. And that sensor reading is pretty faint. You had to be right on top of it to get anything. Base sensors wouldn't pick it up."

Shaila clambered down to the floor of the gully. "You know an awful lot about the equipment around here."

"It's my job," Greene said simply. "I cover space exploration. And remember, I'm former JSC. I still have friends inside. I keep up on things."

"I'm sure you do," Shaila said.

Greene turned toward her, the camera momentarily forgotten. "I didn't mean it that way."

"What way?"

"The colonel told me not to ask about it, but I wasn't going to anyway."

Shaila's heart started beating faster. He must have misunderstood her snark for something else. "Ask about what?" she finally said.

"*Atlantis.*"

The word hung between them for several seconds. "Good," she finally said. She saw compassion on his face, and was surprised at how much the look pissed her off.

Greene turned back to his camera and started walking again, the line of static still in view. "That whole thing will come out eventually, but it won't come from me," he said nonchalantly.

Shaila stood stock still for a few more seconds, fists clenched, before she finally started walking after him.

Greene went on calmly. "What sucks is that the JSC does so few exploratory missions to begin with. And when one goes south, they cover it up, and send the survivors out to pasture. Or, in your case, to Mars."

"I don't have all the details, but I don't want them. It would jeopardize what little real science JSC still does. And it wouldn't be fair to those who didn't make it back. Or to you, for that matter." He paused to see if Shaila would respond; she didn't. "Anyway, you don't have anything to worry about from me, Lieutenant."

They walked on in silence for several more minutes, climbing up the other side of the gully and onto a plateau. One of the base's AOO sensor poles was about three hundred meters ahead, and they were on course to walk right into it.

"Maybe it's some kind of interference from the equipment up there," Greene said.

Shaila struggled to bring her mind back to the task at hand. "Still doesn't explain the narrow band," she said. "I assume that equipment would give off EM omnidirectionally, just like anything else."

"True," Greene said. "But anything's possible. It's the start of an explanation."

Sure enough, the line led right to the pole. Greene started walking faster, and Shaila had to skip-jump to keep up with his long strides.

When he stopped suddenly, about four meters from the pole, she nearly ran into him. "What is it?" she asked, annoyed.

"I lost it."

Shaila looked at the flip-screen, which showed a perfectly pristine view of the tower ahead. "Where did you lose it?"

"Don't know. Let's backtrack."

They turned and retraced their steps, easy enough in the red dirt despite a light Martian breeze. It only took about four strides before the line reappeared.

"There we go," he said. "And it didn't just stop. It turned."

"Turned?"

"Turned. Roughly 36 degrees to the left, away from the base. Looks like it's heading off that way."

Shaila pulled a map of the area from her datapad, half-expecting the line to lead directly to the mystery cave. Instead, it headed off…nowhere. If the line had previously slid neatly between the base and the mining ops, this new line basically headed off into Mars' no-man's land. "There's nothing out that way," Shaila said. "No mining ops, no nothing."

"Does it intersect with another tower?" Greene asked.

"No, don't think so. And besides, the line turned before we reached the tower." She turned to look back at where they had come from. "Let me see that camera."

Greene surrendered the holovid to Shaila, who went back to the point where the line diverged. "Look at that," she said, pointing to the flip-screen.

Right where the line angled off, a small ball of static appeared, slightly wider than the lines itself. As Greene took the camera back, Shaila used the sensor pack again. "And it's omnidirectional, too," she said.

Greene looked down at the readings. "There's something under there."

Shaila frowned. "So it would seem." She flipped channels on the comm. "Jain to McAuliffe, over."

"McAuliffe to Jain, go ahead," said Finelli, who had the day's ops watch.

Her first instinct was to have the base tell Stephane and Yuna that they'd be delayed again, and to ask to speak with Diaz. After all, this was a random encounter with an EM field, and the cave also carried an unusual EM signature. But after a moment, Shaila knew that getting the 'bot to the cave and figuring out what was going on down there was still her biggest priority.

"Finelli, have Adams suit up and head out to these coordinates with a shovel," Shaila finally said. "There's something buried under the terrain here. I want him to dig it up and bring it back under quarantine. Over."

"Roger that," Finelli said. "How will he know where to dig?"

Shaila took out her roll of duct tape and made a quick X with two strips. She pinned it to the ground with the pen she kept in her carry-all, then placed rocks on each of the four ends. "Tell him X marks the spot. Jain out."

"Now wait just a minute," Greene said, his voice rising. "I want to know what this is."

Shaila walked off toward the rover again. "Sorry, Doctor. Duty calls. Chances are, whatever's going on in and around that cave is going to take priority."

"Lieutenant, I shouldn't have to remind you that I've been afforded total access here," Greene protested, hurrying off after her.

Shaila turned back to him. "Look, doc. This is interesting, OK? Not part of our usual day-to-day. But there's a cave out there that's doing some *really* crazy shit, and I need to figure that out." She started to stalk off again, but turned back. "And I'm going to need to borrow that camera."

Greene considered her skeptically for a moment before handing over the camera. "OK, but I play ball, and this EM field we've found turns out to be something interesting, I want in. And I'll want it on the show."

It was probably the best deal she was going to get. "Fine, pending the colonel's approval. Until then, don't distract my people with this. It's probably nothing, and we have far more serious problems to deal with. Clear?"

"Clear. Can I have my holotape, at least?"

"Hell, no." Shaila gave him a flash of a wicked smile and headed back toward the rover again, tripod in hand and a frustrated holovision personality in tow.

CHAPTER 9

March 15, 1779

Father,

We are back in the Void, and the questions that have disturbed me of late have lessened, though as we approach Earth, I am certain they shall arise once more. At the moment, however, we are preparing splash down again upon our native seas. Coming home has always brought cheer to a sailor's heart, and so it is aboard Daedalus, *though I fear we may not be able to tarry long should the Admiralty order us to continue our investigations.*

As our days away from Venus amass and the sun wanes in apparent size, I find there is much to be said for the resumption of normal duty in the wake of hard action, for it shields the mind from worry and distress. Plus, the company of our fine officers has been a solace and boon, and I've actually found our Dr. Finch to be more congenial than I had first thought him to be...

With Miss Baker locked under guard in the forward area of the ship that used to be the alchemical laboratory, Andrew Finch had little choice but to embrace the rough but earnest bonhomie of the wardroom, where he was forced to take up residence during the young woman's stay aboard *Daedalus*.

This was problematic for a number of reasons, not the least of which was the tremors and sweats he occasionally and randomly endured as his vices seeped from his body. Being an alchemist, and an uncommonly good one at that, the loss of his hookah was not the loss of all opportunity. However, the loss of his privacy meant there was rarely, if ever, occasion for the kind of self-medication that, at the very least, would soothe his nerves and ease his transition into a more healthy life. Not that he had actually opted for the latter, but somewhere between Venus and Earth, he found himself actually curious as to what such a life might be like, given the lack of alternatives.

And even in his darkest moments, sleeping in an ill-fitting hammock with the snores of Lt. Plumb echoing in the tiny wardroom, Finch was forced to admit there was something refreshing about the camaraderie he experienced in residence there. Yes, manners were coarse. Fulton and Plumb, in particular, held little in the way of formalities or suavity, while Weatherby's bookish earnestness was, at turns, off-putting or humorous. But the officers simply accepted Finch's presence as a matter of course, as if bringing Finch into the fold and making of him a friend and comrade was the most natural thing to do.

Having blackballed numerous candidates from his private clubs for simply being of poor lineage, this instant sense of belonging discomfited Finch to no end. What would his friends in London say about him drinking with these men, who were no better than the sons of farmers or shopkeepers? And what would he say back, now that he had sampled and indeed enjoyed their company?

It was all too much to contemplate, especially while he spent his days poring over books in vain attempts to divine the goals and needs of the fiend Cagliostro. Finch knew that he was probably one of the foremost alchemists in England, certainly the best currently working for the Royal Navy, but Cagliostro's place in the pantheon of great alchemists was assured, by sheer knowledge if not morality.

So when he was not buried in his books and charts and coming up against frustration after frustration, Finch gladly endured the companionship of the wardroom. On this particular evening, as he had heard regularly for the past several Saturday nights, Lt. Plumb raised his glass and said, "To wives and sweethearts." And in response, all in the wardroom—including the midshipmen, who all too easily fell into their cups—responded, "Wives and sweethearts." And a moment later: "May they never meet!"

The uproar of laughter arrived on cue as tankards of grog clanked together. Finch participated, though with a certain bemused reserve—it was naval tradition for such a toast on Saturdays, Weatherby told him, and so long as he was to remain enslaved in His Majesty's Navy, Finch promised himself to try to at least be as tolerant as possible, despite the repetition.

"I must disagree with this toast," Plumb exclaimed after the laughter subsided, "even though it be tradition. For those of you who juggle both sweethearts and wives, I commend you for your energies!" At this, laughter once again ensued. "No, not those energies!" Plumb went on. "That is but a simple thing, and far more pleasurable, compared to all of the letters, the presents, the attention your multiples of women will want! No, gentlemen, you may keep your wives, and your sweethearts if you wish. As for me, I'll just find a new wife in each port, and be divorced before I set sail again!"

More tankards clanked, and Finch knew the grog had fueled the frankness with which Plumb spoke. Certainly, Finch was no prude, and would be the first to admit as such; he believed he could give any Navy man spirited competition in the ways of debauchery. But he saw Weatherby's heart was not in the jest, and knew immediately the cause. Unlike the others, Finch included, Weatherby had a poet's outlook on life and love, and it was quite evident that his thoughts were upon someone far closer than Earth.

Cigar in hand, Finch followed Weatherby to the quarterdeck when the latter man took the evening watch—perhaps the other reason Weatherby had not imbibed as much as his fellow officers, though it seemed such mindfulness was more the exception than the rule in the wardroom. "Looking forward to seeing Earth again, Mr. Weatherby?"

"Perhaps not under these circumstances," Weatherby said. "I find it hard to believe that we must rely upon the word of a traitor to help us solve this riddle."

"One man's traitor is another's patriot, Mr. Weatherby," Finch said. "And the captain is correct: Dr. Franklin has a reputation for being quite upstanding and morally sound. I should think you would've liked that."

"Apparently the moral imperative of loyalty to one's king and country does not enter into your equation, Doctor," Weatherby replied.

"Oh, I've no use for this particular conflict," Finch said. "Let them go. We can continue trading with them, and without the expense of providing for their defense." Seeing Weatherby's deepening scowl, the alchemist tried a different tack. "And how is our Miss Baker faring? I understand you had the watch before dinner."

"As well as can be expected, Doctor," Weatherby replied. "I continue to be amazed at her strength. She has held up well under innumerable trials. She tells me her life has not been an easy one."

Finch nodded as he lit his cigar. "Yes, she's told me this as well," he said, then paused for a moment to think. "Lieutenant, perhaps I am overstating things, but I dare say you've become quite fond of her."

Weatherby's face turned a bright crimson, evident even in the dim light of the lamps, and Finch could not help but chuckle at the young officer's attempt to maintain his composure.

"Oh, come now. We are men here!" Finch continued. "She's beautiful and quite intelligent."

"That she is," Weatherby murmured while staring straight ahead. "However, the notion is simply not one that I might pursue. We have much demanded of us in the service, Doctor. And whilst my origins are not of the aristocracy, I feel it would do my career no good whatsoever to find myself pursuing a mere household servant."

Finch raised an eyebrow at this. "Your ambition is a credit to you, Mr. Weatherby, but surely the Royal Navy can be accommodating of a man who follows his heart in such matters. So long as propriety is maintained, such a match would not hinder you, would it?"

"I do not know, to be honest," Weatherby said. "I am a few years off from having to make such decisions, but I know of very few captains and admirals who achieved such rank without seeking a wife of appropriate station. Social standing and patronage are becoming increasingly more important to an officer's career, much as we might wish it to be based solely on merit."

"Well, then, perhaps it's for the best," Finch said. "Of course, I'm a mere third son of a relatively minor noble house. I'm rather expected to sully the family name somewhat." He gave the young officer a wink, which was returned with a small smile. "Her circumstances could be quite an impediment should all come out."

Weatherby turned to the doctor at this, confused and a little alarmed. "What circumstances are these? You seem to imply more than you're saying, sir."

Finch grew serious. "Mr. Weatherby, there may be nothing to it at all, but I will say this: I spent two months at Elizabeth Mercuris. There are matters I have heard of that should not have been spoken of, and I am loath to repeat them. But there is a saying amongst your sailors, something akin to still waters running fast?"

"Running deep, Doctor," Weatherby corrected him.

"Oh, fine then. My point is such, and you may consider taking the advice of a self-confessed scoundrel for the half-pence it is worth. You're an upstanding young man, and I dare say a good one besides, for they say the devil knows good when he sees it." He leaned in close for a moment. "A fine alchemist once said, 'A prudent question is one half of wisdom.' So until you know all, Mr. Weatherby, I suggest you keep asking questions of her."

"Now you have me quite at a loss, sir." Weatherby's gaze was penetrating, and his face grew stern.

Finch straightened up with one of his broad, sometimes infuriating smiles. "Mr. Weatherby, it is merely advice. I find the girl compelling as well, but it has been made plain to me, most embarrassingly I might add, that my feeling is not returned in kind. I have no wish to insert myself where I am not wanted, nor do I wish to imply anything there may not be. So consider it advice from a man older and more experienced than you, though I will say you are likely the wiser. She had undergone much indeed, and it is likely worth your time and effort to determine exactly what her life has been like over the years, should you finally wish to pursue her."

Weatherby grimaced. "This must be some province of the aristocracy, Doctor, to speak so plainly about such delicate matters."

"No, merely my own province, nothing more," Finch replied with a puff of his cigar. "There are few in the Known Worlds whom I may truly call friend, and I have been a true friend to fewer still. Honestly, Mr. Weatherby, I've not the faintest idea how to go about it."

Weatherby pondered this comment for a time before saying, "I do believe your concern is heartfelt, Doctor. Thank you."

"Not at all," Finch replied simply as he watched the sun-currents stretch out before the *Daedalus*.

"So, then," Weatherby said with the air of a man changing the subject. "How exactly was it made plain to you regarding your feelings toward Miss Baker?"

Finch, surprised, turned to see the younger man smiling broadly. Perhaps he was not such a humorless caricature as Finch had thought.

"Never you mind, Weatherby!" he grinned. "The matter was brought up, discussed briefly and summarily dispensed with, nothing more."

"Come now, Doctor," Weatherby said. "Did you use your little charm potion upon her and she found you out?"

"What potion is that?" Finch said, a hint of defensiveness in your voice.

Weatherby was quite pleased to have one over on the doctor. "I saw you place it on your tongue when you spoke to the Venusians. It was some sort of elixir to make your words more amenable to them, was it not?"

"Well done, Mr. Weatherby! That is exactly what it was. You've been reading up quite well. And yes, I may have used it for such amorous pursuits in the past. But not with Miss Baker, I promise you."

"Well, then, your encounter with her must be an even more interesting tale," Weatherby said, prodding his fellow officer good-naturedly.

"Not even if you returned my hookah and my privacy would I tell you," Finch vowed. "I am wholly unused to such patent rejection, and do not wish it to be attached to my otherwise pristine reputation amongst the ladies!"

Weatherby smiled. After the man's genuine, if clumsy, expression of concern, Weatherby hadn't the heart to tell him that his hookah was tossed overboard weeks ago to drift aimlessly in the sun-currents between Mercury and Venus.

July 26, 2132

The little six-wheeled robot seemed to take in its surroundings. It swiveled its head left, then right, then in a complete 360-degree turn in each direction. Its "neck" likewise telescoped from a mere ten centimeters to nearly a full half-meter and back again, and angled itself up and down. Then, the 'bot moved forward about a meter, then back a meter. Ultimately, it did a small donut in each direction.

"I am satisfied," Stephane pronounced from fifty feet above the cavern floor. "The *Dolomieu* is ready."

"The what?" Shaila asked. She looked over at Stephane, guiding the 'bot with a joystick attached to a small portable computer.

The geologist looked up at her and grinned; she was a bit relieved to see a smile after last night. "The *Dolomieu*. Named for the French geologist Deodat Dolomieu. He discovered dolomite, you know."

"What a lovely name!" Yuna said, shooting Shaila a wink and a grin. "I never thought to name it."

"You are not French," Stephane said. "We name everything. I am sending you images from the main full-spectrum camera. You two may watch as we go."

"Send it my way, too," Greene said. "I can feed it directly onto the recording."

Shaila watched as the little 'bot headed between the sensor suites, and noted that its camera-head was pointing forward—not down—and that Stephane opted to fully extend the probe's neck, so that it could approximate the height of a person. It didn't seem to be much of a show, though Greene was glued to his camera's flip-screen regardless.

Then the 'bot shook slightly. Stephane stopped the probe and swiveled the camera head around to focus on the ground next to the 'bot.

The rocks in the cave were still rolling.

"Thought so," Stephane said. "At least we are still going in the right direction. And the rocks are not too big." He swiveled the camera to look behind the 'bot, but saw no major impediments—like large boulders bearing down from the recesses of the lava tube. "All right. Moving forward now."

Shaila watched the cave roll past as the *Dolomieu* progressed. "Tough to get my bearings here," she said over the comm. "Is it me, or does it look different again?"

"The low levels of seismic activity continued overnight," Yuna said. "I imagine we've had a bunch of rocks rolling around in there for hours how."

The *Dolomieu* continued down the cave, with Stephane pausing to swivel its head left and right at regular intervals. Yuna kept tabs on the radiation and EM readings, both of which were increasing slightly as the 'bot went deeper inside. Within a few minutes, the little probe had gone past the furthest point the astronauts had explored in person, and the lights from the sensor suites began to dim.

"Here there are dragons," Stephane intoned with fake seriousness. Everyone else ignored him.

Ten minutes later, the probe was nearly a kilometer further along, and despite the ebbing light, the scenery was little changed—rubble on the floor of the cave, the rock strata visible along the walls, elevated levels of Cherenkov radiation, ambient electromagnetic fields and seismic activity that increased with every rotation of the *Dolomieu*'s wheels. Yuna noted a slight rise in atmospheric pressure, but there were no real problems to contend with—yet.

Suddenly, it seemed, the video feed showed a near-vertical pile of stones in front of the probe. "What's that?" Shaila asked.

"It is something in our way, obviously," Stephane responded, sounding peevish. "One moment. We will go around."

The *Dolomieu*'s head-camera pivoted to the left. And the obstruction stretched off into the dark. Stephane swore in French into the comm, then swiveled the camera around to the other side.

Same thing. Stephane tilted the camera upward, toward the ceiling of the cave. The rocks were at least two meters high, if not more so, as it was difficult to discern the top of the wall from the darkness of the cave beyond.

"OK, what the hell *is* that?" Shaila asked.

"It is…a wall," Stephane answered.

"Bullshit," Greene muttered. Shaila looked over at him; he was holding his datapad in both hands, staring intently at it with a stunned look on his face.

"Confirmed," Yuna said, her voice quiet. "The rocks are piled up at an angle of roughly 89 degrees, and there is very little deviation along the length of this…structure."

Shaila turned to Yuna suddenly. "I swear, Yuna, if this is some miner's idea of a joke, I'm kicking all their asses off this rock."

"Oh, Shaila, I don't think that's the case," Yuna said, a chiding tone in her voice. "I mean, who would take the time to build a wall down there, of all things?"

"*Somebody* built this," Shaila said. "Rocks just don't pile up into a god-damn wall on their own, now do they?"

"Yes, they do," Stephane interrupted.

"Dammit, Steve," Shaila barked, turning to face him. "Now's not the…" She stopped when she saw him furiously tapping at his datapad.

"I just sent you the video," he said simply, a few moments later.

Both Shaila and Yuna looked down on their datapads. *Dolomieu* had been looking off to its right, toward the ground. The camera tracked a rock, about twenty centimeters in diameter, as it rolled—*uphill*, Shaila reminded herself—toward the wall.

And then it rolled right up the wall toward the top.

"Christ," Shaila breathed.

Stephane switched the video feed back to live, and immediately found two other rocks to track. They, too, rolled up the wall, disappearing over the edge.

Nobody spoke for several minutes. They watched the rocks, one every thirty seconds or so, roll past, roll up, roll out of sight.

"OK," Shaila said, struggling to resume some kind—any kind—of control of the situation. "Double check and be sure we can't get around this thing. Go to either edge."

Stephane dutifully guided *Dolomieu* to the left, where the wall of rock tightly abutted the lava tube. It was the same on the other side. He also tried to look over the wall, but it was too high, even with the 'bot's "neck" fully extended.

Meanwhile, the ambient electromagnetic energy, Cherenkov radiation, seismic activity and atmospheric pressure continued to rise, albeit by scant fractions.

It took a solid half hour before they ran out of ideas. "All right, bring her in," Shaila ordered. "Let's get the 'bot up here."

"Should we not leave it there?" Stephane asked. "We can tie the video feed into the base computer."

Shaila pondered this. "Tempting. But that's an active cave down there. You think the lifting arms are strong enough carry a sensor down to the wall?"

Stephane grinned. "This I like. It is worth trying."

They watched as *Dolomieu* turned and made its way back toward the skylight, which appeared as a small, pale shaft of light piercing the darkness in the distance. It took several minutes before they could pick out the sensors in the darkness, and Stephane piloted the 'bot to the nearest one.

And then the screen went blank.

"*Merde*," Stephane muttered.

Shaila walked over and peered over his shoulder. "What happened?"

"I do not know," he said, pressing icons frantically on the screen. "I have nothing. She is dead."

"Dead?" Yuna asked.

"Dead. No communications, no control, nothing." He threw his hands up. "Gone. Poof."

Shaila dialed up the remaining sensors in the cave—none of them were able to penetrate the darkness far enough to clearly see the wall off in the distance. Likewise, the sensor range wasn't where it needed to be, either. "All our existing assets are in the wrong place," she said.

She started walking over to the skylight, peering down into it. "Seismic?" she asked.

"Steady," Yuna replied. "Shaila, you're not thinking of going down there, are you?"

Shaila tested the ropes that remained tethered around the skylight. "Maybe."

Yuna hop-skipped over, a worried look on her face. "I know you want to get a camera back on down there, but the colonel said nobody should risk it."

Shaila turned to address Yuna, whose maternal-worried look immediately consoled and angered her all at once. "Look. There is a *wall* down there. A wall. Rocks rolling uphill, building a wall all by themselves. And our only chance of getting eyes on it just went dead."

Shaila looked toward the others. Stephane looked worried, but she could tell he'd back her up. Greene looked hopeful; Shaila figured he wanted more footage.

"I'm heading down there," she said finally. "Anyone who objects can bring it up with the colonel. And nobody follows me down there, no matter what. That's an order." She grabbed one of the ropes and hooked it to her suit. "Yuna, give me whatever readings you can from the sensors already down there. Especially seismic."

Taking a deep breath, she started lowering herself back into the darkness.

CHAPTER 10

March 24, 1779

Father,

Like many of those who sail the Void, I have often dreamed of visiting the fabled ring-cities of those Saturnine aliens who call themselves the Xan. Of course, they are also a most insular and un-welcoming breed, and with the journey to Saturn long and arduous, it is unlikely that I should ever cast my eyes upon them. Yet I imagine I would feel more welcome and much less different than I felt walking amongst the French on the streets of Paris.

I am surprised to find so many English speakers here, many of whom possess unmistakable London accents. I certainly expected a handful of Ganymedeans and other colonists sympathetic to the rebel cause, for the French king has made no secret of his desire to see our colonies parted from us. Yet there are gentlemen and ladies from England as well, and they peruse the shops and cafes here freely, as if without care for the politics of the day. Another province of the aristocracy, undoubtedly. I, for one, would never have come willingly, but such is the increasing strangeness of our quest that I find myself here regardless.

Why the carriage upon the road to Passy had been stopped, none within or without could really say, but the gendarmes had stopped it nonetheless. To passers-by, either entering the grand city of Paris or taking their leave of it, it was something best not contemplated. Those therein would certainly either be allowed to go upon their way—or they would be found out and made to pay for whatever slight they had perpetrated against His Majesty, King Louis XVI of France.

Those inside the carriage were, quite surprisingly, not acting against the king whatsoever. But they had reason to be nervous regardless.

"I can't understand it," Finch said to his compatriots. "Do we have the mark of Cain upon our brow? Or worse, of England?"

Captain Morrow gave him a harsh shushing. "Be quiet, man!" he whispered. "We managed to avoid the constabulary in Le Havre. This will not be a problem."

Morrow sat back in the coach seat and pulled down upon his civilian waistcoat, adopting a look of amused perturbation, much as any gentleman would adopt should his coach be stopped by the city's authorities for no good reason. Miss Baker looked nervous, but took to fluttering her new fan before her; amazing how a new dress and a fan could turn a chambermaid into a gentlewoman, for she fit the part exquisitely. Weatherby, seeing no other valid course of action, tried to adopt Morrow's countenance. But he could not help but think that Le Havre was quite different from the French capital.

It had seemed easy enough over the past three days. They had rowed ashore under cover of twilight, reaching the small farming village of Heuqueville just as the Moon rose—their timing could not have been better. Pleading a broken-down coach, they arranged a ride into Le Havre upon a farmer's cart, and enjoyed a fine dinner there. Morrow seemed quite happy to allow Plumb to take *Daedalus* into Portsmouth to deliver a report to Admiral Sir Thomas Pye—old "Goose Pye," as he was known to many in the Navy, with all the regard the nickname implied. Indeed, Morrow was quite genial and witty at dinner that night, and Weatherby found himself proud to have been allowed to see this side of his commander.

The next morning found them in a coach bound for Paris, where they arrived the following afternoon. Posing as Ganymedean sympathizers, it took but a few inquiries to determine Dr. Benjamin Franklin's locale—the village of Passy, on the road to the great Palace of Versailles. They also discovered that Franklin had just been recognized as the United States of Ganymede's ambassador to France. Ambassador, indeed! Weatherby found the very notion ludicrous.

Thankfully, he was pondering that very thought, with something of a smirk upon his face, when the gendarme commander appeared at the door to the coach once more. "My apologies, gentlemen and lady," he said in

French, which Weatherby was barely able to follow. "But you must understand, we do not allow travelers upon the road to Versailles lightly."

"I understand completely, monsieur," Morrow said with a genial smile, his French seeming perfect to Weatherby's ears. "But we are not bound for Versailles, but for Passy."

The gendarme frowned. "You are not French," he said flatly, not sharing Weatherby's assessment of Morrow's skill.

"No, we are not, monsieur," Morrow said. "We are from Boston, on Ganymede, and we have business interests here that we must address with our new ambassador."

"Do you have papers to that effect?" the gendarme demanded.

"I am afraid not," Morrow demurred as Finch and Weatherby shot each other a nervous glance. Weatherby had secured a pistol behind him, but he knew that using it would be a last resort and a thin chance of escape. "We were hoping—"

Suddenly, Miss Baker leaned forward, fanning herself, which prompted the very tips of her fan to glow alchemically in the night sky; it was an effect she had added to her fan while upon the road between Le Havre and Paris. "William, darling, what is all this?" she interrupted coquettishly in English, flapping her fan before her. "I am absolutely *starving*. Can we not go to Franklin's house tonight?"

"I don't know, my dear," Morrow said, unable to keep a smile from his face. "This gentleman seems to think we should not be upon the road." He turned to address the gendarme in French. "Please, sir, my wife is hungry, and we do not wish to be late to dinner."

The gendarme looked at Miss Baker, who gave him a winning smile and, to Weatherby's shock, a wink. "Well," the gendarme said. "It is not far. But you will stop there, yes? Otherwise, you will be held in the village of Versailles should you go there."

"Of course, monsieur. We are staying at Passy tonight. Merci!" Morrow said. He quickly closed the door, then rapped on the roof of the coach. The driver immediately snapped the reins, and the coach lurched forward out of Paris, with Miss Baker giving the gendarme a little wave of her fan as they passed.

"Well played, mademoiselle," Morrow said, his grin growing broader. "If I weren't mistaken, I'd say you were born and bred a gentlewoman."

Miss Baker snapped the fan shut, extinguishing the lights at its tips. "I've seen my share of them," she said, her affected airs extinguished just as quickly. "I can manage witless privilege well enough."

They all had a laugh at this—even Morrow was a commoner by birth, while Finch seemed to delight in this stab at the aristocracy regardless of his own lineage. And Weatherby could not help but allow his gaze to linger on Miss Baker, even as hers took in the scenery of the French countryside.

The village of Passy, but a short distance from Paris, was quite handsome, having a number of noble homes therein. They learned in Paris that Franklin was staying at the Hotel de Valentinois, a palatial home offered to the Ganymedean commissioners by a sympathetic and successful French merchant. It was a fine house with many windows, situated on a hill with a splendid view of the river, surrounded by gardens and trees.

Franklin was staying in one of the smaller buildings adjacent to the mansion proper, a pavilion called Basse Cour. Weatherby was surprised at how easy it seemed to gain access to the place, though they had learned in Paris that Franklin was a very welcoming sort, and saw many of his countrymen and French supporters at all hours. What if they were assassins, hoping to remove one of the rebels' greatest leaders? Now there was a thought. But Weatherby quickly put it out his mind, reminding himself that he was a Royal Navy officer under orders, not some dishonorable ruffian.

They were greeted at the door of Basse Cour by one Edward Bancroft, who identified himself as secretary to the Ganymedean commissioners. Unfortunately, Bancroft reported that the ambassador was not feeling well and, at any rate, was about to sit down to dinner. Morrow stressed the importance of their meeting the ambassador, even going so far as to claim they had messages of importance from Philadelphia, the Ganymedean capital, but Bancroft still put them off.

Finally, Morrow gave the man a hard stare and said, "It is most unfortunate, sir. You should know that the weather in Boston bodes ill for the harvest this year, especially the tobacco."

This caused Bancroft to visibly start. "Ah. I see," the man said. "This visit of yours, then, is something of an embassage?"

"Of a sort," Morrow said simply. "Our request for an audience does not encompass the current political situation."

Bancroft looked uncomfortable, but finally relented. "Come in, and if you would, please wait here."

The secretary bustled off into the house while the party from the *Daedalus* stood waiting in a marble entry hall with a fine staircase.

"Captain," Finch said, "if memory serves, tobacco is not grown in or around Boston."

The captain merely smiled and said, "It is a bit of game-craft, Doctor. This Bancroft is our man, and has been for some time."

"A spy?" Weatherby asked, perhaps a little too loudly, earning a stern glare and a shushing from Morrow. A few minutes later, Bancroft returned and, despite the look of worry on his face, ushered them into a beautifully decorated salon that boasted tapestries, gilt and a warm fire. Therein, they were introduced to Dr. Benjamin Franklin.

He was an elderly man, looking at least sixty to Weatherby's eyes, with a balding pate and long graying hair upon the sides. His girth bespoke of a love of dining and drink, and while he moved slowly as he rose to greet his guests, there was fluidity to his movements that hinted of dexterity and grace that yet remained to him. His eyes were bright between his rectangular spectacles, and his smile had a bit of mischief to it. For an ambassador, he was dressed most plainly, in but a simple waistcoat, linen and breeches, though the fabrics appeared to be of fine quality. He also wore an evening robe to ward off the chill.

"Edward tells me this is most important," Franklin said as he extended his hand. "You'll forgive me, however, if I must make this an abbreviated visit, as I am not entirely well." The man's congenial smile hid something, Weatherby thought, though he was not at all sure what that might be.

"Of course, Ambassador," Morrow said. "I am Captain Sir William Morrow of His Majesty's Ship *Daedalus*. May I present Lt. Thomas Weatherby, Dr. Andrew Finch and Miss Anne Baker?"

Franklin nodded, his smile disappearing quickly, as he sank back into his chair. "I see. I thought I knew your face, Captain. We have met before, in London, I should say. You were naught but a midshipman, if memory serves."

"A mere fourth lieutenant," Morrow said, trying to brighten matters with a smile. "I found you to be a most gracious person then, and I hope to impose upon your good graces now with a most vexing issue."

"A vexing issue, is it?" Franklin said, looking at each of their faces in turn.

"Well, I should think that you are not here on behalf of King George or his government, at least in any official capacity. With the utmost respect, Sir William, you are all far too young to be negotiators on his behalf."

"Indeed so," Morrow replied.

At this Franklin nodded and sighed, looking down at his waistcoat. "Very well, then. Where will you be taking me?"

Morrow started. "Excuse me, sir?"

"Please, Sir William, let us not hide behind decorum now," Franklin said. "It is well that you introduced yourself so plainly, but do not stop there. I must assume by your dress and your late arrival, under the cover of darkness and with few people at my house, I will be leaving here your prisoner."

Morrow took a small step backward, and raised his hands upward slightly—in surrender or placation, it seemed. "Dr. Franklin, I can assure you that our intentions are both peaceful and honorable."

The old man shifted in his chair. "You'll forgive me, sir, if this is not as reassuring as you might wish. If you are not here to bring me to England, or otherwise mishandle me, then please state your purpose here plainly."

"Our mission does not fall within the realm of the current political situation," Morrow said, "but instead involves the investigation of terrible crimes, the murderous person who perpetrated them, and matters pertaining to the workings of alchemy."

"I see. And this young man here," Franklin said, nodding at Finch, "is insufficient to the task? I see his hands, quite literally, in the Great Work as much as mine."

Weatherby glanced down at Finch's hands and, for the first time, noticed the light stains and marks upon them, likely the product of dealing with alchemical solvents. "You honor me, Dr. Franklin," Finch said, genuine modesty in his voice, "but my small knowledge is not up to the task at ferreting out the motives of our quarry, the man who calls himself Cagliostro."

This remark seemed to finally penetrate Franklin's mien of imperturbable skepticism. "I know that name, and it is one I had hoped never to hear again!" he grimaced. "He was recommended to me upon my arrival here as an alchemist and physician, for my knowledge in the Humanis school is not what it should be. Yet soon after he arrived for an interview with me, I found he had secured a few of my books upon his person. Needless to say I had him summarily dismissed from my presence! So what has this cad done now?"

At this, Miss Baker spoke. "I am sorry to say, good sir, that he is the murderer of my master, and your friend, Dr. McDonnell."

The last shred of Franklin's reserve dissipated, and he became visibly distraught at this news. "Oh, God in Heaven! Poor Roger dead? At Cagliostro's hand?" He spent a few moments gathering his composure. "And you must be the one of whom my dear friend Roger wrote most ardently and favorably." She smiled at this, and Franklin extended his condolences to her, prompting Weatherby to wonder as to the nature of the relationship between Miss Baker and the deceased, and Finch's veiled allusions as well. His musings were cut short as Franklin, sitting up suddenly, asked: "The Mercurium?"

"Gone, sir," Morrow answered, seemingly unperturbed that Franklin knew of McDonnell's efforts on behalf of the Crown.

"And what else?" Franklin demanded.

"Books on the topics of Venus, Jupiter and the Xan," Finch replied. "Furthermore, the foul criminal slaughtered an innocent village of Venusians in order to obtain the rare va'hakla flower."

This prompted more silence and deep thought from Franklin. "Very well," he said finally, before turning to shout out the doorway. "Edward?"

The secretary entered the room once more. "Yes, sir?"

"We're having guests for dinner," Franklin said. "Please see to the arrangements. Oh, and tell those outside that they may stand down for the time being."

"Very good, sir," Bancroft said, hurrying out of the room.

"Those outside?" Weatherby said.

The Ganymedean smiled. "There are old men, and there are revolutionaries, sir, but there are few *old* revolutionaries. And one does not become such without knowing when to take precautions."

Finch nudged Weatherby and nodded toward the window, whereupon the young officer spied two men in the shrubbery—aiming muskets through the window at the Englishmen.

His attention was drawn back to the seated Franklin, who uncocked a pistol pulled seemingly from nowhere and set it upon the table.

"Well then," Franklin said, rising slowly from his seat. "Before we dine, there is something I would like to show you, for your unfortunate news fits all too well into some of my alchemical inquiries of late. If you please?" He waved his hand toward a door into the rest of the house before tottering off.

With an arched eyebrow, Morrow motioned his officers and Miss Baker to follow.

July 26, 2132

This is amazingly stupid, Shaila thought as she lowered herself into the lava tube for the third time. The first two times she was in here, she was in an earthquake. She wasn't feeling particularly lucky about the third.

Yet seeing the wall at the end of the cavern drove her to climb down that rope. She thought back to her training, the holovids and, in some cases, 2-D videos of exploration on a dozen planets and moons. Nothing—*nothing*—came close to what she saw on the 'bot's video feed.

Yes, it was stupid. As her boots crunched down on the cavern floor, she fully expected the cave to fall down on her head at any moment. But she had to see it. Had to record it. Had to know what was going on. It was why she went into space. For the first time since all this craziness started she felt certain of things, and it was no use denying the impulse. Moreover, she *knew* the answers were down here. Somehow. If she had paused to take stock of that certainty, it would've scared the hell out of her how logically baseless it was. But she was in no mood to contemplate.

With Yuna reporting no increase in seismic activity or radiation levels, Shaila set off into the cave as fast as caution allowed, which resulted in a kind of shuffling hop-walk, her feet staying close to the cavern floor. She would've loved to just bounce her way to the sensor—it would've taken only a minute—but there were still plenty of rocks rolling around in the cave, and it was hard to see them in the dim light. She paused a moment to take a sensor reading on one of them as it languidly rolled past her feet, but there was no discernible difference between the rock and the rest of the cave.

Except, of course, that the rock was moving to begin with.

"Give me an update," Shaila said, continuing her shuffle.

"Nothing material," Yuna replied. "Then again, we're using the existing sensors, not the 'bot, so it's hard to determine what you might experience when you get closer. But for now, you're in good shape."

"Roger that."

Shaila arrived at the last sensor suite in the array. A quick scan of the sensor's touch screen revealed all was in working order. She wrestled the sensor into her arms, cursing as she did so; on Earth, it would've weighed 50 kilograms, but on Mars, it was a mere 17 kilos. Still, it was bulky as hell. She took a few tentative steps forward—and slipped on a rock rolling out under her foot, barely catching herself.

"Shit!" she swore reflexively.

"What? What is it?" Stephane asked.

"Easy, Steve. I'm good, all's well," she replied. "Can't see my feet carrying this thing. Got caught up with a roller underfoot, that's all."

"Be careful, will you?" Stephane replied, sounding peeved.

"Didn't know you cared," Shaila said, smiling despite herself. "Just going to have to take it slower, that's all."

Shifting the sensor in her hands, Shaila started forward once more, carefully sweeping her feet in front of her with each step as she proceeded into the darkest part of the cave, her helmet lights the only illumination. The wall was still a couple hundred meters ahead of her, making for very slow going. At least the light from the previous day's cave-in was giving her a better sense of location within the cavern.

"I see the 'bot," Shaila reported. It was ahead of her, about 45 degrees to her left. "No lights on it. Probably no power. I'll check it out when I come back."

As she progressed, she saw higher piles of rubble on each side of her, even as the path before her seemed to be less strewn with rock. It was as if there was a path of some kind laid before her, leading to the wall. That was nonsense, of course. But then, the wall itself wasn't supposed to be there, either.

Finally, off in the distance, she began to make out the dim outline of the wall. After confirming once again that there were no spikes in seismic or radiation activity, she steeled herself and took a step forward.

Another rock skittered into her boot, causing her to jump slightly. She lifted her boot and watched it roll out from under her, toward the wall. The rock, about 15 centimeters in diameter, rolled up to the wall and then, defying gravity itself, rolled right up the vertical surface, disappearing over the two-meter high top.

"Creepy," she said, the radio carrying her voice to her colleagues above. "I wonder what's on the other side."

"Is there a way to see over it?" Stephane asked.

"Don't know. Let's get this sensor down first." Shaila kept moving forward until she found a spot she felt would allow for maximum camera coverage. "Greene, how's this for placement?" She figured that, with his background, he should know a thing or two about camera angles.

"Good. We can see about twenty meters of the wall, top to bottom, too."

"All right. Status, Yuna?"

"Rate of increase unchanged," Yuna said. "Atmospheric pressure now up to point-one-eight psi—that's a record for Mars. Seems the increase is mostly nitrogen at this point."

"Which means?" Shaila asked.

"No idea," Yuna said. "A gas deposit, maybe? Planets can still surprise you, even when you think you've seen it all."

"So I've heard." Shaila put the bulky sensor down on its stubby, sturdy legs. "Sensor's down. How's it look?"

"Perfect," Stephane said. "Now please get back here."

Shaila gazed at the wall in front of her. "Not yet. I'm already here. Might as well have a look." She stepped around the sensor and walk-shuffled over to the wall. It looked like a loosely packed pile of rocks that nonetheless seemed to be almost perfectly straight and smooth. Looking left and right, she saw that the walls of the cave itself had changed somewhat, with two large indentations forming on either side, just before the wall. This was definitely an unstable cave—she should've been running for the skylight, if she hadn't been so stupid to come down in the first place. But if the very cave itself was changing, then it stood to reason that the ravine nearby had also been part of the changes going on. That was, oddly enough, reassuring.

"Do not touch anything," Stephane warned. "We don't know how stable it is."

Shaila stopped about a half meter in front of the wall and leaned in toward it. "All right, let's see. Certainly seems like just a pile of rock. Surface is rough and uneven. Doesn't seem to be anything holding it together." She looked to her left and right. "Seems pretty straight, though. I'm impressed. How's seismic?"

"Unchanged," Yuna said.

"Good. Hang on." And with that, Shaila crouched down low…and jumped.

On Earth, the average person can jump about two-thirds of a meter. Shaila was in better shape than the average person, and enjoyed the benefit of Mars' low gravity. She jumped nearly two meters off the ground, and looked straight ahead to see what was over the wall.

"Oh, my God!"

"What?" Stephane said. "What is it?"

Shaila pulled her portable sensor out and adjusted its settings so it could capture video and send the feed up to her colleagues. "This is crazy. Look."

She jumped again, the sensor slightly over her head.

Before her feet touched the ground, she heard the gasps over the comm. "What the hell is that?" Greene asked, sounding awe-struck.

Shaila jumped a third time. Before her, she saw the ghostly outline of a second wall, set off from the first by about twenty meters and cloaked in a pink-grey light from the new hole in the ceiling of the lava tube, where the surveyors had fallen. Above that second wall, she thought she might have seen a third.

"It's a structure of some kind," she said.

She crouched to jump again, but was interrupted by Yuna. "EM and Cherenkov readings are starting to climb higher than baseline. I really think it's time to go."

Shaila thought about this a moment. The first two quakes were preceded by a blue flash. That represented a buildup of enough Cherenkov radiation to result in the appearance of blue in the visual spectrum.

A buildup....

"I'm out," Shaila said, turning and hop-skipping back through the cave. "Update your readings as I go."

She hadn't gotten more than fifty meters before Yuna came on again. "EM and Cherenkov levels at the wall still rising slightly higher than before."

"Seismic? Psi?"

"Rate of increase unchanged."

Shaila kept moving. "You think my proximity to that...thing...seemed to bring about the increase?"

"Possible, but without further testing, it's hard to say," Yuna said.

"Should I go back and test it?" Shaila said.

"No! Too dangerous," Stephane interrupted. He was really starting to get nervous, Shaila thought. Then again, she thought she probably ought to be far more concerned that she currently felt.

"Don't worry, I'm leaving and—wait," she said. "The 'bot." She spotted it and headed over. "I'm going to have a quick look, see if I can bring it along."

She skidded to a stop in front of the disabled probe and knelt down before it, sensor still in hand. "No power. Something fried it."

"We have a camera on the wall, Shaila. I really think you should just leave it and get back up here," Yuna said.

Shaila grabbed the 'bot by its still-extended neck and lifted—a little too heavy and bulky to carry. She then pulled on the neck, watching as it rolled along with her arm. "Negative. The wheels aren't frozen. It's coming with me."

She began to pull *Dolomieu* along with her, which slowed her down slightly. But she felt salvaging the 'bot was the best option. If they could figure out what happened to it, they could fix it up and use it again.

She continued hop-shuffling back—less hop, more shuffle now—passing the first of the sensors they had placed the last time. Here, the cave was more recognizable, with the detritus of the earthquakes far more random and scattered. Exactly what you'd expect. Not structured at all.

"Cherenkov spike," Yuna reported. "Fifteen meters, bearing oh-nine-zero."

Shaila looked off to her right and immediately recognized the pile of rubble there. "That's where Ed got buried," she said. It was also where she heard her own voice in her head, and that was enough to get her moving. Shaila let go of the 'bot and covered the distance in a few hops. "Did the rad levels spike again just now?"

"No, elevated but steady," Yuna said. "What are you doing?"

Shaila knelt down in front of the rubble. "I thought I saw something first time we were down here, after we moved Ed." She started to use her gloved hands to sweep away the rocks. "I wonder if it's there. Maybe it's causing the spike."

There was no comment on this from Yuna or Stephane; they probably thought this was an unnecessary detour and a rather bad idea. They were probably right, but Shaila kept digging.

Two minutes later, her gauntlet brushed against something flat. "Found something," she said, brushing dust and rock from the surface, finding the edges.

"What is it?" Stephane asked.

"...where I shall leave it."

The voice came into Shaila's head just like it had the first time—but this time it wasn't hers. It was a man's voice, barely heard in her mind, as if she was eavesdropping on a conversation occurring in another room, or on the other side of the cave. She paused to look around, but found nothing. Her heart started to race, and for the first time, she wondered whether the immensity of everything going on was really starting to get to her.

"Shaila?" Stephane asked again. "What did you find?"

Shaila shook her head to clear it, then slowly lifted the object from the rubble. "It's a book."

She turned it over in her hands: Leather cover, slightly beaten up from the quake; fine quality pages....

"Say again?" Yuna said.

"There's a book down here," Shaila replied. "I wonder if Ed brought some kind of notebook or something with him." She flipped through the book, but couldn't find any writing anywhere. "It's blank." She pulled out her sensor and waved it over the journal. "You're right. I have elevated EM and Cherenkov readings centered on this. Higher than ambient, but not enough to give me any kind of blue light."

"Suggest you leave it and get moving," Yuna said, a slight quaver in her voice. "The cave's still unstable."

"Negative," Shaila said, sliding the book into her carryall. "It's coming with. I'm outta here. Get a rope lowered so we can get the 'bot back up there and—"

She looked down to see pebbles skittering past her feet, bouncing slightly off the cavern floor. And she caught a flash of blue from somewhere she couldn't quite place.

"Shay!" Stephane called. "Move!"

Shaila jumped up and dashed toward the skylight, leaving *Dolomieu* behind. She didn't need to see the dust cascading down from the ceiling to know what was coming next.

She didn't make it in time. A huge weight crashed into her back, sending her sprawling down onto the cavern floor. The last thing she saw was a large rock falling inches from her helmet visor.

CHAPTER 11

March 24, 1779

Since the dawn of history, alchemists have always been circumspect regarding the location of their laboratories. In ancient days, they were shunted off to the edge of settlements, respected for their abilities yet feared as well. Those fears have never been entirely misplaced, for more than one building—indeed, more than one city—has burned due to a moment of carelessness or overreaching ambition on the part of an alchemist.

This, Weatherby considered, likely was why Dr. Benjamin Franklin was granted a pavilion away from the main house of the Hotel de Valentinois. For even such a luminary as Franklin could have a mishap. And indeed, as the group from the *Daedalus* proceeded into the basement of Belle Cour and into Franklin's laboratory, the disarray in Franklin's workspace bespoke of mishaps large and small, or so it seemed.

"I apologize most heartily for the mess," Franklin said as he opened the door and ushered his guests inside. "I had not expected to be entertaining here this evening, I assure you!"

"Not at all, Ambassador," Morrow said as he carefully stepped into the room, his nose wrinkling at the stench that assaulted him, akin to rotting eggs mixed with strong vinegar. "Though I confess I am unsure why we are here."

Franklin tottered into the room and made straight for the large furnace in the middle of the chamber, where he opened a compartment and, using a fireplace poker, stoked the materials inside. From Weatherby's reading—for he had made a study of basic alchemy as part of his supervision of Finch—he knew this to be the athanor, a special furnace for alchemical creation.

"It is often better to show, Sir William, than to tell," Franklin said as he closed the athanor's door. "And given Dr. Finch's expertise, and the burgeoning knowledge of your Miss Baker, I'll wager, they may aid in translating my work better than I might alone."

Weatherby was quite sure he had no idea which wonder Franklin might show them, for it seemed the room was full to bursting with alchemical amazements. Shelves adorned every wall, brimming with a wide variety of glass containers and earthenware, as well as jars containing powders, liquids and, it should be said, a wide variety of plants and animal remnants. Mixed in with these were enough books to fill a university, it seemed.

There were also two notable features to the room, aside from the shelves and a couple of long worktables. One was a clockwork orrery, one far larger and more ornate than was used aboard *Daedalus*, and the table next to it was covered in papers and notes. The other was a curtained-off corner of the room, which Weatherby knew to be Franklin's oratorium, where he would likely read and meditate upon his workings. More religious-minded alchemists would have a private altar as well, but he never saw such a feature amongst Finch's belongings, and did not take Franklin for being overly pious, given his politics.

"First, some refreshment!" Franklin said. He walked over to a small table near the curtained area, which contained glasses and a decanter of wine, pouring five glasses and distributing them to his guests. "To strange bedfellows!" he said, raising his glass. Everyone raised theirs as well, though Weatherby's heart was not in it. But he sipped just enough wine to be polite. Finch, however, merely sniffed the wine and lowered it without drinking, which Weatherby took as a good sign; even Finch's decadent ways did not prevent him from declining to drink with a traitor to the Crown.

Franklin then approached the room's main worktable and immediately started stacking books and papers. "Now then, I am not one for grand workings. While I enjoy discussing theory, I prefer far more practical applications of the Great Work. And once such working I performed just a few days ago was a simple tincture to aid my good friend, Madame Brillon de Jouy, in balancing her humours." Franklin blushed slightly. "She is, not to be indiscreet, rather partial to fire and earth."

Finch and Miss Baker smiled knowingly at this remark, leaving Weatherby rather perplexed. Finch leaned over and whispered to Weatherby: "His friend, it seems, is ruled by her passions." Finch's arched eyebrow left Weatherby with no further confusion in the matter.

Meanwhile, Franklin had placed two retorts upon his table; these were large glassware containers with long stems, and stoppers upon each. "I had created a similar mixture before, and wanted to keep it on hand, so I made a second batch. It is a relatively simple working, one that involves countering the effects of Venus. As such, I included a pinch of powder from Mercury's ores and a bit of *althak* plant from Venus, putrefied so as to reverse its effects."

The ambassador held up one of the retorts. "This was my original working, and the green-grey color you see here is the desired outcome. This would aid Madame Brillon in keeping her focus on more practical matters, while calming her other humours." Again, the old man flushed slightly as he set down the container and picked up the second. "As you can see here, this new elixir is nearly black!"

Morrow simply frowned at this. "I'm sorry, Ambassador, but I still do not quite understand."

Franklin nodded. "Of course, I apologize. Allow me to demonstrate. Dr. Finch, would you assist in drawing out some of this elixir?" He went over to a small cage upon one of his shelves, which contained a number of rats. Clucking softly, he managed to seize one of the rodents, bringing it to the table, where Finch had used a small dropper to gather up some of the foul-looking liquid. Taking the rat's head between his fingers, Franklin drew the creature's mouth skyward, where it was met by the stopper. A single drop fell into the creature's mouth.

Franklin set the rat down upon the table, where it was immediately seized by tremors. After thrashing about for less than half a minute, it keeled over—dead.

"As you can see, this poor creature's humours were unbalanced in quite the other direction," Franklin said drily. "Now, why would this be?"

Not even Finch had an answer forthcoming, so Franklin gestured toward the orrery and walked toward it. "As you may be aware, our workings are governed by the movements of the planets, so it behooves the alchemist to pay mind to his astrology. Naturally, when I encountered this result, I thought that Venus and Mercury were simply in opposition to each other, or to some other force. But I saw nothing here that would indicate such."

"So why would your working have failed, then?" Miss Baker asked, her curiosity regarding alchemical matters quite evident. "If you had followed the same procedure, you should have had the same outcome."

"Exactly!" Franklin said. "But I did not. And whilst I won't bore you with the researches I have conducted since, I have been able to come up with but one possible answer. It is my supposition that the powers of each of these planets has been magnified of late. A working including both of them—few workings tend to include both spheres, mind you—would result in such an over-powered and utterly useless elixir."

Weatherby nodded. "And it seems Cagliostro has powerful materials from both worlds," he murmured. "But what does that mean?"

"I cannot say until I hear of your travels in detail, young man," Franklin said. "And for that, I think we should retire upstairs to dinner."

And so it was that, minutes later, Weatherby partook in perhaps the oddest dinner of his life, hosted by a traitor, though a genial and generous one at that. The pheasant was quite delicious and, despite himself, Weatherby ate heartily. Morrow, meanwhile, relayed all that had happened since learning of Dr. McDonnell's death on Elizabeth Mercuris, with Finch and Miss Baker chiming in as needed. Weatherby, still feeling uneasy and unsuitable to the company, remained mostly silent.

Franklin, for his part, was most keen on learning every detail, and quizzed Miss Baker upon her late master's work, her answers to which were once again most detailed and exacting. Finally, over a dessert of pudding and port wine, Franklin spoke once more.

"So, Dr. Finch," the ambassador said. "You of all people should know why I am indeed highly concerned about these recent events. Are you familiar with the importance of the two stolen substances, the va'hakla flower and the Mercurium?"

"I am to some degree, sir," Finch responded. "Mercurium is the distilled essence of Mercury itself, and there is a case to be made that the va'hakla plant, being as rare as it is, may play a role in distilling the very essence of Venus. These essences would govern all of the humors of their respective worlds, and portions of the zodiac besides."

"Indeed," Franklin said. "Distilling the very essence of a world could very well increase the mystic powers of all materials from that world, which could very well be why my working failed so spectacularly. But I will also say this: having heard your story, I now believe that these essences may not be the only ones Cagliostro requires. I dare say that this madman is embarking upon a terrible working indeed. I believe that Cagliostro means to collect the essences of many more of the Known Worlds, if not all of them."

Weatherby saw a genuine look of concern—possibly even horror—on Finch's face, and noted that Miss Baker was similarly distressed as Franklin elaborated. "The Great Work of Alchemy, lady and gentlemen, is based upon the concept of *essences*. Certain materials in alchemy represent the larger occult forces at work in the universe, and by stripping away the crude matter surrounding these materials, their true essences may be obtained. The tail of a lizard, for example, is used in a regenerative elixir because the lizard can naturally re-grow said tail—the lizard has the *essence* of this ability within it. Thus, the alchemist, if truly gifted in the Humanis school, can refine this essence to reproduce the effect in a person. Now, think about the properties of these rare alchemical items, those that have distilled the very essence of an entire planet!"

"But to what end, sir?" Morrow asked, looking slightly perturbed. "It's all well and good to engage in such pursuits, but we haven't the slightest ideas as to what purpose they would be employed, do we?"

"The purposes are many, Sir William!" Franklin said. "Since the motions of the planets rule our workings to a large degree, he who has the essence of those worlds in alchemical form can, under the right circumstances, bring the divine quintessence of Creation to bear, and possibly shake the very foundations upon which the Great Work is based! Every humor and impetus in the universe would be open to him!"

"So what is his aim, then?" Morrow countered. "Does he work on behalf of a foreign power? France or Spain, perhaps? Surely such alchemical wonders would turn the balance of power throughout the Known Worlds, and it is that balance that most concerns me here, not some theoretical arcana."

Franklin smiled, shaking his head ruefully. "I must honestly state that the danger Cagliostro presents is one not tied to politics. Whether he is in the employ of a nation or simply furthering his own ambition is immaterial. Cagliostro, I believe, has only his own agenda in mind, whether or not he has accepted the backing of a nation."

"He has two such essences," Weatherby said, his pique breaking down as his interest grew. "How many more does he require?"

Finch answered before Franklin could. "One for each of the Known Worlds remaining to him: Earth, the Moon, the Sun, Mars, Saturn, and Jupiter."

"I fear he may already have at least one other," Franklin said, a distressed look upon his face, "that of Earth."

"How do you know this?" Morrow snapped.

"Some years ago, this Cagliostro was the student of perhaps the greatest alchemist among mankind, the one who calls himself the Count St. Germain. They traveled together for a time, and St. Germain saw promise in young Cagliostro, and took him as his apprentice. A short time later, St. Germain made his crowning discovery, the Philosopher's Stone. Are you familiar with it?"

Everyone nodded; even Weatherby had heard of the wild tales surrounding this prized alchemical discovery. It was nothing less than the means to transmute lead into gold and, some said, the means to transmute the very soul of the alchemist into something far more sublime and, perhaps blasphemously, divine. Likewise, the tales of the famed Count St. Germain were many, though most were too fantastic to be given much in the way of proper consideration.

"The Philosopher's Stone is many things, but most importantly, it may very well be the Earth's planetary essence," Franklin said. "It was a supreme accomplishment for St. Germain, perhaps the greatest working ever done by man. I had occasion to meet the Count not two years past, when he recommended a young officer to our cause on Ganymede. Yet the Count himself was in a most foul humor, and when I pressed him as to his disturbance, he confided in me that his student, this very same Cagliostro, had fallen in with a new mentor of some sort, one of mysterious origin and means. Cagliostro stole the Stone and went off with his new teacher, leaving St. Germain years of work ahead of him to replicate his discovery."

"And so our criminal has three of these essences. How many more might he possess?" Morrow said.

"Well, the essence of the Sun is quite simple, for it is simply the light and warmth which it gives off, so we may consider that among his prizes. Now, given the thievery from my poor colleague's library, I would venture to say that he has yet to visit Jupiter or Saturn," Franklin said. "As to the latter, he will have an extraordinarily difficult time dealing with the Xan people upon their home world. As you know, Captain, they do not wish to truck with us except in the most limited fashion. I can count upon my fingers the number of times they have accepted a delegation from humanity, and none have even laid eyes upon them uncloaked. With their advanced engines and alchemy, he cannot take what he needs by force, either.

"So I find it highly doubtful that he would attempt to bring about a working that would envelop the Xan as well as mankind," Franklin said. "To do so would be true madness, and Cagliostro is many things, but not a fool. Thus, I should think he will indeed make for Jupiter, and it is there that we might, with luck, find this devil. My friends, I must thank you most heartily for bringing this matter to me. I see now that your words are true and your mission quite just."

"We appreciate that, Ambassador," Morrow said genially. "I know such a leap of faith could not have come easily."

Finch cleared his throat. "I dare say faith had little to do with it. Isn't that right, Dr. Franklin?"

The ambassador gave Finch a sidelong glance and a cunning smile. "Indeed, Dr. Finch. Why did you not say anything?"

"Because trust is all too fleeting when people are at war," Finch said. "And because we genuinely need your help."

Morrow turned to Finch with a look of alarm on his face. "Explain yourself, Doctor."

"I detected an unusual scent within the wine served in the ambassador's laboratory, which is why I abstained from it," Finch said. "A hint of earthy and minty notes, along with a touch of something floral—pennyroyal and violet, yes?" he asked Franklin.

"Well done, Dr. Finch," Franklin said, his smile growing wider.

"As I thought. These herbs are associated with Libra, and as such can govern truth-telling, among other things," Finch said. "The ambassador, I think, simply wanted to assure himself of our veracity."

Franklin clapped his hands. "Exactly right! And I've also found that this particular admixture does wonders for the digestion as well. Sir William, you have found a most worthy alchemist indeed!"

Morrow was less impressed. "Dr. Finch, we will have words about this later," he said ominously.

Finch merely nodded, while Weatherby glared at him with utter disdain.

At this the meal ended on a somewhat awkward note, but Franklin nonetheless offered them rooms for the night. "We may be on different sides when it comes to politics, lady and gentlemen, but there are some matters that are far beyond the conflicts of ideology and government," he told them. "And I should hope that hospitality may be as universal as the Great Work. In any event, we must be united against Cagliostro. While he may not know we are onto an inkling of the work he intends to do, his escape from Venus has ensured he will move quickly now. So sleep well here tonight, and tomorrow we shall make for Le Havre with all due haste."

"We, Dr. Franklin?" Morrow asked. "Surely you don't intend to accompany us."

"My good Captain, I must insist upon it," Franklin replied. "There are perhaps only a handful of students of the Great Work who are adept enough to divine Cagliostro's ultimate goal. In fact, I should say that there were three, up until poor Roger's demise. Now there are two: St. Germain and, without undue boastfulness, myself. And only the Almighty knows where St. Germain is."

"Ambassador, you would put yourself in the hands of His Majesty's servants to do this?" Weatherby asked incredulously. "We are at war, after all. By rights, we should deliver you to London for your crimes against the Crown!"

Morrow winced, but Franklin merely smiled. "My dear boy, I certainly would not wish that, of course, but these are dark times indeed. I have already determined that you are men of honor, thanks to the elixir placed within your wine. So if you can vouchsafe for the suspension of the conflict among us and my return to Paris unmolested by agents of the Crown, then yes, I shall do it."

Part of Weatherby felt chagrined, for here was someone quite ready to suspend his political leanings for a greater good. On the other hand, he forced a truth elixir upon them as well. "My apologies, sir," he said simply.

"Not at all, Mr. Weatherby," Franklin said, giving the younger man a clap on the shoulder. "You are a credit to the service, I have no doubt. So what say you, Captain? Shall I accompany you, or shall I be forced to make arrangements on my own? For either way, this is a matter of critical importance, and I feel most obligated to unravel it."

Morrow shot Weatherby another hard look before responding. "I shall still have to report on this to the Admiralty, Ambassador. Your service and cooperation will be noted, as will our agreement to bring you back to France and resume the political status quo when we are done. Is this acceptable to you, sir?"

"Of course. In fact, you may relay your message through Edward if you like. I understand he's quite adept at such communications."

This shook Morrow visibly, albeit for the barest hint of a moment. He quickly regained his composure. "I do not understand."

Franklin's smile was both genial and mischievous. "Captain, I am well aware that Edward Bancroft is in the employ of King George's servants. It's all right. You may use him for your message."

"But Dr. Franklin, if you know the man is a traitor to your cause, why keep him in your employ?" Weatherby asked, now even more confused as to the workings of spies and politics.

"Mr. Weatherby, I shall respond to your question with one of my own. If you knew that it was likely your enemies were spying upon you, would you rather know the identity of the spy and keep him close, or do away with his presence and risk a spy with whom you are not familiar?"

Weatherby could not help but concede the point, though he despaired at the transparency Bancroft obviously showed in his duty to England, and hoped other spies in His Majesty's service were far more adept at concealing their allegiances.

On the other hand, as Morrow pointed out after Franklin retired for the evening, the situation must be dire indeed. "Obviously, Franklin is a passionate supporter of his cause, ill-advised as it might be," Morrow noted. "And yet he has quickly given up an immense advantage against his enemies by revealing his knowledge of Bancroft's activities. Whatever Cagliostro has planned, it must be quite serious for Franklin to exhibit this much concern."

We are back aboard Daedalus *as I write this, with an avowed traitor to England as our honoured guest. Mr. Plumb was successful in obtaining our orders from the Admiralty—we are to make haste for Jupiter, and attempt to track down the miscreant Cagliostro, particularly to obtain any Mercurium he may possess, along with the formulae for its production and the means by which Chance escaped directly to the Void from Venus. We may enlist help from any*

Royal Navy vessel we encounter as well.

I can see Earth from the gunport in the wardroom as I write. I shall miss home dearly, for although it was a pleasant surprise to visit unexpectedly, the visit was all too short. I fear it may be a long time yet before I see her again.

July 26, 2132

Shaila heard the soft beep-and-hum of the medical sensors before she even opened her eyes. In her half-conscious state, she nonetheless seized on two likely facts: one, she was back on base, in the medical berth; and two, she was going to catch hell for her jaunt in the cave.

She opened her eyes and saw Diaz looking down at her, the colonel's face lined with worry and frustration. *Right on both counts.* "Ma'am," Shaila murmured.

"Lieutenant," Diaz said. "How you feeling?"

It was a good question. Shaila paused a moment to take stock. "Sore as hell. Chest hurts. Knee feels fucked up."

Doug Levin entered her field of vision. "Not bad, kiddo," the doctor said. "Bruised ribs, cracked kneecap. You missed the concussion, though."

"That explains the dizziness," Shaila said with a weak smile. "So much for the medical career."

Diaz raised her eyebrows. "We're gonna have a talk about career later, Jain. For now, you should be thankful you didn't get your skull cracked open. That was the biggest quake yet. There's a kilometer-long crack in the roof of that lava tube, and now there are three new ravines around it. Fucked up thing is, they're going off in different directions nearly in a straight line."

Shaila fought to focus. "The sensor at the wall?"

"Gone," Diaz said. "We've only got two boxes left up and running in there, and all they seem to be doing is measuring increases in EM, radiation and atmospheric pressure."

Shaila nodded. "How'd I get out?"

"Durand. Soon as the quake stopped, he was down the rope before Yuna and Greene could stop him," Diaz said. "And I've had to order him back to work so he'd stop hanging around here moping after you."

"Really?" Shaila said. "Maybe he's not such a piker after all."

"His heart's in the right place, but he's young and dumb and has problems following orders," Diaz said. "Sound familiar?"

Shaila nodded. "A little."

Diaz gave Levin a glance, and the doctor took the hint, busying himself elsewhere as the colonel took a seat on Shaila's bed. "I told you I was running out of plays, Jain. Now I've got you disobeying direct orders not to go down into that cave."

Shaila wanted to explain why, but the words wouldn't come. The sense of *rightness* she had felt in the cave was evaporating quickly. And she was damned if she was going to talk about voices in her head with her pissed-off C.O. Or some old book, for that matter. "I know. I'm sorry. You saw the holos?"

"Yeah," Diaz said, relenting a moment. "Crazy shit. Steve and Yuna are busy slicing the data seven ways to Sunday. But in a month or so, it won't be our problem anymore."

Shaila struggled to sit up. "What do you mean?"

"We packed everything off to Houston after they hauled you back here. JSC is sending a full survey team, launching tomorrow. They'll be here in a little more than four weeks."

This wasn't entirely surprising, given the fact that some kind of structure was spontaneously building itself in a Martian lava tube. But it still pissed Shaila off. "Well, we've got four weeks to figure it out."

"No, we don't," Diaz said. "That cave is hands-off from now on. The ground is too unstable to even get close. So we'll make do with the sensors we have and let the survey team handle it when they get here. Yuna and Steve will keep at it as best they can without going back down there," Diaz said. "You, on the other hand, will go back on duty."

"But—"

"No buts, Jain," Diaz said, standing. "You disobeyed my orders and went and got yourself laid up, and endangered Durand and the rest of your team in the process. You're out. You can focus on getting the base spruced up for our visitors."

A million arguments flooded into Shaila's head, but between the previous night's reactor scare and today's adventure, she knew she was playing with a short deck. There were no other options but acquiescence and humility. Besides, she had the journal, and possibly the EM fields to figure out. Technically, neither was an explicit part of the investigation. "All right," she said quietly "Sorry, ma'am."

Diaz eyed the younger officer warily for a moment. "All right. For the record, I'm glad we got the holo, and I'll chalk this up to young-and-dumb, meaning it's not going on your record. But you've officially used up all the goodwill and rule-bending you had coming to you."

"Aye, ma'am," Shaila said. "Thank you."

Diaz nodded and left, leaving Shaila to wonder just how long she'd be able to maintain a career at this rate.

An hour later, Shaila was on her feet, much to Levin's consternation. Her knee throbbed in protest every time she tried to put much weight on it, but Martian gravity was kind to injuries, and barring a direct order, she wasn't about to spend the rest of the evening moping around in bed. A few hops around the medical berth were enough for her to get the hang of one-legged propulsion, and she was out the door five minutes after that, Levin's warnings about taking it easy ignored as she skip-hopped down the corridor to the Hub. There were things to look into.

Unfortunately for her, the first person she ran into was Harry. And he was not happy.

"This is how you iron things out for me?" he grumped without preliminaries. His frown lines were deeper than usual, and the bags under his eyes belied his stress levels. "You realize what we're having to do now?"

She gave him a hard look and kept going as fast as her knee allowed. "I've been laid up, Harry. So no, I've no idea."

"JSC has imposed top-level safety precautions. You know what that even means?" He didn't bother waiting for Shaila to respond as he fell in beside her. "It means I can barely extract a tenth of what we're used to doing at the sites we already have because of all the safety checks, and Diaz isn't letting anybody within twenty kilometers of that cave. We have to drive way out of our way just to get to the damn sites now. How long are we going to have to do this?"

"Beats me," Shaila said, a true statement that nonetheless brought on a little sense of satisfaction. "Like I said, I just got out of medical. And it's not my problem anymore. Diaz took me off the investigation."

Harry fixed her with a truly withering gaze. "I thought we had an understanding."

Shaila stopped and turned to him, more than happy to find an outlet for all her anger and frustration. "*You* had an understanding. I didn't say 'boo' about it. Besides, I understood you wanted me off this investigation anyway."

"That's before I realized you're basically all I've got, Jain, and that ain't saying much," Harry growled, his finger pointing at her chest while he stared, red-faced, into her eyes. "If we can't get out from under these stupid safety regs and get back in that cave, everything goes to shit here. And my report to HQ isn't going to be kind to anyone, especially you."

Shaila frowned right back at him. "Threats instead of bribes, Harry?"

"Both. You want the money? Then do something productive to get us back up to speed again. Otherwise, I will fucking torch your career. My guys are pissed. The foremen can barely keep them in line. You want them taking over? It's four weeks before we get backup, and they're ready to cut some corners to get back on schedule. I hear Alvarez is—"

Harry's rant was cut off by the shrill cry of klaxon alarms piercing the normal din of activity in the Hub. "Christ! What now?" Shaila said.

It didn't take her long to find out.

McAuliffe Base had four twenty-person emergency transports available—enough to get everyone off planet—located in the back of the Hub. All you had to do to get off Mars was to hop in, press a few buttons, and the computers would automatically start a launch sequence and plot a course for insertion into Earth orbit.

And a group of eight miners was busy shoving past anyone in their way as they clambered into one.

"Shit." Shaila immediately tried to dash over, and nearly fell onto her side. She lurched back to vertical and began one-hopping over, her comm already in hand. "Ops, this is Jain. Override emergency launch sequence!"

The miners quickly got aboard, one of them punching Lt. Adams squarely in the face in their effort to get out. Shaila couldn't immediately recognize anybody in the mass of dirt-and-stubble faces, except for Alvarez, already at the controls. Idiot.

"Roger," Finelli responded. "Attempting override now."

Shaila made it to the transport hatch just as it began to close, and immediately felt a meaty fist hit her squarely in the chest, sending her sprawling three meters backward, right into Harry. They both fell backward onto the deck, a tangle of limbs and obscenities.

Suddenly, Stephane appeared in her field of vision, making for the door as quickly as he could, one of the company's laser drills in hand. He propped it between the closing hatch and the doorway, likely hoping that the obstruction would circumvent the launch cycle and freeze the transport in place.

Shaila knew it wouldn't work. "Steve! No!"

An eruption of airflow burst around her head. The transport hatch itself was closed, but the drill succeeded only in keeping the airlock open. And now McAuliffe's atmosphere was rushing out into the freezing Martian surface.

Stephane managed to press his back against the wall, holding on to one of the equipment lockers to keep him from getting sucked outside. He looked to Shaila with terror. "What do I do now?" he yelled.

With a grimace, Shaila leapt upward on her good leg and allowed the flow of air to whoosh her toward the hatch in seconds. She aimed herself right at the laser drill, which was already starting to crumple under the pressure. Grabbing the tool in both hands, she swung her lower half toward the door and, using both legs, pulled for all she was worth. Stephane joined her and they heaved together.

A moment later, Shaila was on her ass, at least five meters from the hatch, a destroyed laser drill in her hands. The hatch was closed, the atmosphere saved. And her knee was killing her.

"Shay!" Stephane scrambled off the floor a few meters away and ran toward her. "Are you all right?"

She tossed the drill aside and lay back on the decking. "I've been better. What the hell were you thinking?"

The Frenchman's face grew red. "I was trying to stop them," he said, indignant.

"Leave it to the pros next time, will you?" She clambered ungainly to her feet, brushing aside Stephane's outstretched hand. "We could've been killed." She plucked Stephane's comm out of his breast pocket. "Jain to ops. Status."

"Override failed," Finelli reported, frustration evident even over the comm. "Transport launched."

Her shoulders slumped. "Roger. Jain out." She shoved the comm into Stephane's hands. "Well, we're screwed now." She saw Harry walking over, fury on his face, and met his stare with one of her own. "Don't," she said sharply, stopping him in his tracks. "Do *not* say a word."

With that, she hopped, one-legged, toward the stairs leading to the command center. For the next hour, she coordinated damage control teams, grilled her subordinates on what happened and issued a report to Diaz, who was grim but surprisingly subdued. The colonel dismissed Shaila without comment, leaving her even more frustrated.

Having little else to do, and with her knee protesting vehemently, she slowly made her way back to her day room, resisting the urge to stop by Levin's office for some painkillers. She was in a foul enough mood to appreciate the lingering pain, and her record was in enough tatters without it seeming like she was looking for some chemical R&R after the shit hit the fan.

Shaila's day room was just as she left it—a total mess. Coveralls and exercise clothes were strewn about. The couch/cot contraption—which did neither function particularly well—was considerably mussed. Atop the cheap armoire-dresser against the wall was a small statue of a ten-armed Indian woman—Durga, a favorite of Shaila's mother—between two candles, all of which were half-covered by a Birmingham City Football Club scarf. Shaila's desk had a holopicture of her parents upon it, but little else besides data chips and a couple of datapads scattered across the surface. The holopic of her one-time artist boyfriend was firmly buried in a desk drawer, along with four years of memories and a good year's worth of disdain.

Given that she had little in the way of personal effects, the note on her desk stood out: "Il ya un cadeau pour vous dans le laboratoire de confinement.—Stephane."

Naturally, she had no idea what it said, though she figured it had something to do with the base containment lab. Why couldn't he have just sent an e-mail? Regardless, her datapad helped her with a quick translate query.

"There is a gift for you in the containment lab.—Stephane."

She eased herself down onto her daybed and frowned. If this was some convoluted, Gallic attempt at seeking forgiveness—or worse, more ill-fated flirtation—Shaila would shove him out an airlock, sans suit.

Nevertheless, it only took five minutes' worth of staring at Durga's serene smile and wavy arms before she was up again, hopping awkwardly to the containment lab. Unlike the main lab, it was rarely used; there was little on Mars these days that required the kind of quarantine the lab afforded. She entered to find the lights on, which wasn't too surprising, as Stephane had likely been in there a short time ago.

Her eyes were drawn to one of the lab's two containment units. Inside, lit from overhead, was the book she had found, sitting closed and looking for all the world like a refugee from an ancient library. The computers were already running a diagnostic on it, and Shaila ambled over to take a look at the readout, grateful that Stephane had secured it for her.

The book was, in essence, exactly what you'd expect from an old book. Mostly organic—the leather cover and paper would certainly be the culprits. Some trace iron and other organics—likely the ink. A light emanation of Cherenkov radiation…

…was sure as hell not what you'd expect. Neither were the trace electromagnetic field readings.

Shaila turned, excitedly, and in doing so jammed her knee into the lab's small worktable. Swearing viciously under her breath, she grabbed at the small metal box that had started falling due to the impact. Hopping on one foot, she caught it before it hit the floor and started to place it back on the table, until she noticed the rust-red dirt clinging to it.

The box was roughly a half-meter long, half again as wide. On either end was a pair of protuberances that immediately caught her eye. One looked like an emitter nozzle that Shaila had seen on any number of lasers, including the drill she had wrenched from the airlock door not too long ago. The second was a tube of some kind that uncomfortably reminded her of the barrel of a very small gun.

She set the box back on the table. Someone had already taken the screws out of the sides of the box and, most likely, had opened it. Shaila did the same, half expecting to be electrified or irradiated at this point in the very long, tedious day.

Instead, she found what appeared to be someone's engineering experiment. She immediately recognized the guts of a high-end laser drill, attached to the two emitters on either end of the box. The tritium batteries were a given, too, and they looked like they'd been wired together in a very ad hoc kind of way. But then she spotted a small containment field generator, attached to a simple glass vial. And she had no idea why the length of the lower half of the box was surrounded by a series of well-polished mirrors which seemed to focus light toward the tubes at either end.

The door swished open behind her and she started, almost whacking her knee again. Frowning, she turned and saw Evan Greene enter the lab.

"Got turned around?" Shaila asked, trying to keep the suspicion out of her voice as she casually reached over to dim the containment unit's light over the book. Greene didn't need to know about that one right now.

"Actually, I was hoping you'd be here," he said with his customary grin. He keyed the door shut behind him. "I see you found our little contraption."

"From our jaunt this morning?"

"Yeah." Greene's face turned serious. "I think you have a problem here, Lieutenant."

"What kind of problem?"

Greene walked over and picked up the device. "I assume you got the drill figured out. You know what the other thing is?"

"No, but I bet you do."

"It's a directional electromagnetic field generator," he said, sounding a touch too dramatic for Shaila's taste.

"That makes sense," Shaila shrugged. "That explains the fields, right?"

Greene sighed. "No, it doesn't make sense. In order for this particular device to work, you need more generators out there to create a link. It'll only work in tandem with others."

"So there's more of them out there?"

Greene put the device down and used the workstation to call up a map of the outside terrain. There were several markings on it. "We found the device here, right? And it angled off 36 degrees in this direction. If you figure there are emitters on either side of this thing, you can get a 36-degree angle from one to the other." He traced his finger off into the distance, the computer creating a red line in its wake. "That means that there are at least two more devices on either end of this angle, right?"

"At least," Shaila said, starting to follow along. "And the other points on the map?"

"A decagon. A ten-sided geometric shape. It doesn't make sense to create an angled linear EM field, because most practical uses would generally be point A to point B. But what if it were a ring, and these lines were long enough...?"

The computer filled in a series of red lines, forming a ring across the

Martian terrain.

The lava tube was inside the ring.

"How certain are you about the placement of these boxes?" Shaila asked.

"Certain? No way. But we know that the line you and I followed was at least three kilometers long. Even if all the lines were just three kilometers, the cave would be just outside the ring. And I'm betting it's inside."

Shaila looked hard at the little box on the table. "Where'd this come from?"

Greene picked it up again. "That's the other thing. This is totally home-brew. Tritium batteries scavenged from pressure suits and datapads. Magnetized iron alloy coating on the directional focus mirrors—probably came from older laser drills. The box looks like an old sample case. And all the serial numbers have been removed."

That last bit sealed it in Shaila's mind. "So somebody built those out of spare parts, specifically so they couldn't be traced, and built a ring of directional EM fields out in the middle of nowhere."

"Exactly," Greene said. "Now, there's a million perfectly good scientific uses for a ring of EM energy. But inside this particular ring, it seems like all hell's breaking loose."

CHAPTER 12

April 17, 1779

Father,

We are past the path of Mars and have successfully navigated the treach-erous Rocky Main. Thankfully, our Captain led one of the most recent expeditions to map the boulder-islands of the Main, which stretch between the paths of Mars and Jupiter. So while transit may be burdensome to others, it did not require much in the way of effort on our part.

I fear my purpose for this journal has been well diverted from the original, having become far more of an adventure story than a narrative of life in the service of King and Country. However, these are most unusual days, and I am compelled to continue now in this new vein, in the hopes that my writing may not only entertain and illuminate you, Father, but also may serve as a record of these quite singular events.

Of course, during the long transit between worlds, the mundane comes to the fore. But even now, our guests aboard ship have made even these days event-ful....

Midshipman O'Brian gripped his sword with white knuckles, his face pale as he parried one swift blow after another. He retreated along the main deck, his form faltering under the steady rain of thrusts and swipes from his opponent. His position was untenable—he would soon be backed up against the stairway to the quarterdeck, where he would be forced to ascend the stairs backward whilst under the barrage of canny moves by his surpris-ingly adept opponent, who showed little inclination to give ground.

But he would gain ground regardless. He made a daring gambit, parrying his opponent's blade widely, hoping his strength would be the greater despite his young age, and thrust forward. As he hoped, his opponent retreated just a hair's breadth, giving the young man enough time to resume the offense.

With renewed vigor, the midshipman furthered his attack, thrusting, parrying and riposting back across the main deck toward the bowsprit. Yet, he noted, his opponent did not panic or lose form. Instead, O'Brian watched a brilliant parry-riposte combination that came under his blade, forcing his arm wide. The young man hand to practically fall backward, scrambling to maintain his footing, as his assailant once again began to press forward.

"Mister O'Brian!" boomed a voice from behind him. "What in God's name are you doing?"

The midshipman turned round and stood at attention, forgetting his battle and opponent entirely. There stood Lt. Weatherby, and with him Dr. Finch. The former looked most aggrieved and angry, whilst the alchemist bore a look of supreme amusement.

"I, um, well, sir, I mean to say that—" O'Brian stuttered. "It weren't my idea, sir."

O'Brian's opponent walked in front of him, placing herself between him and his lieutenant's wrath. "Come now, Mr. Weatherby. Just a bit of sparring, is all." Miss Baker smiled sweetly, and O'Brian saw Weatherby's anger give way to a small smile and awkward frustration.

"Miss Baker, you could have done yourself a grave injury," Weatherby said gently, as if parenting an errant child. "O'Brian here has been training for some time now."

"She's better than me, sir," O'Brian said brightly, but quieted quickly as his superior's withering look returned.

Miss Baker turned and handed over her blade to the midshipman. "Thank you, Mr. O'Brian. That was most refreshing." She turned back to Weatherby, smiling primly. "I trust dinner was as well, Mr. Weatherby?"

Weatherby's mouth moved, but no words came out; the only sound came from Finch, who could not stifle his laughter for long. "Miss Baker," Finch said, "I must thank you for the entertainment."

The young woman frowned. "Did you find my form so amusing, Doctor?"

"Oh, not at all. I've no doubt you could skewer half the men aboard," he replied, his insouciant grin unabated. "The amusement comes from once again rendering my lieutenant speechless." Weatherby wheeled on Finch, who suddenly became quite keen to depart. "Come, O'Brian. Best to let me have a look at you after such a ferocious onslaught."

The midshipman looked up at the doctor as the latter approached. "She didn't lay a scratch on me, sir, I—" The young man's protests were cut off as Finch grabbed his collar and dragged him below, leaving Weatherby alone with Miss Baker.

"Ah, well, then, Miss Baker," Weatherby said, looking for something, *anything* to say. "I trust you're unharmed."

"Quite so, Mr. Weatherby," she said with a smile. "Thank you for your concern."

He waved his hand to allow Miss Baker to go first, and they began their now customary stroll down the main deck. "Not at all. How is it that you learned to fence so well? 'Tis an uncommon skill for a woman, to be sure."

"Elizabeth Mercuris is a difficult place," she replied, frowning slightly. "One must learn everything one can in order to survive, lest your very future be cut all too short."

"Ah, well, I see," Weatherby said, though he didn't quite understand her statement. "And, what of your future, once our task is complete? We are indeed headed for Jupiter and her moons. There may be some opportunities for you there if you wish it."

"I suppose I should think on it more than I have. But I honestly do not know what will become of me," she said, her smile fading. "It's rather new to actually have a future to look forward to. But I have no idea what I will make of it."

"What of a family, perhaps?" Weatherby said, not realizing the full gravity of his words until they were spoken. He suddenly felt as though he were venturing upon the frozen Thames at winter—never a safe endeavor.

However, Miss Baker misunderstood him. "I have no family to speak of, Tom," she said, falling into a familiarity that had grown over weeks of conversation. "Perhaps I will stay in one of the Jovian colonies after all. I understand they are more tolerant of a woman on her own. Who knows? Perhaps I can make some small business of my alchemical skills."

Weatherby raised his eyebrows at this. "Had Dr. McDonnell taught you that much?" he blurted out.

She turned and smiled at him coyly. "Why, Tom, you do not think I have it in me to be a great alchemist? Or perhaps a swordswoman instead?"

He hated how that smile so quickly robbed him of rationality and confidence. "No, of course not. I mean, you have skill with the sword. And with alchemy, it seems. I, um, simply meant to suggest, well…perhaps I am not entirely familiar with life in the colonies."

"No, I daresay you are not," she replied. "But I am, and I've survived it. And with the knowledge Roger—I should say, Dr. McDonnell—has given me, I can make my way well enough. One way or another."

"Was it that hard?" he asked, trying to mask his curiosity with compassion.

Her eyes drifted downward to the deck. "I lost my father to the mines when I was eight, and my mother to the pox when I was twelve," she said. "I did what I needed to do, and I picked up some skills, as you just witnessed. Thankfully, in the end, Roger took me in, gave me a home, helped me greatly."

Weatherby was struck not only by the story, but the familiarity she had with her employer as well. "I'm sure he was most kind to you," he said, for want of nothing better.

She looked up with a hardness in her eyes. "As I said, he helped me greatly, and I him."

"I see."

"No, Tom, I don't think that you do, but that is a conversation for another day, I think," she said. She then looked down at his sword, her smile returning. "So. With my swordsmanship no longer in question, do you think we might put my alchemical knowledge to the test, then?"

He followed her gaze. "What did you have in mind?"

"Give me your sword. You shall have it back the next time you stand guard over me."

"I should hope so," he said, unbuckling the scabbard from his belt. "The men haven't been in port for quite a while!"

She laughed at this, then took the blade in hand and drew it. "A fine blade, Lieutenant. But we shall see what I might do with it. Could you escort me to the alchemical laboratory?"

Weatherby left her at her impromptu quarters; unsurprisingly, Finch was nowhere to be found, his story about O'Brian an obvious ruse to begin with. Their parting was awkward, as it seemed neither wished to be the one to say good night. Finally, Weatherby took his leave when he saw O'Brian having returned and tarrying nearby, as it was his watch to begin with.

After that, Weatherby decided to retire for the evening, but found his curiosity kept him from sleep. Miss Baker was, perhaps, all of seventeen, maybe eighteen at most. She had spent at least a year in the employ of Dr. McDonnell, and Weatherby felt it safe to assume that her feelings toward her former master, while mostly compassionate, were mixed at times. And that left a space of…four years? Five? It was a long time for a girl to be orphaned, especially on an outpost like Elizabeth Mercuris.

"I did what I had to do." Images of a young Anne Baker, beggar's bowl in hand, haunted him as sleep came. He resolved to be more cautious with his feelings toward her until he learned all he could of her troubled past.

Morning arrived abruptly in the form of a rather loud and exuberant midshipman. "Mr. Weatherby! Mr. Weatherby! Wake up!" Forester shouted.

"What? What is it?" Weatherby asked, feeling suddenly panicked. "Are we under attack?"

The boy merely laughed. "No, sir! Miss Baker is asking after you. She's setting up a demonstration!"

Weatherby swung his legs out of his hammock. "A demonstration? A demonstration of what?"

"Alchemy, sir!" The boy headed for the door. "We're told it's to be quite spectacular."

"I see," Weatherby grumbled, running a hand over his face. She was headstrong, certainly. Were he more awake, and perhaps of a more self-reflective personality, he might admit such stubbornness was part of his burgeoning attraction. "Go on, Forester. I will be up in a moment."

After splashing some water on his face, Weatherby grabbed his hat and coat and went above decks, where he could see a small crowd of idlers on the main deck, looking forward toward the bowsprit. There, Miss Baker had set up a table and had one of the 18-pound cannon balls upon it. "Ah, there you are, Lieutenant!" she called as he approached. "Let him through!"

The idlers parted and allowed Weatherby to move forward. "I did not think you would make such a spectacle of this," he said quietly, trying not to allow his foul mood enter his voice.

"Nonsense," she said sweetly. "If I am to make a name for myself as an alchemist, I need to start somewhere."

"Very well, then," he said. "I hope, for your sake, this comes off well."

She handed him his sword. "If you please, Mr. Weatherby." Her tone was one of challenge.

He looked at the blade. It caught the sun and stars particularly well; if nothing else, she had polished it perfectly.

"Now then," she said, loud enough to be heard on the main deck below. "Let us see if I've been successful. I'm but a woman, so surely I am quite unable to test the blade properly." The onlookers had a laugh at this; the tale of her bout with O'Brian had obviously spread. "Take your swing, sir." She motioned toward the cannon ball.

Weatherby looked to see at least twenty men on the main deck, all rapt attention. Even Captain Morrow and Dr. Franklin were looking at him from the quarterdeck. He felt a stab of panic at the thought of seeing her working fail before everyone. "Miss Baker, are you quite sure?" he asked.

She put her hands on her hips. "Swing, Tom," she said with quiet intensity.

"Very well." He took his position in behind the table, facing the crowd, praying that whatever happened would not embarrass the young woman too greatly. Rearing back with the blade in both hands, he sliced downward.

A moment later, two halves of a cannon ball fell to the deck upon either side of the table, followed quickly by the two halves of the table itself—and then the blade, which embedded itself into the deck planking by more than six inches.

A cheer erupted from the men, and even Morrow and Franklin could be seen applauding and talking amongst themselves on the quarterdeck. Weatherby heaved and pulled his blade from the deck.

"Shall we deem this a successful test, then?" Miss Baker asked.

"My God, I should say so," Weatherby breathed, looking at his sword with new appreciation. "It cut so cleanly!"

"Don't forget your scabbard," she said, handing it to him. "It's been similarly treated. This blade will slice through any other scabbard you would use."

He carefully sheathed the sword. "I don't know what to say. I am in your debt."

"Not at all, sir," she said, nodding to the crowd. "When we arrive at a friendly port, these men here will say more than enough about it. And that was the point."

"Very clever," Weatherby said. He then quietly added: "You have given your future far more thought than you first let on."

For once, the young woman blushed. "Perhaps so. And perhaps we may yet discuss it further, you and I."

Weatherby smiled and, alchemical marvel in hand, found himself quite entranced, caution thrown to the solar wind.

July 26, 2132

Shaila knew she should've been unnerved by the prospect of strange, home-brewed technology secretly buried near the base. Instead, as she presented her case to Yuna and Stephane, she felt downright euphoric. It had been a bad day all around, and here, she thought, was *something* that could begin to explain what the hell was going on.

The good feelings didn't last very long.

"Shaila, I know you want to be a part of this investigation, but I really think these boxes you and Dr. Greene discovered aren't related at all," the older woman said, a kindly smile on her face. It was the smile that hurt the most, perhaps, with its mix of worry and concern. It was the kind of smile you give overly imaginative children or frightened old people, and it pissed Shaila off to no end.

"Yuna, there is a ring of these boxes all over our ops area," Shaila said, trying to sound reasonable. "We're sure of it. And that ring and those ravines could very well encompass the lava tube. It's throwing a ton of energy and EM fields all over the place. You can't tell me that's a coincidence!"

Shaila didn't realize her voice had carried over the mess hall, but the stares quickly made it evident. The JSC astronauts looked at her with worry, while the miners whispered among themselves, half-lidded eyes pointed in her direction.

"Shaila, I commanded this base on two separate tours, back in the day. You know how many little experiments we had going on, before Billiton came over? Why, everyone had some little project to tinker with, and the stuff that failed probably didn't get recorded. Who wants to be embarrassed by something like that?"

"So you're saying it's some kind of old experiment?" Shaila said, disbelieving.

Yuna smiled again. "You're stuck on Mars, without even mining ops to keep you busy. Of course you tinker some. And remember, we did have some U.S. military types who came to play around with some top-secret things. Could be something of theirs, too."

Shaila looked up at Stephane, trying to keep her face straight. "What do you think?"

The geologist frowned into his dinner. "I do not know," he said simply.

"That's it? You do not know?" Shaila didn't mean to mock his accent, but it came out that way regardless.

"Yes, I do not know, Shay. Theoretically, you could generate an electromagnetic field area big enough to create a kind of tremor, I guess, but—"

"See?" Shaila smiled at Yuna. "It's possible."

"*But*," Stephane continued. "Look at the box you found. Old batteries from pressure suits and datapads? You would need fusion reactors for enough energy to create an earthquake."

"So you don't think it's anything," Shaila said, eyes downcast.

Stephane looked genuinely concerned. "If we cannot find other causes, we can look at your theory. For now, there are far more realistic things to consider. But what about the book?" he asked, baldly changing the subject. "What have you found there?"

Shaila shrugged. "Haven't looked at it much." In fact, the only thing she did was to password-encrypt the containment unit's controls, in case Greene got too curious.

"You should. It is an amazing story," he said.

Shaila finally looked up. "I flipped through it in the cave. It's blank."

"No, it's not," Stephane said, a genuine grin on his face.

"Fine. I'll give it a read," she said dully. "Thanks for hearing me out, guys."

She quickly got up and headed for the tray return, then out the door.

"Shay!" Stephane jogged up behind her and awkwardly avoided plowing into her, sending them both down the stairs to the Hub.

"Jesus, Steve! What is it?" She managed to land on her good leg, and grabbed Stephane's coverall just in time to save him from face-planting on

"I do not think you are nuts," Stephane said. "I just do not know if these boxes are really anything we should look at now."

"They are," Shaila said, willing herself to believe it as much as her voice implied. "This can't be a coincidence, and I'm going to track them down." Shaila let go of his coverall and, with a nod, jumped down the stairs toward the Hub, turning briefly at the landing to face him one more time. "And thanks for saving my ass back at the cave."

She jumped down the second set of stairs before he could respond; it was hard enough leaving him there like that. It was good—great, really—that he was taking ownership of the investigation in her absence. But…she really wanted someone to believe her. And the two most likely candidates just put her off completely.

As she walked through the Hub, she noticed that the banter between miners was far more subdued. They were clustered together more, talking animatedly but quietly. Two junior JSC astronauts stood guard over the remaining emergency transports, something Shaila had recommended to Diaz earlier. Good to see that some of her ideas weren't crap. But the looks she got from the Billiton crews made the hairs on her neck stand up on end. They were getting just a tenth of their usual haul, and that wouldn't be sustainable for more than a few more days, most likely.

After that, well…Shaila had her doubts. To be fair, in the history of interplanetary resource extraction there had been exactly one riot: the 2107 Freeport Vale Riot. Roughly 125 men were promised good money if they went to work on lunar extraction. Problem was, the company's geologists were taking a gamble on the site chosen—the strata seemed promising, but their sensors couldn't penetrate far enough to confirm it. Three men died as they spent two months digging into the lunar crust; the promised veins of minerals never showed. The Freeport Vale geologists and project leaders never made it back to Earth, and the surviving miners all had similar memory loss as to how the honchos died.

Shaila knew things at McAuliffe were far better than a generation ago on the Moon, but as she made her way down the corridor and passed several Billiton personnel—and no JSC people—she was acutely aware of how outnumbered they'd be in the event things got interesting.

When she got back to the containment lab, Greene was nowhere to be found, but he had taken the precaution of locking down the EM device in the other containment unit. He had to have been worried, since he would need Shaila or some other JSC officer to unlock the unit for him if he wanted another look at the gizmo.

Shaila flopped down into one of the room's three chairs, put her feet up on the work bench and filed through e-mail on her datapad. Harry was creating a holy ruckus, CC'ing everyone in JSC about his failing quotas and McAuliffe's "unreasonable and unwarranted" safety requirements; he probably knew the details of Freeport Vine better than she did, so his hell-raising wasn't entirely surprising. Scrolling down further, she saw that someone in JSC actually agreed with him—the diggers would be back to standard safety protocols tomorrow, so long as they stayed well away from the cave. At least that might get some of the hard cases back on the job. Idle hands, after all….

A cargo ship was due in tomorrow, the *Giffords*, bringing a new rotation of six miners and a few tons of consumables that would get the base through the next few months. Shaila saw her subordinates had handled the preparations pretty well. Of course, the new blood wouldn't make up for the eight miners who bailed earlier in the day, so even without the harsher safety regimen, Billiton would still fall behind quota. Maybe the six guys who were due to rotate out would be convinced to stay.

Shaila tossed the datapad on the table in disgust. It didn't matter. The biggest thing to happen on Mars since *Spirit* and *Opportunity* landed, and she wasn't in on it. Nobody *wanted* her in on it. She rubbed her hands over her face in exhaustion. Maybe they were right. Time to hang it up, maybe go work for United Airlines on the Earth-Moon run. Of course, with her luck, she'd end up on the Dallas-Cleveland run.

She forced herself to get up and address matters at hand. She wouldn't give up on the two pieces of the mystery she had left to her. She couldn't.

The EM device appealed to her far more than the book, despite whatever Stephane found written in it. She remembered a holoshow about ghost hunting—funny how they never seemed to find solid evidence of the afterlife—that said high EM fields could create feelings of paranoia or hallucinations. Maybe that's why she was seeing and hearing things in her head. She put that out of her mind quickly, however. It wasn't something she was interested in dealing with, and if she told someone about it, with her record on *Atlantis*, they'd send her home in a straightjacket.

Instead, she walked over and took a look at the book, sitting closed inside the unit. Opening and reading it would be a huge chore; the unit's manipulator claws were far better suited to handling rock samples than turning pages. So she simply programmed another sensor analysis, followed by a computerized comparison with the one she took earlier. At least she could see if the Cherenkov and EM readings were changing or not. It would take a little time to crunch the numbers, so she could let that run while she followed up on the linear EM problem.

Shaila brought one of the lab's workstations to life. She knew Diaz wouldn't be happy with her withholding information about the EM device or the book, but it seemed to be the quickest and surest path to some kind of redemption. Or at least the surest way to feel like she still mattered.

Straightening up as the screen flickered to life, Shaila dialed up the base's pressure suit beacon log. The base computer kept tabs on everyone who EVA'ed on the surface, going back two years. She and Greene had wandered pretty far from the access road to find the EM device's location, which wasn't near any mining ops or JSC sites. Thus, anyone who showed up on the beacon log prior to today would automatically be a person of interest, as the police holodramas liked to say.

Shaila put the database on map mode and centered in on the area where the device was found. Adams was there that afternoon, along with Greene, and she saw her own beacon, along with Greene's again, from their trek earlier in the day. A couple of JSC engineers passed by that spot three months prior, but didn't linger at all—they were doing maintenance on the nearby AOO sensor. Then nothing for a good five months…

…until Harry Yu showed up exactly in that spot.

Shaila double checked the data to be sure. Going back for the entirety of the log, Harry was the only other person to linger at that location for more than a few seconds.

"Son of a bitch," Shaila muttered. She quickly filtered out all other beacons and expanded her search area to the entire McAuliffe area of operations—three hundred square kilometers of bleak Martian turf. Turned out Harry spent a fair amount of time outside, but the vast majority of it was confined to access roads, mining ops sites and a few of the bigger survey trips. So Shaila filtered out those locations as well.

She got two more hits. Both of the new locations were well outside the normal Billiton sites, and were rarely explored by JSC as well. In fact, if there was a middle-of-nowhere within McAuliffe's sensor grid, those were two good candidates.

Shaila singled out the three sites on the map and cleared the rest of the data, and stared intently at them. They weren't at 36-degree angles to one another. And they were anywhere from fifteen to forty-five clicks apart.

But…

Shaila traced her finger around the map, encapsulating the three points into a ring. It turned out to be a pretty big area, at least 60 kilometers in diameter.

And just as Greene had guessed, the lava tube was inside that area.

Shaila keyed the comm. "Jain to Greene, over."

A few seconds passed before he responded. "Greene here. What's up, Lieutenant?"

"You want to grab some more shots outside tomorrow morning?" she asked.

To his credit, he got the hint within five seconds, tops. "You know, I think I do."

"Meet me in the Hub at oh-eight-thirty. Jain out."

Shaila turned back to the screen, intent on running a second suit-beacon search for anyone who had been anywhere along the ring-line she had drawn on the map. Before she could start the search, however, she was interrupted by a chime from the computer near the containment unit.

She rolled her chair over to the unit holding the book and quickly scanned through the comparison the computer had done between her initial scan and the one just completed. The book continued to radiate electromagnetic energy and Cherenkov radiation at constant levels, while nearly every other metric remained the same…

Except the book now weighed 0.6 grams more than it did when first scanned.

Six-tenths of a gram wasn't quite a rounding error, even with McAuliffe's slightly antiquated equipment. Unfortunately, she hadn't thought to do a more thorough chemical composition scan earlier—and really, why bother when books are made of paper, right?—so it was impossible to tell exactly how the book gained weight.

Shaila recalibrated the containment unit's sensors to include the chemical composition data, then set it on a regular loop—if the book gained weight regularly or if it suddenly spiked, she'd know about it. And if it were simply a glitch, which was most likely, she'd know that too.

She was about to turn back to her suit-beacon search when she eyed the book's cover one more time. It was nice looking, well-weathered leather, and looked like it had been hand-made. Books hadn't really been published on paper for nearly a century, but there were still some folks who slapped down hard-earned terras for something they could put on a shelf. Shaila never really understood that.

But this book seemed different even from the vanity books still published on Earth. Taking the unit's manipulator controls, she gently nudged the claws toward the book and, with more than a little effort, managed to flip the cover open.

The first page had a single word—"Weatherby"—on it. Shaila figured it was easy to miss that.

The second page—reached all too slowly by dragging the claw lightly across the surface of the first page—was covered in neat penmanship, addressed to someone's father. How she missed that, she didn't know. Shaila started reading.

"*Father,*

You have often asked me about my life in service to His Majesty's Navy, and I have endeavoured to tell you as much as I can, but often detail escapes me..."

Shaila stopped and re-read the first few paragraphs.

"Mercury?"

CHAPTER 13

May 2, 1779

Father,

These are strange days. I do not know if this journal can any longer serve as a present to you, as the situation we find ourselves in is one of the utmost sensitivity. Yet I am driven to continue with my chronicle, in the hopes that my thoughts on recent events may help others to perhaps better understand the extraordinary events in which we find ourselves.

And so, I write this while HMS Daedalus sits in port—in Philadelphia, capital of these so-called United States of Ganymede, where we will soon be forced into captivity. And yet we are not captives. Truly, it is a hard thing to explain, but I shall try to do the situation some small justice herein before we embark upon what I am sure will be one of the stranger episodes in the annals of diplomacy.

Weatherby stumbled slightly on the cobblestones of the streets, his balance poorly aided by the manacles he wore and the darkness surrounding him. Truly, he had little idea how Capt. Morrow walked so straight and tall, even while at musket-point, or how even Finch could navigate the darkened streets of Philadelphia with seeming grace. For his part, Weatherby simply wished for nothing more than to turn around and hit the Ganymedean soldier who prodded and pushed him along the streets at musket-point, but he was under very strict orders to cooperate fully. Besides, he thought rather glumly, he had used up much of Morrow's goodwill and forbearance, if not all.

This circumstance was, sad to say, a continuance of the ill fortune that seemed to plague both *Daedalus* in general—and her second lieutenant most particularly—since leaving the Rocky Main behind. Four days prior, as they entered the Jovian system, the *Daedalus* was caught in a roiling Void storm. These were common enough—about as common as severe thunderstorms on Earth—but had little in the way of the latter's merit. At least an Earth-bound thunderstorm would produce fresh water, always a welcome gift aboard ship. Void storms had nothing in the way of rain, unless a torrent of sun-motes counted as such, and these could certainly not quench thirst. They instead stung faces and charred wood to a small degree, like the embers cast from a fireplace, carried away by the wind.

And there was plenty of wind in a Void storm, as well as roiling currents, black clouds that blotted out the stars, and seemingly twice the lightning of its planet-bound cousin. Naturally, it was in this stew of foul weather that Mr. Plumb had ordered Weatherby to inspect the mainmast sail rigging—some sixty feet above the pitching deck. The officers regularly inspected the sails and rigging, but it was a task with which Weatherby had never become wholly comfortable, and the violent pitching of the ship made the task far more onerous.

Yet it was the men of Weatherby's division responsible for the sails on this watch, and there would be Hell to pay if they were other than perfect. So he joined his men above, carefully inspecting each line, sail and spar. All seemed to be well.

He had begun to make his descent to the relative safety of the deck when the ship lurched violently, swaying at least sixty degrees upon its keel axis—she would've sank had she been at sea instead of Void. As it was, Weatherby clung to the hempen rigging near the mainmast and hung on for dearest life, eyes screwed shut in fear—and prayer.

But a sharp crack had sent his eyes open wide once more—was it cannon fire? Here in the storm? There was a sharp cry to his right, followed by shouts from the deck below. And as Weatherby turned to trace the sound, he could feel *Daedalus'* momentum slowing

Next to him, the mainmast spar was hanging at a terrible downward angle, taking the wind right out of the mainsail. And there were two men of his division now atop the stilted spar, tangled in a mass of rope, canvas and broken wood that kept them from falling to the deck—but also trapped them and threatened to send them careening off into the Void if the spar gave way completely.

Weatherby began to climb upward once more, but the billowing sailcloth was catching the solar wind in all the wrong directions, and the Void storm continued to pitch the ship, almost throwing Weatherby off into the Void before he had climbed but a few feet. Saving himself by just one tightly clenched hand, the young officer managed to regain his footing and proceeded upward once more, wrapping his forearm around the rigging at each step. A shower of sun-motes swept past his face, momentarily stinging his eyes and blinding him, but he shook his head and hauled himself onto the firing platform at the intersection of the mainmast and the mainsail spar.

Off to larboard, Weatherby could see that the two men—Lamb and Weller were their names—were busy trying to untangle themselves from the wreckage of the mainmast and their own body lines, now tangled and likely compromised by the accident. Weller was the nimbler and more experienced of the two, while Lamb was a pressed man who had barely been aboard six months. Lamb was also closer to the firing platform, making Weatherby's decision easier. He grabbed an extra body line from the mainmast and tied it around his waist before venturing onto the broken, sloping spar toward the two trapped men.

"Hold fast!" he called out as he inched his way up the wooden beam, clutching at the dangling ropes from above. "Do not move about! I'm coming!"

Lamb immediately stopped pulling at the rope and canvas around his leg, looking to Weatherby with fear and hope combined. Weller, however, kept trying to unravel his body line, which had tangled up around his arm—even though he was half-dangling from the very end of the spar, with naught but hard deck and vast Void beneath. "Weller, stop what you're doing!" Weatherby called out, but to no avail; either Weller couldn't hear his officer over the wind and lightning, or the experienced tar trusted his own skills over that of the younger man.

Then the ship bucked violently once more, nearly throwing Weatherby off the spar entirely, with only a rope between him and the deck below. He held on tightly, trying to stifle the protest from his stomach and nerves, and continued upward. Lamb, panicking, had begun to pick at his ropes once more, while Weller seemed to be getting free on his own—experience was winning out.

After what seemed an age, but was likely but a minute, Weatherby reached Lamb and pulled out his dirk, slicing through the offending ropes that kept the man bound to the wreckage of the mainsail. The lubberly man—why Lamb was assigned to the sails, Weatherby could not venture—clumsily grasped the rope around Weatherby's waist and held on dearly as the officer cleared the wreckage away, freeing his leg. "Go back!" Weatherby shouted over the gale. "Head for the firing platform! Crawl along the spar!"

Lamb nodded desperately and began crawling downward, nearly shoving Weatherby off the spar in the process in his haste. But he could see that Lamb's caution was an asset—so long as the spar held, he could make it to the firing platform and, from there, easily descend to the deck, even in the Void storm. Weatherby watched his progress for a few more moments before turning to Weller.

Weller was gone.

Aghast, Weatherby looked and saw rope, broken wood and canvas dangling from the spar just 10 feet ahead. The man had managed to free himself. And then—

Weatherby looked about, but saw no trace of the man, not even upon the deck below. But he did see Lt. Foster below, waving for him to come down. Even from his precarious perch, Weatherby could see his fellow officer's head shake sadly. There would be no further rescue.

With resignation, Weatherby began inching his way back down the spar. He looked back to see Lamb had reached the firing platform, and was hugging the mainmast desperately as the ship swayed and heaved. This sight was quickly obscured, however, by the mainsail, which blew up and around Weatherby's body. The young man cried out in surprise, and quickened his grip along the spar, but he could feel the sail's weight dragging at him.

Then something hard and sharp—likely a piece of wood—sank into Weatherby's hand. With a shriek, he released his hold for a bare moment. A quick gust of wind, a shower of dust motes and a massive pitch to starboard did the rest.

Weatherby fell as the mainsail sloughed off him, dropping twenty feet in an instant before his lifeline caught him, prompting him to nearly retch as it bit into his stomach and spun him upside down. Before he could gather himself, the rope swung him around in a wide arc—and he barely had time to blink before he saw the strong oak of the mainmast rushing up to greet him.

Then all was black.

The next sight Weatherby enjoyed—and he enjoyed it very much, for it meant he was alive—was a wooden ceiling. The next sensation was far less agreeable, for it seemed his entire body had been severely bludgeoned.

He turned his head to the right, prompting a throb of protest in his brainpan, and saw Dr. Finch mixing some sort of alchemical elixir at a bench next to him. The doctor turned and, seeing Weatherby was awake, smiled genuinely. "You're an incredibly brave and utterly stupid man," he said.

"More the latter," Weatherby murmured. "Lamb? Weller?"

The doctor sighed. "Mr. Lamb is fine. Nothing an extra ration of grog cannot cure. Mr. Weller is missing and presumed lost to the Void."

Weatherby nodded, closing his eyes for a moment. He remembered Weller as one of the more businesslike of the crew, highly skilled and respected if not widely liked. He wished he could remember more of the man, but that was all that came to him.

"Do you know how the repairs go?" Weatherby asked.

It was Captain Morrow who answered; Weatherby had not seen him, but he had been standing on the other side of his cot the entire time. "The repairs proceed, Mr. Weatherby. Our most vexing problem remains why they were necessary in the first place."

Morrow's tone was gentle enough, but the question was unmistakable. "Sir, I checked the sails myself," Weatherby said. "All appeared proper to my eye prior to the engagement."

Morrow nodded soberly. "So say those aloft as well. But the mainsail, the maintopsail and most of the rigging along the mainmast is a run now. Mr. Plumb has already begun investigating the wreckage to ensure there was nothing amiss aside from weather."

The captain fixed Weatherby in his eye as he continued. "I have given you a commendation for valor in the log, Mr. Weatherby, and it is well deserved. But should an oversight on the part of you or your division be responsible for the sail giving way so completely, I will be forced to note this in the log as well." Morrow turned to Finch. "How long before Mr. Weatherby can return to duty?"

The doctor looked discomfited at this. "He has suffered a sharp blow to the head. I should like to keep him here for the rest of the day, but if you need him sooner, I shall do my best."

Morrow nodded. "Best you can, Dr. Finch." And with that, the captain took his leave with a last glance at his young second lieutenant, whose pained expression did little to pierce Morrow's inscrutably neutral mien.

"Ah, the service," Weatherby said, laying his head back on the pillow and trying to ignore the throbbing. "One good deed deserves a poor one."

"So it would seem," Finch said in genuine sympathy. "Even if one of your men had been sloppy, 'tis no reason to punish you for it."

"They're my men, Doctor, and it is up to me to ensure they perform their duties well," Weatherby said quietly. "But I tell you, all aloft really did seem well in hand. I'm sure Mr. Plumb will agree."

Finch applied a compress to Weatherby's head, one that made his scalp tingle to a degree—something laden with alchemical treatments, no doubt. He then traced a few sigils upon Weatherby's brow using some sort of clear oil. "Are you quite sure you wish to make a career of all this?" Finch said with a small grin. "I should imagine piracy would at least be more fun."

Weatherby could not help but smile back. "True, but if you think our bilges smell bad, I imagine they're far worse aboard a ship like *Chance*."

"Anything at sea or Void, I believe, will have a certain putrescence attached to it," Finch said, seemingly enjoying the banter. "Take for example, the smell associated with this whole notion of equality among officers in the wardroom. Imagine the son of a shopkeeper in charge of a nobleman!"

"My father is a shopkeeper," Weatherby said, his grin growing wide. Any further rejoinder was cut off by the sound of the ship's bell and the marine drum—they were beating to quarters.

Weatherby bolted upright, doing his best to ignore the throbbing dizziness produced in his head. He tossed aside the compress, grabbed his hat from Finch's workbench and, despite a string of pleading and obscenities from the doctor, carefully picked his way up above decks, grabbing onto whatever he could to maintain his balance as the ship pitched.

Except, when he ascended to the main deck, Weatherby could see they were out of the storm, and Jupiter loomed large across the entire larboard-side horizon. The pitching was due solely to his lack of balance at the moment. He looked up to see seamen scrambling over the mainmast rigging, attempting a slapdash repair to the mainsail that would at least give *Daedalus* something in the way of maneuverability, if not speed. Willing the doctor's alchemy to hurry into effectiveness, Weatherby quickly picked his way across the deck toward the ship's stern—until he nearly bumped into a burly sailor blocking his path.

It was Lamb, giving him a pronounced salute. "Mr. Weatherby, sir, I can't begin to thank you enough, sir, what you did for me. I'm in your debt, sir."

Weatherby gave the man a small smile and put his hand on his shoulder. Even with his head throbbing, he knew others among his division were watching this exchange. "I would've done it for any man aboard, and I know you would have done so for me. Now go and mind your station."

Lamb saluted again and scurried off, leaving Weatherby feeling immensely better about nearly everything—until he took a step and nearly keeled over the side. Grabbing at the rigging, Weatherby staggered forward, ascending the few steps up to the quarterdeck and presenting himself to Morrow, who acknowledged him with a bare nod before turning back to his conversation with Dr. Franklin.

"Ambassador, you must recognize you're asking a great deal of me," the captain said crossly. "And there is no guarantee that the captain of that ship will agree to it."

"He will, I promise you," Franklin said. "It is critical we avoid a battle here, Captain. It would only distract us from our goal of apprehending Cagliostro!"

"And what if this is a trap, after all?" Morrow demanded. "First our mainsail gives at a critical moment, and now a Ganny frigate bears down upon us. Tell me, sir, that you've not had a hand in this!"

To his credit, Franklin remained calm. "Sir William, should I wished to have your vessel captured, I could have easily misdirected you whilst you were in Paris, and I would be home now, sitting by my fire, playing chess!"

The look of confusion on Weatherby's face must have been evident, for Lt. Foster took it upon himself to take Weatherby's arm and lead him back down to the main deck and his battle station. "Ganny sighted," Foster said quietly, pointing off to starboard, forward of the ship. "She must have kept station at the very edge of the storm, hoping for easy prey."

Even without his glass—or much of his wits—Weatherby could see the Ganny off in the distance, and he could tell it was already much larger.

With her mainsail greatly diminished and outgunned as well, *Daedalus* would be easy prey indeed. Hence, Weatherby assumed, Franklin's plea for negotiation with his fellow rebels, for it would likely save them all.

A few minutes later, with Weatherby's gun crews at the ready and the Ganny nearing all too close to firing range, it seemed Franklin finally won over the captain. "Secure the guns and stand down!" Plumb called from the quarterdeck.

A moment later, Weatherby saw that *Daedalus* had struck its colors, replacing the Union Jack flying from the quarterdeck with a single white sheet.

Surrender.

Weatherby's own discomfiture was echoed in the murmuring of the men around him, but even in his still-dazed state, Weatherby could see the sense in it. With Franklin aboard, the Ganny likely would allow them safe passage or, at the very worst, allow them to make repairs and leave the Jovian system under escort. Better that than to fight a 44-gun frigate with but 28 guns and a crippled mainmast.

Minutes later, the enemy ship was close enough to identify as the *Bonhomme Richard*, which appeared to cheer Franklin greatly. Weatherby saw the Ganny approach cautiously, guns at the ready, and the men of his own division frowned and murmured as they watched. *Daedalus* had not unfurled a sail, and the guns were run back in. She was naught but an easy target, and Weatherby had to sternly order his men to remain quiet and motionless, lest the Ganny find an excuse to open fire.

Soon, Morrow and the enemy commander—Weatherby could not help but think of the Ganymedeans as anything else—were exchanging shouted words through speaking horns. Morrow brought Franklin to the ship's railing, and enjoined him to shout through as well. Yet instead of seemingly pacifying the Ganny's crew, the guns were still drawn, and the shouting grew more intense.

Ultimately, the two ships drew alongside each other. Morrow ordered the men to stand at attention, hands visibly at their sides, while the Ganny's crew could be seen training their muskets and cannon upon them. A gangway was secured between the two vessels, and some two dozen Ganymedean marines flooded onto the British vessel, followed by what appeared to be the Ganny captain.

"Appeared" seemed appropriate to Weatherby, for this man was dressed in one of the more outlandish military uniforms he had ever seen. The man's hat was wrapped in gold braid along the edges, and his coat was likewise heavily adorned with braiding, piping and a surfeit of brass buttons. The man's waistcoat was the brightest red Weatherby had seen outside of an actual fire, and the buckles on the Ganymedean's shoes were perhaps three sizes larger than they needed to be.

Nonetheless, Morrow had come onto the main deck to greet him, and even ordered the men to pipe this popinjay aboard as if he were an allied commander instead of a traitor to the crown. "Captain," Morrow said formally, "I am Captain Sir William Morrow of His Majesty's Ship *Daedalus*."

The man nodded curtly. "Captain John Paul Jones of the United States' Ship *Bonhomme Richard*. Do I know this ship? Were you 'round Mercury two months past? There was a merchant vessel there that had behaved most curiously, as if attempting to escape us, and I would've taken her if not for the interference of an English frigate, much like this one."

Morrow smiled graciously at the Ganymedean. "With all due respect, Captain Jones, I believe it is better to focus on the present and future." Weatherby knew that Jones would not take kindly to being informed that *Daedalus* had indeed fired upon his ship—especially if Jones somehow knew that the engagement had robbed him of the opportunity to capture LeMaire.

"Very well, then," Jones said dismissively. "Where is Dr. Franklin?"

"Right here, Captain," Franklin said from behind Morrow. "And once again, I assure you that I am here of my own free will, and neither harm nor ill-fortune has befallen me."

Jones nonetheless looked put out. "I am quite afraid I do not understand your presence here, sir. And Captain Morrow, since you are outgunned and already have two dozen of my men aboard your ship, I am unsure why there needs be a conference at all."

Morrow refused to take umbrage at Jones' pointed remarks. "Nonetheless, Captain, I would invite you to my cabin to confer with myself and Dr. Franklin. This way, please." Morrow held out his hand toward the great cabin, and Jones marched toward it, acting as if he had already captured the ship.

The three men emerged an hour later, with Morrow looking perturbed,

Franklin looking concerned and Jones smiling ear to ear. He approached the gangplank once more, shook hands with Morrow—who returned the gesture most perfunctorily—and reboarded his own ship.

"Take down the plank and prepare to make sail," Morrow ordered. "We're following *Bonhomme Richard* into Philadelphia. Officers and Dr. Finch to report to my cabin in ten minutes." And with that, Morrow stalked off into his cabin, the door slamming behind him.

Plumb, Weatherby and Foster immediately began issuing orders, and found they had to raise their voices more than usual, as it seemed the men were somewhat dumbfounded at the scene that had just transpired. Nonetheless, they soon had *Daedalus* on the proper course, following the larger Ganymedean vessel—into the very heart of the rebellion itself.

Shortly thereafter in the great cabin, Morrow and Franklin revealed their plan. "Suffice it to say, the situation is quite imperfect and our course embarked upon only under great duress," Morrow began. "However, we are sailing to Ganymede, and into Philadelphia itself, as a captive of the Ganymedeans."

All assembled gasped, even Plumb, but Franklin was quick to follow up. "Now, let me be clear. This is captivity in appearance only, as it seemed the best way to secure Jones' cooperation and allow us to fully engage the resources of my countrymen in our quest."

"But sir," Weatherby said, addressing Morrow, "could we not have simply enjoined Jones not to discuss our presence here, and proceeded to Philadelphia on our own, perhaps in disguise?"

Morrow glared at Weatherby for his lack of decorum, but answered regardless. "That certainly would have been far more preferable, but we are well outgunned and damaged besides. In order to keep this Jones fellow from shooting us out of the Void entirely, we had to effectively surrender the ship. Once he came aboard, Dr. Franklin convinced him of our intent and goals. And yet…" Morrow had to steel himself to continue. "And yet, Captain Jones preferred to escort us into Philadelphia, so as to assure himself of Dr. Franklin's continued safety and security."

The lieutenants, to a man, appeared mortified, whilst Dr. Finch merely smiled. Naturally, Weatherby thought, Finch would enjoy such gamesmanship.

Franklin elaborated on the plan and its foundations: "Captain Jones is ambitious, certainly, and would love nothing more than to have 'captured' an English vessel. Yet if we are to ascertain whether Cagliostro has visited Ganymede, and to garner the help of my countrymen, then we have little alternative other than to follow Jones' demands."

"But no Ganymedean has ever captured an English ship!" Weatherby blurted out. "Surely this cannot be our only avenue!"

Morrow stood up and leaned over his desk, fixing the young man with his most stern and terrifying gaze. "Mr. Weatherby, it is the most expedient avenue that allows us to make progress upon our quest. And I expect you—all of you—to behave accordingly, and urge the men to do the same. I will not repeat this again."

Weatherby's face flushed red as he nodded. "My apologies, sir."

Morrow stared a moment longer before continuing. "We shall be in Philadelphia in three days. At that time, we will present ourselves to the authorities there to discuss the matter of Cagliostro. Once we have completed our inquiries, Dr. Franklin has guaranteed that we shall be free to continue on elsewhere as we see fit. And if that guarantee is not enough to appease his countrymen, then I promise you all we shall earn our freedom by force if need be."

Morrow issued his orders: All weapons were to be stowed and the men cautioned to behave accordingly as they followed the Ganny into the enemy capital. The officers were dismissed, but Morrow had Weatherby tarry behind.

"Sir?" the young man asked nervously, knowing full well what was about to come.

The captain stepped around from his desk and planted himself mere inches from Weatherby's face. "Mr. Weatherby, I fully expect that I shall not have to defend nor reiterate my orders to you ever again," he said.

"Aye, sir," Weatherby responded, his back stiff and eyes fixed on a point just below the captain's eyes.

"I had originally thought to leave you in command of the ship whilst Plumb and I ventured ashore to meet with the Ganymedeans. Yet with your outburst here, I see now you are most unready for such a task. So you will accompany us instead, so that I may keep my eye on you and you may yet prove some worth to me. But I warn you, I will not tolerate anything further from you. Have I made myself clear?"

"Aye, sir." A thin sheen of sweat began to gather on Weatherby's brow.
"Good. Get out."

Weatherby saluted and quickly retreated, only to be met by Lt. Plumb outside the great cabin. "With me," the first lieutenant ordered, and Weatherby dutifully followed him down into the wardroom, where Forester and O'Brian were lounging about whilst off duty. "Get out, you buggers," Plumb snarled. The youngsters needed no further exhortation.

After they clambered out the door, Plumb wheeled on Weatherby and put a massive fist into the younger man's stomach, sending him sprawling into the wall, coughing and clutching his midsection.

"Now you listen to me, you little shite," Plumb hissed. "Captain's too good a man to say it, but you're a prissy little bastard, too full of yourself. Your head's caught between your books and that damned girl we have aboard. If I ever catch you questioning the captain again, I swear I will break every bone in your body. You got that, Tommy boy?"

Weatherby nodded, still sputtering and trying to catch his breath. Before Plumb stalked out, he boxed the young man's ear for good measure, which sent the junior officer to the deck, unconscious once again.

Three days later, marching through the midnight streets of the rebel capital, Weatherby's head was still tender, despite Finch's best efforts. It wasn't the first beating he had endured during his time in the service, but it was perhaps the most effective, given his previous injury from the adventure on the mainsail spar. While Mr. Plumb had found no wrongdoing on the part of any man aboard, Weatherby had chosen not to speak one whit to him nor Morrow since then. Although he continued to question the wisdom of any surrender to these traitors, he kept his opinions well concealed. Or so he hoped.

Yet even while brooding over the intolerable situation, Weatherby found himself surprised at the neat and orderly city before him, for he expected the heart of rebellion against the Crown to be a place of the worst sort. Philadelphia's streets were broad, the buildings almost uniformly brick. There were many parks and open spaces, and a cheerful bustle of late evening activity as the *Daedalus* "captives" made their way toward the Pennsylvania State House, led by a proud John Paul Jones and a cloaked and disguised Benjamin Franklin. The taverns seemed particularly boisterous, and there was a steady stream of people about—even a few free Venusians, it seemed—doing business under Jupiter's unblinking eye. The gas giant was at least ten times larger in the sky than was the Moon as seen from Earth. Next to it, tiny Io was an angry crimson dot, Europa a small white snowball.

It took but ten minutes for the *Daedalans*—Morrow, Anne, Finch and Weatherby—to arrive at the Pennsylvania State House. It struck Weatherby as too small and parochial to be the very epicenter of planetary rebellion, but it did have a certain charm regardless. It was but two stories tall, primarily red brick, with a pitched slate roof and a tall, white wooden bell tower. St. James Palace, it was not.

Once inside the building, Franklin took off his hat and cloak, much to the surprise of those present inside. They were, of course, immediately sworn to secrecy and pressed into service. The word was passed regarding their arrival, and soon Franklin and Jones were invited into one of the hall's main chambers, therein to consult with their conspirators, Weatherby guessed. The *Daedalus* party remained in shackles, under armed guard, in an anteroom. Morrow was silent, and thus they all were.

After this private meeting, which lasted many minutes, the Englishmen were ushered into the room—some kind of parliamentary chamber, though rudimentary at best. There they found Franklin and Jones in the presence of two others, one of whom sat at the room's central desk looking quite dour, and the other, attired as a military commander, who ordered their manacles removed and rose to greet them.

The man behind the desk was John Jay, the current President of the Second Ganymedean Congress and, thus, the political leader of the rebellion against the Crown. The officer identified himself as Major General Benedict Arnold, commander of the Ganymedean forces in the Philadelphia area.

Weatherby forced himself to greet both men cordially, and perhaps succeeded in some small part. Morrow and Finch, of course, were far more gracious, which Weatherby attributed to their more cosmopolitan experiences, and Anne was greeted with naught but kindness. Weatherby would have argued against her accompanying them, but Franklin thought it useful, and the young officer was in no position to argue the point.

President Jay was obviously ill at ease with their presence—or perhaps simply perturbed at being roused in the middle of the night—but Gen. Arnold was genial and accommodating. Weatherby assumed this was professional respect and courtesy when not engaged in conflict, something most officers aspired to, yet few achieved.

"There has been activity here in Philadelphia pertinent to our quest," Franklin said with nothing in the way of preamble. "There has been murder, and theft besides!"

Morrow looked surprised. "But how can we know it is Cagliostro?"

"Who else?" Franklin said. "The goals and the means fit the crime. General, would you be so kind as to give our guests a summation of what has transpired?"

"Of course," Arnold said. "Dr. Franklin told us of the *Chance*, and while no such vessel has made port here, a similar one, calling itself *Liberte*, was here just two days' prior. I remember its name only because of the terrible events discovered in the wake of that ship's rapid departure.

"Our harbormaster reported that *Liberte* had come in from Io, and certainly she smelled most prodigiously of sulfur, I'm told. But the harbormaster was surprised to find very little Ionian sulfur-iron aboard; as you know, there are few exports from that blasted world, and that's one of them. But it's not for us to tell a captain how best to do business, so the ship was allowed to make port.

"Not four hours later, the ship suddenly made sail without warning," Arnold continued. "Again, this would not be taken amiss in most respects, except that shortly thereafter, we discovered a most heinous crime had been committed. As you know, gentlemen, the rare Aquila gemstones can only be found here on Ganymede, and are mined in the western parts of Virginia and Pennsylvania. As our chief port, Philadelphia sees much trade in these valuables.

"As I was saying, a terrible crime was discovered shortly after the ship's departure. Jonathan Wilkes, one of the most prosperous men in the Aquila trade, was discovered dead in his warehouse, with his most recent shipment of gemstones taken. While the latter is a great monetary loss, this murder is far more onerous. I should think that this Cagliostro person may be responsible, if the *Liberte* is indeed your quarry," the general concluded.

Morrow considered this thoughtfully. "This does appear to fit in with the *modus operandi* of our quarry," he said. "Then again, Aquila are quite valuable, are they not? How do we know that this is not simply mere theft, and unrelated to our task at hand?"

Arnold nodded in acknowledgement of Morrow's question. "Method, of course, is everything, Captain. Wilkes kept his stones in perhaps one of the finest iron chests ever wrought, at least to my eyes. It was Ionian steel, thick enough that the chest, no bigger than your sea chests, had to be carried by four men."

"Ah, I see it," Finch said. "You found the chest corrupted and seemingly melted."

Franklin flashed the young alchemist a winning grin. "Well done, Doctor! Cagliostro used a bit of his stolen Mercurium to hasten the corruption and rust of the iron. He must have been at wit's end to use such telling means to open the chest, for it puts us squarely on his trail once more."

"But where does this trail lead?" Jones asked. "Once again, I remain unconvinced. Yes, this Cagliostro is a fiendish sort. But he could be anywhere by now."

"He has been to Io," Franklin said. "And now Ganymede. I suspect he wishes to visit the other two Jovian moons. That leaves Europa…and Callisto."

At this the room hushed a moment. Callisto was the express province of the denizens of Saturn, those enigmatic creatures that called themselves the Xan. Sir Francis Drake was the first to encounter them in his charting of the Jovian system two centuries past, and was told in no uncertain terms that colonization of that world would not be permitted. Since then, embassies and expeditions had been sent regularly by the great powers of Earth, and all were summarily rejected without even being received by the Xan in person.

And of the handful of martial expeditions that were launched, it sufficed to say that the Xan's alchemy and knowledge far outstripped that of humanity, much as humanity's was far superior to that those of the Venusians. The belligerents were never seen again.

"We cannot go to Callisto again, Franklin," President Jay said finally. "Our embassy was rejected just last year. I doubt they shall appreciate another such visit."

"We shall go, then," Morrow said. "England's ties with the Xan are tentative, certainly, but we are an established power amongst mankind."

Jones turned on Morrow. "I am still not quite convinced we should let you go, Captain," the Ganymedean said. "Whatever this rogue has planned, it does not change the state of affairs between England and Ganymede, and you and your men have seen too much of our city already!"

Franklin drew himself to his feet, leaning heavily on his stick. "Captain Jones, we have discussed this. This matter is far more serious than the current conflict! We must be allies in this!"

"Do we indeed?" Arnold said from his seat, leaning back and eyeing the English delegation warily. "With all due respect to our guests, if this Cagliostro fellow is amongst Jupiter's moons, then he is our problem. With your help, Dr. Franklin, I believe this is a matter that the United States can manage on our own."

"And in doing so, we increase our naval power considerably with the capture of an English frigate," Jones added.

Franklin looked aghast, but Weatherby saw the guards in the room had taken a firmer grip upon their weapons. And President Jay, seated behind his desk, began to nod slowly.

For once, even Finch looked upset. A shame, Weatherby thought, that it took rank betrayal to finally perturb him.

July 27, 2132

The rover sped across the Martian plain on what passed for a beautiful morning on the red planet. Shaila was oddly chipper; despite the reactions she got from Yuna and Stephane, she was still convinced that the strange EM boxes were key to solving whatever was going on. Moreover, she was actually out doing something about it instead of sitting on her hands or making the base look pretty.

Of course, she also had to explain to Diaz why the hell she was suddenly so chummy with Evan Greene, especially since she had all but wanted to hide from him the day prior. The colonel approved their EVA, but made it crystal clear to Shaila that while Greene was cleared for the investigation of the lava tube, she was not. Of course, if Diaz knew Shaila was withholding a potentially pertinent clue to this mess—even if no one else thought it was pertinent—she'd be on the next transport back home.

But Shaila was energized now. Her career could very well be ending anyway. Might as well go out with a bang. Besides, she had enjoyed reading the journal the night before, and was eager to see what Greene thought of it. On the one hand, she thought it was stupid to think that the book was related to the EM fields, because it made no sense. But the fact was that she thought she saw it the first time, and then it was there the second. It was beginning to creep her out, no matter how strange and intriguing the book's writing had become.

"Benjamin Franklin? Ganymede? Crazy," Greene mused as he read the transcribed journal from the passenger seat. Shaila had the computer photograph and transcribe each page as she progressed, and downloaded it to Greene's datapad before they left McAuliffe, copying Yuna and Stephane as well. She wanted them to know she was at least doing something.

"Oh, I know," Shaila said over the comm. "A Royal Navy officer's personal log from 1779…in space…with alchemy…and reptile men on Venus. Awesome, in a drug-induced sort of way."

Greene smiled. "Well, I'm no book critic, but I've read better. More importantly, how'd this thing get in that cave?"

"Don't know," Shaila admitted. "It was me, Steve and Kaczynski the first time, and Yuna was down there the second time. Far as I know, that's it."

"Huh. You writing a novel?"

"Oh, no. I'd be horrible. As for anyone else, I don't think Stephane could manage the idioms, and Kaczynski isn't romantic enough. Yuna? Doubt it, plus I think I caught a glimpse of it before she got down there. That means someone put it there, and someone managed to tag it with both Cherenkov radiation and an EM field. Who and why?"

"Good question," Greene said. "I mean, first off, you don't just go and 'tag' something with this kind of radiation, or with an EM field without a discernible source. Pretty interesting, really."

"You're the scientist. I'm sure you'll come up with something," Shaila said. "Any theories on the box we dug up?"

"Yeah, but it's pretty out there," Greene admitted. "When there's nothing in the mainstream that seems to work, you have to go to the fringe."

"Hey, I've got earthquakes on Mars, geographic features shifting all over the place and a big-ass wall building itself in a cave. Go for it," Shaila said.

"Fair enough. Let me tell you about tachyons. A tachyon is a hypothetical subatomic particle that can travel faster than light."

"Except that nothing can travel faster than light," Shaila interrupted.

"Like I said, hypothetical. But quantum physics allows for the possibility that space and time are not universal constants, and thus allows for the possibility of faster-than-light particles."

"So how does a particle get to move that fast?"

"It's a chicken-and-egg thing, really," Greene said. "Do you bend space, and thus seem to bend time as well? Or do you bend time, and thus move through space at a seemingly faster-than-light pace? Or is the distinction moot?"

"I vote moot," Shaila said as she deftly guided the rover around an outcropping of rock. "So are tachyons the cause of this faster-than-light movement?"

"More like a byproduct," Greene said. "The more energy you expend— and you'd have to expend a lot to start warping space-time—the stronger tachyon emissions you'd get. And as you already know, when you have charged subatomic particles moving faster than the ambient light around them, what do you get?"

Shaila grimaced. "Cherenkov radiation. And if you expend energy in those quantities, you're probably going to get some residual EM fields, too."

"Bingo. Well done."

"So what are you saying? That there's some kind of space-time rift going on here?" Shaila asked.

Greene paused and looked hard at Shaila. "Umm, no. Not at all," he said, sounding as if Shaila wasn't taking his findings seriously. "But I imagine that someone might be playing around with a lot of energy. And those boxes generating the directional EM fields could very well be some kind of primitive particle accelerator, designed to speed up particles, smash them into each other and create huge amounts of energy that could theoretically shed tachyons.

"Of course, we can't actually detect tachyons because they're still theoretical," Greene added. "But we can see the Cherenkov radiation. Now, I don't know why this book would have similar readings, but it's a start."

Shaila felt he might be onto something. Smashing up molecules would probably do the trick, energy-wise, especially if you managed to weave it through the Martian terrain. "So what the hell is a homebrew particle accelerator doing on Mars?" Shaila asked.

"Hey, I just came up with the theory. Up to you to prove it," Greene said.

"Well, it's the best explanation I've heard since this whole thing started,"

Shaila said. "Particle colliders can throw off some serious energy. If it's not properly shielded, well, I can imagine it might shake things up around here."

"Yeah, but I ran the numbers. If this thing is a particle accelerator, it's still not powerful enough to cause earthquakes, unless it hit some pretty specific geologic points. My thinking is there's something still missing in the equation."

Shaila glanced at the rover's readout. "Only one way to find out. Coming up on the coordinates now."

A light breeze swept across the Martian plain as Shaila pulled the rover to a stop about ten meters away from the coordinates she got from Harry's suit beacon log. They'd have to do some poking around, because the coordinates were a bit too broad to pinpoint the exact locations, but that's why she brought Greene's once-confiscated holocam with them. They got out of the rover and started surveying the area—Shaila with a sensor pack, Greene with the holocam. Shaila tried to look for signs of Harry's visit, but it had been months ago, and even with Mars' weak atmospheric pressure, the light breezes and subsequent dust devils—a problem for Mars explorers since the first 21st century rovers touched down—would've been more than enough to erase boot and rover tracks.

After a few minutes, they decided to tackle things in a much more methodical manner. They spread out several hundred meters apart, moving in a zigzag pattern toward each other to cover the maximum amount of territory.

"It was easy to find last time," Shaila said about ten minutes later. "What the hell's the problem now?"

"Maybe the boxes were shut down somehow," Greene said, his eyes fixed on his cam screen. "I mean, who knows whether this thing's been on the whole time, or whether we just got lucky?"

"It's out here somewhere," Shaila said. "Keep going. Harry *was* doing something out here."

Another fifteen minutes later, the two met by the rover, having covered 500 square meters of territory without so much as a beep from the sensor or a glitch on the holocam screen. "Maybe we're not going about this the right way," Shaila said. "Let's switch. I'll go back where you came from with the cam, you head to where I started with the sensor."

Greene handed over the cam. "Just don't erase the tape, OK? This could still be big."

Shaila's rejoinder was cut short by a sudden flare on the holocam screen. There was a flash of very familiar static off to her left. "Greene, I got something."

She turned in the direction of the flicker she saw, and was rewarded with a vision of the rover, about four meters away. There was a very thin line of static running under it.

And the line was growing bigger.

And brighter.

And Greene was only a meter or so away from the vehicle.

"Greene, jump away from the rover!"

"What?" he said, turning toward her.

"Jump away from the rover! Now!"

He didn't need further prompting, leaping as far back from the rover as he could—several meters thanks to Mars' gravity—and landing on his side. Shaila saw her holocam's viewscreen turn white, and she could feel it start to vibrate in her hands.

And then it died.

A wisp of smoke curled up out of the camera. She looked up and saw a very similar trail emanating from the rover's electrical motor.

"Greene, report," Shaila said as she leapt toward the rover.

"I'm here," Greene said. "Sensor pack is offline, though."

"Suit check," she said curtly.

"Checking," Greene said as he got to his feet. "All systems normal."

She finished her jump-sprint over to him and nonetheless took a look at his chest and gauntlet monitors. "You're all right. I think we just saw a major EMF spike."

Greene fiddled with the sensor pack once more. "Yeah. Right before the sensor was scrambled, it recorded a large buildup of EM energy. And it was directional."

Shaila looked over his shoulder at the screen. The data showed a linear spike of energy that appeared to travel toward their area...and right under the rover. Then the signal scrambled for several seconds. By the time the sensor's computer righted itself, the energy spike was gone.

"That'd explain the holocam," Shaila said, holding it up. "Fried. Most civilian holocams aren't rad-hard like our suits."

"Yeah, but a sensor pack? The rover?"

Shaila shrugged. "Turns out we parked the bloody rover right over the line. Probably too much for the shielding to handle. And the sensor pack didn't fry. It just got confused for a bit."

Greene holstered the sensor. "Well, we found our EM line. But now we don't have a rover."

Shaila grinned at that. It was well over 25 kilometers to base. "Oh, come on. Lovely day for a walk in the sun."

"Can't we just call and have someone come get us?" Greene said, sounding slightly petulant.

"And explain to Diaz what we were doing out here?" Before Shaila could continue, her comm beeped.

"McAuliffe to Jain, McAuliffe to Jain, priority one, over." She recognized Finelli's accent.

"Shit," Shaila said, keying her comm. "Jain here, McAuliffe, go ahead."

"There's been an accident at Billiton Site Six," Finelli said. "Multiple injuries. Report there immediately to assist. Over."

Shaila looked at Greene with dread. Site Six was an underground mining operation in the foothills—and right on the border of the decagon they had mapped out last night. "Our rover's malfunctioned. We'll have to go by foot. You have rescue teams on the way? Over."

"Yes, ma'am," Finelli said. "Please get there as best you can. McAuliffe out."

Shaila keyed up a map on her datapad. "Six kilometers. Let's get moving. Maybe we can hook up with the rescue team on the access road."

"You think it's related," Greene said. It wasn't a question.

"If it is, I'm going to bring Harry up on charges," she replied, already bouncing across the terrain at full speed.

CHAPTER 14

May 2, 1779

So it was that our gambit failed. I suppose our only fault was in trusting these Ganymedean insurrectionists to keep their word. I admit, I am especially disappointed with Doctor Franklin, of whom I had begun to think better. Of course, we may have underestimated the influence he has upon his fellow traitors.

I am reminded of a tract I saw amongst the crew aboard HMS Egmont not two years ago, where, as you recall, I served as fourth lieutenant. This tract, inexplicably called "Common Sense," was one in which the cause of Ganymedean independence was put forth. The greatest fanfare came in describing the military potential of the colonies. But I say that if Jones and Arnold are the best these rebels can muster, then they are an honourless lot and our victory is all but assured.

And yes, the seaman who had this tract in his possession spent considerable time in the brig.

"Don't you have anything better to do than to write in that blasted diary of yours?" Finch asked, quite perturbed as he saw Weatherby, seated on the floor, scribbling into his journal.

Weatherby looked up at Finch and gave him a small smile. "We have been in here but a half hour, Doctor," Weatherby said. "And I thought we agreed we should allow the guards time to relax before making our move."

The two were inside a painfully small room in the attic of the State House, with Morrow and Anne presumably held elsewhere upon the premises. The scene in the parliamentary chamber had devolved quickly—Jones and Arnold had ordered the *Daedalus* officers taken prisoner—without pretense, this time— while Franklin protested vociferously and the supposed leader of the insurrection, President Jay, said nothing at all, tacitly allowing the Englishmen to be detained.

At first, they could still hear the occasional voice raised in anger below as they waited, but there hadn't been such an outburst in some time. Weatherby had already tested the room's security, such as it was, and knew it was only a matter of time before they could act. There could hear two voices directly outside the door, and Weatherby was hoping he'd hear one of the sentries leave. In the meantime, he had taken to writing once more, while Finch nervously paced about the room.

Some minutes later, during which Weatherby continued writing and Finch continued pacing, they heard a set of footsteps receding across the attic and down the staircase. "It's time, Doctor," Weatherby whispered. "Whenever you're ready."

Finch quickly produced a number of small pouches and vials from about his person, tucked away more than five hours ago at Weatherby's suggestion. "Morrow shall have us in the brig if this does not come off well, you know," Finch said as he began mixing substances. The smell of jasmine and other, less pleasant odors began slipping into the air.

"Fortune favors the bold," Weatherby said. "The Greeks said that, did they not?"

"Romans," Finch corrected with a smirk. "Though I must say, I am continually impressed with your literacy, especially considering your horrible breeding."

"Must do something whilst we wallow in the mud, I suppose," Weatherby said as he rose and slid toward the door, pressing his ear against it before turning back to respond.

Finch finished his working and poured a now-noxious mixture over his hastily doffed neckerchief, while Weatherby secured his pencil and journal on his person. The two approached the door from either side, Weatherby taking the cloth from Finch's hands. "Simply over his face?" he whispered.

Finch nodded and began knocking at the door. "Get me out of here!" Finch bellowed. "I cannot take being in the same room as this loutish peasant any longer!" Weatherby raised an eyebrow at this, while Finch grinned wickedly.

The door opened, and one of the guards entered, musket in hand. "All right now, lads, what's all this?" Weatherby was on him in a flash, placing the cloth over his mouth and holding on as best he could, while Finch grabbed the musket and began wresting it away. The man struggled mightily, his cries muffled by the cloth, until he finally relaxed and, a moment later, went limp.

"How long will this last?" Weatherby asked as he grabbed the musket and returned Finch's neckerchief.

"Fifteen minutes, perhaps," Finch said. "After you, *sir*."

Gripping the musket, Weatherby slowly entered the hallway, edging toward the stairway and stopping in order to listen for anyone coming. Hearing nothing, he made his way to the stairs, Finch in tow, and began descending. He had thought to find where Morrow and Anne were being held, but the resulting scuffle could endanger both unnecessarily, and while the State House was somewhat small for a government building, he did not know it well.

But he knew where he had been. And from the muffled voices floating upward as they descended, Weatherby knew that the Ganymedeans were still debating below. The flickering light from the double doors leading to the parliamentary chamber was further proof—and Weatherby was gratified that those inside no longer felt the need for additional guards.

Weatherby paused a moment to listen. There was Franklin's voice, still outraged. There was Arnold, calm and seemingly reasonable. Jones remained loud and abrasive, while Jay seemed to be growing in both fatigue and impatience. Weatherby pondered a moment whom he'd aim for, but really, there was only one suitable candidate.

"Now, Doctor," he whispered. Finch opened the door.

"Gentlemen!" Weatherby called out, entering the room at a brisk pace, his musket aimed before him. "We've found your hospitality quite wanting!"

Before Arnold or Jones could react, Weatherby strode to the Ganymedean naval captain and placed the barrel of his musket upon the man's chest. "Weapons on the floor, if you please," he said calmly. "The doctor will collect them."

"What are you doing, Weatherby?" Franklin demanded. "I am trying to secure your release!"

"And I thank you, Ambassador, but we've already secured it," Weatherby said, his pounding heart belying the confidence with which he spoke. "No thanks to this man here, who so easily reneged on his word."

Jones' face darkened. "Do not test me, boy," Jones snarled. "I'll have you hang for this."

"Then you compound your own dishonor, sir," Weatherby replied. He saw Finch had secured everyone's weapons, and was aiming a pistol at Arnold.

"What is it you want?" Jay asked from behind his desk.

"Nothing more than to resume our negotiations in a far more equitable manner," Weatherby said. "And for that, I would ask that Captain Morrow and Miss Baker be brought here forthwith."

Jay looked to the lone sentry and nodded, and the man—a boy, really, no older than fifteen—quickly left the room. Weatherby assumed he would return not only with Morrow and Anne, but with pistols to their captives' heads and reinforcements as well.

"Mister…Weatherby, is it?" Arnold said. "You must understand, our two nations are at war. And we must look to our own affairs. Having you here presents both problems and opportunities that we cannot fail to address."

Weatherby nodded. "I can appreciate the strategic issues, General. However, the promise of safe conduct we were given has not been upheld. And no matter the conflict between us, I find that utterly inexcusable, as does the good ambassador, I'm sure."

Weatherby looked over at Franklin for support, but the old alchemist merely frowned. "You should have let me argue for you," Franklin scolded as Morrow and Anne entered the room.

"Mr. Weatherby," the captain said in a tone of voice quite calm considering the circumstances. "Report, if you please."

"Securing our release, sir," Weatherby replied. "Yourself and Miss Baker are well?"

"We're fine, Tom," Anne said cautiously. "But the guard has raised the alarm. Whatever you're doing, time isn't with us."

Jay smiled grimly. "So you plan to negotiate at musket-point, boy, with half the Ganymedean army aimed at you? Perhaps try to bring us back to London for trial? Or will you fire and decapitate the rebellion against the Crown right here and now?"

Weatherby, for his part, had anticipated this argument and had mentally dismissed it whilst still captive. And yet…here he was, with the leadership of the Ganymedean rebellion literally within his sights. What a demoralizing blow it would be to haul this "president" back to England for trial!

He looked to Morrow, who eyed Weatherby with an inscrutable gaze. Perhaps he was making the same calculation. Perhaps not. But he hadn't issued any orders, either.

Weatherby breathed deeply, trying to clear his head. Things were so much simpler when the enemy was easily identified, and the battle lines drawn cleanly. Would a victory against the rebellion here create opportunity for something far worse to occur?

"Tom," Anne said, her distress mounting. "They're coming. Do it quickly!"

Weatherby's finger tensed on the trigger...and then relaxed. Ultimately, he had given his word. Unlike Jones, Weatherby aimed to keep his.

"You're absolutely right, Mr. Jay. I cannot negotiate in such a manner," the young lieutenant said. He lowered his musket and placed it upon the table next to Jones. Finch likewise lowered his pistol.

Morrow smiled, any doubt about Weatherby's gambit erased. "Gentlemen, never let it be said that officers of His Majesty's Navy are without honor or decency. Now, then—I believe we should address the matter at hand with some alacrity, before the sun rises and all of Philadelphia sees our ships upon the river."

The ensuing negotiations went surprisingly well, Weatherby thought, especially given the presence of some forty armed men now outside the building. His actions seemed to have a profound impact on Gen. Arnold, who abandoned Jones' ploy and agreed to allow the *Daedalus* safe passage out of Philadelphia. President Jay likewise agreed to let the matter pass, in a kind of *status quo ante*. Jones, however, remained completely pig-headed— so much so that Jay himself, as head-of-state, had to order the Ganymedean captain to remain in port for 48 hours.

Minutes later, the *Daedalus* officers, accompanied by Anne and Dr. Franklin, quickly dashed through the Philadelphia night en route to their boat. "I do apologize, Captain Morrow," Franklin huffed quietly as they walked. "I knew Jones was ambitious, but I did not think him blinded by it."

Morrow gave a rare smile. "Too many officers are," he said. "It takes a brave man to capture a ship, but a braver man still to give up glory for the greater good. I hold no ill will against you, sir. We have more information, and have made good our escape. That is better than I had hoped for but an hour ago."

The captain then turned to Weatherby, who was assisting Anne over the rough-hewn cobblestones. "And Mr. Weatherby, I confess I am unsure as to whether I should commend you for your initiative or reprimand you for taking an unnecessary risk."

Weatherby's stomach turned. "I'm sorry, sir. I thought it best to be prepared for any eventuality. Thus, I asked Dr. Finch to bring with him some admixtures that might effect an escape, if need be."

They reached the boat, moored to one of the smaller quays, and started helping Franklin and Anne aboard. "A wise course, Mr. Weatherby. But I would appreciate it if you would be so kind as to apprise me of your contingencies next time."

Weatherby looked directly at the captain, preparing to own up to whatever punishment Morrow would issue. Yet he was surprised to find Morrow wearing a small grin.

"Aye, sir," said Weatherby, unsure as to the best response.

"And me as well, Lieutenant," Anne said, smiling broadly at him. "I've a strong constitution, but I very nearly fainted in there!" Weatherby laughed at this, as the thought of anything rattling her to that degree was nothing short of comical.

With Weatherby and Finch on the oars, the boat quickly arrived at *Daedalus*, whereupon the officers and alchemists—Anne among the latter—gathered in the great cabin to discuss their next move while the crew prepared to make sail.

"Divining the alchemical essences of the Known Worlds has long been a goal of modern alchemy," Franklin said as he sipped a glass of port to fortify himself at this late hour. "I often wondered whether the Aquila stone might be such an essence, or if the essence of Ganymede could be distilled from it. It is exceedingly rare. You could dig through thousands of pounds of coal before finding even the tiniest of these stones. I have no doubt that Cagliostro feels as though this stone is critical to whatever working he has planned."

"And if it is," Finch asked, "to what end would it serve? I do not even know what the alchemical essence of Ganymede would even represent."

"True," Franklin allowed. "I would imagine it could represent the great mineral and agricultural wealth of our world, and as such, could play a role in workings having to do with soil, farming, growth and perhaps even money. However, more importantly, we must bear something else in mind that occurred to me back in the State House. Cagliostro has been to Io! That is the the foremost piece of this puzzle!"

Franklin looked expectantly at the others, but was greeted with naught but fatigue and confusion. "Meaning what?" Morrow snapped.

"I'm sorry, Sir William, I do get carried away on these matters!" Franklin said. "But it is a fact that obtaining the alchemical essence of Jupiter itself is no small task. Even gaining samples of Mighty Jove's winds is difficult in the extreme. But what if…what if you had the alchemical essences of the four main moons of Jupiter? One, perhaps, for each element?"

Anne suddenly sat up stock-straight. "My God, it could work!" She looked from Franklin's smiling face to Finch, who also expressed surprise and recognition.

Morrow, however, was less impressed. "Really, would you learned alchemists mind telling we simple sailors what's going on?"

"Sorry, sir," Finch said. "Alchemy, as Dr. Franklin has noted, is based on the premise of essences, but it is also based on the notion of *sympathy*, wherein a composite of various elements can stand in for greater truths and essences. In many ancient workings, the four primary elements—air, earth, water and fire—can be combined to create the fifth element, the *quintessence*. Now, if you took that theorem and applied it to Jupiter, you could very well recreate the quintessence of the entire Jovian system through its four primary moons."

"Yes, I see it now," Anne said. "Europa would, of course, represent water. Io is fire. Ganymede, given the gemstones, would be earth. And that leaves Callisto representing air."

"Exactly!" Franklin said. "And, of course, that means Cagliostro will indeed be heading to Callisto. Whether or not he stops at Europa first is immaterial. We shall meet him there, I have no doubt, so it is to Callisto we must go."

"And what if the Xan object to our presence?" Weatherby asked.

Morrow leaned back in his chair as he spoke, looking tired. "According to reports given to the Admiralty, most ships are met by one of their vessels and politely asked to remove themselves from the moon. It is only when a ship is seen a second time that more…permanent…measures appear to be taken. Thus, we can at least be assured of one chance at contact, and we must hope that an embassage from both His Majesty and neighboring Ganymede will be sufficiently impressive to allow us entry."

Despite these words, Weatherby thought he saw a glimmer of doubt in his captain's eyes.

July 27, 2132

Mining on Mars was an exercise in very simple economics, with few of the mitigating factors that mining elsewhere entailed. Aside from a bare handful of "Martian environmentalists" who held out hope for life on the red planet, most people didn't care what Billiton Minmetals did. Indeed, there was more backlash on lunar extraction than Martian exploitation. Nobody wanted to look up into the night sky and see the Man in the Moon marred by strip mining.

So when Billiton mined the Martian ice cap for deuterium, whole blocks of ice were lasered away for processing. Strip mining and open-pit mining for other minerals became quite common. Over the years, the landscape around McAuliffe Base became littered with debris from recovery and smelting operations.

Yet some minerals were too deep for these more intrusive measures, and the palladium and titanium found at Billiton Operations Site Six were among them. So as mankind had done for centuries, the miners there dug tunnels and shafts, working in near darkness kilometers below the surface.

To be fair, most of the work was done by machine, and there were only a handful of people at Site Six to program the remote laser drills that did most of the heavy work in the dozen or so shafts and tunnels in the mine. These finely tuned lasers would bore into the walls, vaporizing the bedrock and leaving the valuable ores mostly unspoiled. These would then be scooped up and sent via robotic mine cars to the site's main chamber.

Jack Heath was one of these new generations of miners, more comfortable with a computer than a pick—though he was quite ready to have a go with the pick as well. Jack grew up poor in west Texas, served four years in the U.S. Army, then quit college two years in after his parents died. Feeling adrift, he answered a Billiton job posting. Three years later, the simple guy who hadn't left Texas until joining the Army was drilling on Mars. He had a girlfriend and marriage plans.

But today his mind was on the drill in shaft seven. It was acting up, and he had traveled down the tunnel to figure out what happened to it. He didn't come back alive.

Ed Kaczynski grimly told anyone who would listen about Jack's short life as a pair of JSC astronauts pulled his body out of the rubble and into the main chamber. The reinforced pressure suit that saved him from instant death under the falling rocks ultimately failed him with a small leak. It had taken a half hour for rescuers to reach him—still a pretty impressive response given the distance from McAuliffe and the volume of rock that had to be vaporized in order to reach him.

But Jack Heath was cold, the liquid in his body half evaporated, by the time they found him. Shaila looked down at the desiccated body and remembered his smiling face—he grinned in a very American, cowboy way, she thought. He had a penchant for really bad action holos, she remembered, and was a big fan of the violent curiosity that was American football.

At least there was only one death to contend with. The collapse around the mining site was fairly impressive, with several tunnels and shafts irreparably damaged, and millions of terras in equipment lost. A few other Billiton folks suffered minor injuries—broken bones, concussions and a few depressurizations that were caught in time. Shaila, who linked up with the rescue team on the access road with Greene in tow, did her best to coordinate the response, but there was little she could add at the moment—except for one thing.

"Jain to McAuliffe, where's Harry Yu?"

"McAuliffe to Jain, we don't know," Finelli responded. "Assume he's en route to your position."

"Check the suit beacon log," Shaila ordered.

A few moments passed before Finelli came back on. "He was at your location about an hour ago, but that's the last we have from him. Must be some sort of beacon malfunction. We will look for him here and have him contact you."

"Screw that," Shaila said. "I want him detained. Find him and confine him to quarters. Jain out."

Another voice came over her comm. "That seems a bit much, don't you think?"

Shaila looked around and saw Yuna approaching the rescue team, her face drawn and haggard. "Not at all. He's responsible for this," Shaila said.

"This what, exactly?" Yuna asked, that maddening, maternal look of concern back on her face. "I don't follow."

Shaila and Greene filled her in on their search for the boxes, and the huge energy spike that fried their rover's engine. "The linear EM field's we've theorized would cross right through this site," Greene said in conclusion, showing Yuna the map Shaila had drawn up the night before.

"Did you find the box there?" Yuna asked.

"No," Shaila frowned. "Soon as the spike came through, the shit hit the fan here and we hopped over to help."

Yuna shook her head sadly. "It's still all very circumstantial, Shaila. I know Harry can be a handful, but I'm not sure that he would be responsible for this. Even if the boxes were some kind of experiment, who's to say the energy spike you saw triggered all this?" Yuna seemed quite upset by what had happened—understandable, Shaila thought, since she had probably gotten to know a lot of the miners during her years on Mars.

Shaila looked around at the main chamber. Levin was doing medical checks on a number of miners, while her ops team was busy patching suits and getting people out of there and back to base. "There's never been a collapse before, Yuna," Shaila said. "Why would there be one now?"

Yuna pointed toward shaft seven. "Ask Stephane." The Frenchman was coming out of the tunnel with Harry Yu's mining chief. Both of them looked shaken.

"Once again, I cannot explain this," Stephane told them a few moments later. "The shafts were very well made. And of course, there is no seismic activity here. So I cannot say why we would see a collapse, except for the fact that there may be some sort of energy involved. Look here." Stephane pulled out his datapad and pointed to a map of Site Six. "There are collapses here, here and here," he said, pointing to three areas on the map. "They are in an almost exact straight line from one another."

Shaila looked over at Yuna with satisfaction. "And that's the line on the map, Yuna."

The older woman shook her head, looking even more distraught. "This has to be some kind of mistake. I can't imagine what would even cause this."

"Well, we're going to find out," Shaila said, spotting a new group of Billiton workers entering the main chamber. She could see Harry Yu's face among them and immediately hopped over to him.

"What the hell happened here, Jain?" Harry said. His usual put-upon look was gone; concern and worry lined his face. "I heard one of my guys is dead?"

"Yeah, that's right. Jack Heath," she said, spitting the words at him.

Harry looked taken aback. "Oh, my God." He turned to look at Stephane, who came up behind Shaila. "Durand, what happened?"

Shaila cut the planetologist off with a wave of her hand. "You know damn well, Harry. Where you been this morning?"

"What do you mean, where have I been?" Harry said. "I was doing paperwork on base when one of my ops sites collapsed!"

"Wrong answer." She pointed at Harry's chest. "Where's your suit beacon?"

The mining executive looked down, but couldn't see his chest through the bulky suit, and instead used his hands to feel around. "What the hell?" he muttered.

Shaila, meanwhile, flagged Adams, who had accompanied the rescue team. "Lt. Adams, escort Mr. Yu back to base and confine him to quarters. The colonel and I will have a chat with him when I get back."

"You have got to be kidding me!" Harry shouted. "I've got a crisis here!"

"Save it," Shaila said. "You've done enough today. Adams, get him out of here."

The young lieutenant approached Harry, taking him by the arm and pulling him back toward the entrance of the mine. Harry staggered along with him, looking back at Shaila with anger and confusion.

Shaila watched him go with a satisfied smirk. Bastard.

Greene sidled up next to her and pressed a comm button on her gauntlet, switching her to a private channel. "You know you're pushing it here, Lieutenant," he said.

She wheeled on him, but the look of concern on his face sapped her anger almost immediately. "You saw the logs. You know he was out there, he and his people. They put this EM ring out there."

"The correlation's weak," Greene countered gently. "On the face of it, there still isn't enough energy to prompt a collapse, either here or at the lava tube."

Shaila frowned. "Then we'll find wherever that extra energy is coming from. And I'll bet Harry knows." She was about to elaborate when she felt a tap on her shoulder. She turned to see Stephane, tapping his helmet. She quickly switched channels. "Yeah, Steve."

He simply held up his sensor pack. There were trace readings of Cherenkov radiation and ambient EM fields. "It is here, too."

Shaila nodded and patted him on the shoulder, then—with a wicked grin toward Greene—went back to finish coordinating the rescue team. Whatever was going on, Harry Yu was going to pay for it big time.

CHAPTER 15

May 4, 1779

*F*ather,

    Having been upon the seas of Callisto for but a day, I may say with certainty that I know why the Xan have kept this world, above all others, for themselves, as it is nothing short of a Paradise.

I have sailed many seas, but never have I seen such crystal clear oceans, nor have I felt such sweet, steady breezes. The lands we have seen thus far are unspoiled, verdant and lush—and seemingly untouched by the hands of either man or Xan. The seas teem with life, but we dare not take harvest of the strange fish or turtle-like creatures we have seen, for we know not if this would upset the denizens of this world, or even sicken us should we try to eat them. I personally had to remind Dr. Finch—twice—to refrain from disturbing these animals. He has finally satisfied himself with scribbling madly in one of his journals and frequently consulting Dr. Franklin about this particular sea creature, or that singular tree spotted upon the shore. The rest of us go about our duties as best we can, trying to keep from becoming distracted by the new world around us....

"And that is how you mark noon on Callisto," Weatherby said to the gathered midshipmen, pointing to his sextant. "You must always remember to account for your path 'round Jupiter, as well as the position of the Sun, when marking noon here. Understood?"

The mids nodded, though really only O'Brian seemed to grasp the concept clearly. Forester would likely catch up later, when reviewing his navigation book, as he always did, and Anne, still attending the classes regularly, would likely master this concept as she did all others. The other three mids, ranging in ages from twelve to twenty, seemed quite lost, and Weatherby would not be surprised if they needed to review a text whilst buckling their shoes.

Then again, Weatherby had to look up the procedure himself, so rare was keel-fall on the Xan's Jovian colony moon.

Finch gave a yawn as the mids fiddled with their sextants. Weatherby could sympathize, to a degree—the calculations involved in navigation, while complex, were likely child's play to any alchemist worth his salt. Furthermore, the doctor's interests lay more with the planet itself, and the Xan in particular. Those enigmatic aliens also concerned Weatherby, which is why he had the doctor attend the mids' class, despite the rote repetition of basic mathematics.

"And now, let's pay attention to Dr. Finch," Weatherby said with a small smile. "Doctor, if you would, please tell us what you might know about Callisto and the Xan."

Looking as if he were just awakened from a nap, Finch scowled at Weatherby but nonetheless rose from his seat to take Weatherby's place at the mizzenmast. "Best to keep it simple," Weatherby whispered as they passed. Finch's scowl simply grew deeper, but he at least made a go of it.

"Very well then, Mr. Weatherby. Callisto and the Xan," Finch cleared his throat. "Now, we English discovered the Xan here on Callisto back in 1578, thanks to Sir Francis Drake. There had been landings before, it seemed, by the Spanish, and Drake had been issued a letter of marque by Queen Elizabeth to pursue them amongst the Known Worlds. For whatever reason, the Spanish either never encountered the Xan, never made such an encounter public, or the Xan dispatched them forthwith once they arrived here. So it is Drake who is credited with making peaceful contact with them—at the very same port we now sail for, I should add. Of course, it's the only port we've ever been able to find here.

"Of that first encounter, we gleaned little, and have gleaned little more since," Finch said. "Drake saw a single Xan here on Callisto, and this worthy was said to be exceptionally tall, some say ten feet or more, but completely obscured by heavy robes. Subsequent encounters have all failed to produce even this sighting, as the Xan now opt for complete secrecy, speaking only through melodic voices that cannot be pinpointed to any source—a marvel in and of itself.

"While here, Drake was told that Saturn, not Callisto, was the homeworld of the Xan, and that they lived within cities upon the very rings of that planet. A few intrepid astronomers on Ganymede have claimed to make out these cities when viewing Saturn, but none have submitted enough proof to the Royal Academy to substantiate the assertions," Finch said. He paused to catch his breath, only to see Captain Morrow and Anne, along with Weatherby, listening intently.

Slightly unnerved at his larger audience, Finch continued: "Drake was told that Callisto was something of a retreat for the Xan, used for some kind of philosophical or religious purpose, it is hard to say. What's certain is that Drake was given something of an ultimatum. The Xan claimed Callisto for their own, and Saturn and any worlds beyond as well. Visitors from Earth would not be allowed, as these worthies required their privacy—for what reasons we do not know. Drake agreed to their demands, which was seen as particularly odd, since Drake had quite a fearsome reputation as a privateer. Some believe the Xan had made a display of their greater alchemical insights, or advanced technology, which had frightened Drake so that he immediately set course for Earth once more.

"And that is where things stand today, in brief," Finch concluded. "The Xan politely turn away visitors to Callisto and, should the visitors fail to depart or become belligerent, they are never seen nor heard from again. And on the few occasions that some brave or foolhardy souls have set course beyond the path of Jupiter, they either encountered severe Void storms and were forced to turn back, or they were likewise never found."

One of the older mids, well into his teens, raised his hand. "What about the stories of men on Callisto, Doctor? I hear there's a whole tribe of primitives here that we've never seen!"

Finch smiled. "If we've not seen them, how do we know they're here, Mr. Buckland?" Finch allowed the youngster to look confused and embarrassed for a moment before relenting. "I do not know where the rumor has come from, but yes, there has been much conjecture regarding men on Callisto. Some say they are pets of the Xan, kidnapped from Earth long ago. Others say they are the Lost Tribe of Israel, or refugees from Atlantis itself. All of these seem rather unlikely, but with our access to the planet severely curtailed, I fear the answers shall not be forthcoming."

Young O'Brian was next. "What do you think will occur here, Doctor? I mean, with us here and all."

Finch looked uncomfortably at the captain and Weatherby before continuing. "Speaking only for myself, of course, I would say we shall make our inquiries here, learn very little, and then be asked to leave. And leave we should, most expeditiously, as I'm sure none of us wish to disappear from the Known Worlds forever. But divining the will of the Xan is difficult to say the least, and furthermore, our course of action, naturally, is in the hands of our wise captain."

Weatherby saw Morrow arch an eyebrow at this, and seemed to want to comment, but he was interrupted before he could. "Sighting!" came a voice from the tops. "Three points off to larboard!"

"Sighting of what, exactly?" Morrow muttered as he and Weatherby immediately went for their glasses, peering off the left-hand rail of the quarterdeck. What they saw surprised and amazed them both.

Several miles off was a silver, ovoid-shaped craft, sitting upright upon the waves, with a number of odd bulges upon it and several spindly protuberances around the base. While without visible sails, the ship was moving at a high speed toward the *Daedalus* and leaving no wake behind—as if it were above the planet's gentle waves, not upon them.

Morrow dropped his glass a moment. "Mr. Weatherby, have the men proceed quietly to their stations, but do not beat to quarters. We must not make a show of aggression. And please ask Ambassador Franklin to join me on the quarterdeck at his soonest convenience."

Weatherby wheeled toward his class and repeated the order, propelling the junior officers into motion and having O'Brian summon Foster and Plumb to the quarterdeck. He then went below decks to the midshipmen's quarters, where he found Franklin perusing an old book on Callisto and making notes. "Ambassador, Captain Morrow requests your presence on the quarterdeck at your earliest convenience. We've sighted what appears to be a Xan ship."

Franklin's face immediately turned bright with delight. "We have, indeed! What wonderful news!" The old man grabbed his stick and rose with surprising alacrity. "Lead the way, my boy! I would never have thought I'd live to see one! Did you know they actually may bear some resemblance to conveyances described in ancient Indian texts?"

Weatherby could not help but smirk at this. "Dr. Franklin, I'm sure I've never even seen an ancient Indian text. This way, if you please."

Franklin followed Weatherby through the gun deck as the men quietly took their stations. If Franklin was alarmed by the potential aggression involved, he did not show it, instead continuing his discourse. "Well, Mr. Weatherby, the Hindus have their Vedas, rather like our Bible, and these describe—in great detail, mind you!—the chariots of their gods. And the few sightings we have of Xan ships through the years seem to mirror these descriptions! Isn't that remarkable?"

"Quite so, sir," Weatherby said neutrally as he aided the portly ambassador up the stairs toward the main deck.

The young man's lack of enthusiasm did not go unnoted. "I know the subject is perhaps dry, Mr. Weatherby," Franklin said, pausing to mount the last few stairs, his energy finally outstripped by his enthusiasm. "But I wager we may know much more about these Xan people than we even realize!"

Weatherby aided the ambassador up the few remaining steps to the quarterdeck, whereupon Morrow ordered him to remain there on his glass, and to report all he saw while the captain and Franklin discussed how best to truck with the mysterious, Saturnine aliens. Weatherby was quite surprised to see that, in the few minutes it had taken to dispatch the mids and fetch Franklin, the Xan egg-ship had neatly come up alongside the *Daedalus*, perhaps only two hundred yards off to larboard.

Morrow and Franklin consulted in quiet tones, but were quickly interrupted by a voice coming, as Finch had forewarned, seemingly out of nowhere. "Vessel of Earth," said the voice, loud enough to overcome most conversation yet surprisingly even-toned, with traces of harmonics laced through the words. "We request you state your purpose for visiting Callisto."

Morrow turned to Franklin, who shrugged slightly and smiled. "I've often held honesty to be the best policy," the ambassador said. "I suggest we state plainly that we are in pursuit of a criminal who may have come here to disturb them."

The captain nodded and lifted his speaking horn, but the voice responded before he could even speak. "We know of no criminal that would come to disturb us, Dr. Benjamin Franklin," the voice responded. "Though we are flattered that a man with your reputation would visit us, we must respectfully ask that you turn about and depart our world."

Surprised, Franklin started to reply but was cut off by a gesture from Morrow, who spoke in his stead. "To whomever I have the pleasure of addressing, I am Captain Sir William Morrow of His Britannic Majesty's Ship *Daedalus*. I have come with the full cooperation of Dr. Franklin and his Ganymedean brethren on a mission that concerns us all—including the Xan, if I may be so bold. Several humans and Venusians have been murdered, and several planetary alchemical essences may have been stolen. We feel compelled to apprise you of the situation, and to perhaps seek your aid in resolving it."

There was naught but silence from the Xan at this. Indeed, as the silence dragged on, the officers and guests on board began exchanging worried looks, whispering among themselves. The Xan vessel itself did not seem to move at all, but nonetheless easily kept pace with *Daedalus,* which continued to sail at a respectable seven knots toward the Xan port. At least, Weatherby thought, they were still alive and intact. Morrow eventually had the lieutenants inspect the men—and assuage any of their fears—while consulting with Franklin and Finch regarding the Xan vessel. Anne joined them, and was busy making notes and sketches in a notebook as they all talked.

Weatherby was below decks, quietly upbraiding one of the men for a misplaced powder charge, when the Xan response came, more than an hour after they had last heard any word. "Vessel of Earth called *Daedalus*," said the voice, which seemed as clear on the gun deck as it was above. "We will allow you to make port. Please follow our conveyance to our city and come alongside the southernmost dock. You will receive further instructions there. Do not deviate from your course and speed."

Immediately, smiles and sighs broke out from amongst the men on the gun deck, and Weatherby realized just how much tension had built up amongst the crew. He himself smiled back, giving a few of the senior men a nod. "Seems as though they know proper Englishmen when they see them," Weatherby said to Smythe, who nodded and saluted. The lieutenant then raised his voice a bit more. "Remain at your stations, men, but do not act rashly or aggressively. Let us not unduly frighten our genial hosts!"

A light chorus of laughter followed Weatherby up the stairs toward the main deck, and his confidence grew with his men's approval. Yet his good mood evaporated somewhat when he saw the port that the voice had spoken of. Quickly, he pulled out his glass and ran forward, resting his arm along the railing as he peered off toward the Xan settlement.

The *Daedalus* had been told to come alongside the southernmost dock—because there was another vessel at the northern one. An Earth vessel. They were too far off to make her name, but she appeared to be a three-masted ship with elegant lines and numerous guns—and a flutter of red off a banner at her stern.

Weatherby snapped his glass shut and ran for the quarterdeck, where he found Plumb and Morrow peering through there glasses as well. Morrow, however, saw him coming. "Report, Mr. Weatherby."

The young man caught his breath. "It's the *Chance*," Weatherby said, "I'd swear it."

Morrow nodded, snapping his own glass shut. "Very well, then. Commence docking procedures. Ensure the men remain at quarters, but for God's sake, ensure they do not take any rash measures now!"

So it was that, a half hour later, HMS *Daedalus* sat moored to a dock on the moon Callisto, with a known pirate vessel less than a mile away—the very same ship they had been searching for since Mercury. It was nothing short of galling.

"Naturally, we have found our quarry in the one place we cannot easily take them," Morrow groused from the quarterdeck, where the ship's officers and guests had convened for no particular reason other than to curse their misfortune.

Franklin nodded in agreement, but looked concerned regardless. "I cannot urge you strongly enough not to engage this enemy here," he said. "We know not how the Xan will take it, and they certainly may have the scientific and alchemical means to eradicate us should we try."

"Yes, yes, I know, Doctor," Morrow said. "Yet inaction does not sit well with me here." He turned to his first lieutenant. "Mr. Plumb, you are in command. By no means will you move this ship or open fire unless you are fired upon first. And even then, you must resist provocation until such time as you feel the ship is truly imperiled. Should the Xan or any of their agents wish to board, they may do so, and you will treat them as guests. Am I understood?"

Plumb looked unimpressed, but responded nonetheless. "Aye, sir."

Morrow turned to Weatherby and Finch. "Finch, you're with me. Weatherby, please assist the ambassador and Miss Baker to the gangplank. We shall disembark and proceed to the end of the dock, where we will wait for whatever the Xan opt to do next."

There was no real need to assist them, of course; all parties in question were above decks and eagerly awaiting something to do. The prospect of laying eyes on the mysterious Xan—on the very shores of Callisto!—was too tempting. For a moment, Weatherby worried that he would be omitted from the gathering, but Morrow gathered him in with a gesture as he walked down the gangplank, and Weatherby could not stifle a smile. It seemed his gambit in Philadelphia had helped overcome his earlier indiscretions.

"If it's to be diplomacy," Morrow said quietly to Franklin as they strode toward the end of the pier, "I dare say I shall lean upon you heavily, Ambassador. I doubt I can rely on Mr. Weatherby's gunpoint negotiations here."

Franklin gave the captain a small smile. "I shall do all I can, of course. But I fear that if Cagliostro is already here, and our story heard second, we are at a disadvantage. I can vouch for his ability to be most charming."

The group proceeded to the very end of the dock—a stone dock, but one without seam or masonry—and stopped before a sandy beach of the purest white. There were none of the typical port facilities anyone could see. Instead, there was a pathway made of some kind of hard surface leading from the dock toward the lush tropical forest behind the beach and, finally, to a pair of massive doors in what appeared to be a city wall, some two hundred feet along. The wall itself blended in so perfectly with the foliage that Weatherby could not be sure how far it extended. Beyond that, a handful of spires and domes protruded from the verdant canopy. These looked well maintained, and bore some small resemblance to pictures Weatherby had seen of both India and Japan, while mimicking neither.

Once the group reached the end of the dock, the doors opened, and a pair of human men walked through them, starting to make their way toward the *Chance*. They were unaccompanied, and did not once look back at whatever wonders the Xan city may have held for them. Both were dressed quite finely, one as garish as the other was understated.

Recognition dawned upon Weatherby almost immediately. "Captain, I saw that man on the beach on Venus. I dare say it is LeMaire!" he whispered.

"More than that," Franklin added. "Unless my eyes deceive me, the other is Cagliostro."

Weatherby's hand moved toward his sword as the better-dressed man stopped, looked at their party, and began to walk toward them. Morrow motioned for the group to stay and wait. "Do not make a show of force," the captain ordered. "I have no doubt we are being observed, by whatever means."

The young lieutenant took a hard look at the gentleman as he approached. He was of middle age, dressed in fine clothing and a perfectly powdered wig. He had heavy eyebrows and a pronounced nose, and while he walked with alacrity, he appeared quite well fed. His full lips bore a smile that hinted at both seeming friendliness and a certain foreknowledge.

Finally, the man stopped about ten feet away and bowed deeply to them. "How refreshing to find some of my fellow men on Callisto," he said by way of greeting, speaking perfect English with a slight Italian accent. "I would not have expected it, given the Xan's reputation for isolation."

Franklin was the first to speak. "I think we may dispense with the pleasantries, Cagliostro. Surely you remember me, do you not?"

The man squinted at Franklin a moment before breaking into a wide smile. "Of course! The esteemed Dr. Benjamin Franklin! I trust you are well? How is your gout?"

Franklin practically sputtered out his reply, his face turning red. "You fool! We know what you have been doing! What is it that you have planned?"

Cagliostro turned toward the city gate, an eyebrow raised. "I have no idea what you mean. I have been simply visiting the Xan as part of a Grand Tour of the Known Worlds. My reputation as an alchemist must have preceded me, for I found them to be most gracious."

At this, Morrow spoke, his words hard as flint. "Sir, your ship was spotted at Elizabeth Mercuris, and on Venus, where terrible crimes have been committed. You are also implicated in crimes upon Ganymede as well. I command you to surrender to us to answer for these."

The alchemist was undaunted, and indeed made a good showing of surprise in his response. "Surely there has been some grievous error, my good sir. As I have said, I am merely taking my tour, nothing more. The good creatures here may tell you that I've done nothing amiss on Callisto whatsoever. And if you seek to implicate me in some manner of criminality, I must ask what proof you have."

Anne, who had been somewhat obscured behind both Franklin and Morrow, shouldered her way in between them. "I have seen you with my own eyes!" she said, her face a mask of fury. "You murdered Roger McDonnell and took his Mercurium. I even let you into his house!"

If Cagliostro was taken aback at the sight of the girl, he refused to show it. "Really, now, miss. I must protest. Yes, I did indeed visit the esteemed Dr. McDonnell, and I vaguely recall you might have answered the door." He paused and smiled. "In fact, I do remember you being in something of a state at the time, were you not?"

Anne's face turned a bright red, and she looked upon the verge of tears. "I heard the struggle. I heard him die! Murderer!"

"Murder?" Cagliostro said, sounding shocked, though Weatherby swore his face did not show it well enough. "Don't be silly, girl! We argued, and I left, and that is the end of it!"

"And what of Venus, sir?" Morrow demanded, stepping in front of the distraught woman. "That ship there was seen escaping the site of a massacre of an entire tribe of Venusians!"

Cagliostro turned to regard the *Chance*, and Weatherby could see several men from that ship approaching across the beach, looking ill-intentioned and well armed. "I admit, my choice of conveyance for my travels is perhaps not the best, but if that vessel is implicated in any such incident, it was not of my doing."

Weatherby had quite enough. "You, sir, are a liar, thief and murderer!" he stated firmly. "Come with us peaceably, or we shall take you by force!"

Cagliostro actually smiled as Morrow placed a warning hand on Weatherby's shoulder. "Truly, young man, force would be unwise. The Xan do not take conflict lightly," the alchemist said, turning once again to see his shipmates now well at hand. "Indeed, should you try to apprehend me, and my friends here intervene, well...I dare say the Xan would likely do away with us both quite thoroughly.

"And besides," the alchemist continued, turning toward Morrow and Franklin, "will you take the word of a whore against mine own?" Cagliostro fixed Anne with a hard stare. "I'm sure you do not wish me to explain the exact state in which I found you that evening, do you? Or the circumstances from which Roger McDonnell rescued you?"

Weatherby nearly drew his sword at this, but Finch and Morrow grabbed his arms in time. "Easy, Tom," Finch whispered. "Not here."

Anne, however, was not so restrained. She hastened up behind Morrow and all too quickly slid his sword from its scabbard. In an instant, its point was at Cagliostro's throat. "You *will* come with us," she cried, her tear-streaked face warped into a snarl.

The beach quickly echoed with the sound of a dozen pistols and muskets being cocked, and not just from Cagliostro's band of unwashed brigands. Weatherby could hear the weapons aboard *Daedalus* as well.

"Tuez-les?" one of the pirates muttered, his pistol aimed squarely at Anne's chest.

"Attendez un instant," Cagliostro said softly before turning his full attention to Anne. "Go ahead, child. Strike me down. And you and those with you *will* fall, either to the shots of my comrades or the arcane power of the Xan. I'm not quite sure which would be worse."

Weatherby's attention shifted from Anne's trembling sword-arm to the pirates. A few of latter seemed quite ready to act and be done with it, all-powerful aliens notwithstanding. One in particular seemed particularly eager and twitchy, and Weatherby could not help but note that his pistol was pointed right at Anne.

Yet despite her visible distress, Anne's voice remained surprisingly calm—a calm Weatherby recognized from seeing seasoned officers in battle. "What's worse, signore, is allowing you to live," she said firmly. Weatherby shrugged off Finch's and Morrow's hands, which had loosened already, and walked forward to stand next to Anne...

...just as she raised her arm back to strike.

Weatherby saw the pirate's hand tense. He knew.

The shot rang out just as Anne's arm began to swing forward, and Weatherby shoved her aside for all he was worth. The blade fell into the pure white sands of the Callistan beach.

And Weatherby fell beside it a moment later, excruciating pain piercing his chest.

"Weatherby!" Finch shouted.

Weatherby looked up to the crystal blue skies, a vibrant hue such as he had never seen. He desperately wished he could breathe properly.

And then with an odd thunderclap, everything went dark and cold.

July 27, 2132

Col. Maria Diaz finished reading Shaila's report on her activities and tossed the datapad on the table, regarding the younger woman with a tired yet piercing stare. Shaila stood tall, comfortably at ease, sure in the knowledge that she had pieced the puzzle together, squarely placing the blame at Harry Yu's feet.

"All right, Lieutenant," Diaz said. "Tell me why I shouldn't bust your ass back to Earth."

"Ma'am?"

The colonel slowly got up from her chair and went around her desk to stand in front of Shaila. Despite being a few inches shorter, Diaz loomed very, very large. "You were ordered back to active duty and off the investigation, were you not?"

The protest immediately pushed its way front-and-center in Shaila's brain. The EM device was not the cave, and although she suspected they were related, she had no proof—at least, not until Stephane detected the Cherenkov radiation in the mining tunnels.

Diaz, however, didn't seem to be in the mood to split hairs over her orders, and technically, Shaila was still concealing the book from her as well. "I was, yes, ma'am," Shaila said.

"And then," Diaz continued, "you took a civilian out to a site where you suspected unknown technology was buried. You endangered him and you managed to fry a rover—and believe me, we could use that rover right about now.

"And *then*, you responded to the only fatal mining accident in Martian history by arresting the executive in charge?" Diaz asked.

"I did," Shaila said, trying to project more resolve than she felt. "The nature of the device in question, combined with his suit-beacon record in locations where devices were known or theorized to be, led me to believe that he had knowledge that these devices were placed there, and perhaps did it himself. Given the results we saw at Site Six, it was either gross negligence or willful endangerment. Ma'am."

"You do realize the complete and utter shitstorm you've unleashed, do you not?" Diaz asked.

At the time, of course, it really hadn't occurred to Shaila to consider the potential fallout for her, her boss and JSC's relations with a company that represented a large chunk of the command's budget. But she was getting the message loud and clear now. "I do, ma'am."

"And your theory is that this ring of linear EM fields, generated by ten of these devices, is some how channeling potentially destructive energy around an area of Mars, right in our area of operations," Diaz said. "And you have no idea why."

"Yes, ma'am," Shaila said. "I'm willing to bet Harry knows."

"BET?" Diaz shouted, causing Shaila to jump slightly in her at-ease stance. "You're willing to *bet*? Jesus Christ, Jain! I've got a man dead, earthquakes and tunnel collapses and strange EM fields all over my ops area, and you're *betting*? What the hell?"

It seemed a bad time to say much of anything so Shaila continued to stare straight ahead.

Diaz gathered herself again before continuing. "Where's Harry now?"

"Confined to quarters, ma'am, without computer or comm access," Shaila said.

Diaz punched a button on her desk. "Ops, this is Diaz. Harry Yu is no longer confined to quarters, with my apologies. Out."

Shaila's heart sank. She stared straight ahead, avoiding the return of Diaz' gaze.

"You're lucky we're undermanned and dealing with a mine collapse, otherwise you'd be headed back to Earth, with or without a rocket under you," Diaz said. "As it stands, you're relieved of duty for the rest of the day. I don't care what you do, just stay out of my hair while I deal with this crap. I'll be lucky to save the base, let alone your sorry ass."

Shaila nodded, trying not to lose it entirely. "Yes, ma'am. I'll have Finelli run the rescue ops and pull Washington in to cover him."

"Fine," Diaz said, looking up at Shaila intently. "You're smarter than this. You should've come to me first, but you don't *trust* anybody. Maybe that's understandable, with *Atlantis* and all, but just because I reprimand you and take you off the investigation doesn't mean I'm automatically your enemy. In fact, I'm probably the only friend you got left here, except for maybe Steve. But now, even if I think you might be onto something, I can't follow up on it because you're a liability."

"You're right, ma'am," Shaila said quietly. "I'm sorry."

"Damn right you are. Dismissed."

Shaila quietly walked out of Diaz' office. The officers in the command center were pretty busy, what with the fallout from the mine collapse and preparations for the *Giffords'* arrival in a few hours. She should've been there with them, leading them.

She quickly turned on her heel and made for the stairs.

Not knowing quite what else to do, or where to go, she made her way through the Hub toward her day room. Maybe staring at the ceiling would help. But the whoosh-swish of the airlocks distracted her—it was the wrong time of day for so many people coming in, and despite knowing that it wasn't an ordinary day, she turned to look out of habit.

Jack Heath was coming in for the last time.

Six pressure-suited miners bore his body into the Hub in two neat rows of three, an honor guard for the fallen. Someone from JSC should've been there, but it seemed everyone was managing one crisis or another. Shaila walked over to where the miners had gently placed Heath's body, just as Ed Kaczynski pulled his helmet off.

"I'm sorry, Ed," she said simply.

She had never seen him look so sober, in every sense. "Thanks, Lieutenant. Looks like you were right about those safety regs after all."

She shrugged. "Glad someone thinks so, for all the good it did."

"Yeah, no kidding. Some fucked up shit going on here, Jain. I—" Kaczynski stopped and looked past Shaila's shoulder, his eyes narrowing. "You self-righteous son-of-a-bitch!"

Before she could react, Kaczynski leapt past her and flew across the Hub as fast as Martian gravity could carry him. His target was Harry Yu, who had just entered from the Billiton corridor.

"You sent us in there!" Kaczynski shouted. "You risked our lives, you little prick!"

Shaila immediately jumped off after Kaczynski, even as Harry, wide-eyed, put his hands out in front of him. "How the hell was I to know? I swear to God, there was no reason to—"

Kaczynski's fist finished Harry's sentence for him.

"Ed, no!" Shaila grabbed the back of the old digger's pressure suit and yanked hard, pulling him away from Harry and sending him flying two meters across the room, even as the rest of Heath's honor guard ran toward the fracas.

Shaila turned toward the miners, putting herself between them and Harry. "He's not worth it," she said. "Don't do this."

She felt a hand on her shoulder shoving her out of the way. "I don't need you to protect me, Jain," Harry snarled, wiping a trickle of blood from his face and sneering at her. "It's *your* goddamn fault this happened!"

Shaila wheeled on him. "Don't you dare," she said, fists clenched.

"Me? Don't *you* dare to try to weasel out of this," he parried before turning to the miners. "You want to know what's going on? Me, too. But JSC didn't want to play ball with us. So now Mars is falling apart, Jack's dead, and they're *still* not telling us what we need to know to do our jobs safely! Instead, they put *this* fuck-up in charge!" He jabbed his finger right at Shaila.

Shaila's hands weren't as big as Kaczynski's paws, but her training more than made up for it. The right cross she landed on Harry's jaw sent him sprawling.

She turned to face the miners again, her mind reeling, her fists clenched. "Come on, then!" she called out. "Anyone else care to comment?"

The voice from behind her made her jump. "Shay. No."

Her fist cocked, she spun around again to find Stephane standing there, his pressure suit still on. He had been among the honor guard. And she had very nearly taken his head off.

"Come on," he said gently, placing his hand on her arm. "We need to leave. Now. Yuna will handle this."

Shaila could see Yuna already talking quietly but firmly with Kaczynski. If there was anyone one base whom everyone could agree to listen to, it was Yuna Hiyashi. She still looked extremely upset—perhaps more so than she did in the cave—but it already seemed that Kaczynski was backing down somewhat.

His pressure suit still on, Stephane half-pulled, half-lifted Shaila toward the JSC laboratory wing, leaving a few stares in their wake. She saw Adams racing down the stairs from the command center, likely dispatched to figure out what was going on. Someone would tell him that she had flattened Harry, she knew. And really, that would be that. End of career. Game over.

Stephane keyed the entry to the corridor and quickly pulled Shaila into the nearest available room, the containment lab. "All right," he said, looking out the door's tiny window into the hallway. "I do not think they are coming to arrest you."

He flashed a saddened smile at her, which she found herself actually mirroring—despite the anger that had her hands shaking uncontrollably. "Not yet. Thanks for that."

"Maybe you should have let them kill Harry, yes?" he said as he began to strip off the bulky pressure suit he still wore.

"Maybe. Just reflex, I guess. Military training." She slumped down in a chair and stared vacantly at Stephane's efforts to dislodge himself from his gauntlets.

"Yes, well, it did not hold up for very long," he noted. He finally got a gauntlet off—and threw it to the floor. "Damn it, Shay. What the hell are you doing?"

She glared at him, her attention refocused. "What do you mean?"

Stephane ripped the other gauntlet off, cracking the seal in the process. "You go off on your own. You do not tell people what you are doing. Even I know there are rules here, and I am just an academic. You are an officer! And yet you trust no one."

Shaila kept her gaze riveted, but felt her insides sink. "You're the second person to say that to me today."

"Then it must be true," he said. "I do not know what happened to you, but they say you were on *Atlantis*, yes?"

Shaila's eyes narrowed. "Who's 'they?'"

"People here, the miners and the JSC people. They say the mission went wrong. And I think to myself, 'This could explain it.' Because what JSC says happened and what you are doing here are two different things."

Shaila didn't respond, instead simply turning her head away to stare off into space again. Perturbed, the Frenchman continued.

"Fine, you do not want to tell me. And I do not care what really happened out there. The story everyone heard about *Atlantis* is fine for me, too. It was supposed to go to Jupiter, but it had an accident in Earth orbit and lost everyone on board except you.

"But you know what? I care that *you* made it back. And aside from rare moments when you actually smile, you are not happy. Anyone can see this." He leaned in toward her. "So if I can help you—with Diaz or Harry or anything else—I want to do that. But you need to let go of your 'tough guy' act and let me."

Shaila stared at him, hard, struggling to regain her mental balance. "You're a good guy, Steve," she finally said. "You really are. But you have no idea. You just don't."

"So tell me." It was both a command and a plea.

Shaila shook her head sadly. She was about to speak again when a small chime from the containment unit interrupted. She lolled her head around to look at the readout. "Looks like the book's gaining weight again."

"The book is gaining weight?" Stephane asked.

"Yeah," she said, sliding onto her feet. "Sorry. Didn't tell you that, either. Fractions of a gram. I had the computer ping me the next time it detected a change."

Shaila walked over and keyed the unit's security. She left the book open the previous evening, and was certain that the right-hand page was two-thirds blank. Yet it was filled with writing, something about traveling to Callisto, of all places. She could've sworn Weatherby—she couldn't help but think of the author by name—was being held on Ganymede.

She brought the manipulator arms to life and started slowly flipping pages. "Stephane, what's the monitor say about weight?"

He was trying to pull the suit's torso piece off, but gave up and leaned over the workstation next to the unit. "Two hundredths of a gram. No… wait. Three hundredths."

"It just gained?"

"Yes, it seems so."

Shaila kept flipping, until she finally came to a blank page, on the right hand side of the book. She looked to the left…

…and froze.

"Stephane," she whispered.

He looked up, then peered over her shoulder into the unit.

Seemingly out of nowhere, words appeared.

"To Mr. Weatherby, senior,

I am Dr. Andrew Finch, a shipmate of your son aboard HMS Daedalus. *In hopes that you may one day receive this journal as Thomas intended, I have taken upon myself the terrible duty of informing you of your son's untimely passing. Know that he served bravely to the very end, giving his life to protect another's. He was truly a credit to His Majesty's Royal Navy and, more impor-tantly, to his family."*

The words kept appearing, though in a different script than the careful, neat handwriting the rest of the book featured. Regardless, it was as if an invisible hand was taking pen to page.

"Am I crazy?" Shaila asked?

"If you are, so am I," Stephane said quietly, almost reverently.

Shaking her head, Shaila quickly reached over and pressed a button to activate the unit's holocorder, to capture video of the book as it wrote. A second later, she hit the comm switch.

"Jain to Diaz, over."

A moment later, Diaz responded, shouting into her comm to be heard over what seemed to be an angry mob. "This had better be good, Jain. I've got half a mind to arrest your ass right about now."

"Understood," Shaila replied absently, not really caring about anything else anymore. "Please report to the containment lab soon as you can. Jain out."

"What? You gotta be kidding me!" Diaz snapped.

Shaila thumbed off the comm and turned back to the book.

It kept writing.

CHAPTER 16

May 4, 1779

To Mr. Weatherby, senior,

I am Dr. Andrew Finch, a shipmate of your son aboard HMS Daedalus. In hopes that you may one day receive this journal as Thomas intended. I have taken upon myself the terrible duty of informing you of your son's untimely passing. Know that he served bravely to the very end, giving his life to protect another's. He was truly a credit to His Majesty's Royal Navy and, more importantly, to his family.

Whilst I certainly was a great nuisance to him in my first days aboard ship, I grew to admire his many positive virtues, no doubt instilled by his upbringing. In many ways, I owe my life now, however short it may yet be, to your son's sense of honor and his unerring ability to set me aright.

Finch poured his heart out onto the page before him, describing his time aboard *Daedalus* in great detail, hoping it would give Weatherby's family some sense of comfort when faced with the loss of their son. To his very great surprise, he himself felt better writing it as well.

Finally, he set the pencil down on the table and looked over to where Weatherby's body lay in repose. The lieutenant was pale, as to be expected, though Finch noted earlier, during a frantic examination, that rigor had not set in. Yet there was no pulse or heartbeat, and the pistol round had struck the young man squarely in the chest. Finch knew death when he saw it, and Weatherby was most certainly in God's hands now.

The lack of rigor mortis was Finch's only clue to the time that may have elapsed since the incident on Callisto's shore. He played the scene repeatedly in his head: Anne Baker moved to cut down Cagliostro, one of the Italian fiend's hirelings fired a pistol, and Weatherby shoved Anne away in order to save her life, taking the round intended for her. Weatherby collapsed, Finch ran to his aid.

Then there was a sharp slap of sound that reverberated across the beach. Finch thought he recalled a flash of yellow as well. And then all was dark and silent.

He awoke, most improbably, in an impeccably decorated bedroom that echoed the height of fashion in London when last he visited home. The furnishings were expertly crafted and polished to a brilliant shine, the walls were exquisitely papered and gilded along the edges, and the carpets appeared to be woven by the finest hands in Turkey or Persia. There was a fire already lit in the hearth, candles upon the desk at which he now sat, and the bed in the corner of the room was covered with some of the finest linens he had ever seen. And that is where he found Weatherby's body, the dead man's journal secure in his pocket.

Three hours. That was the reasonable expectation for the onset of rigor. So it had been less than three hours since the beach, but he hadn't a more precise measure; his pocketwatch had stopped seemingly at the moment when he lost consciousness.

Aside from the late Lt. Weatherby, Finch was alone. After his futile attempts to revive his shipmate, Finch had tested the single set of double-doors in the room. They were locked, of course, and would not give. Not even when he used the fireplace tools upon them. Not even when he tried to hurl the desk into them repeatedly.

There were no windows, either. Where one would expect them, there were mirrors instead—mirrors of uncanny craftsmanship, better than any he had ever seen, mirrors which reflected his sadness and anger perfectly upon him.

Where was Captain Morrow? Dr. Franklin? Anne? What of the *Daedalus*? And of Cagliostro, for that matter? Franklin had warned that the Italian could be most charming, and with his innate cunning and his alchemical skill, Finch thought it quite possible that Cagliostro may have simply waltzed past the Xan and off Callisto altogether to further whatever fell plotting he had in mind for the Known Worlds.

Was this, then, the fate of the French and Ganymedeans in Queen Anne's War? Were they forever imprisoned in facsimiles of their Earth-bound comforts? Whatever the case, Finch was grateful to be alive, but knew that the hour could come when that would no longer be the case. To the Xan's eyes, the emissaries from *Daedalus* were the aggressors. It was Anne who drew on Cagliostro first, who was more than willing to strike at that bilious wretch and set her life aright again—and in doing so, save the Known Worlds from his scheming.

Perhaps it was that act that sealed all their fates.

He did not blame her for her actions. Finch had been upon Elizabeth Mercuris for months, and it was a small and gossipy place. The fact that Roger McDonnell had taken up with a young streetwalker was, in that environment, a mild scandal at best. Finch had watched Weatherby grow fond of the young woman and did not wish to begrudge him of it. Weatherby might never have known of her past if not for Cagliostro's cruel jab, and Finch had hoped that even if the lieutenant had heeded his advice and learned of it, he could look past her sin and embrace her as she was now. Of that, he harbored doubts, however. Weatherby could be—rather, was—very prudish at times. Or maybe he simply possessed a morality that all too often eluded Finch. Who could say?

Finch leaned back and slammed shut Weatherby's journal. He had written enough for Weatherby's father to know what became of his son. Perhaps if he were imprisoned longer, he would write again. Perhaps future scribblings would chronicle Finch's own descent into madness as the hours stretched into days and the solitude and anxiety gnawed at his soul.

The damned Saturn-dwellers could have at least afforded him a hookah to dull his mind, Finch thought. But then he looked over at Weatherby and found himself ashamed for entertaining the very notion. It seemed to tarnish the young man's legacy.

"Andrew Finch."

Finch stood quickly at the sound of his name, sending his chair backward onto the floor in his haste. The voice—once again layered with harmonies unlike any he had heard—seemed to come from somewhere above him, yet gently filled the room. And it had nearly scared his ghost right out of him.

He paused a moment before responding, considering how best to address a disembodied voice. "I am he," he said finally.

"You have not been able to heal your comrade." It was not a question.

Finch thought this odd, somehow, since if the Xan—for this is whom he assumed was speaking—knew his name, they would likely know Weatherby was already dead, would they not? "He passed on before I could attend to him," Finch said.

"And your skills could not revive him?"

"No, his heart was pierced. Death was quick."

"Death is never so quick as that," the voice said. "It has not been long."

"So you say, but to my eyes, he is beyond reach," Finch said.

The voice paused a moment before resuming. "We had thought you were capable."

Finch looked up at the ceiling, fists clenched. "If you hadn't bloody well rendered me unconscious and hauled me here, I might have had a chance!"

"And there would have been even more blood staining on our shores," the voice said, the harmonics tinged with saddened minor chords. "That, we could not allow."

"No, of course not," Finch muttered.

The voice paused once again, this time for several seconds. When it returned, the cadence was slightly faster, more aggressive, and the minor chords seemed tinged with anger. "We requested solitude. You have ignored this request."

"Our need was great," Finch countered. "But surely you already know this."

"And how would we know that?"

"Since I am still among the living, and that you expected I would be able to heal my lieutenant, it stands to reason my other shipmates are alive as well. And since you're interrogating me, it also stands to reason that you have interrogated at least some of the others. I only hope you imprisoned Cagliostro as well."

"Count Cagliostro was not the aggressor. He was allowed to leave as he came," the voice said, this time laced with a quavering tenor that, to Finch's ears, sounded of hesitancy.

"Then you're damned fools, the lot of you!" Finch shouted.

"Where is the Sword of Xanthir?"

"The what?"

"The Sword of Xanthir."

Finch threw up his hands. "I've no idea what you're talking about."

Another pause, then: "You will wait here."

Perplexed, Finch bent down to pick his chair off the floor. "I shan't be going anywhere, it seems," he said, primarily to himself. He flopped down at the desk again, mulling over his first interaction with the enigmatic Xan. It did indeed stand to reason that his colleagues were in similar straits. Furthermore, it seemed that the Xan were not as all-powerful as they were assumed to be, as it was clear that Cagliostro had duped them somehow.

And then Finch threw his head back and laughed ruefully, the idea hitting him squarely in the brainpan. Whatever the Sword of Xanthir was—beyond a blade, obviously—Cagliostro's men likely made off with it whilst the Italian sought to charm the Xan with whatever seemingly innocuous falsehoods he had created. Yes, it would've been difficult, but even Finch could contemplate a number of alchemical solutions that might be applied to the task of thievery.

And the arrival of *Daedalus* provided a perfect foil. Anne's aggression—with Cagliostro goading her along—closed the circle neatly. Cagliostro was off, and now all aboard *Daedalus* would be made to take the blame.

The most learned men on Earth had little knowledge of the Xan's melodic language, but "Xanthir" implied, at least to Finch's mind, something *of* the Xan. They called themselves Xan, after all, and Saturn was named Xanath in their tongue. So the blade held not only some great import for them, but may have very well been *from* Saturn.

Thus, by visiting Callisto, Cagliostro might have managed to get a piece of Saturn itself for his plot. Now his foul working could very well include *all* the Known Worlds, and the results could alter the very nature of Creation.

"Oh, Weatherby," Finch said sadly, looking at his friend's body. "Perhaps 'tis best you won't live to see this. We've botched things cleanly for sure."

A click from the door drew Finch's head around sharply. The knob was turning.

He stood quickly, casting about for something to use as a weapon, then mentally scolded himself. Whatever might happen, he doubted it would be anything close to what he might expect.

He was right.

The door swung open and Anne strode into the room, her simple dress swirling around her. "Where's Tom?" she demanded, looking determined.

"What?" Finch stuttered. "How did you...?"

But she had already seen Weatherby's body on the bed and wheeled out of the room as quickly as she had entered. "He's in here!" he heard her call from beyond the doorway.

Finch peered out the doors and found his room was at the end of a long hallway, lined with perfectly smooth walls and lit by glowing orbs of light affixed to the ceiling at regular intervals. Anne had ducked into another room along the hallway's length, and was already returning to Finch's room—with someone Finch didn't recognize in tow.

"Over here," she said as she entered and strode past Finch. With her was a very tall man, dressed in the very fine yet simply adorned clothes of a well-to-do gentleman. The man's long dark hair was drawn back in a ponytail, and his eyes shone behind the sharp features of his face.

Those eyes....

"Bacon?" Finch asked. "Surely it isn't you, is it?"

The man followed Anne to Weatherby's side, but turned to spare Finch a small smile. "Well done, Dr. Finch," he said. While "Bacon's" crude accent was gone, replaced with one far more genteel, Finch knew the voice regardless.

"Can you save him?" Anne said, gripping Weatherby's cold hand as she knelt beside the bed.

"I believe so," the gentleman replied. He reached into a small purse at his side and withdrew an aquiline stone and a vial of liquid. "You drive a very hard bargain, girl."

"Yes, I do," Anne said simply. "Please hurry."

Shaking himself out of his incredulity, Finch rushed over to the side of the bed, standing over "Bacon." The stone and the liquid in the man's hands looked utterly unfamiliar to him. "Rigor's not set in, but that's all I know," Finch reported.

"Plenty of time," the man muttered. "Girl, keep his mouth open."

Anne reached over and pried open Weatherby's mouth as the man held his stone over it. He flipped the vial's stopper off with his thumb, then poured the liquid over the stone, allowing it to drip into Weatherby's mouth. The liquid quickly eroded the stone into nothingness. "It is done. Close his mouth."

"Now what?" Finch asked as Anne freed Weatherby's jaws.

The man stood and regarded Finch carefully. "I assume you have simple tinctures of iron oxide among your stores, Doctor?"

"Yes," Finch said, confused. "But—"

"Mix the tincture with Ionian sulfur powder and a touch of Venusian *pre'lak* extract, and administer it back aboard your ship," the man said gruffly.

Finch's confusion grew. "That mixture would dissolve metal!" he exclaimed. "Why would I give him such a thing?"

"Because his heart will heal with the musket round still inside," "Bacon" said, as if explaining the alphabet to a very slow child. "The iron oxide, combined with the sulfur, will break down the metal in short order, while the *pre'lak* will keep it from breaking down his blood as well. Do you follow now?"

Finch's eyes widened. "My God, that's brilliant."

"Don't get too excited," the man said as he returned his alchemical tools to his purse. "In most cases, it's far easier to get the round out of the body first, because if the wound is still open when you apply the mixture I described, the air around the wound would cause the surrounding tissue to break down quickly. Remember, Doctor—everything has an effect on everything else."

"Of course," Finch said, closing his eyes and trying not to snap back at the man. Causality was perhaps the most basic tenet of the Great Work, and his pride was threatening to burst forth at the man's chiding. "What is that stone you used?"

The man frowned. "It is an inferior creation, an earlier attempt at a greater success that was later taken from me."

The realization dawned on Finch like a thunderbolt from Zeus. A greater success...taken from an obviously accomplished alchemist...on the same world where Cagliostro was found....

Dumbfounded, he regarded the man with new eyes.

"It's...*you*," he said slowly. "Of course! You, of all people, would want Cagliostro caught!"

The man gave a little smirk. "You've a sharp mind when it's not addled by drugs, Dr. Finch. Your time amongst naval discipline has been good for you."

"Indeed it has, despite my best efforts to the contrary," Finch replied before turning to Anne. "Did he effect our release, then?"

The girl looked slightly uncomfortable. "Well, no...."

"She did," the man said flatly. "She managed to convince the Xan of your good intentions, and mine as well. And I can tell you she's a keen negotiator. I significantly reduced my alchemical stores to revive this man—in return for my very life."

"But how?" Finch asked.

"Later," the man said curtly, looking over Finch's shoulder toward Weatherby. "I believe he's coming out of it."

Finch and Anne moved to Weatherby's side just as he began to stir. "My God, that hurt," Weatherby groaned softly.

"Weatherby!" Finch breathed as he knelt by his lieutenant's side. "How are you feeling?"

The young man opened his eyes and looked about. "Far better than before." He cast his eyes around the room and fixed them on Anne. "You're all right?"

"Yes," she said, fighting back tears. "Welcome back."

"Back from where?" Weatherby asked, eying "Bacon" suspiciously. "And who is that?"

"I am the Count St. Germain," the man said. "We need to get you on your feet. The Xan are waiting for us, and I imagine they have some explaining to do. If my theories are correct, they are as much to blame for Cagliostro's fell mission as the man himself."

July 27, 2132

"Jain, I've got two officers in sickbay, the mess hall's been trashed, and I personally beat the shit out of somebody just to prove a goddamn point. We'll all be lucky to get off this rock in one piece. Now what the fuck... Oh."

Diaz' voice trailed off as the door to the containment lab closed behind her and she saw the book, which had thankfully obliged Shaila—and her career—by continuing to write itself in Diaz' presence.

Diaz stared for several long minutes, well after Finch's journal entry had finished. Then she simply hit the comm button. "Ops, report."

"Ops to Diaz, Adams here. We've managed to contain the miners to the lower Hub and their dorm wings," the young lieutenant said nervously.

"We're holding the stairs to the upper dome and the doors to the JSC wing. So far, no further incidents."

"Good," the colonel said absent-mindedly. "Call me if it gets worse. Have Greene and Hiyashi report to the containment lab. Diaz out."

After that, Diaz fell silent, her fingers steepled in front of her as she stared at the book, seeming to dare it to write again. Shaila could see the red on her knuckles and idly wondered which malcontent miner Diaz punched. When Greene and Yuna arrived, it fell to Shaila to show the others the video recording of the book's writing, which was met with the same quiet bewilderment from each of them.

Now, they waited. Yuna and Greene sat in the room's other two chairs, while Stephane and Shaila leaned against the worktable. Nobody looked at each other. Their eyes were unfocused, their thoughts kept to themselves.

Finally, Diaz turned around to address everyone. "Well, then." She stopped, paused, and visibly gathered herself. "We all know what we just saw. And unless the chef's been sneaking hallucinogens into the mystery meat, this is absolutely 100 percent real." The joke had the desired effect, producing smiles and the barest hint of relaxation.

"First off," she continued, "this lab is completely locked down for everyone except you guys. And Dr. Greene, I really hope I don't have to say anything extra to you."

Greene got the message clearly. "Colonel, even if I came in here with a crew and recorded it, nobody on Earth would believe me," he said quietly. "Some things just..." His voice trailed off as he ended his thought with a shrug.

Diaz nodded. "Good. We need you on this. We're way out of our league here." There were nods from around the room. "So what we're going to do now is, we're going to go around, one at a time. I want to hear your thoughts. Obviously, I don't care how crazy they seem, because we're way outside the box here anyway. Jain? You found this book. Talk to us."

Shaila looked up at her boss and, for once, had a profound appreciation for her. Diaz didn't ask whether the book was fake, nor did she exclude Shaila, even after everything that went down earlier that day. So she took a leap. "Well, you said to think outside the box. I'm going to trust you on that."

"About damn time," Diaz said with a tired smile. "Go."

Shaila looked around the room. Most everyone was still staring off into space, but Yuna looked at her with concern—probably expecting another career-ending moment. So be it. "We've got three things going on here, by my count. We've got earthquakes that shouldn't be happening, a bunch of buried devices creating a ring of linear EM fields, and now…this thing," she said, nodding toward the containment unit. "I think they're related."

"I think we pretty much assumed as much at this point," Diaz said. "You guys even found Cherenkov radiation at the collapse today, right?"

"It's more than that." Shaila stood up and walked over to the book, looking at the neat handwriting again, as if to draw strength from it. "The energy that fried the rover and seemed to be involved in the collapse—it seemed to be following the EM ring. But that device we dug up, it couldn't have generated that kind of energy."

Shaila looked to Greene, who nodded and picked up her line of reasoning. "Right. If there is a ring out there—and that seems to be the case, by the way—and if it really is a particle accelerator, it still couldn't singlehandedly cause the collapse at the mining site. And it couldn't cause the earthquakes we've felt over the past few days."

"Exactly," Shaila said, warming up to the subject. "So where's the energy coming from?"

The room fell silent once again.

"And," Shaila continued, "while we're at it, where's the energy coming from to create the writing in this book? We're not detecting it within the containment unit. And we can't pinpoint the source of the Cherenkov radiation. So if the energy isn't here, it's got to be somewhere else."

Diaz looked at the book again quizzically. "All right, I'll bite. Where?"

Shaila pointed at the book. "From wherever that book came from. And I'm betting that the energy that's ripping up Mars right now is being unleashed from there, too."

"Yes, but where is 'there?'" Stephane asked.

"From whatever world Weatherby is—was—writing from," she concluded, surprised at the pang of sorrow she felt at his apparent death. "Another dimension of space-time, I suppose. And we may have to accept the possibility that there's some truth in there, and that this Cagliostro guy, or somebody else, is actually doing something that's affecting us here."

More silence. Shaila looked at each person in turn. Stephane seemed both intrigued and amused, while both Yuna and Diaz fixed her with expressions of deep concern, seemingly for her mental health. She was glad that she had refrained from mentioning the strange stuff that filtered into her head while in the cave, because that probably would scotch the whole thing.

But Greene…when Shaila looked at him, she could see his wheels turning.

So could Diaz. "Dr. Greene, your turn."

He straightened up in his chair and smiled slightly, almost seeming embarrassed. "I remember this show, an old 2-D show from the beginning of the 21st century. This quantum physicist was talking about how you could theoretically access a…well, a parallel dimension," he said, turning slightly red as he carefully pronounced those last two words. "He said you needed a huge amount of energy, and came up with the idea of using asteroids to create a massive particle accelerator around the entire asteroid belt. He figured he'd either create a bubble universe spliced off from our own…or open a doorway to another dimension, a parallel universe.

"But what he didn't figure, I suppose, was the possibility of having someone on the other side of the door trying to do the same thing," Greene continued. "If you were doing things on both sides, then your energy price tag would be a lot lower." He looked up with an embarrassed smile. "Theoretically, of course."

"So you're saying Jain's right?" Diaz said, sounding a bit stunned.

Greene shrugged. "Hell if I know. I mean, give me enough time and I can come up with a variety of theories to explain everything that's going on here. But right now, Jain's theory seems to be the only one that fits *all* this strangeness. I mean, there's all kinds of space-time variables that don't make sense, but still."

For all the emotion she felt at being vindicated in front of her commander like that, Shaila settled on a simple nod in Greene's direction, which he returned in kind.

Yuna was unimpressed, however. "Colonel, I would strongly recommend against adopting any theories at the present time," she said, "especially ones that would take what's written in that book at face value, or ones that rely on theoretical particles that we can't even test for. There are far too many actual questions that need answering before we delve into the realm of… of fantasy!"

"Well aware, Yuna," Diaz said. "I'm going to have to report to Houston on this, and I'm less than thrilled at the idea of saying, 'Hey, guys, we think we've got a parallel universe pushing through here on Mars.'" That got the laugh Diaz intended, and even Shaila chuckled. "However, I'm not going to dismiss that theory out of hand, either. It goes into the pot with whatever else we come up with. Now, what do we—"

Diaz was cut off by the sound of the base alarm, which filled the room with a loud, nerve-jangling dissonance. "Col. Diaz, Col. Diaz, report to the command center immediately. Col. Diaz to the command center immediately." It was Finelli, and he sounded stressed.

"Christ, what now?" Diaz said as she turned to the others. "All right. Adjourned for now. Greene, welcome to the team. You, Steve and Yuna try to come up with some kind of testing scheme for the book, the EM devices, all of it. Jain, you're with me." Diaz took one long stride to the door and wrenched it open, and Jain hustled to follow her.

The two officers bounced down the corridor quickly, with JSC personnel flattening against the walls to let them pass. But before they got to the Hub, Diaz stopped and turned quickly to her subordinate; Shaila had to grab the wall to keep from plowing into her.

"Look, you had a good theory back there, OK? It's crazy, but Greene seems to think you're on to something," Diaz said quietly. "But you're not off the hook. If it's hitting the fan, I need you. But dammit, I need you on the ball. Read me?"

"Aye, ma'am," Shaila said. "Thank you, ma'am." The "thank you" seemed inappropriate, somehow, but Shaila's sense of relief—from Greene backing her up, from simply being *needed*—prompted it to come out.

Diaz nodded and the two officers bounded into the Hub, covering the vast room in a dozen quick leaps en route to the command center. As she ran through, Shaila saw a couple groups of miners loitering near the equipment lockers and, across the way, four very nervous looking junior officers standing watch on the emergency transports and the stairs to the upper part of the dome, weapons in hand.

McAuliffe had a half-dozen handheld microwave emitters on base to help police the civilian population. They used a focused microwave beam to overload the target's nervous system, knocking them out for about 15 minutes. And the pain was excruciating, too, though there was no lasting damage done. The emitters—dubbed "zappers" by everyone on base—had been gathering dust for years. Until today.

A few of the miners loudly lobbed invectives and threats toward the officers, who stood their ground quietly with zappers at the ready. To Harry Yu's credit, he was among the miners and appeared to be trying to calm them, though he still had a moment to regard Shaila with a furious look, one made a bit more palatable by the bruise on his jaw from her fist. Shaila ignored him and, a moment later, she and Diaz entered the command center to find nearly everyone on watch at their emergency stations. "Report," Diaz barked.

"Incoming transport has lost power a hundred clicks out," Finelli reported from his ops station. "There was a massive energy surge outside, and the transport was caught in it."

While Shaila jumped over to the ops console, Diaz slid into her seat and pulled out her datapad. "Send me a visual," she ordered.

"Negative," Finelli responded. "Overhead MarsSats are offline. Same with half the outside sensor grid."

"Say again?" Shaila said.

"Sats and sensors are out. Gone. Fried," Finelli said, frustration entering into his voice. "Right when the transport got hit, so did our gear."

Diaz keyed a button on her datapad. "Transport, this is McAuliffe. What's your condition? Over."

The radio crackled a moment before a response came back. "McAuliffe, this is transport *Giffords*. We have no flaps, no rotors, only thrusters, and our electronics are out. Radio is on backup. We are inbound without the ability to stop. Over."

"Shit," Diaz said. "Stand by, *Giffords*. Finelli, what's their course?"

"Can't tell yet. But they were heading for the pad earlier. Don't know if they made their turn. They could end up on the surface or crash right into the base."

Shaila, meanwhile, was pulling up a schematic of the *Giffords*. It was a small crew-and-cargo ship, capable of carrying a couple of tons. It used a combination of heat-shielding, an inflatable front cone, massive retractable wings and dozens of small rotors to navigate the tricky path to the Martian surface. Without rotors or attitude control, it could only plow into the surface or try to blast back into orbit.

The manifest showed it was carrying food supplies—enough to feed the base for the next three months—and empty ore containers.

There were also eight people aboard—a pilot, co-pilot and six miners.

Shaila opened the comm again. "*Giffords*, this is McAuliffe. What's your fuel situation? Can you make orbit again? Over."

"Negative," the transport replied. "We were late getting off, so we were told to burn the reserves getting here. Over."

Cheap bastards. "Roger that. Stand by." Shaila turned to Diaz. "I got a plan B."

Shaila quickly filled Diaz in. It would be tricky, especially without any visuals to help guide the ship in, but it would have to do. If nothing else, it would spare the base. "All right, Jain. Your show."

"Aye, ma'am," she said, reopening the channel. "*Giffords,* this is McAuliffe. You got enough radio bandwidth to link me to your controls? Over."

"Roger that, McAuliffe. You can have the stick, for what it's worth. So long as we get down in one piece, you can have whatever you want."

Shaila called up the holographic virtual control panel the base ops people used to guide ships in for landings. Most pilots preferred to land on their own, but it was a handy backup. She linked the radio into the VR panel and a moment later, she was surveying the ship's readouts as if she were sitting in the cockpit, while her headset and force-feedback gloves allowed her to hear and "feel" the controls as if they were in her hands.

It didn't look or feel good. Main fuel was nearly tapped—maybe 10 percent left, and they needed at least 40 percent to achieve orbit again. Wing flaps and rotors were gone. Controls were completely unresponsive in her hands. On the bright side, landing thrusters remained on backup. Hopefully, that would be enough.

Shaila stabbed a button and got no response. "*Giffords*, I need you to go back and manually open the rear cargo door, then cut the gear loose," she said.

"Say again?" The pilot sounded incredulous.

"Open the rear cargo door! Now!" Shaila ordered. She heard a faint echo in her headset, but couldn't spare the time or attention to care about what it was.

"Roger. On our way." Twenty seconds later, the pilot came back on. "Cargo door open, cargo is loose, over."

Shaila activated the two forward landing thrusters. She hoped that, between the thrusters and the remaining lift in the wings, the ship would start to nose up.

And when the cargo shifted....

"We're nosing up and losing cargo," the pilot reported. "Lift won't be enough to land, though."

Shaila left the forward landing thrusters on and diverted the remaining fuel to them. "Roger, *Giffords*. Just trying to get you vertical."

"Vertical?!" the pilot barked. Shaila ignored him as she watched as the attitude readout climb higher. Forty percent angle. Fifty...sixty...seventy.

Finelli turned to the colonel. "I have a visual now. Some of the outside sensors are back up."

"Give it to us," Diaz said.

Shaila watched out of the corner of her eye as another readout came to life, showing the image of the little ship from a faraway vantage point. It was still flying, and its nose continued to rise.

Yet it was slowing down, and that was the point. Problem was, it was also starting to drop. Fast.

"OK, *Giffords*. Prepare for main engine fire."

"What?" the pilot screamed. "We won't make orbit!"

"Just hang on," Shaila said. She watched as the nose got up to 85 percent—and dipped slightly. The controls in her hands started to vibrate a bit, and she was getting feedback on her palms as she tried to keep the ship vertical. That was all the thrusters were going to give her.

"Firing main engines," she said. "Twenty-five percent thrust."

A moment later, the large nozzles at the base of the ship roared to life. But the *Giffords* continued to fall alarmingly fast.

"Shit. Increasing engine to 40 percent," Shaila ordered.

"We're still falling, McAuliffe." The pilot sounded like he was barely keeping it together.

"Ramping up main engine thrust to full," Shaila said. She tapped the ship's landing thrusters in an attempt to keep the ship as vertical as possible. "Any emergency chutes left?"

"First thing we tried," the pilot said.

"Thousand meters," Finelli reported from his seat next to Shaila. "Still falling."

"Engines at 65 percent," Shaila said. "I'm showing your rate of descent is reducing."

"Not enough!" the pilot yelled.

"Crap. All right," Shaila said. "Full engines—now."

Shaila saw the ship's engines spit gouts of flame…just as it fell out of the camera's view. "My visual's gone!"

Finelli's fingers scrambled across his workstation. "I can't find them!"

Shaila saw alarms going off on her VR controls; the ship's hull integrity was starting to weaken under the strain. "*Giffords*, what's your status? Over."

Silence.

Shaila turned to Diaz, who looked straight ahead, her fingers steepled in front of her. "Try again," she said.

"*Giffords*, come in. Over."

The VR controls suddenly winked out. Shaila's fingers flew across the workstation as she tried to access them again.

It wasn't working

"Ma'am, I think we've lost them," Shaila said quietly.

It was at that moment that a soft boom was heard from outside the base. Shaila closed her eyes. It didn't sound good.

She opened them when the radio crackled back to life. "McAuliffe, this is *Giffords*," the pilot said jubilantly. "We are on the surface. Repeat, we are on the surface. Over."

Shaila slumped in her chair as the command center erupted in cheers. "Roger that, *Giffords*. What's your status?" she said.

"Well, we landed on our engine nozzles, then fell over on our back. And we missed the base by only about three hundred meters. But fuck it, we're alive. Over." They could hear cheering aboard the ship as well.

"Roger that, *Giffords*. Welcome to Mars. We're en route to your position now. McAuliffe out," Shaila said, beaming while her crewmates slapped her back and mussed her hair in celebration. She could also hear cheers emanating from the Hub. She looked over at the ops board—and found that someone had put the entire radio exchange on the base-wide intercom, so that every pissed-off miner could hear what was happening loud and clear—hence the odd echo in her headset.

That's when Shaila started shaking a bit. Damn good thing nobody died.

"All right, people!" Diaz shouted above the din. Nonetheless, she was smiling pretty broadly as well. "Jain, get a team out there for some search-and-rescue. Finelli, get with engineering and figure out what the hell happened to the MarsSats and sensors. I want them back up and running ASAP."

Shaila got up and headed for the door, but Diaz reached out to lightly touch her arm. "See what you can do when your head's on straight?" the colonel said.

"Yes, ma'am," she replied. "Big risk putting that on the 'com. What if they didn't make it?"

"You're a *pilot*, Jain," Diaz said with a slight smile. "Go outside and get 'em."

Shaila turned to go, but Finelli stopped her. "Lieutenant, wait!" He held up a datapad, showing a map of the outside sensor array in the base area of operations. "What *is* this?" he asked.

More than two hundred sensors were offline.

And the outage was in a perfect circle, almost directly centered on the lava tube. The perimeter was nearly identical to the presumed ring of EM energy Shaila had laid out for Diaz earlier that afternoon.

"It's a big fucking problem," Shaila said, her euphoria draining away. "Get that image to Diaz. She's going to need it."

CHAPTER 17

May 4, 1779

Weatherby staggered out into the hallway, his arm around Finch's shoulders for support. He felt weak, as if his blood were only now resuming its normal course through his body—which, he now understood, was precisely what was happening. However, the Count St. Germain insisted that Weatherby was *not* dead all that time, despite his lack of heartbeat. He'd been close, of course—bare minutes to spare, really—but alive enough to be revived through St. Germain's queer little stone.

"Mr. Weatherby, good to see you up and about," said Captain Morrow as he stepped into the same hallway from another room. "I trust the wound was not severe, then?"

Weatherby couldn't help but smile. "I'm told it was a close thing, but here I am," he replied. "You've met my savior?"

"I have. You and Finch were the last ones to be fetched," Morrow said. "Ah, there's the ambassador now. Shall we? We have an appointment with the Xan."

Franklin stood up ahead, looking far less distressed than he was upon the beach. Indeed, he was staring up at the ceiling, at one of the glowing orbs that illuminated the hallway. "I daresay they might have done it," he murmured as the group approached.

"Done what?" Anne asked. She looked up with curiosity.

"Harnessed the forces of electricity!" the ambassador said excitedly. "I cannot think of anything else it might be. Do you not hear the low hum that permeates the hallway? It comes from these lights. And the light is steady, without fail. Even the greatest alchemical light sources must needs falter at some point, and I dare say—"

St. Germain pushed his way past Weatherby and Finch and continued down the hallway. "Really, Franklin. There are far more important matters at hand."

Frowning, Franklin tottered off after him. "You still have yet to explain your presence here, Francis. I pray to God you've had no hand in the theft of this sword they're on about."

"Of course not," St. Germain said dismissively as the group hustled to follow the two alchemists. "You know very well why I'm here. I've followed that bastard across the Known Worlds to this spot. And now the Xan have thwarted me from not only stopping him, but from cleaning up *their* mess as well!"

"And what do you mean, exactly, my lord?" Morrow asked, stressing the title slightly. St. Germain's assumed peerage was something of a mystery, after all, as the crowned heads of Europe either claimed him or rejected him regularly, and often depending on the particular tale at hand.

"I've no wish to repeat myself, Captain," St. Germain said. "All will be revealed soon enough."

Weatherby, Finch and Anne fell back from the others as Morrow and the others attempted to glean more from the recalcitrant St. Germain. Weatherby was still moving slowly, his limbs struggling to regain their strength. "Tell me, Miss Baker, how did you secure our release?" he asked quietly as the shuffled toward the end of the corridor, where a large archway promised entry into a far more cavernous space. "Were you not the one who would have struck Cagliostro down?"

"Well, yes, Tom, I was," she said, turning red. "As hard as it might be to believe, it seems as though I'm the very first woman the Xan here have encountered. The fact that I accompanied you upon the beach here was seen as something of a curiosity, and I was immediately brought to one of those salons, and they asked me many questions."

Finch nodded, huffing slightly under Weatherby's weight. "Yes, well, I could see that. What ship of war or exploration carries women? But still. How did you convince them?"

The girl merely shrugged. "I really don't know. I stated our intentions plainly. They asked me about my alchemical knowledge, of which I have a little. I told them of Cagliostro's plot, about the planetary essences. The voice left for a long time after that, and when it came back, it somehow judged me worthy, I suppose. They said something to the effect that we were more knowledgeable and 'enlightened' than they had first believed."

Weatherby frowned slightly at this. He only now remembered Cagliostro's words on the beach, and his heart ached from more than a mere pistol shot. Apparently, the Xan had a different definition of moral enlightenment than humanity. "And St. Germain?" Weatherby asked, eager to change the subject. "What of the former Mr. Bacon?"

"They believed he had stolen their sword on his own. They caught him in the city here, sneaking about. I recognized him from a portrait Roger had of him in his study," she said. "They seemed to be quite impressed with the notion humans could be merciful."

"Only when we're not shooting at each other," Finch quipped. "And… oh, my." He fell silent as they passed the archway and entered a new and utterly alien chamber.

The room was massive; Weatherby estimated it could hold a three-story building inside with ease. The vaulted ceiling was arched, somewhat in the manner of a cathedral, but without nave or steeple. It was also windowless, the light coming from several glowing orbs set in the walls and ceiling, high above. Every surface was hewn by a strange, hypnotically veined pink stone completely unadorned, incredibly smooth and highly polished.

And this massive hall was completely bare, save for a single object in the center—a table-like structure, five feet tall, five wide and easily twenty feet long. It looked, to Weatherby's eyes, like an altar, and he suddenly feared that they could become a sacrifice to some heathen, Saturnine god. Upon the table was a simple stand of some sort, much as one might see a sword stand on Earth. It held nothing, however.

"This is the Temple of Remembrance," said the now-familiar voice, sparkling with beautiful harmonies that echoed throughout the chamber. "It is here that we remember what we once were, and strive to evolve beyond it."

St. Germain had walked to the center of the room and now stood mere feet from the table. "You are missing something," he said. Whether it was a challenge, an inquiry or mere observation, Weatherby could not tell. "I assume Althotas' student took it."

"You know much, son of Earth, including a name we do not say lightly," the voice said, its chords echoing minor keys. "Gather and watch."

"Who's Althotas?" Finch whispered to St. Germain. He was met only with a deep frown and a shushing sound.

The lights in the room dimmed, save for one directly above the altar—given that this was a temple, Weatherby felt justified in calling the table such. This light began to swirl oddly, coalescing into a large orb hanging over the altar. Shapes soon appeared. Before long, an image of the Known Worlds, as if seen from the far reaches of the Void, appeared clearly in view—some twenty feet in diameter.

"Long ago, there were two civilizations in the Known Worlds," the voice said. "We are, of course, an elder race, with 20,000 years of history. And there was another, a race of beings whose name we will not speak here. They were of the planet you call Mars, and they were an aggressive, warlike race, as we were earlier in our history."

The images shifted, showing a lush, verdant world. Long, spindly green hands worked fields, built buildings—and forged blades. As much as Weatherby tried, he could not make out faces, or even full bodies. An arm here, long limbs there. It was as if they were being deliberately concealed from view.

"It was only a matter of time and innovation before we met, five thousand years ago, and we soon fell to quarreling and, later, outright war," the voice continued. "For two hundred years, we battled these Martians. I am most ashamed to say that both sides acted with equal abandon. Millions died. Worlds were razed. Trails of blood were left across the Void."

Once again, the images shifted. The green hands took up weapons, the blurry bodies charged, meeting other creatures in battle. These others were covered in strange armor, it seemed, and they too could not be fully realized to Weatherby's eyes. There were fires, the clash of metal, flashes of multicolored lightning, explosions in the Void—and screams no man could possibly reproduce, let alone want to hear ever again.

"Then came a singular Martian warlord, perhaps one of the most brilliant military and occult minds ever seen. His mastery of the mystic arts was immense, and it was said he could even master Death itself. He rallied his people and went upon the offensive. We lost these very moons and our other holdings, and suffered heinous attacks upon the very satellites of Great Xanath, the world you call Saturn."

A flotilla of strange Void vessels, with bloated hulls, broad wings and sails at all angles, swooped in toward Saturn. Aboard one of them, a green-skinned fist clenched a wickedly barbed blade of alien origin.

"We were at a loss, so we delved deeply into our alchemical and occult lore. We created machines of unspeakable destruction to combat this creature, and we drove him back to Mars—but at a terrible price. An entire world, a colony of these Martians, was destroyed."

Weatherby watched in horror as other ships—their silver ovoid hulls marking them as Xan to his eyes—gathered around a pale blue world. A moment later, this world exploded into a billion shards of rock, destroying the ships.

"Soon, desperation became his, and fearing an end to Mars itself, he turned to Earth, where your people were just barely evolved into sentience. Appearing as gods under the direction of their warlord, the Martians taught you some of their lore and prepared to turn you—all of you—into new soldiers in their battles against us. And so we did the same, attempting to win new allies among your people."

Images of primitive men appeared. They wore skins and coarse linen, feathers and beads and rough-hewn metal jewelry. They were seen in deserts and forests, mountains and swamps, all looking up at the blurry, green-tinted beings before them, or armored beings of impossible height. And they seemed to listen intently.

"But this warlord was too late. Even as we competed for your loyalty, we launched our final offensive, turning Mars into the barren world you know today and decimating the Martian people. It was our last, greatest crime that we committed genocide against them on a massive scale—such a crime that we ultimately stopped our mindless raging and adopted the customs and philosophies that keep our past in check, allowing us to better ourselves."

The armored beings were seen marching across a red desert toward a basalt citadel. Flames set the horizon aglow, while green-skinned bodies lay at their feet, their blood turning the red sands purple.

"Yet we had one more crime to commit. We captured the warlord, forcing him to watch as we eradicated his people. Instead of putting him to death—

for what was death to one so powerful as he?—we did something far worse. Using our darkest and most secret lore, we created nothing short of a hell for him, a place between worlds in which he would suffer an eternity of torment. They say his screams were heard even after the portal to this realm was sealed."

Weatherby saw green-skinned hands, chained. Robed figures surrounded the alien. And a bright light flowed into the room, with only a last, terrible cry piercing the silence.

The light before the altar faded, the orb disappearing as the room's lights began to shine brighter.

And now, someone stood behind the altar, prompting the assemblage of humans to gasp and step back.

This figure was tall—at least nine feet in height—but still shaped like a man, with discernible arms and a head and, Weatherby assumed, legs. It was hooded, however, and cast in shadow besides. A glimpse of pale salmon beneath the hood? A wisp of something that seemed like a cross between hair and…tentacle? Weatherby could not say, and he drew his eyes away despite himself.

"We call this the Temple of Remembrance because we need to remember what we once were, so that we do not become so again. Many of our kind make pilgrimages here in order to maintain the calm within themselves," the voice said. This time, it emanated directly from the creature—the Xan—standing before them, and its harmonies were laced with minor chords and regret. "Here, upon this altar, was the Sword of Xanthir, forged from the diamond core of our ringed homeworld. It was the bane of all Martians, and it was used in the occult rite that sealed the warlord away from our worlds forever."

St. Germain cleared his throat. "Your seals were not entirely effective, it seems," he said, attempting to be gentle and only partially succeeding. That he had the temerity to talk at all struck Weatherby as monumentally arrogant.

"We have told you our story," the Xan said. "You, son of Earth, need share yours now."

St. Germain turned slightly so he could address both the Xan and the delegation from *Daedalus*. "Very well. First of all, I must apologize for not having announced myself upon my arrival in your city, but the opportunity to do so was unavailable to me, considering the nature of my mission, for I came here to intercept and stop the fiend known as Cagliostro. And to do this, I had to stow away aboard *Daedalus* when I spied your ship in Philadelphia. So I must offer my apologies to you as well, Captain Morrow." St. Germain nodded at Morrow, who frowned deeply, before continuing.

"I met Cagliostro seven years ago. He was brilliant, a most gifted alchemist, and I admit I was blinded as to his character by his talent. I took him on as an apprentice, hoping that his unconventional thinking would help me unlock the secrets to finding the Philosopher's Stone—the very essence of the planet Earth itself.

"We were indeed successful, producing the Stone not two years later. But Cagliostro soon became sullen, for I guarded the stone carefully, concerned that others might take this accomplishment and use it for their own ends. He became more erratic in behavior and temperament, and soon after, it became clear to me that we could no longer work together effectively. I ended his apprenticeship and told him to be on his way. I felt that I had kept enough of the Stone's creation from him that he would not soon easily replicate it."

St. Germain looked down at the floor as he continued. "Indeed, it seemed as though he could not, so he opted instead for mere theft. I awoke one morning to find my mystic defenses breached, the Stone missing. He even left me a note, mocking my limited appreciation for his skills and the potential of my Work. And he said that his new master—one called Althotas—would teach him far more than I could."

St. Germain turned to address the Xan directly. "Althotas is the warlord you speak of, is he not?"

"Yes," the creature intoned. "And it would seem that he works now to free himself. The rituals used to create his prison are lost to us. We turned our back on the darker arts millennia ago. It is possible that time, and the growing aptitude of humanity's alchemists, has lessened the power of our working. It may be that he has projected his consciousness into our world, and has found a means of freeing himself entirely, with help from Count Cagliostro."

"And yet you let him walk out of here not long ago," Morrow said, entering the conversation after long minutes of rapt silence. "Have you not issued chase?"

"We have, but his vessel is too rapid, and his ascent to the Void too fast. Furthermore, it is forbidden for us to follow him beyond Callisto," the Xan said. "We have sworn to remove ourselves from the worlds you occupy, and we shall continue to do so.

"However," the Xan added, pausing. "Should Althotas effect his release, we may be forced to take action. There are those among our people who would welcome the return to our old, violent ways. And in the ensuing battles, the cost to Earth itself may be dear."

The creature raised its arm, revealing a dark pink, three-fingered hand—more pincer-like than human—and pointed at the group. "It falls to you to stop Cagliostro from unleashing Althotas. In doing so, you may prove your mettle upon the larger stage, and earn the gratitude of our people. That is the will of our leaders."

Franklin coughed a moment before stepping forward. "Then we had best be on our way. But I must ask this question: We know so little of your city here, and less of your homeworld. How would Cagliostro know that such a treasure was housed here?"

The creature paused before answering, its harmonies laced with a slight dissonance. "You are perceptive, Dr. Franklin. We do not know, but any potential answer we may explore is disconcerting at best."

"Indeed," Morrow said. "It would seem our quarry may have had assistance from quarters other than this Althotas fellow. Whatever the case, I promise you, we shall tend to our affairs and bring this villain to justice. I respectfully suggest, however, that you tend to yours as well. As you said, there are those among you who would welcome a return to your warlike past," Morrow concluded.

"Again, perceptive," the Xan replied. Another door opened along the right wall. "You are forbidden from walking among our people, or those who live beyond our walls. This tunnel will take you back to the city gates, and your vessel. Now go, with our wishes for success."

Morrow nodded and, gathering his delegation with a sweep of his arm, led them from the temple.

"Captain," Weatherby whispered as he walked along, his chest feeling better even as his mind grew more troubled. "If Cagliostro's ship can ascend to the Void from anywhere, and outrun the Xan as well, how are *we* to catch him?"

Morrow frowned. "I do not know, but we had best find a solution quickly. It seems the very Earth itself is now at risk."

July 27, 2132

It was past dinnertime before Shaila Jain managed to return to the Hub, tossing her helmet in the equipment locker with tired satisfaction. It took the better part of three hours for her and the rescue team to cut through the hull of the now upside-down *Giffords* to get the crew and passengers out, and there were still a few tons of cargo to contend with. But everyone was alive, and that's what counted.

She slowly slid the pressure suit off her tired body, feeling every second of the past seventy-two hours in her bones. She lost count of the odd mishaps McAuliffe had endured, though three remained foremost in her mind—the wall in the cave, the book writing itself, and Heath's death. As she saw the miners gathering in the Hub to welcome—and perhaps warn—the new-comers, she added potential rioting to the list. During the rescue ops, she learned that the two injured JSC officers were pummeled in the mess hall by at least six miners, and that four of them had to be taken down with zappers, in addition to the one Diaz personally thrashed.

Shaila could easily see that the diggers still didn't look happy, but the loss of the *Giffords* and the AOO sensors was enough to make them more scared than pissed. Scared would make them more pliable—theoretically. Either that, or they'd really go batshit. On the bright side, more than a few of them gave her a nod as she passed through the Hub. There were a handful of smiles. And someone gave her a friendly pat on the shoulder too. That didn't mean they still wouldn't go batshit, of course, but perhaps Shaila's rescue—and Diaz' gamble—bought them a bit of goodwill and time.

Thus, Shaila couldn't help but feel pretty good as she cautiously climbed the stairs to the command center; her knee was better, but it would oc-casionally send a pang or two up her leg to remind her all was not well. She was learning to ignore it.

"How we doing, 'Rico?" she asked Finelli as she entered the command center.

"MarsSats and sensors still down. Dr. Hiyashi told me to tell you there's no new activity, but I have no idea what she means," Finelli said. "Do you?"

"Yeah," Shaila smiled weakly. "Need-to-know, Lieutenant. Where's Diaz?"

"She's in with Harry and Dr. Durand," Finelli advised, nodding his head toward Diaz' office.

Shaila nodded and knocked anyway. "Come," Diaz said, her voice muffled by the door.

Inside, Harry was sitting in Diaz' guest chair, looking mightily pissed, while Stephane scowled at him as he leaned against the bulkhead. "What do you mean, we're not going back outside?" Harry was saying—shouting, really.

Shaila tried not to smirk. "Sorry to interrupt, ma'am. All hands aboard *Giffords* secured. No major injuries, but we'll pack 'em off to Levin to be sure."

"Thanks, Jain. Sorry, Harry, you were saying?"

"I was saying that you can't shut us down!" Harry said after a sharp glare toward Shaila. "Those guys out there rioted this afternoon because of the shit going down here. You got two of your guys in sickbay and six of mine knocked cold with zappers. And now you want to tell them to sit on their hands and play nice?"

"I hear they rioted for other reasons, no matter how much you want to turn this on us," Diaz countered, fixing Harry with a hard stare. "And no, I don't want them sitting around. I want them sent home."

"All of them?" Harry cried. "You can't be serious."

Diaz turned to Stephane. "Dr. Durand, your assessment of the safety of mining ops?"

Stephane shifted his stance along the wall, clearly uncomfortable with being put on the spot. "When you see what happened in the lava tube, and the ravines, and now at your Site Six, you see none of the usual triggers for seismic activity. You do not see tremors, tectonic shifts, any of it. They are very localized and they should not be so. The quake that killed Mr. Heath should have been felt all the way here at base. And it was not.

"So," Stephane said, drawing a deep breath. "The quakes are not confined to one area, and there is no way to tell when or where they may appear. My official report is that it is unsafe to mine anywhere in our area of Mars."

Before Harry could argue further, Diaz leaned forward and called up a pair of images on her computer screen, both maps, and started pointing at the first one. "OK, you know that device I told you about? Here's where it was found, Harry. Here's the suit-beacon logs showing where you and your people were hanging out, which coincides with the EM ring we believe is out there." She then pointed to the second one. "And here's our sensor outage. Coincidence?"

"Right, and your suit-beacon data is totally infallible." Harry groused. "I mean, when Jain had me fucking arrested in the middle of an accident...." He paused to try to contain his anger. "I didn't have my suit beacon on. I didn't notice it was missing."

Diaz seemed to consider this. "Jain, how easy is it to tamper with a suit beacon?"

Shaila had to think back to the manuals she skimmed on the topic when she first arrived. "Taking them off would be easy. Switching them with another suit? Probably not too hard. I mean, you'd need to play with a few different suits, and someone might see you do it and start wondering. But it's possible."

Harry held up his hands in faux supplication. "If that's not at least reasonable doubt, I don't know what is."

Diaz was about to reply when she was cut off by a loud voice from outside the door. "I don't give a damn who's in there, kid, she's gotta see this now!"

Diaz slid a tired hand across her face. "Kaczynski." She hit a button on her desk. "Finelli, let him in." The colonel nodded to Shaila, who rose and went to the door, ready to let him in—or knock him out, as needed.

A moment later, Kaczynski hustled into the room as respectfully as his bulky frame would allow. He was followed by someone else; Shaila recognized him as one of the miners that came in aboard *Giffords*.

"Sorry to disturb you, Colonel," Kaczynski said, "but you really gotta see this." He held out a small data chip.

Diaz reached over and took it, eyebrows raised. "Holovid?"

"Yes, ma'am," he replied. Shaila thought he was being unusually respectful. Or maybe it was something else altogether. "Tony here—this is Tony, by the way—he shot this as he was incoming on *Giffords*."

Diaz slid the chip into a reader on her desk. "OK, but this better be good."

A holo image sprang to life, hovering a half-meter off Diaz' desk. It showed the view out the *Giffords* window as it entered the Martian atmosphere. The sky lightened, and the familiar geography of Mars unfolded.

"Pretty. Nice angle," Shaila quipped.

"Keep watching," Kaczynski said.

The image continued, with more Mars, more landscape. There was some chatter about finding booze on base.

Then the screen went white for a second—exactly the same way Greene's holocam blanked when it hovered over the EM lines outside.

When the holoimage refocused, Shaila could hear the *Giffords* alarms going off, the passengers starting to ask questions, shouting. The camera panned to the interior of the craft, where she could see at least one of the passengers assuming the useless tuck-and-cover position. The camera panned back to the window.

"Oh...." Diaz quickly hit pause.

The frozen image was wholly unfamiliar. It showed a very long trench, at least five meters wide and several kilometers long. A series of other trenches branched off it at 45 degree angles, stretching off to the edges of the frame.

And at the head of the main trench was a pyramid.

"Three guesses where that is," Kaczynski said. When Shaila looked up, she saw his eyes were wide, his face drawn.

"Our cave," Shaila said.

"Far as I can tell. Check out the foothills over to the left," Kaczynski said, pointing at the little screen. "And that's the access road. It fits."

Shaila nodded as everyone studied the pyramid. The image was a little pixilated, but she could see the structure clearly—a full six tiers. The lava tube itself looked completely collapsed, which would explain the ditch...in part. That ditch looked a hell of a lot longer than the lava tube was.

In fact, it reminded her of a canal.

A Martian canal.

And the other ravines that had inexplicably appeared near the lava tube were transformed into other canals. They all pointed toward the pyramid.

Diaz stared hard at the image, then zoomed in on it. "Looks like...wow. Like Chichen Itza or something."

They stared for a few moments longer. The resolution was crap, but Shaila could still make out the fact that the pyramid's bricks were large—far larger than the stones in the cave had been. They also seemed to be intricately decorated—carved, maybe, or even painted—with images that she couldn't quite make out. The four-sided pyramid was topped with an odd circular structure that gleamed in the weak Martian sunlight. There were also various places on the walls that caught a similar gleam. Maybe it was gold?

Harry broke the silence and looked over at Shaila. "And you're sitting there thinking I had something to do with *that*?" he asked, with a touch of reverence completely outside his usual bombast.

Shaila ignored him and turned to Diaz. "I think Ed's right. We'd need sensors back to confirm it, but that…structure…appears to be right where the lava tube was. And that canal, or whatever, would roughly correspond to the length of the cavern. Right, Steve?"

Stephane was staring intently at the image, eyes wide and a slight smile on his face. "I recognize the landmarks. *Mon dieu*, it is incredible."

Shutting down the holoprojector, Diaz leaned back in her seat and signed. "Well, we don't have sensors. We don't have overhead coverage, either. Houston's already having kittens. Now this?"

"What are you going to tell them?" Shaila asked. It wasn't exactly protocol to ask, but hell, there was a pyramid out there. What's normal?

"At the moment? Just sensors and sats," Diaz said. "They'd see that anyway. The rest, well…I want to chat with Harry here first."

"And I'm telling you, I'm not involved in this, and neither are my people," Harry protested.

Kaczynski and Tony looked around and shifted slightly. "Maybe we ought to go," Kaczynski grumbled quietly.

Diaz smiled. "Tony, thanks for the vid. Why don't you get yourself some dinner? Ed, I'd like you to stay, if you don't mind." Tony quickly hurried outside, leaving Kaczynski fumbling with his hands next to Stephane. "Ed, I need you to be frank with me," the colonel said. "I assume some other folks have already seen this vid?"

"Yeah, and the rest probably heard about it by now," he said.

"How much of a shitstorm am I looking at?"

Kaczynski barked out a little laugh. "Between all the crap so far today and this thing? Ain't no regs say we gotta work under those conditions. Look, your girl here"—Kaczynski nodded toward Shaila—"did some fine work. I don't think anybody's ready to start something big now. But with this shit? A pyramid? If I were you, I'd lock down those transports good."

Diaz nodded. "I'll do one better than that," she said, turning to Harry. "You've just had a mining collapse. Someone, whether it's you or someone else, has been tampering with suit beacons, which is a big deal around here. And someone, again you or someone else, managed to place a ring of linear EM fields around my area of operations that took out half our sensor grid and three of our satellites. It's going to take us months to deal with just those issues, let alone a giant fucking pyramid of unknown origin—which, by the way, is totally unofficial and is not to be discussed. But until all that's dealt with, you've got no mining ops here."

Harry's mouth opened to protest, but closed after a second or two as Diaz continued. "I'm ordering an emergency evacuation of all Billiton personnel. No matter what happens in the next few days, nobody's going to let you back outside. So your people are going home. And I'm sure JSC is going to debrief each and every one of them when they get back to Earth."

"I'd like to stay," Harry said weakly. "Someone has to keep an eye on the company's interests."

Diaz frowned. "Honestly, I'm not sure I trust you around here right now, Harry."

"You can cut off my comms. Monitor computer use. Kick me out of my office. Whatever. Someone needs to stay here," he said.

Diaz looked over at Shaila. "What do you think, Jain?"

Shaila thought about it for a moment. The old maxim about keeping your enemies closer seemed apt. "He stays in the JSC corridor. All his passwords are revoked. He gets nothing from his office from this point forward, and he has zero access to any computer, workstation or datapad. Not even a calculator. He gets e-mail privileges once a day, under supervision."

"Agreed," Diaz said. "Harry, you stay. Your people are gone." She turned to Kaczynski. "I know your guys are scared, pissed, whatever. I really need you to do your best to keep them in line as best you can while we get 'em out of here. If not, I'll zap all y'all to hell and back again. Got it?"

Kaczynski nodded. "I'm more than happy to get off this rock and let you talk to the little green men. Doubt you'll get much argument from anyone else, either."

"Good. Thanks, Ed. Harry, get moving. I'll be sounding the order in a few minutes."

Harry gave Shaila one final, withering stare before leaving the office, Kaczynski in tow.

"What a bastard," Diaz muttered. "Be sure to relay that bit about his comms and computers. And be sure to tell everyone that Greene and Yuna aren't part of the evac. We'll need them."

Shaila was already tapping out orders on her datapad. "On it. At last count, we have 58 Billiton employees, including the eight guys that just came in, and three 20-seat transports. Oh, and we have Greene's cameraman and producer, making sixty. That means when they leave, we're stuck here at least another four weeks." *While Mars figures out whether it wants to tear itself apart or not*, she thought.

She looked over to Stephane, who returned her gaze with a small smile and a shrug. "At least it will not be boring."

Diaz looked down at her hands, seemingly weighing her options. To Shaila, the colonel suddenly looked very tired. "No kidding," she said quietly. "All right. Sound the emergency evac. Let's get 'em out of here."

CHAPTER 18

May 4, 1779

F*ather,*

The Void is vast—so much so that a ship could sail for months without so much as spotting another vessel. It is only with our alchemically-treated looking glasses, as well as the bright beacon lanterns we hang about the ship, that we are able to see, and be seen by, other vessels.

Yet it has been our fate to come across yet another ship in the Void as we left Callisto. Our path took us past Ganymede once more, en route toward the worlds beyond the Rocky Main, and that is where we spotted a sister ship of His Majesty's Navy—one that very quickly moved aggressively towards us. Even Captain Morrow wondered why a fellow ship would do such a thing before remembering that Daedalus *was disguised as a Ganymedean privateer!*

It had seemed a perfectly good idea at the time, as these things often are. With Jones and *Bonhomme Richard* likely back in the Void—and the rest of the French and Ganymedeans unaware of their mission or illustrious passenger—Morrow and Plumb had thought that disguising *Daedalus* as a Ganny would dissuade any would-be attackers, especially as the work upon the mainsail was newly completed and not as thorough as a repair in port might be. The disguise was simple enough, requiring but two watches of painting and several hands put to sewing the Ganymedeans' garish striped flag.

What they did not count on was encountering another English vessel so close to the routes patrolled by the Ganymedeans and their new French allies. Yet they were barely away from Callisto's pull when a ship of His Majesty's Navy was spotted—and given the other ship's change of course, they were likely spotted in turn.

"Run up the white flag and our true colors as well," Morrow ordered from the quarterdeck while still keeping his glass upon the English ship sighted off to starboard. "Have the men stand down from the guns, hands raised. It shall do us no good to be shot at by one of our own!"

As Plumb relayed the orders and a pair of men raised a white banner from the quarterdeck, Morrow turned to Weatherby. "I have need of your eyes, Mr. Weatherby. Stay on the glass and watch the other ship carefully, and relay all that you see."

Weatherby complied, wondering why the captain would not prefer his own experienced eye; while Weatherby was widely considered to have the best sight of any man aboard, it was rare that Morrow did not train his own glass outward as well. Instead, Morrow stood right next to him on the starboard rail, looking out at the smaller Royal Navy vessel as if he could see it perfectly well.

The other vessel was a 12-gun brig—a two-masted ship half the size of *Daedalus*, primarily used by His Majesty's Navy for scouting missions and planetary patrol. She was likely on the hunt for Ganymedean shipping or smugglers in the Jovian system. As the little ship moved at speed toward *Daedalus*, Weatherby thought it quite brave of the little ship to attempt an engagement with a full-sized frigate. Brave or foolhardy, perhaps.

Then the warning shot came.

Weatherby spotted the small plume of flame from the little brig's foremost starboard gun. Moments later, all aboard *Daedalus* saw a gout of purplish fire speed altogether too close to the port side of the ship, accompanied by an incredible roar—an alchemical hull-piercing round, further enhanced with a rather spectacular and obvious noise-maker. It would have been comical had the other ship not been English.

"What is she doing?" Morrow said quietly, with obvious exasperation.

While Weatherby felt Morrow's question was wholly rhetorical, he felt obliged to reply. "She's turned about 20 degrees on her keel-axis, sir. About 15 degrees downward as well. I think she means to come out under us."

"Get those guns in!" Plumb roared from the quarterdeck. "She's one of ours, even if she don't know it yet!"

Another puff of smoke and flame emerged from the little brig's starboard side, and a second round—this one of pinkish flame, the mark of a fire-starter round—came uncomfortably close to the top railing of the quarter-deck itself, mere feet from where Weatherby stood with his glass. He took two steps back, nearly plowing into the captain, though even Morrow was more startled than annoyed.

"Take in sheets, bring the planesails and ruddersail in," Morrow ordered. "Complete stop. Have then men stand down. I want no movement on deck."

As Plumb relayed the captain's orders, Weatherby watched the English ship grow closer and closer, as if she planned to ram the larger ship for no sane reason at all. Weatherby turned to report once more, but saw Morrow now with his glass out as well, and the other vessel was well close enough for him to see. Soon, it would be altogether much too close.

Seemingly at the last moment, the little brig dipped downward to lar-board, continuing its keel-axis spin in order to sail directly under the now-dormant *Daedalus*, exposing the frigate's lower hull to the brig's guns. Even with just six guns firing, it would be enough to spread iron, wood and fiery death to all belowdecks.

"With me, Mr. Weatherby," Morrow said calmly. Weatherby hastened to Morrow's side as the captain walked to the quarterdeck's aft railing. A moment later, the brig emerged beneath them, her guns pointing straight up at them from a distance of no more than 35 yards.

"Dear God," Weatherby breathed.

"Train your glass upon the quarterdeck," Morrow said, a bare hint of chastening in his voice. "Look for anything beyond the ordinary."

"Aye, sir," Weatherby replied. There was much beyond the pale in this encounter, but he did as instructed. As he watched, he could see a pair of lieutenants upon the quarterdeck, one of whom wore the braid of a post-captain—a lieutenant typically promoted to the command of smaller vessels such as these. The post-captain had his glass likewise trained on *Daedalus'* quarterdeck.

Finally, as the little brig passed into the distance, Weatherby could make out a name. "She's the *Badger*, sir," he reported. "I see an officer on the quarterdeck with his glass. Likely the post-captain." Suddenly, Weatherby saw the other officer drop his glass and smile. A minute later, as the *Badger* sped off into the distance, she likewise ran up a white flag.

"I wonder what he saw," Weatherby said. "Any privateer can muster up captured uniforms."

"A very valid point, Mr. Weatherby," Morrow said with a smile. "But even if we had indeed been captured by the Ganymedeans, the rebels would be quite hard pressed to muster up my face, imperfect as it might be, which is why I stationed myself here as she passed. It is worth becoming known amongst your peers in the service, in those rare cases they may mistakenly wish to shoot at you."

Weatherby nodded and saluted as *Daedalus* prepared to come amidships with *Badger*. The captain was in fine spirits, leaving Weatherby to wonder whether Morrow had something in mind for this little brig.

A half-hour later, the *Daedalus* welcomed the commander of the *Badger* aboard, a young lieutenant just a few years older than Weatherby himself, one Horatio Nelson. "A good man, this Nelson," Morrow had told his officers prior to his arrival. "He was a mid with me aboard *Carcass* in '73. He's well connected, of course. 'Tis no small thing to go from mid to post-captain in six years. But he's a good sailor. I imagine he might have a decent future, if he can avoid shooting his comrades out of the Void."

Morrow and the wardroom officers met Nelson as he came aboard. Weatherby thought he cut a dashing figure, though he seemed to possess a surety about him that wasn't entirely appropriate. The line between confidence and hubris is often one seen after the fact by the one who crosses it, Weatherby felt.

"I had heard your ship was captured, Captain Morrow," Nelson said after the formalities were over. "We've had privateers disguising themselves as English vessels for weeks now. I nearly opened fire on you!"

"You were right to be on your guard, Mr. Nelson, given our necessary ruse," Morrow said. "She's a smart little ship, your *Badger*. May I ask your orders?"

"We are to interdict enemy shipping around the Jovian moons, sir. We sail from Port Royal. We left port but a week ago."

Morrow considered this. "Well, then, Nelson, as senior commander on the scene and duly authorized by the Admiralty, I may have new orders for you," Morrow said. "Would you join me in my cabin? Mr. Weatherby, please request the presence of all our guests and pass the word for Mr.

Plumb and Dr. Finch, if you please."

Soon thereafter, a most notable gathering was held in the great cabin. Morrow presided, flanked on either side by the mystic luminaries Benjamin Franklin and the Count St. Germain. Nelson was also granted a seat, as was Anne. Plumb, Finch and Weatherby were left to stand. Introductions were made throughout; Nelson acquitted himself well despite the surprise of meeting a traitor to the Crown, followed by the greatest alchemist known to mankind, all in the space of a few moments.

Weatherby caught Anne trying to meet his gaze, but he turned away each time, Cagliostro's taunts echoing in his ears—and her denial of his claims notably absent.

"Our situation seems dire, my friends," Dr. Franklin said finally. "We may safely assume that Cagliostro's plans have gone far too well for him, and that he has the planetary essences of Mercury, Venus, Earth, the Moon, the four Jovian moons, and Saturn—the latter without even having to visit the place! Given that he schemes with an ancient Martian, and dares not approach Saturn, we may assume his destination is Mars."

"So our course is set," Morrow said. "We should proceed with all haste, since it's clear his vessel is the faster."

"Agreed, Captain. But we must be cautious," St. Germain warned. "Franklin and I have not had much opportunity to discuss matters since leaving Callisto, so we have yet to divine his motives. Given his ties to Althotas, I suspect that Cagliostro's plan has something to do with Mars, but a notion of his exact working escapes us, beyond the freedom of this Althotas person."

"It is a difficult thing," Franklin added. "Each of these planetary essences are, in and of themselves, most powerful. Many of them would, theoretically, cancel each other out. Others may produce any number of wild effects that would overshadow whatever goal Cagliostro may have. To place all of these in balance and harmony is a herculean task, especially to further his apparent goal."

After a few moments of silence, Franklin rose slowly from the table; his exertions on Callisto had aggravated his gout, but his mind remained undimmed. "Captain Morrow, may we retire to the quarterdeck, if you please? I should like to see your orrery once I have obtained some books from my quarters."

A few minutes later, the assemblage gathered upon the quarterdeck before the *Daedalus'* clockwork model of the Known Worlds. "How long should it take us to make Mars?" Franklin asked.

"We are unfortunate that, as of now, Mars is traveling on the other side of the sun from Jupiter," Weatherby said. "About seven weeks, I should say."

"Mr. Weatherby, could you use this to give us a sense of where the planets will be in seven weeks' time?" Franklin asked. Weatherby nodded and, with some hasty calculation, moved the planets ahead accordingly.

Franklin, Finch and St. Germain studied the position of the planets intently, and soon the alchemists were engaged in a lively discussion, while Anne looked on, listening intently.

"The six-pointed star, then?" Finch asked.

"Mercury is out of position for that," the Count said. "What of the Rosa Crusis?"

"No, I can't see it," Finch said. "Saturn would have to be at least six degrees further along."

"Then I should think it's the Tree of Life," Franklin said. "It is certainly the most powerful of alignments. That ought to please him, the scoundrel."

"It should, but none of the planets are in position for it," Finch said, holding up one of Franklin's books. Upon the page, Weatherby saw a strange array of lines and circles—the circles were obviously the planets, and the lines connected them in some sort of alchemical manner, he supposed.

Yet there was something to the drawing that caused Weatherby to study it, and the orrery, intently. While the alchemists flipped through books and continued arguing, Weatherby circled the orrery for several moments, crouching over it, until he gasped in recognition.

"There is indeed a pattern on the orrery, My Lordship," Weatherby said. "Look there. Do you see it?"

"Stay out of this, young man," the Count snapped. "You know not of what we speak."

"Francis! You could stand to be kinder," Dr. Franklin said before turning to me. "What do you see, Mr. Weatherby?"

"Well," said Weatherby, "this diagram is such that Mars is off to the right, yes? Well, I will admit that it does not hold true as such. But if you look at this pattern and put Mars at its center, then you might have better fortune with it."

Dr. Franklin looked closely at the orrery, and the Count began referencing each planet in his book. Finch, meanwhile, looked over at the young lieutenant with a large smile upon his face. "I think you've cracked it, Weatherby."

"So it would seem," the Count said flatly. "The alignments match, though there are two spheres missing when there should be only one."

Immediately, the alchemists launched into another a vigorous debate. After a few minutes, it seemed Morrow had heard enough. "All right. Would one of you kindly tell we ignorant fools what you have found?"

Dr. Franklin responded: "I apologize, Captain. You see, the Tree of Life represents one of the oldest alchemical formulae we know of. It comes from the Jewish people and their Kabbalah study, which has informed our Great Work for thousands of years. There are ten major spheres in the Tree, most of which represent various planetary alignments. In most workings, the Sun is at the Crown, the uppermost sphere, though Earth may be in this place at times.

"Now, in the pattern that your Lt. Weatherby has discovered, you see that yes, the Sun is at the Crown, but Mars is at the center, here, what we call the Daath."

"Yes, yes, I see it," Morrow said. "But what does it mean?"

"I cannot say with certainty, but if Mars is his destination, than I would say that he wishes to alter the pattern of the Tree. Given Mars' destructive qualities, I imagine this might be undertaken to create an unmaking of something, likely something immense."

"Like the imprisonment of this Althotas person," Dr. Finch said.

"Indeed," Dr. Franklin said. "If the Xan imprisoned him in some sort of Hell between worlds, then this working would free him. But with the powerful materials at hand, there could be a risk of unleashing more than just one soul. He could crack open the very gates between our world and others beyond, perhaps even Hell itself!"

"We don't know that," St. Germain said. "All we know is that this is a clue to his working, nothing more. And there are two spheres still missing."

The group fell silent once more, leaving it to Anne to speak up. "What of the Rocky Main, m'lord?" she asked St. Germain.

The Count looked at her with surprise and thinly veiled disdain. "What of it? Why are you even here, girl?"

"She is as much an alchemist as we," Finch replied as Anne scowled at the Count. "I can vouch for her knowledge. She was apprenticed to Dr. McDonnell."

"Apprenticed?" St. Germain said. "Are there no men left in the universe who can understand the Great Work? All right, elaborate, if you would."

Anne straightened up as she spoke. "Well, I was thinking about what we saw in the temple. There was a planet there, one that the Martians held, that the Xan completely destroyed. It appeared to me that what's left of that planet could be the Rocky Main. If Cagliostro needed the essences of *all* the Known Worlds, would he not need something from the Main as well?"

"That may have some validity," St. Germain remarked with a frown. "Some of us have long theorized that the Main was once the legendary planet Phaeton. But if there are workings that might involve this world, why have I not heard of them?"

Dr. Franklin reached over and actually slapped the Count in the back of the head in a very grandfatherly way. "Because you, and Roger, and so many of us hoard our knowledge like old dragons upon piles of gold, that's why!" he scolded. "We work alone, when we should be working together!"

"Yes, yes, I've heard your democracy in alchemy discussion before, Franklin. I'm still not going to any more Masonic meetings. So let us suppose Cagliostro may need the essence of Phaeton, though I've no idea what that might even look like. What then?"

Franklin turned to Weatherby. "Lieutenant, from what you know of the *Chance*'s travels, can you estimate how long it might take for them to travel from Callisto to the edge of the Main?"

Weatherby pulled out his journal and, flipping to the back page, began performing the necessary equations. "They can make the Main in two and a half weeks, Doctor. If they're straight on to Mars, it might take them six or less."

Franklin, in the meantime, was flipping through books of his own with Finch and St. Germain looking on. "Very good. Now, let us plot the largest islands in the Main, shall we?" Weatherby smiled at the reference to islands, as the Main consisted of nothing but barren rocks, ranging in size from pebbles to small worlds, floating in the dead of the Void.

After a few minutes, there were four coins upon the orrery. "These are the four largest, then—Pallas, Ceres, Juno and Vesta," Franklin said. "Look how they are so close together, within a few days' sail of each other. I believe that, as with Jupiter, he may attempt to fuse pieces of these islands together to recreate the essence of Phaeton itself."

There was silence on the quarterdeck as this sunk in, with the alchemists present nodding in agreement—and the naval officers simply looking confused. "So, then, what does that mean, exactly?" Morrow finally asked.

"We have time, Captain!" Franklin said jubilantly. "Cagliostro must traverse the distance between these four points, or otherwise tarry amongst the Main to gather whatever he needs. Even if he loses but a few days, it is to our advantage. And if he must, as I've presupposed, gather materials from the four largest islands, then we may catch him before he reaches Mars, so long as we head for the red planet straightaway."

St. Germain nodded. "Neatly done, Franklin. Neatly done, indeed." He then turned to Anne. "My apologies, miss. It seems your notion had merit after all. And the grouping of these four islands so close to one another would fit neatly into the Tree of Life diagram that this young man here discovered."

Morrow nodded and addressed the officers present. "Mr. Nelson, I believe it is time for you to return to the *Badger*. I am placing you under my command, with orders to escort *Daedalus* to Mars." Nelson saluted and, making his good-byes quickly, re-boarded his ship.

"Mr. Weatherby, make your heading Mars. Full royals, stud'sels and planes, if you please. If this Cagliostro is toying with such dangerous forces, I shall want to be there ahead of him."

I rushed to comply with the captain's orders, but not before spotting a most peculiar sight off the starboard side, which was facing Callisto. I saw a small light rise from the moon, and unless my eyes deceived me, it originated from the very same spot where we had met the Xan. This light rose quite quickly from the planet and, once it made the Void, went past Jupiter at a respectable speed.

A quick calculation made its course apparent—Saturn. I told the captain at once, and he merely nodded. It seems the Xan, he said, were racing to inform their superiors of what had transpired of late.

So while we are heartened that we may yet catch Cagliostro, should he tarry among the rocky islands of the Main, I am convinced our mission rests upon a knife's edge. Should he succeed, this madman will not only unleash a powerful evil—but could unleash the Xan upon all of us as well. The emissary on Callisto said his people were once warlike. I pray they do not become so again.

July 28, 2132

Shaila stalked the halls of McAuliffe Base, zapper holstered but loose, looking for signs of trouble as the evacuation got underway. Each group of miners—in the mess hall, in the barracks corridor, in the Hub—represented potential trouble. Would they drink the last of their contraband booze and get unruly? Would some of them refuse to go? Would some try to commandeer a transport and leave before everyone else was ready?

She walked, and looked, her focus sharp despite her exhaustion.

And she saw no trouble brewing whatsoever among the sixty souls about to take a long, uncomfortable ride back to Earth.

Sure, the JSC personnel did get some pretty hard looks. A few choice words were thrown around just within earshot. And a kind of sullen indignation permeated all the Billiton personnel—the kind of ornery frustration usually reserved for lawyers, dentists and government tax agents.

Yet despite the anger and frustration, the miners seemed to be handling the evac well. There were no protests, no disputes. They just packed up, as ordered, with very little fuss.

"You're damn right they're behaved," Kaczynski said when Shaila asked about it. He was lined up with 17 other miners and Greene's two holovid colleagues, all waiting for the last transport. "The new guy, Tony, wasn't shy about what he saw today. Between that and what killed Jack, they're scared shitless."

Shaila nodded, studiously ignoring the clinking sound from Kaczynski's duffle bag as he gestured. She didn't begrudge him a drink in transit; four weeks was a long time to be stuck on an emergency transport with 19 other people and exactly zero privacy. "Just surprised, is all," she replied. "I'd have thought some of them would petition to stay."

Kaczynski shrugged. "We're gonna be at least a couple weeks without digging anyway. And we can't figure out that collapse at Site Six if the whole damn planet's gonna quake up. Throw in a pyramid? Screw that. I know I'm outta here. I'll go dig on the Moon, maybe do some asteroid wrangling for a change. There's plenty of work that don't involve this shit."

Shaila nodded. "All right, then. Thanks for keeping 'em calm, Ed. Safe trip home, OK?"

Kaczynski extended his hand to her. "You'll be bored without us."

The light above the emergency transport hatch turned from red to green. "All aboard!" Adams called out from the hatchway. "Next stop, big blue marble!"

Shaila laughed as she shook Kaczynski's hand. "Kids."

"Glad he ain't with us. Good luck, Lieutenant." For once, the utterance of her rank didn't come with any snotty overtones.

"Thanks. Go hit a beach for me."

Shaila watched the men file into the cramped transport, duffle bags in hand, then headed up to the command center to supervise the launch. The two other transports had already taken off and achieved Mars escape velocity. At least Earth was in the right position—it could've been up to eight weeks otherwise.

The transport sealed itself and began its long procession to the launch pad, carried on a set of rails. From there, it was a simple matter of issuing the computerized order to launch—the course was automatically updated by McAuliffe's computers on an hourly basis.

From the observation window in the command center, Shaila watched the little transport's engines roar to life, and saw it slowly lift off the pad. She kept an ear on her ops team, who were busy tracking the vehicle through the thin atmosphere and into space. Escape velocity was achieved, and within twenty minutes the transport had settled upon its final course. Four weeks from now, it would enter Earth orbit, and JSC would send a shuttle to pick them up and bring them home.

Well, not home per se, Shaila thought. If everything that was happening on Mars was as…big…as Shaila thought it was, the debriefings would take a few days. She thought back to her own experience with debriefings and scowled. They could be altogether awful.

"All right, lock everything down," Shaila said as she turned to her ops officers. "We're back on normal watch. Good job, everyone."

Stifling a yawn—it was just after midnight—Shaila headed for the door. She was stopped by the sound of Washington clearing his throat. "Umm… ma'am?"

"Yes, Washington?"

The young man stood up from his station to address her, looking every bit as awkward as the new recruit he was. "Ma'am, is there any way you can tell us what's going on? I mean…it's really been hitting the fan, you know? And we just sent the last emergency transport out the door. We're kind of stuck here now."

Shaila turned and leaned up against one of the workstations. "You're right," she said quietly. "And I bet you guys heard a lot of stuff today from the diggers, right?"

There were murmurs of assent and nods from around the room. It made sense—Shaila and Diaz had asked a lot of them, but with zero in the way of explanation. If she was feeling stressed, tired and scared, how would they be feeling without even an inkling of what was going down?

"All right. I'll talk to Diaz. Let's circle back here in fifteen," Shaila said.

"Way ahead of you, Jain," came a voice from behind her.

Shaila turned to see Diaz entering the command center—with a huge chocolate cake in her hands. In a day full of strange sights, it ranked right up there.

"Colonel?" Shaila asked, trying to wipe the grin from her face.

"Birthday cake," Diaz replied, setting the dessert on a vacant workstation. "My partner sent it. I turn 50 next week—and not a goddamn word from anyone about it!" Soft laughter filled the room before Diaz continued. "You guys really did great today, and I figured you deserved a treat—and an explanation."

Ten minutes later, the room was filled with loud conversation, muffled only by cake. Shaila saw that Yuna, Stephane and Greene had joined the party, though Diaz seemed to be keeping them busy, probably getting herself updated. Shaila hadn't seen Stephane all throughout the evacuation process, and despite her best efforts to convince herself otherwise, she kind of missed him. She also saw Harry quietly walk in, looking drawn and haggard. Usually, he entered the command center as if he owned the place—which, in a way, he did. Now, he simply gave Diaz a small nod and, after looking around hesitantly for a moment, slowly made for a vacant tracking station along the back wall. She almost felt sorry for him…but not quite.

"OK, attention on deck!" Diaz yelled. "I know it's been crazy, and I know you've heard a lot. You deserve to know exactly what's going on, so here it is."

The room immediately fell silent, every pair of eyes on the colonel as she set her plate down. With a few taps on her datapad, Diaz called up the holovid of the pyramid on the command center's main viewscreen.

"This is what's out there," Diaz said. "Dr. Durand estimates it to be at least 50 meters tall, give or take, and each side measures 100 meters or so."

Shaila looked at her teammates. Every single one of them was riveted to the screen. A couple of jaws threatened to brush the ground.

"Three days ago, there was an earthquake within a lava tube on this very site," Diaz continued. "Yesterday, we discovered there was some kind of wall within that cave, and we captured this holo, showing how it was being built."

Diaz switched to the holovid Shaila had taken of the rocks rolling through the cave—and rolling right up the wall. It still gave Shaila a shiver when she saw it.

"Today, we've had the collapse at Site Six, the sensor outage, and of course, the pyramid sighting. Dr. Durand and Dr. Hiyashi here—ably aided by Dr. Evan Greene, our newest recruit," Diaz said with a smile and a nod toward the holovision host, "have been unable to capture any more images of the pyramid from our MarsSats. The three remaining satellites still have telemetry and are relaying communications back to Earth, but for whatever reason, their cameras are offline."

Diaz stepped forward into the command center, looking at each of her junior officers in turn. "We believe all these events are related somehow, but I gotta be honest with you. We don't know why this is happening. We're working on the 'how' first, and we're making progress. We've also sent off everything to Houston. Can't imagine what that mission meeting's going to look like."

More laughter spilled forth, breaking the tension. Shaila, however, noted that Diaz had omitted two key pieces of information—the existence of Weatherby's journal, as well as the EM ring outside the base.

"So that's why we kicked Billiton off Mars," Diaz said. "Who made this pyramid? I have no idea. Obviously, when you see an artificial structure on Mars, you think little green men. But I want to caution you that we just don't know yet. Let's remember that the Chinese, the Islamic League, the Russians—they all visited Mars before this base was established. And the U.S. and E.U. militaries played some games down here too. I won't sit here and say it's just a man-made thing, because we don't know. But I'm not saying it's Wookie or Klingon, either.

"As most of you know, Houston dispatched a survey team here two days ago. They're still about four weeks out. Given how eventful today was, I have no clue what's going to happen tomorrow.

"What's more, thanks to Mike Alvarez and his band of malcontents, we lost a transport earlier. So with everyone else gone, we're staying on Mars, no matter what. I've requested two more transports from Houston, and I expect they'll send them ASAP. But that still keeps us here for the duration.

"So here's the deal," Diaz concluded. "With Billiton gone, there's a lot less routine stuff to do, but there's a shitload more interesting stuff going on. You're needed here. Each and every one of you is going to have to step up in a big way, and I know you will."

Diaz looked at each officer, one at a time, and to a person, they all looked back at her steadily. Shaila knew, right then, that they wouldn't have any problems with the crew. They were a good, dedicated bunch. And Diaz was a pretty damn good leader.

"Tomorrow," the colonel said, "we're going to figure out a plan to study this thing. In the meantime, engineering will try to salvage *Giffords*. If shit goes down in a big way, that boat's our only ticket off Mars. The rest of you will work on getting our sensors back on line. Right now, though, go get a centrifuge spinning and get some rest. We're back at oh-eight-thirty, ready to work our asses off. Dismissed."

Diaz strode into her office while Shaila watched the junior officers closely. None of them sat by themselves. None of them even left right away. Instead, in groups of three or four, they called up the video and the pyramid image—and started theorizing.

"Yeah, but here's the thing," Shaila heard Washington ask someone from engineering. "This had to start somewhere, right? Even before the first quake. So what the hell triggered it?"

Shaila knew that answer: the homebrew particle accelerator that Harry—or someone else—buried under the Martian surface.

Then the proverbial light bulb went off in her head. *But what triggered the EM fields to kick on?*

Idea firmly in mind, Shaila hustled out of the command center, brushing past Harry as he sullenly watched the hubbub. There was still work to do.

CHAPTER 19

June 12, 1779

Father,

    After our eventful sojourn in the Jovian system, we are en route to Mars and have returned to the typical patterns of shipboard life. The men have drilled for battle every day now, so that if Fortune is with us and Chance *has tarried amongst the islands of the Main, we shall meet her and answer her superior firepower with more rapid, disciplined shots than a gaggle of pirates could hope to muster. We've also shed our Ganymedean disguise in favor of the black and yellow of His Majesty's Navy, for I believe all of us wish to engage our quarry as true Englishmen.*

    Obviously, this is no typical transit. Those of us who met with the Xan and encountered Cagliostro are haunted by the ghosts of the past: the brutal wars that utterly destroyed one planet and razed another, the power that these Saturnine aliens still likely possess, and the fell working that would see this Althotas released upon the Known Worlds once more.

    Personally, I am haunted by other matters as well....

"Weatherby, for the love of God, why do you not at least talk to her?" Finch demanded.

They were taking a stroll upon the deck after dinner, Finch smoking one of his caustic little cigars. This was not the first time Finch had brought up the most unfortunate Anne, but Weatherby remained firm in his stance on the matter.

"Doctor, I will thank you to mind yourself," Weatherby said tersely. "I have nothing to discuss with Miss Baker."

"Rubbish. You stand your watch over her with naught but detachment, bordering on ill manners. You do not address her at dinner, and when she speaks to you, your answers are frustratingly minimal and terse. What is it, man? Has the bloom fallen off the flower so much since Callisto? Even with the past being what it is, you could do far worse."

Weatherby scowled at Finch, but said nothing as he continued to stroll past the larboard-side guns. Finch allowed this silence, knowing in his short acquaintance that the young officer was a private individual, and one who would not easily bare his soul.

After a few moments, they came to the ship's bow, where they could see light seeping from the planks underfoot—the alchemical lab was right under them. "How are our guests getting on?" Weatherby said, his change-of-subject clumsily wrought. "The forward area is small to begin with."

"Oh, they are peas in a pod," Finch said, for once taking the hint. "And most intriguing company besides. Dr. Franklin's explorations into the forces of electricity have fascinated me. My knowledge of mechanics actually surpasses his, but the Count's knowledge leaves us both severely wanting. I am learning much, to be sure, as is Miss Baker. We may yet contribute something to the coming battle."

"Oh? How so?"

A brief flash of light erupted out of the gunports below. "Dr. Franklin says he was inspired by the Xan's seeming mastery of electricity," Finch explained, nodding toward the flash. "I dare say he shan't rest until he finds an alchemical means of harnessing it himself. Truly, he and St. Germain are most remarkable."

A small smile crept across Weatherby's face. "You're not one to admit a deficit of knowledge, Doctor. They must truly be among the great alchemists of the age."

"Indeed. I would suggest you try to keep the ship intact in the coming engagement," Finch said lightly. "Should they fall, I should hate to be the one to advance mankind's knowledge of the Great Work on my own."

They laughed together, turning to walk along the starboard side, back toward the quarterdeck. They could see a handful of boulders from the Rocky Main on either side of the ship. The Main was not as dense with debris as the chapbooks and broadsheets would have the Earth-bound believe, but the lookout watches had been doubled for the duration of their transit, so that *Daedalus* could evade collision if need be.

"I think, Mr. Weatherby, I will retire early," Finch said about halfway back to the quarterdeck. "I've put you where you need to be."

"I don't follow," Weatherby said, his attention drawn back to his companion from the cratered, pitted rocks in the distance.

Behind Finch, he could see Anne slowly walking toward them.

"Mr. Forester was a bit in his cups at dinner this evening," Finch said with a knowing grin. "I prescribed rest for him, and assured the young man you could be relied upon to take up the remainder of his watch discreetly."

Weatherby scowled. "You're a meddler of the worst sort."

"Most assuredly." Finch winked at him, then walked off toward the hatch to the gun deck, nodding at Anne as he went.

Weatherby and Anne stood apart for a few moments before she broke the awkward silence. "I did wonder why Dr. Finch kept filling that boy's glass."

"Indeed," Weatherby allowed, his eyes focused on the planking at Anne's feet. "He may yet infect us all with his decadent ways."

Anne walked past him, back toward the bowsprit, leaving a swirl of dress and hair in her wake. "I find his heart to be in the right place, even if his judgment is lacking," she said.

Weatherby kept pace a few feet back. "I will say he has come a long way from whence I found him."

They walked on in silence, meandering around the main deck in a circle for several minutes. A frigate is large enough for a person to gain exercise under the stars, but not so long that the sights and sounds of the ship do not bore after a short while.

Finally, Anne stopped and turned suddenly, prompting Weatherby to nearly stumble in his effort not to collide with her. "So what is it, Tom?"

Weatherby straightened up, pulling on his coat to smooth it out. "I'm not sure I understand."

Anne scowled deeply at him, anguish beginning to mar the simple beauty of her face. "You must think me a fool, then, for not noticing how you've barely spoken to me since Callisto. You have switched watches with your fellows so that we are never alone together. You treat me distantly and, some would say, quite rudely, even though I bargained with both the Xan and St. Germain to bring you back from death's very door! So I say again, what *is* it, Tom?"

Weatherby felt his heart tighten, seemingly echoing the pistol shot he endured on Callisto. "I have not meant to offend you," he stammered. "I—"

"No, you simply mean to avoid me," she snapped. "You've removed yourself from all kindness, compassion and intimacy. Why?"

"Perhaps now is not the best time," Weatherby said softly, looking at the boards of the deck.

"It is the only time," Anne said. "What sin have I committed against you?"

"You've committed no sin against…me," he said, wishing desperately to be done with the conversation.

"As I thought," Anne snapped, stalking off down the deck before whirling around again. "You would hold my other sins against me, even though I've given you naught but my very best self."

Weatherby looked up at her. "I am sorry, Miss Baker. I know that your life has not been an easy one."

"You know nothing of it," she said coldly. "You write to your father often, I've seen it. Your mother and sisters await you in England. You do your duty and bury your head in your books. You've never known hunger, or thirst, or loneliness. You've never known desperation."

The young officer was stunned by the forthrightness of her words, and the truth of them. "No, I have not," he said quietly.

"You think it a sin to survive?" she went on. "God gave me this life, and then saw fit to inflict the travails through which I've suffered. So should I have wasted His gift and gone to meet Him early, or broken His rules for a chance at survival? What is the greater sin?"

Weatherby regarded the decking once more, at a complete loss for words. His chest ached, his stomach protested, and his mind reeled. But Anne was in no mood to grant him reprieve.

"Yes, I sold my favor on Elizabeth Mercuris," she hissed. "Yes, that is how I learned to use a blade to defend myself, for if I did not, I'd surely be dead already. Yes, that is how I met Roger. And despite how we met, he still showed me kindness, perhaps the first person in the Known Worlds to do so. He educated me, prepared me to make a better life for myself. He was a blessing.

"And you," she added, waving a dismissive hand at Weatherby. "You would judge me for it. Even after seeing Elizabeth Mercuris with your own eyes. Surely the Royal Navy has not beaten all the imagination from you. How would you expect a 12-year-old orphan to survive in such a place? There is no almshouse. No Church of England. No missionary would dare set foot upon the place.

"So tell me, *Mister* Weatherby," she said. "Would you rather I not have been here at all? Or would you rather I have taken the road I chose, if it meant meeting you in the end?"

Weatherby's mind raced, but he could form no words, torn between her past, their present and his future. He could only look her in the eye, the remorse and sorrow in his face meeting her anger.

"Good night, Lieutenant," she said, stalking off toward the stairs leading below.

Weatherby watched her go before slumping down upon the railing, his heart once again pierced—and far more thoroughly than mere shot could accomplish.

Shortly after Anne went below, another flash of light erupted forward, threatening to engulf the entire bow of the ship in bright white light. Laughter and cheers filtered through the Void to Weatherby's ears.

He could hear Anne's voice among them. He watched sullenly as an arc of what appeared to be lightning blazed out of one of the forward gun ports, into the Void—he was too heartbroken to even start at the sight.

July 28, 2132

McAuliffe felt empty—and eerie. Granted, it was well past midnight, and Shaila pulled enough night shifts to know what the base looked like when everyone was asleep. But they weren't asleep—they were gone. She walked through the Hub, looking at the rows and rows of pressure suit lockers. Would anybody be using them again? Would Billiton be able to come back? Or was Mars irreparably broken somehow?

Shaila shunted those thoughts aside and made her way to the containment lab. She had a couple of pings from the computer to let her know that the book had written itself more than once during the evac. And while she wanted to read what happened next—Did Weatherby escape from the Xan? Was that the real Count St. Germain?—Washington's comment had latched onto her brain.

She pulled over a chair and sat down in front of a workstation. There were at least four major instances in which Mars was getting crazy—the initial earthquake with Stephane and Kaczynski; the second one with Stephane and Yuna; the collapse at Site Six; and whatever happened earlier that afternoon that knocked out the satellites and sensor array.

She isolated the time-stamps on every one of those incidents, right down to the millisecond, then opened the sensor database and ran a search over the five minutes preceding each instance. It was a massive task, considering that she was combing through the data generated by every sensor on base, as well as those outside, and looking at every single bit of data generated by those sensors. Full radiation scans, audio/video, radio transmissions—she was looking at the complete spectrum of data available to her.

Shaila hoped that the computer would find some similarity in those five minutes, some miniscule bit of…something…that she could use to track down what was happening. She slumped in her chair. It was a needle in a haystack if there ever was one, and the computer would take a while to crunch the numbers.

The door to the lab opened. "Hello," came a familiar and welcome voice. "Shouldn't you be getting some shut-eye?"

She turned to see Stephane taking a seat next to her. "How? A pyramid shows up on Mars and I am supposed to just take a nap?"

"I know how you feel," she said. "What have you been up to?"

Stephane called up some notes on his datapad as he spoke. "We have analyzed the holovid that miner took. We found some things."

"Such as?"

"Well, it cannot be the result of some natural occurrence. The angles on each of these levels—tiers, is it?—is now a perfect 90 degrees, give or take a minute or two. And each tier is exactly five-sixths the volume of the one beneath it. If that is not an intelligent design, I do not know what is," he said. "I once visited Egypt, and their older pyramids were step pyramids. They were tombs, ancient things."

"Yeah, this reminds me of that, too. Like a ceremonial structure. A tomb, or a temple or something. And those canals?" Shaila shook her head. "Christ, this is crazy."

Stephane sighed, tossing his datapad on the workstation. "So what do you think it is? Aliens?" Shaila tried to see if he was kidding or not, but his face was dead serious.

"It sounds weird, right?" she said. "Aliens. I keep thinking of little green men, pointy ears, bumpy foreheads. But something just sprouted up out there, something that isn't natural. Something that was made by someone. That someone wasn't us—us as in people. So, by definition, yes, that leaves aliens."

Stephane gave a small chuckle. "Oh, my. That would be something. What do you think Houston will tell us to do?"

"I wouldn't be surprised if Houston just orders us right off the planet," she said. "If you were running Earth, would you want a bunch of misfits and newbies making your first contact with an alien species? No, you'd get them on the next ship home and bring in someone else."

"You are not a misfit, Shay. Neither is Diaz. Or Dr. Hiyashi. You could do it," Stephane said earnestly. "Maybe you will."

Shaila slouched further in her chair, watching the computer sift data. "Oh, no. Nobody wants me shaking hands with the little green men."

"Please. You are perfectly qualified to be here, you know. You are trained."

"Stephane, trust me," she said with growing impatience. "JSC does not want me on the front lines of something like that."

The Frenchman threw up his hands, becoming agitated once more. "Why? All I see here is a competent person who is doing very well even though she is facing something very extraordinary. Did you not come up with a theory that even Evan Greene liked? Did you not save lives today?"

"Dammit, Steve," Shaila began, sitting up again, prepared to say something angry and dismissive. She thought better of it after a moment, however. "Stephane…"

He gave her a look that, in any other moment, would've gotten him either punched or kissed. Potentially both. "All right. Please. Talk to me. What happened to you?"

Shaila stood up and began slowly walking around the small room, arms wrapped around her. She took a deep breath before starting, realizing that it felt good to be able to talk about this. Whether it was with him in particular, or just in general, she didn't know. "OK. *Atlantis*. Two years ago. Jovian survey mission. I was the pilot, the number two, even though the official record doesn't reflect that. The reports said we had an accident way before reaching Jupiter, but that was a cover."

"Why?"

"Because the mission was a clusterfuck from the start," Shaila said. "The Chinese were way ahead of us in getting their Jovian exploitation program up and running. Their ships were shit hot—multiple landers, all the bells and whistles, you name it. They would've owned Jupiter space. It would've been their first major win, and they had some heavy corporate backing. Any and all resources there would've been all theirs for the taking.

"So the *Atlantis* program was rushed. Yeah, JSC had been to Jupiter a bunch of times. Hell, Yuna was on the first Galilean survey mission. But we never did anything serious after that. So with all those tensions rising politically between the E.U. and the Chinese, they wanted us to get there first. And we had our own corporate backers who were itching to get one up on the competition.

"So we went, secretly. We launched a full year ahead of schedule, and we went without a few key pieces. But we were going to get there first. And we did, too."

"*Atlantis* actually made it to Jupiter?" Stephane asked, stunned. "*You* made it to Jupiter?"

"For all of two days," Shaila said ruefully.

"I do not understand."

"I'm getting to that. So we're inserting ourselves into Jupiter orbit, and the commander had the stick for the atmospheric braking maneuver."

"Atmospheric breaking?" Stephane asked. "You broke Jupiter's atmosphere?"

"Jesus, no. That's where you use Jupiter's gravity and atmospheric drag to slow the vehicle," Shaila said, smiling despite herself. "Otherwise, you just slingshot off Jupiter and probably head right out of the solar system."

"I see. And?"

"Everything was fine. Our thrusters fired on cue, our heat shield deployed, we hit the atmosphere at the right angle. It went swimmingly until we ran smack into a bloody rock."

"A rock?" Stephane asked. "A real rock?"

"Jupiter's gravity captures asteroids from the Belt, rogue comets, you name it. It even has a ring system, though not as big as Saturn's. So there are rocks out there. And this particular rock was small enough to go undetected—perhaps only four meters by five meters. But big enough to cause a massive problem for us when it hit our midsection."

Shaila paused a moment to gather herself. "We knew going in there could be a potential problem with debris, but the countermeasures weren't ready. JSC figured we could maneuver around anything we might encounter. But when you're in the middle of atmospheric braking, you can't exactly bob and weave. And the right rock came floating by at exactly the right moment. Million-to-one shot, and it was our lucky day."

Shaila smiled sadly at her own joke, but Stephane looked very serious, watching her intently as he listened.

"Anyway, we immediately lost pressurization in the labs, four people gone, just like that. The skipper gave me the stick, went back to assess the damage. That was the last time I saw him. We could've survived the hit intact, but the rad shielding was compromised in several places. Only a handful of compartments remained rad-safe. The cockpit, the forward crew space. That's it."

"How much radiation?" Stephane asked quietly.

"About 8,000 rems."

Stephane nodded soberly. Few people could survive exposure to even a tenth that amount, and even then, their lives would be hellish. "How quick was it for them?"

Shaila closed her eyes once more and continued, haltingly. "Not quick enough. It took about seven hours for the last of them to die. And they were in excruciating pain. They begged me to let them back into the forward compartments. And I couldn't. Not without exposing myself to the radiation. They were already dead, right? They had zero chance of survival. But I had to hear them. Talk to them. Be with them on the comm. All the while, they're dying horribly." She shivered. "Seven people."

Stephane nodded, but didn't say anything. Shaila appreciated that, somehow.

"The impact took out the antenna, so calling Earth was impossible," she said, wiping away a few errant tears and focusing on the story itself. "They had no idea what happened, and I was the only one left. Computers were still functioning, but most of the processing power was in the lab section. It took two days to harness enough computing power to calculate a course home. It was a crap orbit, too—Earth was too far off. So between that and a jury-rigged engine routine, it took thirteen months to get home."

"How did you survive that long?"

She actually smiled at that. "I'm bloody stubborn, I suppose. The crew area had enough food. I managed to get the ship in a spin that would give me at least a little gravity, but the rehab was awful anyway. A month before I could walk again."

Stephane nodded. "You are right. You are stubborn. What happened when you came back?"

Shaila shrugged. "They managed to catch my local comm signals a few weeks out, so they were ready. I figured out a lunar braking orbit, and one of the shuttles rendezvoused with me, brought me back to Earth. There was a review board, of course. I was cleared. They said I did the right thing after, with the crew and all."

"Of course you did," he said.

"Didn't feel like it. I suppose I at least brought their bodies home for burial." She wiped away her tears angrily. "They asked if I wanted out, wanted to start over somehow. How do you do that? This was all I've ever known, you know? I always wanted to be in space. So I said no. And after rehab and a little stint in psych—which was useless and awful—here I am. I applied for other missions, but got turned down enough to know that nobody wants me on board. Nobody knows enough of the details to get the full picture, so there's just this big hunk of dark matter on my record that raises eyebrows." And that, she thought to herself, is why nobody—not even Stephane—will ever know about the visions and voices she heard in that cave.

Stephane weighed his thoughts carefully before speaking. "Shay, darling. What happened was unfair. But you are still a very good astronaut. You brought that ship back all the way from Jupiter, all by yourself. You have such experience now. You must keep trying."

She grimaced. "Trying to do what? Get rejected again for more missions? Maybe they're right. I've thought about leaving JSC, going corporate. I don't know what to do, Steve. Sorry, Stephane."

He smiled. "It is OK for you to call me Steve. Everyone does."

"Well, it's not your name. You deserve Stephane." She gathered herself, wiped her face with her hands, and gave him a smile, the first genuine one she sported in quite some time. "Thanks."

"Not at all. I listen well," he said. "And you, mademoiselle, should get up off of your cute little ass and help us solve all these riddles. You are obviously quite good in a crisis, yes? This seems to be a crisis. Do something about it."

She sighed. "Right. Like what?"

"Your workstation came back with something while you were talking," Stephane said with a grin. "I did not want to interrupt."

Shaila dashed back to her seat. "Bastard," she muttered. She scrolled through the latest results. Some atmospheric changes, some electrical fluctuations again, a few blips of odd radio noise.

Radio noise.

"Look at this," she said, pointing at the screen. "Anywhere from one to six seconds before each incident, there was a brief radio transmission. It's at a really odd frequency, one that wouldn't show up on the usual comm channels."

"Can you find out where the transmissions came from?"

Shaila typed rapidly; the computer replied in seconds. "Two came from inside the base, which is near impossible to pin down. As for the other two, let's see. The second earthquake, with you and me and Yuna, the signal came from…wow. Within five hundred meters of the cave itself."

"So whoever set it off knew we were in there?" Stephane asked.

"Maybe. The other one was the Site Six collapse, and that was, let's see… about six kilometers away, near the edge of where we think the energy ring is."

Stephane clapped her on the shoulder. "That is well done, Shay. But what do we do with this?"

Shaila logged the radio signature into her datapad. "We load this signature into our sensors, inside and out, portable, you name it. If it comes up again, we know it's about to hit the fan."

"But that does not help us pin down the source," Stephane said.

"True," Shaila said. "I figure it's a portable transmitter. And really, the range doesn't need to be all that. Hell, it could be anything with a chip in it, and there's plenty of that around here. I doubt we'd ever find it.

"But, first things first," she added, getting up from her seat. "Let's throw this at Diaz if she's still up. One more thing to pack off to Houston. And I'll upload the signature to the sensors."

The two quickly left the lab and headed for the command center. "Oh, and Stephane?"

"Yes, cherie?"

Shaila grinned to herself. "Keep your eyes off my cute little ass or I'll have you on shit patrol for a month." She tried to approximate his French accent, with comically horrendous results.

The geologist gasped in mock dismay. "It would be easier to stop breathing!"

She shook her head, her smile widening. "That can be arranged."

CHAPTER 20

June 19, 1779

*F*ather, *if you are to ultimately receive this journal, as I fervently hope, know that your son goes now to do his duty, both to England and to all people of the Known Worlds. I am shaken by today's events, but terrified at the task that is now laid before us.*

Once again, I must muster my will and courage to put pen to paper, and I must ignore the bodily pain I endure to do so. Do not fear, Father, for there are those who have fared far worse than I, be they friend or foe. But I must once again order my thoughts and start anew. I have little time before I must lead our men into great peril.

The sun-currents were with us as we departed the Rocky Main, and as Mars began to loom large over the horizon, we spotted our quarry and began to close....

"I believe it's her, sir," Weatherby said, folding his glass. "Her lines match the ship we encountered on Callisto."

"And who else would come to Mars?" Plumb added, still looking through his own glass at their quarry. "There's naught but ruin and sand down there. Most of the canals barely have enough water to keel upon."

Morrow and his lieutenants left the bow and strode across the main deck. "One never knows," the captain said. "It seems the Royal Society or the Jovian Trading Company sends expeditions to Mars weekly in search of some damned thing or another. And the Spanish, of course, continue to seek out gold, for whatever good it does them. Still, I concur. Their course would have them coming from Jupiter, not Earth or Venus. Mr. Plumb, we shall beat to quarters, if you please. Mr. Weatherby, signal the *Badger* to prepare for battle."

Once more, the *Daedalus* erupted into a frenzy of activity, the men executing the plans drawn up in Morrow's quarters over the long transit from Jupiter. The ship's "alchemical society"—as Morrow had dubbed Finch, Franklin, St. Germain and Anne—had prepared extra stores of curatives and alchemical shot for the engagement. They also promised to unveil their new electrical working should a safe opportunity present itself, though Weatherby, upon hearing this, wondered exactly how "safe" would enter into the equation of the coming battle—or to the working, for that matter.

At least the men were well drilled, Weatherby noted. If this was the moment, then they stood to make the most of it. Weatherby looked to starboard and saw *Badger* roughly a half-mile out, her guns at the ready as well.

Weatherby returned to the quarterdeck a hairsbreadth ahead of Foster, both reporting their divisions ready for battle. The Count and Franklin had joined Morrow, despite the latter's entreaty that they station themselves below decks to weather the coming engagement. Neither would have any of it, however.

"Beyond the ship's speed, I doubt Cagliostro has revealed much of his knowledge to these pirates," St. Germain observed. "He was never of a mind to share freely of his work. And he likely believes he was successful in leaving us to take the blame for his crimes against the Xan."

"He very nearly was successful," Franklin reminded him. "It was a canny ploy. But I agree. I doubt they shall have much besides speed to recommend them."

"They remain pirates nonetheless," Morrow cautioned. "LeMaire likely does not have his own alchemist aboard, but he's sure to have laid hands on whatever alchemical workings his victims may have possessed, along with their stores of shot. And boarding her will be difficult as well. We will most certainly be outnumbered when the time comes."

Weatherby nodded gravely. Morrow's plan called for him to lead the boarding party should the opportunity arise. Ideally, this would happen once *Chance* was fully disabled, but that would be a close thing—the pirate was evenly matched against the combined firepower of both *Daedalus* and *Badger*. Only the coordinated effort between the two ships would give them a chance at success.

It was a tense hour before the English ships drew close enough to fire a warning shot. The *Chance* was still well ahead, but protocol called for the warning, regardless. All the officers had their glasses at the ready, peering out ahead to see her reaction.

A moment later, a red flag went up over the enemy ship's stern. Upon it were a white skull and a heart with an arrow piercing it—LeMaire's colors.

"Very well, then," Morrow said grimly. "We have a known pirate in our sights, and that is more than enough. Mr. Weatherby, signal the *Badger* to begin."

Weatherby quickly had a pair of crewmen run up the signal flags necessary to cue *Badger*. Within a minute, the little ship's royals and stud'sels unfurled, and Nelson sped ahead of *Daedalus* to engage the *Chance* off her starboard side.

"This may not work," St. Germain cautioned. "Cagliostro will want to get to the surface at all costs. He may not wish to engage us here."

"Ideally, he will have no choice," Morrow said. "If he turns to engage, so much the better. If not, we have a very good chance to catch up to her before she enters the Martian aurorae. Better to engage us here, in the Void, rather than be swept along the currents to the poles."

Indeed, it seemed LeMaire and Cagliostro had worked through the same calculus, for the *Chance* began to turn to starboard, her guns run out to meet the approaching *Badger*.

"Excellent," Morrow said. "Mr. Plumb, full sail. Royals, stud'sels and planes, if you please."

Plumb barked out the orders, and soon every bit of canvas on *Daedalus* caught the solar wind, speeding the frigate forward. Morrow angled the ship slightly to larboard and ten degrees lower, hoping to catch *Chance*'s underbelly.

Weatherby and Foster were ordered to their divisions, and the young lieutenants walked along the gunnery line to ensure all was well. They were still several minutes away from *Chance*, so Weatherby took the opportunity to duck into the alchemical lab, where Finch was preparing to receive wounded. To his surprise, Anne was there as well.

"Miss Baker, your place is in the hold," Weatherby said sternly. "It is the best protected part of the ship."

"My place, Lieutenant, is where I can do the most good," she said simply, yet coldly. "And that place is here, assisting Dr. Finch with his workings."

Weatherby grimaced and looked to Finch, who merely shrugged. "She's a competent alchemist. Even if all goes to plan, I could use the help."

"A woman's place is not in battle," Weatherby said sternly.

"I'm not leaving," Anne said, pausing from her preparations to look Weatherby squarely in the eye. "And you've neither the time nor manpower to lock me in the brig."

God Almighty, she was stubborn, Weatherby thought. It was oddly attractive. "Very well," he relented. "Do try not to get yourself killed…Anne."

She gave him a little victory smirk and returned to her work, leaving Weatherby to rejoin his division on the gun deck, where Plumb was inspecting the men.

"There you are," the first lieutenant said. "All's well forward?"

Weatherby saluted. "Miss Baker has insisted that she remain there to aid Dr. Finch, sir."

Weatherby was surprised to see Plumb smile, gently and most incongruously. "Lost the argument, did you, Tommy boy?"

Weatherby shifted his feet. "Most decisively, sir."

"She's a brave girl," Plumb noted before casting his eyes along the line of men at their stations. "Your division's in good form, lad. All goes well, you'll get the first shot. Aim true."

"I will, sir. Thank you," Weatherby said as Plumb nodded and returned to the quarterdeck.

Weatherby turned to see Lt. Foster standing next to him. "What was that all about?" the third lieutenant asked.

"I've not the slightest," Weatherby remarked. "Perhaps the moments before battle can soften even the hardest man." He then extended his hand toward Foster—it seemed that now, of all times, the gesture was appropriate. "Best of luck to you, John."

Beaming, the younger lieutenant shook Weatherby's hand eagerly. "And to you, Tom. Let's get these bastards this time!"

Weatherby nodded and released Foster's hand, then turned toward his men, who were already in fine form, waiting for the first shot. He found he had little more to say to them now, or perhaps the words he might have chosen simply didn't do the moment justice. So he settled on one final in-

Michael J. Martinez

spection, going from gun to gun and finding something kind to say to each group, or just a hand on a shoulder. Rooney, Lamb, Smythe…they all had fear in their eyes, certainly. But more than that, there was determination. They knew they had a legendary pirate in their sights, and while not all the men could even grasp the greater evils they were about to battle, they knew well enough that a mad alchemist was no simple miscreant.

Weatherby looked out one of the gunports. *Badger* and *Daedalus* had closed quickly on *Chance*, which continued to tack to starboard to bring its guns up against *Badger*. That would leave its stern and underside unprotected as *Daedalus* approached to join the fray.

The plan seemed to be going well—until *Chance* turned harder still, until it had swung completely around. This served to push the ship against the sun-currents, slowing it considerably. However, it also pointed the pirate directly at the incoming ships, making it a smaller target and potentially allowing it to fire off a broadside as they passed her.

"Damn," Morrow said. "Signal the *Badger*, hard to larboard. Mr. Plumb, hard to starboard for us."

Badger quickly turned in front of *Daedalus*, even as the larger ship turned in the opposite direction. While they surrendered the opportunity to immediately fire upon the *Chance*, they forced LeMaire to decide which ship to fire upon first, ideally giving the other vessel a chance to rake the pirate's weak points.

Chance chose *Badger*, continuing to drift further starboard to bring its guns against the vastly out-classed brig. Weatherby could see Nelson bring his planes sharply lower, trying to avoid the onslaught and potentially cutting under the larger ship. However, *Chance* pulled in its starboard planesail, which rotated the ship and allowed its guns to track *Badger* as it dove.

"Ready the larboard side guns!" Plumb ordered. "Come about hard to larboard, hard down on the planes!"

The men scurried across the main deck to the larboard side, even as the ship tilted and swayed as it pursued *Chance*. Weatherby prayed they would get there in time to distract the pirate from Nelson's little ship, but he knew it was a fool's hope.

The sound of cannon crashed across the Void as *Badger* and *Chance* opened fire upon one another—five guns against twenty-two. The result was horrible in both its predictability and its carnage.

As the cloud of smoke dispersed, Weatherby saw *Badger* floating adrift in the Void, her entire bow nearly shot away, both her masts down and three gaping holes in her midsection. He hoped he was only imagining the faint screams coming across the Void.

At least *Badger's* sacrifice would not be in vain. "Hard upward on the larboard plane!" Plumb ordered as they closed on the stern of the *Chance*. "Prepare to fire!"

Daedalus swiftly closed on *Chance* from under and behind, and while the pirate attempted to complete its turn, its guns had just fired on *Badger*, and it was a poor angle besides. *Daedalus* had the gage and a nearly free shot at its enemy.

"FIRE!"

Morrow's order was echoed by every officer on board, but their shouts were drowned out by the roar of *Daedalus'* guns. Sixteen lines of green alchemical shot raced toward the *Chance*, with at least twelve hitting their marks cleanly, by Weatherby's count. *Daedalus* raced by before Weatherby could see the damage, but the lookout on the quarterdeck reported several holes in her hull, along with at least four guns damaged. Hopefully, the shot had done its job inside the *Chance* as well, where the damage could not be so readily assessed.

"Hard to starboard!" Plumb ordered. "Ready the starboard guns!"

Weatherby raced to the other side of the ship, along with some of the gunners; the others remained to reload the larboard side guns for another shot if needed. Morrow clearly expected the *Chance* to continue to turn larboard, thus bringing the two ships around so they could face each other with a broadside. With its speed, *Daedalus* stood a good chance of making the turn faster, leaving the larger ship without a sound shooting angle once again.

Chance, however, had other ideas.

"She's also coming 'round to starboard!" cried one of the topsmen.

The move would prevent the next broadside from happening quickly as the two ships sailed further apart. And Morrow's turn had the effect of turning *Daedalus* into the sun-current, slowing it as it had *Chance* moments before.

"Ruddersail amidships!" Morrow shouted. "Planes down full!"

The result of Morrow's order was that the ship kept its bow directly in the face of the current, further slowing it, while the currents pushed on the planes to allow the ship to nose upward to a great degree. It was a canny ploy, Weatherby thought. So few commanders thought to fully employ the third dimension available to them in the Void, but Morrow would essentially turn the ship on its stern, where it could pirouette in place and then meet *Chance* in whatever direction it came.

"Tack larboard planesail!"

By drawing one of the planesails in, *Daedalus* began to rotate around, until its underbelly faced Mars directly. Morrow then ordered both planesails deployed at an angle, which not only allowed the ship's sails to catch the sun-current again, but also to get the ship parallel to the orbital plane once more.

Thus, in the space of two minutes, *Daedalus* had turned completely around in place, had regained the current, and now faced its opponent head on.

Except that *Chance* had been busy with its own maneuvers as well.

LeMaire had continued his turn so that his broadside now faced the bow of the *Daedalus*. It wasn't the best angle, but the pirate could get off a free shot at the English ship without much reprisal.

Weatherby looked through the cargo hatch to the quarterdeck, where Morrow stood stoically, assessing the situation. The captain's calm was oddly unnerving, but Weatherby assumed he would possess such a placid demeanor in time. As of now, however, the young officer's stomach was in knots, his nerves on edge.

"Full sail! Prepare to ram!" Morrow shouted. "Boarders at the ready!"

Weatherby rushed up the stairs and onto the main deck to gather his boarding party, some seventy men strong, led by himself and the marines aboard. Pistols, cutlasses and pikes were hurriedly distributed as the two ships closed. *Chance* did not alter course at all, apparently welcoming the coming collision and the bloody battle that would ensue. The damage inflicted by little *Badger* and *Daedalus* was not as much as anyone would have hoped; the boarding would be difficult indeed.

"Twenty degrees to larboard!" Morrow shouted. Weatherby looked up from his preparations to see *Chance* altering course slightly. Morrow responded in kind, and the two ships danced closer together, trying for the best angle in the now-inevitable impact.

Royal Navy ships often drill at ramming and boarding, but few practice such brute tactics as frequently as pirates. A series of minute course changes—dodges and feints, really—gave the *Chance* the upper hand. Instead of plowing cleanly into the side of the pirate, *Daedalus* skittered alongside her, prompting her side to come in contact with the *Chance*'s starboard hull.

"FIRE!"

"INCENDIE!"

Weatherby could hear the Frenchman's order as cleanly as his own captain's. And a moment later, their hulls mere feet from each other, the two ships' guns tore into each other with a fury.

The deck shuddered beneath Weatherby's feet, knocking him to the ground. He felt the impact of cannon shot against wood beneath his feet, and knew that the incoming fire was wreaking havoc throughout the interior of the ship. The screams of men echoed across the Void, but there was no way of telling whether they were friend or foe. All men die similarly, he thought in an odd moment of clarity.

He looked up to find little damage above decks—the *Chance*'s guns were lower than the *Daedalus*'. But he could already see that the planesail was in tatters, and he had little hope for the ruddersail as well.

Hauling himself to his feet, he tried to peer through the haze of smoke toward the enemy ship. Most of the cries were coming from the other vessel; the main deck there bore the brunt of *Daedalus*' barrage.

Then, out of the fog, he saw a number of lines being thrown from the *Chance*, grappling hooks attached. Whatever damage *Daedalus* may have inflicted on the enemy crew, it was not enough to deter them greatly.

Weatherby quickly drew his sword with his right hand, his pistol with his left. "They're coming!" he shouted. "Prepare to repel boarders!"

July 28, 2132

"Never ceases to amaze me just how much crap has a microchip in it," Shaila mused as she waved a sensor pack around over Harry Yu's spare datapad. "This is a total needle in the haystack."

Yuna Hiyashi was busy carefully folding Harry's clothes, wrenched from his closet two hours earlier. "I admit, I didn't think we'd find much here. But I suppose it was worth looking."

Apparently, Diaz had thought the same thing. The colonel was still up at oh-one-hundred, going back and forth with Houston about the dizzying array of strangeness that had plagued them over the past few days. When Shaila presented her discovery of the radio waves before each tremor, Diaz ordered a complete base-wise sensor sweep for the radio signal, which turned up nothing. After that, she told Shaila to search Harry's office and day room thoroughly, and to bring Yuna along as a Billiton representative. The idea was not only to find a "smoking gun" with which to seal the case against Harry, but also to prevent more tremors and problems on the Martian surface—in theory. It was a wild goose chase, but Diaz apparently felt Harry was just as much a suspect as Shaila did.

And so they combed through his office carefully, with sensors and by hand. The sensor was able to detect anything with a battery or microchip in it, and Shaila had gone through every wristwatch, datapad, alarm clock, gizmo and gadget, looking for signs that it might double as a radio transmitter. Shaila was much less respectful of the mining exec's possessions than Yuna, but at least she didn't break anything.

"Would've been bloody easier if it was a nice big box with a button on it labeled 'evil,'" Shaila said, chucking aside the datapad and going over a set of electronic styluses.

"Harry's not evil, Shaila," Yuna said, sounding like a grandmother chiding a toddler. "I don't think anybody's evil, really. Even if he is responsible, somehow, for what's going on, I'm sure he's not acting out of malice."

"Seriously?" Shaila said, tossing the datapad aside. "We've got one miner dead, two others injured along with Kaczynski and me, and you and Steve were totally endangered in those quakes. Plus we nearly lost an entire transport. But hey, he didn't *mean* it, right?" Shaila gathered up the electronics and shoved them into a desk drawer. They had initially agreed that they'd put everything back in its place, but at this point, Shaila didn't care. "And why are you defending him?"

Yuna sat down on Harry's daybed and smiled. "Harry's not all that bad. He's ambitious, and his successes here are pretty tenuous. A hitch here, a delay there, and his bottom line collapses. You'd be skittish, too."

Shaila got up from Harry's desk. "And you still don't believe Weatherby's journal is involved." It wasn't a question.

"I simply don't know," Yuna said, concern plainly written on her face.

"There's so much going on, so many unusual things—your book, the tremors, the pyramid. As a scientist, I want to exhaust every avenue of inquiry before creating a theory. Facts first. Now, let's get this place looking decent."

Twenty minutes later, they left Harry's office and headed back toward the Hub. It was nearly oh-five-hundred, and low-G sleep wasn't much of an option, so they made their way to the galley to whip up something. Sadly, Billiton not only provided miners, but the base cook as well, so the JSC crew would have to fend for themselves—for however long they were stranded on Mars.

"I hope engineering can fix up the *Giffords*," Shaila said as she attempted to figure out the coffee maker. "I want an exit strategy if it really starts going to hell."

"Certainly a good use of our time," Yuna agreed as she whipped up some "eggs" and "bacon"—or, rather, their soy-based, preservative-laden substitutes. "I'm not sure what more we can do out there anyway."

Shaila smiled slightly. "Oh, I don't know about that. If Houston actually lets us, I wouldn't mind going out for a look."

"Outside?" Yuna asked as she slid a plate of food toward Shaila.

"Yep."

Yuna thought about this a moment. "I see one problem right off the bat. The last time something major happened, it took all our sensors and MarsSats offline and nearly brought down a transport. What if it does the same to our electronics? Our pressure suits? I can only hold my breath for so long."

Shaila smiled. "Way ahead of you. We get a piece of rad-hard equipment with some kind of visual marker that lets us know it's working. Maybe a sensor pack that we can have transmit back to our datapads. Then we toss it inside the EM ring and see if it still works or not."

"Interesting," Yuna allowed. "If it doesn't?"

"Well, then, we're properly screwed, then, aren't we?" Shaila said. "But if it works, then we go check out that pyramid. I mean, Christ, it's a *pyramid*, Yuna. How can we not go and see it?"

The two continued debating the merits of an EVA to the pyramid over breakfast, the largest concern being a reprise of Mars' new penchant for earthquakes. Nobody wanted to get caught in another quake, but Shaila didn't see an alternative. She wanted to get out there and see the damn thing with her own two eyes. They were finally interrupted by the base intercom.

"Col. Diaz, Lt. Jain, report to the command center. Col. Diaz, Lt. Jain to the command center," Washington said.

Shaila glanced at her watch—not even oh-six-hundred yet. Way too early for the next crisis, wasn't it? "Come on," she said to Yuna. "Figure you should be in on this, too."

Moments later, they strode into the command center just as Diaz was coming out of her office, looking as if she had slept in there. "What'cha got?" Shaila asked.

"JSC just sent this over and asked me to forward to you two ASAP," Washington said, looking wide-eyed and nervous. "Single image packet."

"I send them a freakin' novel and they send over an image?" Diaz groused. "Put it up, Washington."

A moment later, the command center's main screen flared to life. It was an overhead image of…Mars?

"You have *got* to be kidding me," Shaila said.

The image showed roughly the same area as the sensor outage from yesterday. Inside the affected area, things had changed. Considerably.

The pyramid was in full view now. Six tiers, casting a long southern shadow. Some kind of ditch—or moat?—had formed around the base, with the previously spotted canal leading away from it to the south, toward McAuliffe. Something glimmered in the sunlight in that canal, possibly some form of ice. The canals were not only straight and true, but they looked as though they were well and truly placed there, with care and workmanship evident along the length. In some places, the canals seemed to fade into the Martian landscape. In others, they ended abruptly—right at the edge of the apparent EM field.

One of the canals leading to the pyramid seemed to have something darker in it, like it was filled with something—water, perhaps? It seemed apt, though there was no way of knowing. The canal bisected the surrounding area cleanly, so much so that a couple of sensor poles protruded from the canal itself, as if the earth had been dug out from around the sensors.

Finally, to the north east of the base, there was a small dark patch on the image, roughly oblong in shape, but they couldn't make it out—all they knew was that it wasn't there before. It was situated in some sort of shallow ravine or gully of some kind—one that wasn't on anybody's maps.

"Can we get any better resolution?" Diaz asked.

"No, ma'am. This is the best they've got," Washington said. "Attached message says they actually fired up the old Mars Reconnaissance Orbiter to grab this."

"Really?" Diaz said. "All right. Get this image downloaded to Greene and Durand and the rest of us. Anything else in the message?"

Before Washington could respond, his board lit up with red warning lights. "Sensors picking up something," he said, pressing keys quickly. "Looks like we've got—"

He never finished his sentence.

Shaila grabbed the console in front of her as she felt the ground beneath her feet buck wildly. The whole base suddenly seemed to be built on springs—and someone, somewhere just gave it a shove.

"Report!" Diaz shouted over the klaxon alarms that started shrilling throughout the base.

"Seismic activity!" Washington replied. "Every sensor we've got is lit up. Can't pin down the source."

One of the displays mounted on the wall suddenly tumbled to the floor, shattering despite the low gravity.

As Shaila hung onto the workstation in front of her, watching the base start to fall apart, there was no doubt in her mind where the damn quake was coming from.

CHAPTER 21

June 19, 1779

The line of men waited in silence on the main deck of the *Daedalus*, pistols and swords at the ready, looking into the smoke from the two ships' guns as they waited for the men of the *Chance* to swarm aboard. The old hands waited calmly, having made peace with fate long ago in other battles, or in the swells of storms at sea and Void. The young ones shifted from foot to foot, gripped their weapons tight and stared wide-eyed into the fog.

Yet instead of dissipating, the fog grew thicker. "Steady, men," Weatherby said quietly. "Let them come to us." He was as nervous as anyone, but refused to show it.

At least until the Count St. Germain strolled casually across the deck toward him, as if taking a morning constitutional.

"My lord!" Weatherby hissed. "You should seek shelter!"

St. Germain simply walked right up to him. "In a moment. Franklin asked that I make you this." He handed over a small glass vial.

"What is it?" Weatherby asked, eyeing the vial and the clear liquid therein most suspiciously.

"This smoke is alchemical in nature, a simple measure designed to confound matters when the pirates attack," St. Germain said. "When you first see them about to board, simply throw this down upon the deck, and the air will clear immediately, granting us a moment of surprise. But do not press your attack. I believe we are prepared to aid you from the forecastle first."

Weatherby looked at the little cylinder with appreciation. "Very well, milord. We will wait to advance. Now take cover, if you would, please."

St. Germain nodded and strolled on toward the fo'c'sle, leaving Weatherby to wonder just what the man had seen in life to be so blasé about such imminent danger.

Weatherby turned back to the railing, where he saw some of the ropes thrown by the *Chance* crew begin to move and vibrate as the pirates pulled *Daedalus* closer to their ship. "All right," he whispered to his men. "Wait for whatever comes from the fo'c'sle. When I give the word, first rank fires, then retreats to reload and the second rank fires. Then pikes and swords."

The crewmen nodded and murmured in affirmation as Weatherby watched the ropes carefully, peering into the dark cloud for the sign he needed, whatever form it may take.

It was a grubby hand on a rope, barely visible in the fog, that did the trick.

Weatherby hurled the glass vial to the deck near the railing, where it shattered. Immediately, the smoky fog lifted, revealing several dozen men not twenty feet away, preparing to board *Daedalus* and, at the moment, looking very surprised.

Weatherby turned to the fo'c'sle, where he saw Finch and St. Germain pointing what appeared to be an odd-looking brass cannon at the main deck of the *Chance*. It had numerous protuberances upon it, some of which looked to be made of glass, of all things.

A moment later, Finch furiously turned a crank upon the side of the device—and lightning spit forth from the barrel, cascading through the pirates with a thunderous crackle.

"My God," Weatherby breathed as he saw at least two dozen men fall. The acrid smell of ozone and burnt flesh assaulted his nose.

The flash ended only after two seconds, but its worth had been proven. Weatherby turned back to his men, who were all staring elsewhere—either at the fo'c'sle or the other ship. "Make ready!" Weatherby called.

He saw more pirates move forward to take the place of their fellows. They would still try to board.

"Fire!"

Two dozen pistols fired as one, and another dozen muskets released from the tops, where a number of marine snipers were stationed. Immediately, another score of men on the *Chance* fell to the volley in a chorus of blood and screams, while the rest could barely raise their own weapons.

"Second rank! Fire!" Weatherby shouted, aiming his second pistol as the first rank fell back to reload.

Another score of shots echoed in the Void, releasing more carnage upon the boarders. Several more fell—with some of them careening off into the Void— but there were plenty remaining, and several began to return fire to support those who made it aboard.

"Reload and fire at will!" Weatherby ordered as he scrambled to reload his own weapons. "Pikes at the ready! Prepare to repel boarders!"

With the weapons silenced for the moment, the pirates heaved one last time and immediately began swarming aboard, cutlasses in hand. Without thinking, Weatherby took his unloaded pistol and hurtled it at one of the first to board *Daedalus*, hitting him squarely in the face and knocking him back. His hand thus freed, Weatherby drew his sword and leapt forward into the growing fray.

He lashed out at all and sundry, cutting down pirates otherwise engaged with the *Daedalus* crew. But it only took a few moments for one of the pirates to attack him personally, lunging forward with a scream. Weatherby quickly parried the blade…

…and hewed it cleanly in two.

Both Weatherby and his opponent were stunned, but the pirate recovered a moment faster, tossing his sundered hilt aside and throwing a desperate punch at Weatherby. By reflex alone, Weatherby parried the man's arm with his blade, which had the same effect on the pirate's limb as it did upon his cutlass. In a spray of blood, the man collapsed on the deck, screaming.

"Well done, Anne," he muttered, looking at the blade as the blood oozed off it completely, leaving it shining silver once again. A strategy quickly formed in his head.

He quickly dashed across the deck, hewing through the pirates at will, aiming for weapons first so that his compatriots could handle the disarmed boarders more easily, though at least a half-dozen men fell to his blade as well. A part of him thrilled at the effect his sword had upon the engagement, even as something in the back of his mind rebelled at the bloody carnage he was causing.

A sudden clang of steel on steel drew his awareness back fully, as his blade finally met resistance in the form of another. And before he could react further, a large boot kicked him squarely in the chest—right where he had been shot on Callisto—pushing him backward and prompting him to gasp for air.

A massive man stood before him, dressed in an outlandish red silk jacket and numerous golden baubles. His disheveled hair and unkempt beard could not hide the sneer he offered Weatherby, who quickly recognized the man from Venus and Callisto. It could be none other than LeMaire himself—and it appeared his blade was a match for Weatherby's.

Weatherby assumed the en garde position, but the pirate just stood there, regarding him with the Devil's own smile. "Your sword is better than you are, yes?" he growled in passable English. "Surrender and I may let you live."

Weatherby shook his head. "I decline, sir." And with that, he lunged.

LeMaire swatted Weatherby's blade aside with a deft parry, not even bothering to adjust his stance. Weatherby tried again, and again, but LeMaire was a canny swordsman, and met every riposte with one of his own. Desperately parrying the pirate captain's blows, Weatherby was dismayed to see he was backing up with each move, until he felt the wood of the mainmast behind him.

LeMaire stepped up his attacks, slapping past Weatherby's parries again and again. Weatherby felt his coat rip, felt a trickle of blood on his rib cage—a very close cut that would have been far worse if not for his last-minute parry. Weatherby riposted quickly, catching LeMaire's sword arm with a quick slash. Instead of stopping him, however, the wound only seemed to infuriate the man, who lashed out and punched Weatherby in the face with his free hand.

Dazed, Weatherby could barely make out LeMaire in front of him, sword raised to surely cut him in two. But the pirate was tackled in a blurry flash of blue, leaving Weatherby to shake his head and regain his wits.

It was Lt. Plumb.

LeMaire roared in anger and hit Plumb with the hilt of his sword, sending the first lieutenant reeling and stumbling to the railing, whereupon he was swarmed by a mob of pirates, most of whom had surged aboard *Daedalus* while their captain occupied Weatherby and his alchemical blade. Weatherby regained his senses and moved to help Plumb, but his way was blocked by LeMaire once more, who lashed out with his sword.

Weatherby parried the blow and prepared to riposte, but LeMaire's massive hand was on his face in an instant, pushing him into the mainmast once more. A second later, blinding pain shot through his shoulder, prompting a scream. Looking down, he saw LeMaire's blade sticking out of his body, pinning him to the mast. He heard his blade clatter to the deck, the nerve and muscle damage in his shoulder too much for him to hold on to it.

"So!" LeMaire exulted, standing back to admire his handiwork. "You should have surrendered."

Anguished and in overwhelming pain, Weatherby cast about for help, but his fellows were occupied with the seemingly endless stream of boarders pouring onto the ship from *Chance*. Yet out of the corner of his eye, just over LeMaire's shoulder, he saw Finch and St. Germain upon the fo'c'sle, laboring over their device. It was pointed at the main deck.

Hopefully, they would not labor much longer.

Weatherby saw that LeMaire was now engaged—all too briefly—by a few of the men from *Daedalus*. Grabbing the hilt of LeMaire's blade in his free hand, Weatherby pulled with all his might and wrenched the sword from both the mast and his body, screaming in pain as he did so. He cast it away with all his strength and, by a stroke of luck, saw it fly neatly over the side of the ship, into the Void.

LeMaire saw this and swore in French, his face the picture of rage. Shoving aside two Englishmen, he punched Weatherby in the face once more. The young Englishman felt his cheekbone crack, his teeth threatening to fall from his mouth. His feet failed him and he slumped down to the deck, his back still against the mast.

Even in his daze, Weatherby saw the electrical cannon being aimed for the main deck. He immediately curled into a ball, as low to the deck as his body would allow.

"English pig!" LeMaire roared. "Get up so I may kill you on your feet, you…"

"*Daedalans,* down!" Finch yelled.

Immediately, every English sailor aboard dove for the planking. Looking up, Weatherby saw the flash of white lightning, heard the roaring crackle of electricity. Screams joined the smell of ozone in the air.

And right above him, he saw a lightning bolt quickly pierce the very heart of Jacques LeMaire, who wore a glassy-eyed look of surprise on his face. A moment later, the pirate keeled forward, face-first, onto the deck. Smoke issued from a horrible burn on his back.

Dizzy and weak, Weatherby struggled to his feet, his sword in hand, and looked about for another opponent. However, the electrical cannon had done its job well, and with their captain dead, the surviving *Chance* men were rushing back to their ship, cutting the tethering lines as they went.

Weatherby staggered toward the quarterdeck to report. He only made it about twelve paces before he sank to his knees, his wounds finally overcoming consciousness.

July 28, 2132

Alarms layered upon alarms as the quake continued to shake McAuliffe Base, and Shaila was having a hard time keeping track of them all. Seismic monitors were first. Then the reactor alarms chimed in, prompting an automatic shutdown sequence. The sleeping centrifuges also piped up with a klaxon as they crashed to an emergency stop. Finally, the base's containment alarms were thrown into the shrill mix. Somewhere—probably a couple of somewheres—McAuliffe Base's atmosphere was leaking out—and Mars' carbon dioxide and deadly cold was leaking in.

"We've got hull ruptures in the Hub, Billiton corridor two, and right here in the command center!" Shaila reported.

"Seal off those areas," Diaz ordered as she gripped her command chair. "All personnel to their emergency suits, now!"

Shaila raced over to a closet in the back of the command center, ripping the door open. The emergency suits weren't all that impressive—they only had 20 minutes of O_2 in them, and they wouldn't fight the chill for long—but it was better than nothing. She pulled out three suits and, struggling to keep her feet, started handing them out to Diaz, Washington and Yuna.

"Reactor is offline," Washington said as he grabbed his suit. "We're on battery now. We've got 24 hours."

Then the floor stopped moving.

Shaila looked around carefully, stunned, as the quake subsided just as quickly as it started. She took a cautious breath, saw it fog up in front of her as she exhaled.

"Shaila! Get suited!" Yuna yelled.

But Shaila took another breath instead. It was cold, yes. But not negative

50 degrees Celsius cold. More like…Arctic cold. Survivable. She ran to a workstation and called up sensor data. "Colonel, base oxygen levels remain within tolerances," she reported.

"Say again?" Diaz said as she finished strapping herself into her suit.

"We're cold, but we're not losing oxygen," Shaila reported. "O_2 levels are steady in here." She looked up at the window overlooking the launch pad and EVA staging grounds outside. The window had a massive crack in it—but it was holding. "If we had a real pressure leak, that window should've shattered by now."

Diaz walked over and looked at Shaila's screen. "Get your suit on," she ordered. "Then give me some outside readings."

Shaila finished sliding the suit over her shoulders, snapping the airtight cowl over her head. Immediately, the oxygen from the small tank on her back started feeding her lungs, but she wondered whether it was necessary. The outside sensors confirmed her suspicions.

"Ma'am, I'm reading a massive increase in both nitrogen and oxygen outside," Shaila reported. "CO_2 levels are still beyond Earth norms, but O2 levels are within tolerances. We can breathe out there."

"Bullshit," Diaz whispered. Yet she was looking over Shaila's shoulder at the exact same data. "Sensor malfunction?"

Shaila ran a quick diagnostic. "Negative, ma'am. All sensors systems nominal, except for the ones that fried yesterday."

Diaz stared at the screen a moment longer, then activated the base comm. "All personnel, remain in your emergency suits for the time being. Damage control teams, repair all hull breaches immediately. Seal off all unnecessary areas, including all Billiton corridors. Stand by for further orders."

The colonel turned to walk away—and tripped. She staggered a few feet before recovering herself, then turned to Shaila with a look of confusion on her face. "What the hell was that?"

"Um…you tripped, ma'am."

Diaz shook her head angrily. "No, dammit. I need a gravity reading."

Shaila frowned as she turned back to her station. That was the only thing that the base sensors couldn't measure—nobody really expected Mars' gravity to change. Shaila thought a moment, then started to access the computer that ran the emergency transports; it was a standard-issue plugin module used on the Moon and on space stations as well as on Mars, and it had a gravity sensor in order to calculate proper escape velocities. It took a few creative subroutines and one outright hack, but she managed to get the sensor to play ball.

What she found was nothing short of impossible.

"Ma'am, the transport computer sensors are reading 59 percent Earth gravity," Shaila said quietly.

Washington stood up and, crouching down low, leapt as high as he could, his arm raised high. His fingers barely brushed the ceiling. "Wow. If I did that normally, I'd plant my face up there," he said.

Yuna, meanwhile, slowly walked toward a chair and gingerly sat down. "I wondered why I felt so tired," she said.

Shaila suddenly remembered—Yuna hadn't been in anything stronger than Mars gravity for years. "Oh, shit. What can we do?" Shaila asked as she clambered over to Yuna's side.

"There's a case in my day room, bright yellow—a powered exoskeleton I use for physical therapy," Yuna said, suddenly looking years older. "If someone could get it for me, I should be OK."

Shaila nodded and jabbed a button on the comm. "Jain to Durand, over."

"Durand here," Stephane responded a moment later. "What is going on?" He sounded amazed, worried, concerned—all of it.

"Shut up and listen," Shaila snapped. "I need you to go to Yuna's day room. There's a case in there, bright yellow. Has a suit in it. Get it and get your ass up to the command center now."

"I will," Stephane responded. "Durand out."

Shaila gave Yuna a pat on the arm. "It's coming. Just try not to move until he gets here."

She turned to Diaz, who was sitting at the ops station, looking dazed. "Orders, ma'am?"

The colonel shook her head as if to clear it, gathering herself as best she could. "Washington, get a report out to Houston ASAP. Let them know where we stand, remind them evac is not an option at this time, and ask for recommendations, for what it's worth. Jain, coordinate damage control. Get the place buttoned up again."

Shaila nodded and headed for the door, but stopped to regard Diaz again. "Ma'am, if I may?"

Diaz turned and gave her a weak smile. "Sure. Why not?"

Shaila straightened up. "Once we're buttoned up, recommend we EVA to the pyramid site, ma'am."

"Really," Diaz said, the smile fading. "Why?"

"For one, unless we get the reactor back up, we've got less than 24 hours before we lose battery power and start to freeze. If we're going to investigate this thing, we don't have much time left. And honestly, I still think that whatever's causing this crap is there."

"The guys in Weatherby's journal," Diaz said.

"Aye, ma'am."

Diaz looked at Shaila closely for a moment, seeming to take her measure. "All right. Recommendation noted and officially under advisement. Seal the base, then we'll talk."

"Thank you, ma'am."

Shaila turned to leave, but Diaz spoke again. "Why'd you call Durand instead of Levin?"

Shaila stopped in her tracks. She hadn't even thought about it. There was a crisis, and she knew he'd be nearby. Of course, everyone else was down there, too, including the base doctor.

"Don't know, ma'am," Shaila answered stiffly as she hustled out the door.

Diaz smiled after her.

CHAPTER 22

June 19, 1779

The first thing Weatherby saw when he opened his eyes was Anne, looking intently at his shoulder and dabbing it with some kind of solution that sent stinging sensations through his entire arm.

"There are far worse things to awaken to," he murmured, not fully realizing he spoke out loud.

"Finally, a candid thought out of you," Anne said, the sharpness of her words dulled by the half-grin she bore. "Just stay still while this takes effect."

Weatherby saw Finch standing nearby. "How long?"

"You? An hour. You were the least of our worries, I'm afraid." Finch looked exhausted, and his once-fine clothes were stained with blood and a variety of viscous elixirs.

"The butcher's bill?" Weatherby asked him.

Finch shook his head sadly. "Too high. Thirty-four dead, including Forester. Mr. Plumb is missing, as are three others. I've not bothered to count the wounded."

Weatherby winced. "All too high. The ship?"

"Half the hull's been shot away, it seems. We should sink straight away if we splash down anywhere. The wardroom, galley, the men's berths—all a perfect wreck." Finch shrugged. "We are here, and for that I am most grateful. I understand you were quite the swordsman out there, Mr. Weatherby."

The young man shivered slightly at the memories of battle. "It was more the sword than the man," he said, turning to Anne. "Your work is truly a wonder. Thank you."

Her smile grew brighter. "I can't say the same about your face. I'm afraid you'll bear a scar on your cheek. We've not the curatives to fix it."

Weatherby turned toward the wall, where a looking glass hung. There was a two-inch scar trailing from under his right eye down to his cheek. "LeMaire's damnable jewelry," he muttered.

Anne stood up, wiping her hands. "And that's that. Your shoulder will be sore for a few days, but you should have full use of it."

Weatherby swung his feet off the cot and made to sit up, but had to steady himself with his hands, prompting both Anne and Finch to gently grab his shoulders. "Lie back down, Tom," Finch said. "You've lost quite a bit of blood. You need rest."

"I need to report," Weatherby insisted, waving their hands away. "Any man who can get on his feet will be needed." And with that Weatherby stood...and swayed...and ultimately steadied himself. He gave the two alchemists a winning smile, which was greeted by frowns. "My effects?" he said.

Anne glowered at him, but cocked her head over to the corner, where his hat, sword and slashed coat lay upon a chair. He gingerly walked over, put the coat and hat on with only a few winces, and then buckled his sword to his belt.

"Thank you both," Weatherby said, giving them a salute. He plowed his good shoulder into the doorway as he left, but otherwise made it out onto the main deck with only a little stumbling.

The ship looked horrible. There were gaping holes in the planking beneath Weatherby's feet; he peered through one to see a jumble of lumber where the men's berths once were, and he could even see the Void beneath. Other areas of the deck were cordoned off with rope, likely due to the loss of one or more lodestones affecting the air and gravity in those spots. There was blood spattered everywhere, though at least the bodies of the dead had been removed. Funerals would have to wait.

The masts were in relatively decent shape, as were the main sails. But the larboard side plane was in ruins, and he could see half a dozen men preparing to affix a new spar to it. Other crewmen ran to and fro, carrying lumber or tools or rigging.

One of the men of his division—Weatherby's fogged mind could not place the name—spotted Weatherby and gave him a sharp salute. "Mr. Weatherby's back!" the man yelled. This prompted a chorus of huzzahs amongst the crew on deck, which Weatherby found most gratifying and highly embarrassing. He smiled and returned salutes as he picked his way over to the quarterdeck, where Captain Morrow stood talking with Dr. Franklin and the Count St. Germain.

"Ah, Mr. Weatherby!" Morrow said. "About time you stopped dallying about." Weatherby's heart froze for a moment, until Morrow extended his hand. "Well done in the boarding action, sir."

Weatherby took the captain's hand gratefully. "Thank you, sir. I am most sorry to hear about Mr. Plumb and Mr. Forester."

"As are we all," Morrow said, nodding grimly. "However, it falls to us to carry on without them. So as of this moment, you shall take his place as acting first lieutenant. Mr. Foster shall be acting second, and young Mr. O'Brien shall grow up quickly and be our third."

"Understood, sir," Weatherby said. It seemed ill-mannered to thank the captain for the promotion given its unfortunate circumstances. "Your orders?"

Morrow nodded to Franklin and St. Germain. "Our quarry broke off the engagement in order to make for Mars once more, and these fellows would have me understand that time remains critically short. Thus, we must pursue *Chance* to Mars."

"How will we land, sir? Even if we make the canals intact, we would sink immediately," Weatherby said.

Morrow's face was sorrowful, yet determined. "Dr. Franklin and the Count have determined a possible destination for Cagliostro, based upon his last-seen course. There is an ancient, ruined city in the southern hemisphere, near the pole, that would be something of the ideal place for his working, if I understand correctly, and there are others in that area that might equally suit his needs. Sadly, this locale is still too far north to provide a safe transit through the aurora. And there are indeed few canals there—ones with water, at any rate. Yet given the *Chance*'s head start, we have no choice but to either make for one of the few canals left, or to attempt a dry landing upon the surface. Either way, it must be as close to this temple as we can manage."

Weatherby nodded grimly. Between *Chance*'s advantage and the *Daedalus*' condition, their only option was to attempt a controlled crash landing in either a half-dry canal or upon the the deserts of Mars. "Aye, sir. We shall focus our efforts on repairing the sails, first and foremost."

Morrow nodded. "Lt. Foster has the men at it now. Please relieve him and oversee the work."

Weatherby saluted and hurried back down the stairs to the main deck, pausing to catch himself midway down as he fought a wave of dizziness. Soon, however, he was directing the men in their efforts alongside James, perhaps the most experienced tar any officer could be fortunate enough to sail with.

"She'll hold," James said as he tested the repaired planesail an hour later. "Not sure about the ruddersail, though. Then again, we won't need them for very long, will we, sir?"

Weatherby cleared his throat. "They'll suffice," he said simply.

"I ne'er dry-landed a ship before," James remarked. "Dangerous work, that. Sure 'tis necessary, Mr. Weatherby?"

Weatherby looked to see a number of the crewmen, who had just spent their labors in repairs, nodding along with James, looking worried. Rightly so, Weatherby thought. These souls escaped boarding by a notorious pirate, only to be asked to sail their ship directly into a bloody planet.

"I'm afraid so, James," Weatherby responded. "We cannot often choose our course so readily."

James looked down at the deck, nodding but unwilling to meet Weatherby's eyes. The other men looked on, seemingly wanting more. Weatherby took a deep breath, turning to address them. "I know you have fought hard, and fought well. But there is a fight left to us still," he said. "What's more, there's likely little glory, and no rich prize."

Weatherby raised his voice as he continued. "But it is still a fight, nonetheless, perhaps the most important of our lives. There is a madman loose, one who would see an ancient terror awakened upon us all. And so it falls to us, to we simple men, to step forward as one, to stand tall against whatever darkness this sorcerer may conjure. So we must try, and if *Daedalus* must fall from the skies at last…we shall try to land her squarely upon whatever evil we find!"

To Weatherby's great surprise, the men cheered as one, and resumed their work with renewed vigor. Upon the quarterdeck, Weatherby spotted Morrow looking down on him, a small, satisfied smile creeping across his lined face.

"That was pretty damned good," came a voice behind him. Weatherby turned to see Finch there, leaning against the capstan with his hands folded across his chest. "Hell, I'd even follow you."

Weatherby lifted his hat with trembling hands to wipe the sweat that had gathered upon his brow, his shoulder throbbing even with that modest effort. "Thank you, Doctor. How are our stores of curatives?"

Finch's smile quickly vanished. "Do not play with me. You know well the bill from our engagement."

"Set to work, then, for our plan will cost lives regardless," Weatherby said. "Icarus did not survive his fall. We can only hope *Daedalus* fares better."

July 28, 2132

Shaila stared out onto the Martian surface from a small crack in the Hub's wall, marveling at the fact that the existence of the fissure hadn't spelled instant death to everyone there. Engineering confirmed her immediate reaction back in the command center; the loss of pressure should have blown open any rupture, destroying the base. Instead, she watched as one of the engineers applied a sealant to the crack. A moment later, her view of Mars was gone.

"Integrity restored," Adams reported over the comm a minute later. "Oxygen levels and internal pressure nominal."

"Roger that," Shaila responded, happy with the work. It had only taken two hours for the damage control teams to find all the fissures and cracks in McAuliffe's walls and get them sealed up. "Let's get the heat cranked. I didn't pack a sweater."

She slid the cowl of her emergency suit off her head and took a deep breath. It was still cold, but now more like a ski lodge than the Arctic. And her lungs weren't rebelling, either. Shaking her head at the strangeness of it all, she complimented the damage control team and headed back upstairs.

As she watched the crew bustle about the command center, Shaila was impressed with them yet again. Despite the multiple crises—not to mention the utter weirdness all around them—everyone had performed admirably. The reactor was still down, after all, and without it, survival was definitely an open question, even with a breathable Martian atmosphere.

Diaz poked her head out of her office. "There you are. We good?"

"All breaches sealed," Shaila said. "Internal damage is mostly cosmetic."

"This time," Diaz said with a frown. "Get our science guys up here. I need to show them something."

A few minutes later, Shaila joined Greene, Stephane and Yuna in Diaz' office after scrounging enough chairs for everyone. A frozen holoimage of JSC's director, Vice Admiral Hans Gerlich of the German Navy, hung mutely in the air above Diaz' desk.

"This came in a few minutes ago," Diaz said. "I wanted you to see it first hand."

Diaz pressed a button, and the face of the older, balding man in glasses sprang to life. "Maria, we're still reviewing your data from this morning. Glad to hear everyone's all right. We've also confirmed your atmospheric data using our Earth-based assets, since the MarsSats are still on the fritz. We can't confirm the gravity readings, but we'll certainly take your word for it."

The man took off his glasses and stared into the camera intently. "Frankly, we're just as stunned and confused as you are. What's happening on Mars is breaking every rule of geology and physics we know of. Our people here are practically at each other's throats, debating how this could be happening. For what it's worth, you may tell Lt. Jain and Dr. Greene that their theory has a few adherents here."

Shaila looked over at Greene with a small victory smile, but the physicist merely stared intently at the holo. Unlike Shaila, he was probably used to being the smartest guy in the room.

"First off, you should know we're keeping all this very close. The events on Mars have been classified as Top Secret-Gamma for the duration. Only yourself, Lt. Jain and Doctors Durand, Hiyashi and Greene are to be cleared regarding any new information with regard to these phenomena. And please reiterate to Dr. Greene that his discretion will not only be expected, but enforced."

Greene's eyebrows rose at that. "Geez. All right, already."

"There appears to be no real pattern as to the timing of the earthquakes you've experienced," Gerlich continued. "Thus, it's impossible to say whether or not it's safe for you to remain. We already have our survey team in transit, but they are still more than three weeks out, and at this rate, landing may prove difficult if these phenomena continue to threaten the base, particularly the increased gravity.

"We concur that the structure you've identified is not a natural phenomenon as we know it. And since we do not have any record of anyone building it…." Gerlich's voice trailed off for a moment. "I don't need to tell you what this potentially means, for all of us. This could be the biggest discovery in all human history. I also recognize that your lives are on the line out there. If another quake strikes, you might not be so lucky.

"Your orders are these. If you feel it practical and your engineering group concurs, you have a green light to restart your reactor. Otherwise, do everything you can to conserve power. You may want to investigate using the *Giffords'* batteries and solar cells if needed, unless you feel she's salvageable and can get you off the planet. I strongly recommend you do everything you can to get that little ship up and running, because otherwise, no matter what happens, you're stuck there. If you can salvage her, you may evacuate at your discretion.

"In the meantime, do the best you can to repair any and all sensors you have available, and gather as much data as possible. Send all raw data to Houston for analysis. We're working on some reboot procedures that might get your AOO sensors running again.

"Finally, you are to gather a small survey team and, if safe and practical, enter the sensor outage area and proceed to the pyramid structure. Investigate and assess. If section 138 of the JSC General Operations Code applies, then you are free to perform those duties, as outlined therein, to the best of your ability."

Gerlich sat up and put his glasses back on. "It seems like I should have something more momentous to say, but I really don't. Good luck and Godspeed, Maria. Gerlich out."

The image flickered off, leaving Diaz behind her desk with a wide grin on her face. "Well, then. How about them apples?"

Shaila was smiling too. "I didn't think they'd let us investigate this," she said. "I thought they'd tell us to stay the hell away. And I never thought they'd buy our theory, either."

"It's the only theory that fits right now," Greene said. "Of course, you need a leap of faith to go there, but we were breathing Martian air this morning. So I guess they're willing to see just how far this particular rabbit hole goes."

"What's your take, Yuna?" Diaz asked.

Shaila turned to see the older woman, now wearing a rig of microhydraulic spars strapped over her emergency suit, looking down and frowning. "I honestly doubt we'll find what he thinks we will, but it'll probably be good for all of us to go and find out for certain," she said. "I just hope there isn't another quake. I don't want these young people sacrificed for nothing."

Stephane raised his hand awkwardly. "I have a question, Colonel?"

"Yes, Durand?"

"What is that regulation he mentioned, section 138?"

Diaz turned to Shaila. "You want to tackle that one, Lieutenant?"

Smiling, Shaila pulled up the Joint Space Command General Operations Code on her datapad and scrolled to section 138. "Section 138, JSC Code, reads as follows," she intoned. "'The following section provides regulations and guidelines for JSC personnel in the event they should encounter intelligent life forms not of Earth origin while in pursuit of their duties.'"

Stephane looked incredulous. "We have rules for this?"

"You should see the regs for installing a zero-g toilet," Shaila quipped. "Long story short, we're not to antagonize anyone. If we can communicate with said life forms, we're to offer greetings of peace and goodwill, ascertain their intent and attitude, and offer to open a dialogue. And what's more, we're only to act in self-defense if we're actually attacked—and then only non-lethal force."

"That seems vague," Stephane noted.

"Nobody thought we'd actually need it," Diaz said. "Anyway, we've got some work to do. I'm going to brief the rest of the crew, then try to get the reactor and sensors back online. Jain, have Finelli start salvage ops on the *Giffords*, while you huddle with these guys and come up with an EVA plan. Back here in two hours. Live long and prosper."

Laughter briefly filled the room as everyone got up to leave. One person wasn't laughing.

"Shay, what was so funny?" Stephane asked on their way out.

"What, you haven't seen *Star Trek*?"

"Ummm...*Star Trek*?"

She shook her head in amazement. "When all this blows over and we have some time to kill, you and I are going to sit down and watch a whole lot of old sci-fi shows."

"I like that idea," Stephane said with a grin. "I will bring the wine."

Shaila's inner geek exulted. "You're on."

CHAPTER 23

June 19, 1779

Mars loomed large ahead of the *Daedalus*, the swirling, golden sun-currents visible before the bow as they curved toward the southern pole. Already, the descent had been a difficult one, the currents playing havoc with the gaping rents in the hull. The repaired plane and rudder sails were holding for now, though James was particularly worried about the ruddersail.

"She's dancing about like a French girl, Mr. Weatherby," the bo'sun said, his sure hands gripping the wheel tightly. "It'll be right impossible to keep her full on course."

Weatherby turned to Foster, who was looking at the red planet through his glass. "Mr. Foster, go and fetch three of our strongest men to help James with the wheel," he said.

Foster rushed off, leaving Weatherby to survey the quarterdeck. Morrow stood off to the side of the wheel, surveying the ship's operation, the currents, everything. His posture was sure and steady, but his eyes darted about, and he murmured minute corrections to James as the ship surged forward to the red planet.

Franklin and St. Germain insisted on remaining above decks, and both used spare glasses to survey the planet before them, looking for *Chance* or further clues as to its destination. Finch and Anne stood ready to assist them, each carrying a handful of maps and books about Mars, in case reference was needed. The four alchemists consulted each other quietly, noting this landmark, that canal, some kind of ruin. If Mars was once indeed a verdant world, the Xan's vengeance had been thorough, for all Weatherby could discern was sandy desert and bare rock the color of rust...or blood.

The sky around the ship began to lighten as *Daedalus* entered the atmosphere, and the turbulent currents became even more dangerous. Weatherby could see men on the main deck begin to stumble and pitch as the ship bucked beneath their feet. By rights, everyone should have been below decks, but with a dry landing before them—and large chunks of the lower hull destroyed in the battle—the main deck was their only real option.

"All hands! Secure body lines!" Weatherby shouted over the increasing winds. "Stay low to the deck!"

The men immediately began tying their lines around their waists, and Weatherby and Foster aided the others on the quarterdeck to secure theirs. Weatherby could see the four men on the ship's wheel straining with the exertion of keeping their course true, and the men on the planesails were having a similar time of it.

"We're dropping too fast!" James shouted. "We're too heavy to be landing this far from the poles!"

Morrow simply nodded; Weatherby could see the calculations ongoing behind his eyes. He would still choose proximity to the Martian ruin to a safer landing. Weatherby frowned, looking around for something, anything to do.

The answer came in the form of a cannon that had broken clear of its lines, its carriage wheels rolling it slowly to and fro upon the gun deck, in sight of the cargo hatch. "Captain," he said. "We can lighten the ship. The cannon, the shot, anything that we don't need to land."

Morrow gave a small, somewhat rueful smile. "It cannot harm us, anyway. Do it."

Weatherby strode toward the railing overlooking the main deck. "All hands! Throw the cannon and shot over the side! Anything that is neither food nor medicine must go overboard!"

The food, of course, was certainly an added weight, given that it needed to sustain several score men for weeks at a time. But it felt wrong to Weatherby to cheat the men out of a last hint at survival. Immediately, the men got to their feet and began hurling shot over the side; the cannons took some effort, but they too began to fall to the surface, though they would not likely get all the guns overboard before landing.

Weatherby turned to James with a questioning look. "That helped a little bit, sir," the bo'sun said, still looking quite haggard and worried.

"Mr. Weatherby!" Finch shouted. "A word, if we may?"

Weatherby turned to see the group of alchemists looking upward at the sails, smiling and pointing. "Now is not an ideal time, Doctor," Weatherby said as he joined them.

"It is the best time," Franklin said. "Our Miss Baker here has had a most ingenious idea."

Weatherby turned to her. "What is it?" he said, trying to keep impatience from his tone.

Her frown showed he was not quite successful, but she went on regardless. "The sails above are not critical to this landing, are they?"

"Normally they would be, but our descent is far too rapid to make much use of them," he said.

"Can we not attach the lower spars of the sails on the main and mizzen masts to the masts in front of them?" she asked.

Weatherby looked up, trying to picture what she was saying. Untying the lower spars from the masts, then securing them to the masts before them. As the ship fell, the sails would then catch the wind under them...

...potentially helping arrest their fall.

"It was something I saw in a copy of one of DaVinci's sketchbooks," Anne said, as if trying to convince Weatherby of the provenance of her idea. Yet he needed no further prodding. Weatherby quickly turned and shouted for Morrow and Foster. Thirty seconds later, the men were climbing the rigging, casting lines around each end of the spars and otherwise preparing for a major, and quite dangerous, adjustment in their sails.

The process was painfully slow, and the Martian surface continued to approach alarmingly fast. But from the moment the first sail was adjusted, the ship's descent seemed to moderate. "Well done, Miss Baker," Morrow said. "I doubt we'll get them all rigged, but it may be enough."

A loud rending noise from directly below the quarterdeck erased their optimism. "The ruddersail's gone, sir!" James shouted.

Immediately, the *Daedalus* began to spin and twist in the swirling winds. "Bring the planes in line with the deck!" Weatherby shouted, extending Anne's idea to the sails on each side of the ship. While it did little for the spinning motion, the adjustment seemed to slow the ship further.

Morrow looked over the side of the railing to the surface below. "Get the men down from the tops, Mr. Weatherby," he said. "There's no more to be done there."

Weatherby relayed the order, and immediately the men clambered down, surely relieved to be freed from their dangerous duty. One man slipped on the rigging as the ship bucked ferociously in the wind, but he was caught by his body line and aided by his fellows.

Morrow, meanwhile, continued to monitor their descent, and suddenly ran toward the front of the quarterdeck. "Forty-five degrees upward on the planes!" he yelled.

To Weatherby's great surprise, the ship's spin began to slow, and the *Daedalus* even began to move forward as it fell, so that it was approaching the surface at an angle—a far better prospect than dropping down like a stone.

Of course, this was a matter of degrees. It was still going to be awful.

Weatherby looked over the railing to see the ground rushing up to greet the ship. Something caught his eye in the distance—some sort of dome shape, oddly enough, but it flashed by quickly. A Martian ruin of some sort?

A gust of wind shook the ship, and drew Weatherby's attention back to the peril before them. They were close. "All hands brace for impact!" he yelled. "Move to the center of the deck! Stay down and hold on!"

Weatherby turned to see Anne and Morrow aiding Dr. Franklin in an effort to get him sitting upon the deck, no easy task for a man of his age and girth. But soon they were all sitting, tethered to the mizzenmast and bracing for what was to come. Weatherby looked up and saw Anne's face regarding him. He managed a weak smile that she returned in kind, fear overcoming recent animosity for at least a few moments.

And then the ship hit the planet.

Bodies slid across the decks, both forward and to starboard, as the ship careened onto the surface of Mars with an ear-splitting crunch. Weatherby felt the body line around his waist tighten as he was thrown, wrenching his midsection and causing him to cry out as he was thrown about. The sounds of splintering wood meeting grinding rock and soil surrounded him as *Daedalus* plowed violently across the rust-red deserts. More crunching sounds followed—surely the bow was all but gone by this juncture—and the ship was jolted regularly as it struck boulders and rocks in its path. The screams of the men were audible above the din.

And then, after what seemed like an eternity, all movement stopped abruptly, pitching everyone forward one final time before all was still.

Weatherby was lying on the deck, which was at a slight angle against the Martian surface, noting they must not have landed evenly upon the keel. He chanced to raise his head, positioned as he was against the railing overlooking the rest of the ship.

The bow was indeed gone, an unrecognizable jumble of wood piled up against a rather large boulder. There were men there, across the bow, he knew, but there was no trace of them at all. The remains of sails, spars and rigging hung limply from the masts, while the main deck was strewn with further debris...and bodies.

The men upon the main deck were piled upon each other and tossed about, but there was movement among them, tentative and slow, and the groans and cries of the injured began to rise to Weatherby's ears. In this circumstance, he felt that cries of pain were far more preferable to no sound at all.

Weatherby slowly regained his feet, taking in the destruction of his ship. It took a moment before he noticed that the *Daedalus* was sitting surprisingly low upon the ground, no more than fifteen feet. He looked over the edge and gasped when he saw that the impact had shorn the bilges and the hold clean away. Turning aft, there was a massive furrow upon the ground, strewn with wooden debris, which looked to be no less than three miles long.

And yet...here he stood.

Weatherby smiled even as his hands began to tremble. *Daedalus* had plummeted from the sky, but she had enough of her wings left to bring them safely to the ground.

Almost safely.

"Weatherby!" Finch shouted from behind him.

The lieutenant turned to see Finch rapidly working upon someone, with Anne and St. Germain aiding him. Dr. Franklin was just starting to sit up, so it was not him.

Morrow.

Weatherby rushed to them and saw the captain unconscious upon the deck. A piece of wood some two inches thick jutted out of his thigh, and he was bleeding profusely about the head.

"Report," Weatherby stammered as he knelt at the captain's feet.

"Head wound, severe," Finch said dispassionately. "The leg will keep. I need to stop the bleeding. Have you curatives on you?"

Weatherby reached into his coat and produced three vials, his last. "Can you save him?"

"I don't bloody know," Finch said. "My lab?"

"Destroyed," Weatherby said.

Finch looked up and spotted James picking himself up off the deck. "You there! Help us move him below!"

James scurried over and, with Weatherby's help, moved Morrow into the great cabin, where they laid him upon his dining table. The odd angle of the ship made working more difficult, and Finch swore a great deal as he administered curatives and struggled to save Morrow's life. In that, however, he had the help of not only Anne, but the Count St. Germain as well—and despite no longer having his miraculous little stone, the Known Worlds' foremost alchemist was no mere orderly.

Weatherby and James left the doctor to his work, staggering out of the great cabin and up onto the main deck. There were other wounded, some severely. "James, please ask Miss Baker to come out and tend to the others," Weatherby ordered.

A few minutes later, Anne had enlisted two of the men to help her begin a triage of wounded. The butcher's bill had grown larger on the landing—six dead, another eight unaccounted for, and a score wounded.

Including the captain.

Weatherby walked slowly up to the quarterdeck, his mind reeling. He was greeted there by Franklin. "How is Sir William?" he asked.

"We cannot yet say," Weatherby said dully, looking out over the wreckage of the *Daedalus*.

Franklin regarded the young man closely. "Was it not the great Bard who said, 'Some are born great, some achieve greatness, and others have greatness thrust upon them?'"

"I believe it was, sir," Weatherby replied. "*Twelfth Night*, if I'm not mistaken." He had no notion of how he had managed to remember that.

"Well, then," Franklin said, "I feel the only question before you now is whether you were born to it or shall merely arrive at it now. For I have no doubt, Thomas, that you possess your share."

Weatherby turned to regard the old alchemist with a wan smile. "Whether or not I possess it, I suppose this is my lot."

"Cagliostro is out there," Franklin said, laying a grandfatherly hand on Weatherby's shoulder. "We must finish what we came here to do."

Weatherby nodded soberly. "So we shall."

Finch tells me that Morrow will live, but that he is not likely to regain consciousness for several days. So it is that, in the space of mere hours, I have gone from second lieutenant to acting captain. It is roughly mid-morning here on Mars, and soon I will lead a force of men on an overland march to the Martian temple, accompanied by Dr. Finch and the Count St. Germain. There we will hopefully find Cagliostro and, I pray, stop him from whatever evil plot he has in mind. It is doubtful we will make it in time, for our best estimates put us at least six hours away from the temple. But we must try.

This is not how I expected to serve King and Country. My zeal and enthusiasm of mere months ago seems cocksure and foolhardy now. I do not feel up to this task, but I must see it through regardless.

I can think of nothing more to write herein. Should this serve as my last entry in this journal, Father, know that your son goes now to do his duty, with naught but love for you and Mother and my darling sisters in my heart.

God save us all.

Lieut. Thomas Weatherby, HMS Daedalus

July 28, 2132

Shaila Jain looked down at the datapad in her gauntleted hand, re-reading the last words of Weatherby's journal one more time as she stood between the two rovers that would take her and her colleagues into the unknown. The journal entry had appeared shortly before lunchtime, and the monitoring program she created picked up every word.

Weatherby was on Mars.

Or was he? Yes, Greene insisted that space-time quantum mechanics allowed for the possibility—and she was the one who put him onto the theory. But seriously? Sailing ships? Alchemy? An 18th century Royal Navy officer walking around Mars?

She watched as Greene and Stephane loaded the last of the survey equipment onto the rovers, their now-heavier pressure suits making the job that much more difficult. Diaz had insisted they go outside with the suits on, just in case the newly quirky planet decided it wanted its old atmosphere back. Moments later they were off, with Shaila and Stephane in Rover Two and Yuna and Greene riding with Diaz in Rover One. They tore across the Martian landscape, making a straight line for the edge of the sensor outages—and from there, if they were lucky, right to the pyramid.

Stephane was reading the journal entry as Shaila drove. "How could they go from space to Mars without burning up?" Stephane asked. "Does that not generate a lot of heat?"

"Normally, sure, but 'normally' might not apply here," Shaila said. "I mean, what's a frigate doing in space in the first place?"

"True," he allowed. "And we could be breathing the Mars air ourselves right now if we wanted. Do you really think they are out there, waiting for us?"

Shaila paused a moment before responding. "Caution and objectivity, Steve—I mean, Stephane," she said. "Keep your head on straight and gather the facts as we find them."

"You believe he is there."

Shaila turned to him, expecting to see one of his infuriating Gallic grins. Instead, he looked dead serious. "Caution and objectivity," she repeated. "We're scientists out here, right?"

"Of course," he said, sounding disappointed. "There could be anything out there. But still." He seemed to choose his next words carefully. "There is something I want to say."

Shaila checked to ensure their comms weren't being broadcast to the other rover before responding. "Oh, no," she said. "Don't do it. No professions of undying love or anything like that."

She was surprised by his sudden burst of laughter. "Well, you are certainly feeling better about yourself today, yes? At least this is a good change."

Shaila felt her face go red. "Right. Sorry. Anyway. What'd you want to say?"

"I was *simply* going to say that when we are both done here, I mean on Mars, that I would like to invite you to visit me in France. You have never been?"

Shaila blinked. "You're making *travel plans*?"

She could see him shrug inside his pressure suit. "It seems right, you know, that when you are going off to face something big like this, that you plan ahead for after. It gives you something to look forward to."

"Ummm…yeah. Makes sense, I guess," she said, trying to fumble through an already awkward conversation. "All right. When this is over, you can show me France. Right now, we've a job to do."

"Yes, *Lieutenant*." He folded his arms against his chest in seeming victory.

Thankfully, Shaila only had to endure another five minutes of embarassed silence before they arrived at their first checkpoint. The rovers pulled to a stop about a hundred meters from the estimated border of the affected area. The sensor packs had a range of about five hundred meters, so it seemed safer to get out and walk—slowly—just in case whatever was in there was still frying electronic devices.

"On your feet, people," Diaz said, clambering out of the rover. "Everybody gets a sensor. And Jain, this is for you." Diaz handed her a zapper.

"Really?" she asked.

"Just in case," Diaz said.

"Of what?"

Shaila saw the colonel frown. "If I knew, maybe we wouldn't need 'em, Jain."

"Aye, ma'am." She strapped the zapper to her suit's utility belt.

Standing a few meters apart, the five astronauts began walking slowly toward what they believed was the affected area. It didn't look like much at all, really—a flat rust-red plain with the Australis Montes mountain range off in the distance. The AOO sensor poles were visible all over the horizon, as usual. Shaila's portable sensor pack wasn't picking up anything at all.

Just another day on Mars, apparently—aside from the heavier gravity and breathable atmosphere, of course.

Diaz stopped them about five meters away from the imaginary borderline. "OK, that's far enough. You have our test subject, Dr. Greene?"

"Got it right here," Greene said. He opened a bag and pulled out the oddest piece of exploratory equipment in the history of space travel: a holocam, sandwiched between two standard-issue JSC daybed pillows and held together with duct tape. The pillows were Stephane's addition to Shaila's original solution.

Greene flipped the camera on. "You getting the readout, Dr. Hiyashi?"

Yuna was looking at a datapad. "The camera is transmitting perfectly. Ready to go."

Greene weighed the camera in one hand for a moment, then reached back and threw it into the area, right past one of the blacked-out sensor towers. Even with the heavier gravity, the device was still pretty light compared to Earth. The camera traveled about fifteen meters, then rolled another five meters or so before coming to a halt in a cloud of dust. On their datapads, the McAuliffe crew saw a brief interruption in the camera's transmission—less than a second—where it whited out, much as Greene's holocam had done the first time he and Shaila encountered the EM lines. But other than that, the camera was functioning normally.

Diaz had Greene and Yuna repeat the process twice more, each time advancing another twenty to twenty-five meters into the area. There were no further white-outs, and the camera continued to function perfectly. It wasn't even fully rad-hard.

"It would appear that whatever rendered our sensors blind yesterday is no longer in effect," Yuna finally reported, "though we cannot say for sure if another incident is forthcoming."

"Let's hope not," Diaz said. "For now, I think we're good. Let's get back to the rovers and keep going. But if anyone so much as catches a hint of static or systems interruption, speak up fast."

A few minutes later, Rovers One and Two were off again. There was a brief glitch in the sensor packs as they crossed into the area, but the electronics held up fine otherwise, and Shaila was starting to wonder whether this was just one big screw-up, somehow. That didn't last too long, however. As they progressed into the affected area, both the local gravity and atmospheric pressure continued to climb. Greene theorized that the other dimension, for want of a better word, was overlapping theirs.

Just as Greene was about to launch into a discourse on the many-worlds theory of parallel dimensions in quantum physics, Yuna interrupted—just in time, in Shaila's opinion. "I'm picking up something," Yuna said. "There seems to be both a large amount of liquid water and a great deal of inert organic material about 1.6 kilometers away, just over that little ridge to the northwest. It appears to be in the same position as that unidentified shape in the MRO image we got from Houston."

"Roger that, divert to investigate," Diaz said.

The two rovers swooped off course and headed toward a slight rise in the plain, covering the distance in less than a minute.

"Full stop!" Diaz shouted.

Shaila hit the brakes hard, pulling alongside Diaz' rover just in time to avoid a collision and wondering what the hell happened.

Then she looked up.

About fifty meters away, a large, unnaturally straight ditch filled with water stretched off toward the mountains.

In it, listing to one side, was the wreckage of a three-masted sailing ship.

CHAPTER 24

July 28, 2132

The five astronauts walked cautiously toward the ship, having parked their rovers some fifty meters away. The distance was not only prudent, but it allowed them time to wrap their heads around the sight in front of them.

The ancient ship boasted three masts and at least twenty gun ports on its right side, which was facing the McAuliffe astronauts. Shaila's limited sea training was enough for her to know that the spars and sails and rigging were a complete mess. The ship was listing about ten degrees to starboard, in water that barely covered its keel. There was wreckage strewn behind it—wooden shards and planking, mostly—resting in a shallow trench that, somehow, seemed wrought by hand rather than carved by the ship's descent. Indeed, it seemed the ship had tried to land in one of the area's new canals, but underestimated how much water was there.

"I am not detecting any movement," Yuna said. "There are residual heat signatures, however."

"Heat signatures?" Diaz asked.

"Yes, colonel. Ambient temperature is roughly 4 degrees Centigrade. There are several dozen heat signatures around and inside the...ship...that still stand out from the surrounding air."

"What could those be?" Stephane said, intent on his own sensor. "They seem small, no more than one to two meters in length, some smaller than that."

Shaila took a leap forward, looking intently amidships. The ship's skewed angle allowed her to see the exposed main deck. "I think they were people," she said quietly. "Look."

Everyone looked to where Shaila was pointing, midway between the fore and main masts. There they saw a number of bodies, clothed in little more than castoff rags. Blood was everywhere. A severed arm had fallen from the deck and was floating in the water surrounding the ship.

"Oh, my God," Diaz whispered.

Shaila pulled out the holocam, which allowed her to zoom in on the main deck. "There's, um…six bodies, maybe seven. A couple of them are in… pieces," she reported, trying to keep her composure. "Lots of blood. The bodies appear to have been…slashed, maybe. Torn apart. Yeah, I see some pretty deep gouges in the decking, too."

"What could have caused that?" Greene asked.

Diaz looked over Shaila's shoulder. "Looks like some kind of animal attack."

"Impossible," Yuna said, looking up at the deck with disbelief on her face.

"It is a ship!" Stephane said, gesturing wildly at the vessel. "How can this be impossible, now, when you see this in front of you? What if this is the *Daedalus*?"

"Oh, shit," Shaila said. She handed the holocam to Yuna and quickly leapt away—only to find that the higher gravity wasn't letting her skip-walk as far as she used to go. Nonetheless, she took off at a jog, headed for the stern of the ship.

"Where are you going?" Diaz demanded. "Stay close!"

"I gotta know," Shaila said, undeterred. She did unholster her zapper, however, as she jogged past the stern of the ship. She kept looking over her right shoulder until she stopped about five meters away. There, she looked up to see a red flag dangling from a broken spar. Under the windows of the frigate's great cabin, she read the hastily painted block letters beneath.

"It's not *Daedalus*," she reported, relief evident in her voice as she jogged back to the group. "It's the *Chance*. The pirate ship."

"Oh, that is good!" Stephane said. "I feared the worst."

"Objectivity, Durand," Shaila warned, even though she was just as relieved.

"Yes, of course. But does this not show that the book is really true?" Stephane asked. "Weatherby wrote about the *Chance*. This is the *Chance*, yes?"

"All right, yeah, I believe there's some truth to it," Diaz allowed, her eyes glued to the remnants of human beings bleeding out on the deck of the pirate ship. "But something happened to these poor bastards, and I'm hard pressed right now to say who the good guys are, especially if the British did this."

"Hey!" Shaila said.

"Sorry, Jain. I know the journal *feels* right. But they might not be *your* British, you know? Even if Weatherby is this great, upstanding young guy, who's to say he isn't just plain wrong about it all?"

"I absolutely concur," Yuna said firmly. "We must consider that the situation may not be what it seems. Jumping in and choosing a side could be disastrous."

"Roger that," Shaila said, not quite agreeing.

"All right, back to the rovers," Diaz said. "Whomever or whatever did this could still be around. We'll head for the pyramid and have a survey team come out here later on."

They started trudging back to the rovers, but Stephane remained looking at the *Chance*. Shaila walked back to him and keyed a button on his suit so they could talk privately. "What is it?"

"This is real," he said. "The *Chance*. The *Daedalus*. This Cagliostro person. Aliens. All of it."

Shaila had seen this look before—shell-shocked and trying to cope. Normally, it came in the middle of combat, with people out there wanting to kill you. This was bigger.

Before she could respond, Diaz' voice came on over the com: "Sensors showing movement, possible bogeys less than two clicks off. Smoke sighted. Mount up."

June 19, 1779

At least it wasn't hot.

That's what Weatherby kept telling himself as he trudged ahead across the barren, rock-strewn plain. Having made keel-fall near the southern pole, temperatures there were milder than was the norm for Mars. Indeed, had there been a nice breeze and some fresh air about, Weatherby would have been considerably heartened by the prospect of a pleasant walk. But the wind was more gale than breeze, and suffered from a density of dust that stung the eyes and skins. Furthermore, the plain itself was absolutely interminable, with the foothills of the Sierra del Sur never seeming to come much closer, and only gentle hills—mere inclines, really—punctuating the monotony. Finally, of course, pleasant walks rarely included heavy packs of food, water and ammunition.

It seemed odd, really, that such a momentous quest should involve such drudgery, but Weatherby figured the reality of such things was never quite the same as the adventures published in London, the ones he perused most assiduously during his days as a midshipman. Treks such as these, across featureless, barren deserts, were written away in a sentence, two at most. "They hiked far, and then they arrived." If only, he thought, he could author such an easy, fast journey for himself and the men under his command.

His command. Weatherby felt quite torn about leaving *Daedalus* under Foster's care. It wasn't as though the man was somehow unequal to the task. There wasn't much of a ship left to command, and most of his duty would involve scavenging for lost cargo and fresh water, caring for the now-stable wounded, and securing the ship against intruders. Weatherby did not trust that the pirates would content themselves with Cagliostro's plans, and a crippled ship would make an easy target without fortification.

But the Count St. Germain had been insistent that they depart quickly, and now led the column of sailors and marines forward, striding confidently into the Martian desert with a map and compass in his hands and a surprisingly heavy pack upon his back, aimed squarely for a massive Martian ruin very near the pole itself. Franklin and St. Germain had determined that they had perhaps 24 hours at most before the planetary alignment would take effect, and that in and of itself would last no more than 24 hours. As their current pace, they would barely make the ruins by sundown.

Anne easily kept pace beside St. Germain. Having exchanged her dress for a spare officer's uniform—complete with sword—she had made to depart with the rest of the party without so much as a word. Weatherby's first notion was to order her back to the ship at once, of course, but he barely opened his mouth before her gaze insisted upon his silence in the matter. Never in his time in the service had he seen an officer employ such a withering glare, and he was sure none would quite break his heart and spirit so completely. His stunned silence served as acquiescence enough, and she now seemed to be serving as St. Germain's adjutant, leaving Weatherby to bring up the rear and encourage the column's lone straggler.

"Really, Doctor," Weatherby said, pausing to allow Finch to catch up. "Was there no alternative to bringing such a heavy pack?"

The alchemist grinned wearily from under his burden. "What few curatives we had left were left to tend to the wounded aboard ship," he said. "Should we suffer further casualties, I will need the resources to craft more."

Weatherby nodded and called over one of the men. "Smythe! Come trade packs with the doctor. 'Tis either that, or we carry both the pack and the doctor later on."

Smythe—a full head taller than Weatherby and twice as wide—grinned and lifted the pack off Finch's back as if it were a pillow. He tossed his own sack at the doctor's feet and hurried off to catch up with his shipmates.

"Thank you," Finch said, genuine relief in his voice. "This is my reward for years of vice, I'm afraid."

"Yes, well, 'tis better to abandon vice sooner rather than later," Weatherby said, helping Finch to strap on his lighter load. "We may yet make a healthy man of you."

The two set off once more, serving as a rather ragged rear guard. The column followed no trail, for there was little reason for any of the major powers to establish themselves so far south—or on Mars at all—and thus there were few who traveled this way before them. Yes, the Royal Academy had sent expeditions to the Martian ruins, as did its counterparts among the other European nations. But their investigations yielded painfully few clues as to the nature of the ancient Martians, and there were far more profitable endeavors in the Known Worlds.

With each hour of marching across the wind-swept, dusty plains, Weatherby felt more and more as though he were embarked upon a folly like none other. Yet St. Germain was as sure of their destination as ever, calling it the most logical location considering the materials at hand, the positions of the stars in the Martian sky and what little he was able to glean about the Martians in his studies.

"How fares the Count?" Finch asked, nodding toward the famous alchemist.

"Oh, he marches with the most hale of them," Weatherby said with a disbelieving shake of his head. "I cannot tell whether his workings have given him such vitality, or if he is merely driven to wring the neck of his errant student."

"Both, I'd wager," Finch said, his pace improving substantially. "He told me he plans to strip Cagliostro's knowledge from his very mind once captured."

Weatherby raised an eyebrow. "Can he do that? I thought alchemical knowledge was like any other. One can't simply remove years of study."

"I am not a great student of the Mentis school, so I cannot say for sure. My focus has been on the Vitalis and Materia schools. But this is the Count St. Germain himself. If he says it can be done, it is likely so."

The two marched ahead for several minutes before Finch spoke once more. "Have you had a chance to speak with Anne?" he asked gently.

"Yes," the lieutenant replied quietly. "Before we departed."

"And?"

"It did not go well."

"I am most sorry to hear it. Those who have endured great hardship have a far greater pride than others," Finch said. "And she has endured much indeed."

Weatherby nodded, looking ahead as Anne and St. Germain consulted their maps and compasses, pointing off to the horizon. "Pride is a sin, is it not? And pride in having sinned to survive? We are taught that the virtuous are duly rewarded by God. If there were some sense of repentance for her past, perhaps things would be different."

Finch fixed a hard gaze on his commanding officer. "Is pride in one's virtue not also a sin?"

"I suppose it is," Weatherby said, frowning.

"The Gospel of John, chapter 8, verse 7—it seems appropriate here," Finch said.

"Have I been casting stones?" Weatherby said, half to himself. Then he turned to Finch with a wry smile. "And how is a self-confessed scoundrel so familiar with the Holy Bible to begin with?"

"If one is likely to break the rules, one should have a sense of what they are," Finch replied, his breath still slightly haggard even with the lighter pack. "Makes it easier to ask for forgiveness after the fact. It seems Anne took the same course."

Giving Finch a small smile and a clap on the shoulder, Weatherby finally understood why captains occasionally relied upon one or two officers—or in some rare cases, seamen—to speak freely in all circumstances. What may have seemed to be favoritism was merely a check against ego and hubris, a sounding board for ideas, and a cautionary voice to ward off potential errors. Weatherby found himself hoping Finch would elect to stay in the service, unlikely as that might be. He promised himself he would speak to the doctor about it, most frankly and forthrightly, should their quest be resolved favorably.

Weatherby was helping Finch over a rocky ridge when a scream and several shots pierced the placid quiet of the Martian landscape. Immediately, with thoughts of naught but Anne in his mind, Weatherby drew his sword and pistol and clambered up the slope ahead, leaving Finch behind. What he saw made his blood run cold.

Two of his men lay upon the red, sandy ground, reduced to bloody ruin under the claws of a beast out of nightmare. It was easily the size of a four-and-carriage, its black, scaly hide glistening in the sun. Its head bore two sets of large, yellow eyes under bony ridges, themselves overshadowed by wicked horns, and its double-hinged mouth gaped wide, revealing three sets of blood-stained, razor sharp-teeth. Its hind legs reminded Weatherby of those of a frog, while two forearms sprouted from each forequarter. Each of its six limbs ended with glistening claws the size of a man's forearm.

The beast screamed, a high-pitched howl that assaulted the ear with dissonance, even as its forearms continued to rend the bodies of the fallen crewmen.

Anne and St. Germain were nowhere in sight.

"Fall back!" Weatherby shouted, dashing down the ridge. "Form a line and prepare to fire!"

The *Daedalus* men scattered back to the ridge. Suddenly, from behind a boulder, St. Germain threw something at the creature, which immediately exploded into a cloud of black smoke, blinding it for the few seconds the men needed to regroup. Weatherby saw Anne there as well, crouching next to the alchemist, and felt relief wash over him. His feverish worry broken, he urged his men to stand fast and aim.

A moment later, a score of muskets and pistols fired as one.

The alchemical smoke dissipated, revealing the monster once more as it shook its head, trying to clear its vision. Blotches of yellow appeared on its body, dripping downward. The shots had hit true, but the creature remained upright.

And it was angry, releasing another screeching howl that echoed through Weatherby's nerves.

He immediately had the men reload, and prayed the creature would be stunned enough to allow for a second volley before it leapt forward and slew them all.

July 28, 2132

The rovers plowed across the plain, leaving a trail of red dust in their wake. There was little banter between the astronauts after their departure from the *Chance*. The sensor signals continued unabated, giving them something concrete to focus upon. Otherwise, it all might've been too much to handle. It was one thing to see images of a pyramid on a screen, quite another to see a genuine pirate ship on the surface of Mars.

"Rover Two," Diaz called, breaking the silence. "We're now getting heat readings to go with the movement. Can you confirm?"

Shaila looked over to Stephane, who immediately started fiddling with his sensor pack, which had been ignored while the geologist was deep in thought. "Yes, Colonel," he reported. "At least two dozen readings. One of them is…large."

"Roger that. We're just about there," Diaz said. "Let's park behind those rocks and approach on foot."

A minute later, Shaila pulled Rover Two up next to the others and got out. The gravity seemed to increase as they progressed, and her pressure suit was starting to feel significantly heavier. They all huddled at the base of the rock, staring at the sensor readouts.

"Jesus," Diaz said. "They're moving fast."

A high-pitched noise from over the rocky outcropping immediately drew their attention. "What the hell was that?" Shaila said.

Diaz reached for her zapper, prompting Shaila to do the same. "You three, try to get on top of these rocks and have a look. Greene, go ahead and record whatever you see. Jain, we're going around. Everyone stay close to each other and don't do anything stupid."

As they slowly walked toward the edge of the outcropping, a staccato popping sound filtered through their pressure suits, followed by another high-pitched...shriek?

"Not good," Shaila said, gripping her zapper tightly. She turned back to see the others struggling to get up over the rocks, the weight of their pressure suits making climbing difficult. "I need an environmental reading."

A pause. "Gravity now 85 percent that of Earth. Atmospheric pressure and oxygen levels approaching Earth nominal," Yuna said, her voice thin and tremulous. "Temperature 10 degrees Celsius."

"Roger that." Shaila followed Diaz, crouching down as the rocks sloped toward the ground. Diaz held her hand up and stopped, then stuck her head tentatively above the outcropping.

"Holy shit," Diaz whispered.

Shaila followed suit, then ducked back down, her heart racing. "That's probably what happened to *Chance*," she ventured. "Those uniforms...."

"I see it," Diaz snapped. "As per JSC regs, I'm officially confirming the big-ass creature is hostile. You ready?" The colonel held up her zapper.

"Roger," Shaila said. "Over the top?"

Diaz nodded. "On my mark. Three...two...one...mark!"

The two stood up and turned, firing in the direction of the chaos—and the six-legged monster from hell that was busy tearing up a bunch of guys with pop guns.

The creature roared again, rearing up in pain, tossing aside two men with its flailing forearms. Immediately, it turned, looking for the source of the agony.

"Shit," Diaz said. "Hit it again."

They fired their zappers once more, sending intense microwaves into the creature's scaly body. It screamed and howled, its yellow eyes bugging out, its body rearing up to a height of nearly six meters. Finally, after a full eight seconds of lashing pain, it toppled over, its eyes closed.

"Now!" came a voice from the other side of the creature.

Shaila saw a group of haggard-looking men in grubby clothes rush forward, wielding muskets topped with bayonets. They were led by a way-too-young man in the dress of an 18th century Royal Navy officer, a gleaming sword in his hand. They pounced upon the creature, stabbing it over and over with their weapons. Yellow blood pooled from the wounds and dripped to the ground. Finally, the officer raised the sword high above his head, sending it swooping down across the creature's neck.

It took three swings, but the head soon rolled a half-meter away, severed.

A cheer erupted from the men, but the officer took no part. Instead, he scanned the area for more foes.

And spotted Shaila and Diaz.

"Form a line!" he shouted, pointing his sword at them. The men quickly lined up in front of their officer, getting onto one knee and reloading their weapons.

"What's the plan?" Shaila said nervously.

"Pocket the zapper," Diaz said. "And put your hands up."

Slowly, Diaz walked out from around the rocks, her hands raised, with Shaila following suit. They approached slowly, until they heard the officer's voice filter through their suits once more. "That's far enough. Identify yourselves."

"Go for it," Diaz said through the comm. "You're Royal Navy. Air shouldn't be a problem by now."

"Gee thanks," Shaila muttered. Slowly, so as not to alarm the dozen or so men—and one woman, she saw—with guns aimed at her, Shaila released her helmet seals and, ignoring the alarms on her suit, slowly lifted it off her head.

The fact that the moisture in her body immediately didn't begin boiling off was the first good sign—the breathable atmosphere hadn't gone anywhere. And it wasn't even all that cold.

The officer continued to look at her, perplexed. She latched her helmet to the fastener on the back of her suit—carefully, so as to not cause any alarm.

"Lt. Thomas Weatherby, I presume?" she called out.

Diaz looked over at her in disbelief. "A simple hello would've done it," she said over the comm, the headset of which was still in Shaila's ear.

The man lowered his sword slightly. He was short, no more than 170 centimeters tall, with long brown hair kept back in a ponytail. He looked barely old enough to shave. "I do not know you," he said.

"No, sir. You don't. I'm Lt. Shaila Jain, British Royal Navy."

The confused look on the man's face grew more intense, before giving way to a smile, even as his men, to Shaila's surprise, erupted in laughter. "Please, miss, do not take offense, but I would think I would have heard of it if the

Royal Navy had begun making *women* into officers. Are you a Hindu? What in God's name are you wearing?"

Right. 1779. Try again. "It's a long story. But not as interesting as the one you've written, Lieutenant. We've read your journal. We know about Cagliostro."

Diaz reached out with her gauntleted hand to give Shaila a hard whack on the arm. "Dammit, Jain, we don't know what's going on!" Shaila heard her say in her comm earpiece.

The officer didn't see this, however, as he was talking quietly with two other men, both of whom were dressed as late 18th Century gentlemen, and the lone woman, who was wearing an ill-fitting officer's uniform.

The standoff continued for a few moments longer, until the officer turned back to the astronauts. "Let us say, for a moment, that you have read my journal, even though it remains secured upon my very person," the man said. "Tell me how much of it you have read."

Shaila cleared her throat. "I know about your descent to the surface," she said, prompting a surprised look from the entire group before her. "I know you lost Lt. Plumb in the battle earlier today, and that Capt. Morrow was injured in the crash. And I know that you were just talking with Dr. Finch and the Count St. Germain."

The man, glanced at his comrades, then lowered his sword. "You two, and any others with you, will assemble over there," he said, pointing to an area about ten meters away from both the creature and the rocks. "You will take your…hats…off. And then we shall have a talk, shall we?"

CHAPTER 25

June 19, 1779
July 28, 2132

I t might've been easier if the men from the *Daedalus* had actually been aliens.

Section 138, subsection 1, paragraph 6 of the Joint Space Command General Operations Code states all too matter-of-factly that in an encounter with intelligent life not of Earth origin, personnel should be aware there may be pronounced cultural differences, ones that should be addressed with care and respect for those differing values.

At the moment, Shaila thought that particular regulation was a steaming load of bullshit.

"I am most sorry to say, ladies, that I find your story to be quite incredible. I have seen much of late, but to find an outpost commanded by female officers?" The young officer, who did indeed confirm he was Lt. Thomas Weatherby, shook his head ruefully. "You have me at a loss."

Anne straightened up and turned to Weatherby. "Is it so impossible to consider that women may be as competent as men, Lieutenant?" she said, the emphasis on his rank evident to even the astronauts. "Or am I but a silly housemaid with a few magic tricks learned by rote?"

The astronauts stood together, talking with Weatherby, Finch, Anne and St. Germain—with the business end of a dozen muskets pointed in their direction from less than ten meters away. They had started to relay their story, but they were quickly bombarded with questions about their time, some

350 years later than the voyage of the *Daedalus*, as well as their modes of transportation, the "alchemy" involved in their weapons and, yes, their social structure. Somewhere in there, they discovered that Weatherby's Earth had no North or South American continents. Frustration and amazement abounded, with the former growing more pronounced as the back-and-forth went on.

St. Germain finally interrupted. "Weatherby, we haven't the time to dawdle here. Shoot them, bring them with us, I care not. We must go before Cagliostro completes his working!"

Stephane spoke up for the first time. "We can get you there quickly. We have our rovers. Our, um, carriages."

Weatherby gave Stephane a hard look, regarding him carefully through narrowed eyes. The young officer was already quite disturbed that there were five of these strangely attired people present—including three women posing as officers!—but now... "You are French?" he asked.

"Umm...yes. But you see, in our time, the British and French are allies, and—whoa!"

Stephane's explanation was immediately cut off by Weatherby, who raised his pistol toward the Frenchman, the barrel mere inches from his face. "The British and French are allies, are they?" Weatherby said calmly. "That's perhaps even harder to believe."

"Believe it," Shaila said. Weatherby turned back to the women "officers," only to see the Hindu pointing her strange-looking pistol at *his* face. "Let's not make this hard, Mr. Weatherby," she said, a hint of menace behind her voice.

The click of a dozen muskets came from behind Weatherby's back, prompting a small smile out of him. "It shan't be us to experience difficulty, milady," he said. He did not lower his pistol, leaving Stephane frozen in place with his hands up, palms out, eyes saucer-wide.

Smug bastard, Shaila thought. At least Diaz had her zapper out and aimed as well. On wide-arc, they could probably stun most of them—but probably not all. Yet the situation seemed familiar, and she quickly remembered why.

"Fine," Shaila said. She held the zapper out a moment longer before slowly lowering it. Looking Weatherby directly in the eye, she tossed the weapon to the ground. "We haven't threatened you, Lieutenant. In fact, we saved your collective asses, which means what you're doing right now isn't very honorable." She stared hard at Weatherby, whose hand wavered slightly even as he continued pointing the pistol. She stepped slowly around to stand directly between the gun and Stephane. "We're leaving, and we're going to that pyramid. I'm not even sure whether this Cagliostro guy is as evil as you say, but I'm going to find out, because that pyramid is the center of some bad things happening on *my* Mars. If you decide to start acting civilized, you can join us. If not, you can spend the rest of the goddamned day hiking. But you need to decide. Now."

With that, she turned, grabbed Stephane by the arm, and started walking back to the rovers. Slowly, the other astronauts followed her, leaving the *Daedalus* crewmen stunned.

"Lieutenant," Diaz said quietly, the comm picking up her words clearly. "Care to tell me what the hell you're doing?"

"Winging it, ma'am," she muttered. "Something I read in Weatherby's journal. Ganymede."

"Well, they are not shooting," Stephane noted as he looked back repeatedly. "I can now say that I do not like having a gun pointed at me."

Shaila turned around and saw Weatherby and his alchemists arguing animatedly, with their men standing around, weapons lowered.

"We should be able to at least get out of here," Shaila said. She reached Rover Two, got in, and revved the engine. "Let's go."

Stephane took the passenger seat and Shaila tore off, leaving the other three to pile into their rover. She headed straight for the *Daedalus* contingent, covering the ground in mere seconds and skidding to a stop.

"Last chance, Lieutenant," she said curtly, reaching down to pick up the zapper where she had thrown it. "I can take two, and the colonel's got room for one more."

Weatherby looked at the rover, and then at the hills in the distance, where the Martian ruins were. "And how quickly can your…carriages…cover the distance?" he asked.

"Twenty minutes, maybe less."

Weatherby looked at St. Germain, who nodded, and at Finch, who merely shrugged. The other rover pulled up, with Diaz looking expectantly at the British officers from different centuries.

Weatherby turned to Anne. "Miss Baker, I—"

"Go," she said simply, with something approaching kindness. "There's but room for three, and you need both Finch and the Count with you."

"But your safety," Weatherby said. "Alone with the men?"

She shook her head sadly, smiling. "Have you learned nothing of me at all? After all this time?" She patted the hilt of her smallsword. "I'll be fine. Go."

Weatherby nodded and gave her a small smile before turning to his men. "Mr. Smythe, if you please?"

"Aye, sir?"

"I am leaving Miss Baker in your care. If any ill befalls her, no man here will go unpunished. And after that, you will deal with me. Personally."

Smythe saluted—as did all the men.

"You know," Shaila said, "the wreckage of the *Chance* is about two clicks northwest from here."

Smythe looked at her oddly. "Clicks?"

"Sorry. About a mile, give or take. You can shelter there. We didn't find any survivors."

Weatherby nodded. "Make for the *Chance*. Set up a perimeter and defend yourselves until we return." Finally, he turned to look at Shaila one last time. "Lt. Jain, is it?"

"That's right."

He nodded at St. Germain, who strode toward the second rover. "Well, if nothing else, you certainly talk like a sailor. Dr. Finch, if you please." He motioned for Finch to take one of the back seats. "Given that you have indeed saved our…asses…we shall accept your invitation. Shall we, *Lieutenant*?"

Shaila gunned the motor and took off, the force of which shoved Weatherby into his seat. The officer looked over at Dr. Finch, who couldn't stop smiling at the incongruity of it all.

"I like her," Finch said, nodding toward Shaila as they sped off. "I think the service has held up well over the past 350 years."

"Thank you, Doctor," Shaila said primly. "And we don't slap people around any more either."

Finch laughed heartily at that. "Oh, Weatherby! You wrote about that, did you? And here I was so cautious about not reading your journal, even as I wrote your eulogy!" The doctor leaned forward between Stephane and

Shaila. "Of course, you thus know I am nothing but a wastrel and a terrible influence, much to my eternal pleasure and my lieutenant's immense consternation."

Weatherby grabbed his shoulder and pulled him back into the seat. "You have since comported yourself admirably, Doctor. I was merely frustrated at the time. And besides, that was to be a most private journal, for my father."

"Sorry about that," Stephane said. "When a strange book shows up on Mars dated 350 years ago, you cannot help but read, yes?"

"I suppose," Weatherby said, nonplussed.

The next twenty minutes were spent in a barrage of questions and answers from both sides of the dimensional divide. Weatherby was particularly interested in the zappers—most likely to gauge the relative strengths of their weapons should things fall apart—while Finch was fascinated to discover that the Martian atmosphere was not normally breathable. Shaila was interested in the creature they just slew, which was apparently one of the few indigenous fauna left on Mars, and one that was keen on expanding its diet, according to Finch.

Shaila's comm interrupted the give and take. "Diaz to Jain, come in."

"Jain here, Colonel," Shaila responded.

"Give your guests some headsets. We need to fill you in on what our experts have been chatting about."

Shaila nodded at Stephane, who produced a pair of headsets from the rover's emergency kit. "Gentlemen, if you would put these on, like so." Stephane pointed to his own headset, still hooked up to his suit.

"What do these do?" Weatherby asked, doubt in his voice.

"They allow you to speak to the people in the other rover," Shaila said.

Finch grabbed his and put it on, the wire trailing forward to the rover's control panel. "I say, can anyone hear me?"

"I hear you," Diaz said. "Where's Weatherby?"

Finch grabbed the headset, took Weatherby's hat off, and handed the headset back. "They're asking for you."

The lieutenant put it on carefully, as if he were wrapping some dangerous creature around his head. "Now what do I do?"

"I hear you, Lieutenant," Diaz said. "The Count here and Dr. Greene have been sharing some information. Let's give them a listen. And keep the chatter down. One speaker at a time. Dr. Greene?"

Greene went first. "Well, we're finding some common ground between our modern physics and the Count's alchemy. There are definitely some theoretical underpinnings for both that could allow for multiple universes or dimensions, as well as non-linear space-time constructions."

"The nomenclature is different, of course," St. Germain said, sounding put out that he had to explain himself to his lessers. "In the end, however, both alchemy and their 'quantum physics,' as they call it, can account for the space between spaces, and the joining of those different realms by means of Will and Work."

"However," Greene added, "it seems as though there needs to be folks on both sides of our respective...dimensions, I guess...in order to create a link."

"The boxes. The EM fields," Shaila said.

"So it would seem," Yuna replied, still sounding somewhat doubtful, despite it all. "And the Count here believes that these aliens from Saturn placed this other person, Althotas, between our world and theirs, requiring these two particular worlds to interact in order to free him."

"Why our worlds, then?" Weatherby asked. "Why not any other?"

"Sympathy, as Dr. Finch can tell you," St. Germain said. "Our two worlds are somewhat similar, in that there are human beings, and something of a shared history, different as those elements may be."

"In our 22nd century terms, these particular parallel universes may have shared a common origin at one point, and a particular event that, on the quantum level, split them apart ages ago," Greene added.

"So there are two groups working together in two separate dimensions. How do they know to work together?" Stephane asked. "It is not as though they can talk to each other between universes, yes?"

"Yet Cagliostro has bragged throughout the Known Worlds that his 'ascended master,' as he calls him, has communicated with him extensively," St. Germain said. "I believe that this entity, imprisoned between universes, can yet exert his will into both our realms, though in a limited fashion."

"So who's he talking to here with us?" Shaila asked. "And how?"

"We don't know," Greene admitted. "Given the disparities of the basic principles of time and space between our two universes, Althotas could have laid the groundwork for his reemergence on our side of the portal a very long time ago. Or last week. We just don't know."

"Yeah, but at some point, someone would've had to come to my base to lay out that damned ring," Diaz said. She flipped a switch on her comm. "Diaz to McAuliffe, over."

"McAuliffe. Adams here, over," the base replied.

"Adams, I want you to pull all the suit-beacon data we have going back as long as you can—call Houston for the archives and make it a priority request. Run a search for anybody who's been anywhere in the affected area at any time, with any kind of pattern or regularity, since the very first crew arrived—hell, since the first Mars landing. Combine that search with the radio signature I'll be sending you in a moment. Over."

"Colonel, that'll take some time," Adams said.

"So get started. Diaz out."

Weatherby tapped Shaila on the shoulder. "Who was that?"

"Our base of operations is about 25 kilometers from here. About 15 miles, give or take. We have at least a dozen other people stationed there."

Weatherby sat back in his seat again. "This is truly a wonder," he said quietly, watching the Martian terrain speed by at a dizzying pace.

"I find it gratifying," Dr. Finch replied, clapping the lieutenant on the shoulder. "Cheer up, old boy. Their wonders and our wonders may yet carry the day."

"Yuna, you've been quiet," Diaz said. "What do you think of all this?"

It was several moments before Yuna spoke. "I cannot deny that the theories put forth here have some merit," she said tentatively. "I am, after all, sitting in a rover with the famous Count St. Germain, with my helmet off, breathing the atmosphere of Mars without ill effect. But our assumptions about what has occurred, and what this Cagliostro may be doing, are just that—assumptions. I would recommend we proceed with extreme caution, rather than shooting the place up when we arrive. An alien life form may be arriving in our universe, and I believe we should independently verify its aims before anything else."

"Madam, you fail to appreciate the depths to which this madman will take us," St. Germain said, his voice dripping with scorn even over the comm. "I for one will not stay my hand against him. He has stolen my life's work, murdered several people and a great number of Venusians, and may yet have caused great tension between all of humanity and the Xan of Saturn. If you are able to subdue him with your devices, then I shall acquiesce to that. If not, I will shoot him myself."

A cross-chatter erupted immediately over the comm, with Yuna, Greene and St. Germain arguing vociferously over the proper course of action.

"Stop it!" Diaz shouted. "All of you! That's a goddamn order!"

St. Germain made a tentative sound, as if he were planning on further rebuttal, but stopped. Shaila guessed her commander's don't-you-dare look worked on 18th century alchemists as well as wayward astronauts.

"Now listen up," Diaz said. "If we're attacked, we fight in self-defense. But until such time as we are attacked, we make peaceful contact and try to figure out what's going on. If Cagliostro is there doing bad things, then we take our shot. If it's at all possible to take him alive, we do that." The colonel paused to catch her breath. "Lt. Weatherby, as commander of the *Daedalus,* do you concur?"

The young lieutenant straightened in his seat. "We certainly have disparate views as to the best course of action, but this seems a workable compromise. However, should Cagliostro be an immediate threat, I say his life shall be forfeit in the name of the greater good."

"Fine, so long as we determine that threat on scene," Diaz said. "And again, non-lethal force whenever possible or practical. That goes for you too, Count. Besides, you'll probably want to know where your Philosopher's Stone is. Let's try to keep as many people from getting dead as possible. Meantime, I've got one more question. What happens if Cagliostro is there right now, doing whatever mad-scientist plan he's got going, and we stop him? Will our universes still overlap like this?"

"If his 'working' is the cause, then my guess is that the overlap will recede," Greene said. "How long that will take, I don't know. Our universes started colliding well before Cagliostro even got here, so the whole time continuum is definitely skewing non-linear. If we stop him before he finishes, the overlap could reverse itself at the same pace, or quicker. No idea."

"Or the damage may already be done," St. Germain said. "The rift may be permanent, although I believe it will likely be confined to this area of Mars."

"Nice," Shaila said. "At least we can visit each other."

They parked the rovers about a half kilometer from the pyramid itself, using the foothills of Australis Montes as cover for their approach. Lying down on one of the ridges to stay out of sight, they took in the view ahead.

And it was incredible.

Rising nearly several hundred meters from the ground, the step pyramid was perhaps one of the most ornate stone structures Shaila had ever seen. The six major tiers of the pyramid were covered in additional stonework now—staircases in the middle of each side leading to the top, flying buttresses everywhere, some sort of pillared cupola on top. The entire structure was liberally inlaid and trimmed in what appeared to be pure gold. It was a mishmash of styles, as if each of Earth's ancient cultures had contributed something to the building, yet they all seemed to work together.

"It appears the main entrance is there, at the base where the dry canal leads up to it," Weatherby said as he peered through his spyglass. "I see four men on guard there, pistols and cutlasses. Likely crewmen from the *Chance,* I'll wager."

"At least they won't have reinforcements," Finch said; the astronauts from McAuliffe had filled them in on the fate of the *Chance* en route.

"All right," Diaz said, sliding back under the cover of the ridge. "I'd like to go say hi. Jain, you and Weatherby take up position over there, on that bit of high ground to the left. Yuna, take my zapper and take the Count with you over to the right, behind that boulder. Durand, you're with me, in case I need a translator."

"Wonderful," Durand muttered.

Diaz whacked him on the arm with a grin. "Greene, Finch, stay out of sight."

"So long as my lieutenant concurs," Finch said, pointedly looking toward Weatherby.

"Agreed," Weatherby said. "But you are taking an awful risk, Colonel. They will not be keen on negotiation."

"It's my job to try," Diaz said. "Places, everyone. And remember, non-lethal attacks if need be."

Slowly, the combined force of astronauts and sailors took position around the pathway leading to the pyramid's entrance. Thankfully, the canal had been seemingly carved out of the Martian bedrock, leaving plenty of places to hide along its sides. They managed to get within twenty meters before Diaz radioed ready.

Shaila and Weatherby saw her gingerly step down from the top of the ridge onto the canal bed, aiding Durand down as well. Thankfully, the canal curved slightly, masking them from the entrance until about fifteen meters away.

"Ready, Steve?" Diaz asked over the comm.

"Terrified, but ready," Stephane reported.

Shaila smiled. "Newbie," she said, intentionally allowing Stephane to hear her. He gestured something unkind at her, but she could see him smiling.

"He is not a brave man?" Weatherby asked, nonplussed.

Shaila keyed off her comm before responding. "He's a scientist, Lieutenant," she said, trying not to sound defensive. "He's never been shot at in his life. But he's held up pretty well so far."

The young Royal Navy officer frowned, but said nothing as he watched Diaz and Stephane walk steadily toward the pyramid entrance.

"Hello!" Diaz called out. "We mean no harm!"

"Bonjour! Nous ne veux de mal!" Stephane echoed just as loudly.

Shaila saw the four guards at the pyramid doors immediately go for their weapons, aiming their pistols down the walkway. "They're ready to fire, ma'am," Shaila reported over the comm.

"Roger," Diaz said tersely. "Steve, get up against the wall. How do you say, 'Don't shoot?'"

"Ne tirez pas," Stephane said, huddling against the wall behind Diaz.

"All right," Diaz sighed, then stepped out slightly from behind her cover, arms up. "Si vous plait, ne tirez pas!"

Smoke immediately erupted from the muskets, with the popping sound of their firing reaching Shaila a split second later. Diaz immediately threw herself behind the cover of the wall and started retreating back down the canal. "Plan B, guys!" she shouted over the comm.

"Roger," Shaila replied. "Taking 'em down," she added for Weatherby's benefit. She then aimed and fired her zapper—just as Weatherby's pistol barked. She hadn't even seen him aim.

All four guards went down quickly. Two remained twitching on the ground in immense pain, while two were very still, blood pooling beneath them.

"Shit," Diaz said, running back up the canal as the rest of the group assembled. She wheeled on Weatherby. "What part of non-lethal don't you get?"

"They were firing upon you, madam!" Weatherby said, standing his ground. "Any man who fires upon an ally, let alone a woman, deserves no less!"

Diaz looked ready to clock Weatherby in the head, but apparently thought better of it and visibly calmed herself. "They probably heard those shots inside. That'll make peaceful contact a lot harder now." She held out her hand to Yuna, who surrendered her zapper.

"I have no interest in peaceful contact," St. Germain said, smoking pistol in hand. "He is ripping open a gate to Hell, I tell you!"

"Then I want to see *el diablo* himself before you fire again! You got me, chief?" Diaz barked.

Stunned, St. Germain said nothing.

"Jain and I will take point," Diaz said. "Guys with flintlocks behind us. Use those damn pistols in self-defense only, and only if *our* weapons don't work. Clear?"

Weatherby frowned. "I hope for our sake, then, their numbers are few inside. If not, I will order my men to fire."

Diaz shook her head but said nothing as she turned to the doors and walked toward them. "Hinges are on the other side. No sign of a handle or doorknob." She reached the doors, carved with ornate sigils, and gave them a shove with her shoulder. They didn't budge. "Stone. And heavy as hell. Sensors?"

Yuna held up her sensor pack. "Several heat signatures inside, at least six up against the other side of the door. One of them looks large, and odd. Not moving like the others."

Finch ventured a look at the sensor pack screen. "Amazing," he breathed. "It is as if you can see inside."

Diaz looked up at the door in irritation. "Fine then. Jain, you and Weatherby go around the sides, see if there's another way in."

"That will not be necessary, madam," St. Germain said, kneeling on the ground and fishing through his backpack. "If you can but give me a moment's time, we shall gain entrance through these doors soon enough."

Diaz looked questioningly at Shaila, who merely shrugged. "We're sitting ducks out here, Count, so make it quick," Diaz said.

"Sitting ducks?" Weatherby asked.

"Never mind," Shaila said.

Weatherby gathered the guards' weapons, distributing pistols and swords to the astronauts—all of whom looked perplexed as they weighed the weapons in their hands. As he did so, a very familiar leather-bound book fell out of his pack.

"You know, that could be where I found it," Shaila said, eyeing the book on the floor of the canal. She then caught herself, realizing what she had just said.

It was the same inflection, the same tone, the very same words that had intruded into her thoughts the first time she was in the lava tube, three days prior.

"Miss Jain?" Weatherby asked, stepping in front of her and breaking her reverie.

"What?"

"Found what?" he asked.

Shaila struggled to compose herself. "Your journal. I found it right here, when this was still a cave."

Weatherby stared at the book for a long moment. Despite himself, he was impressed with the Hindu woman's courage and seeming competence, and she had indeed somehow found his journal. If time itself had truly been twisted and bent, then it stood to reason that their aid now was a direct result of their obtaining his diary.

"Then this is where I shall leave it," he said, giving Shaila a small smile. "So you can find it later. Or three days ago. Whichever applies."

Shaila blanched as her mind snapped into focus. *"...where I shall leave it."* That's exactly what she had heard in the cave when she found the book. She thought she was going a little crazy at the time. Now...perhaps not. She couldn't explain why it was happening, but the fact that his words were echoed in her head a few days ago was...OK. It fit.

After a moment, she managed a weak smile. "Thanks, Lieutenant."

The Count, meanwhile, was mixing various liquids and powders from a small kit in his bag. Within a minute, he was vigorously shaking a glass vial of something that smelled god-awful. "Ladies and gentlemen, we should retreat down the canal somewhat."

Everyone clambered back down the dry canal bed and crouched down. St. Germain joined them last, still shaking his concoction. "Put your heads down," he said, throwing the vial at the door and covering his own head with his arms.

Everyone huddled against the side of the canal. Shaila thought there would be some kind of explosion. Instead, there was a loud hissing, effervescent sound that lasted about six seconds—followed by a massive rumbling. Dust and rock billowed down the canal; screams echoed from inside the pyramid.

The explosion came afterward. Shaila felt intense heat wash over them, even from their position away from the doors. And then all was silent.

St. Germain poked his head around the corner to look at his handiwork. "It is done. We must still proceed cautiously, however."

The doors had collapsed inward in a pile of rubble. Shaila could see parts of the doors that looked like they had been eroded by some kind of acid.

"Not bad," Diaz allowed. She then tapped Shaila on the shoulder and pointed to the right side of the door, and motioned for Weatherby to take the left. In a few moments, the group had split up on either side of the doorway, weapons at the ready, as the dust settled.

There was silence from inside.

Weatherby and Shaila peered into the hallway beyond. The doors had collapsed upon four or five men—it was hard to determine exact numbers in the rubble—along with some kind of contraption made from wood and metal, now charred beyond recognition. "Greek fire, I imagine," St. Germain murmured.

The hallway stretched out toward the center of the pyramid, covered in darkness.

Nobody from either century was willing to take chances. The group slowly entered the corridor. Weatherby grabbed a torch from a sconce on the wall, lighting it while Shaila flicked on the flashlight on her left gauntlet.

Together, they crept slowly into the heart of the Martian pyramid.

CHAPTER 26

June 19, 1779
July 28, 2132

Shaila focused her light on the shadows the torch created, tensely anticipating an ambush at any moment. Yet a surprisingly intense part of her wanted to stop, to look at the strange hieroglyphics on the wall, to study and learn about this alien culture.

Thankfully, there was an even more intense part of her interested in self-preservation. She systematically covered the hallway with her lamp, weapon at the ready. Diaz and Weatherby were likewise ready for ambush.

Not everyone in the group had military training, however. "These are utterly fascinating," Yuna murmured. "Count, are these details of rituals of some kind? You see here?" She pointed at one of the pictures of what appeared to be a procession toward an altar of some kind.

"Yes," St. Germain whispered. "And if you look at the position of the orbs above, it is obviously some kind of alchemical—"

"Shut up, both of you!" Diaz hissed. Yuna put a hand to her mouth and nodded at her, while St. Germain merely glared.

The walls of the corridor were smooth, though there were small alcoves placed roughly five meters apart. Some of these held pedestals, others did not. There were columns in between each alcove as well, supporting an arched ceiling that peaked some seven meters above their heads.

Shaila concentrated on the alcoves, while the rest of the McAuliffe officers used their flashlights to check the floors, walls and ceilings. Greene was uncharacteristically quiet; Shaila looked back and saw him recording everything on a holocam, looking focused and, if anything, serene.

A whisper from Weatherby regained her attention. He pointed to one of the alcoves, then held up one finger. She stopped, took aim with her zapper, and fired into the dark.

The shout of a man pierced the hallway as the microwaves scrambled his synapses. He fell into the torchlit hallway, twitching.

And that's when the gunfire erupted from the other end of the hall.

"Down!" Shaila shouted.

Shaila and Weatherby darted behind two of the columns, while everyone else either hit the deck or slid into the alcoves. Ignoring Diaz' order about non-lethal weapons—he wasn't technically part of the chain of command anyway—Weatherby immediately returned fire, though the targets could not be seen. Even Stephane squeezed off a shot with his flintlock. Shaila looked back at him, and he merely shrugged despite the terrified look on his face.

"Weatherby!" Finch shouted. "Phosphor shot!" The doctor threw a small pouch at Weatherby, who caught it cleanly and began to load his pistol.

"What the hell's that?" Diaz asked from her spot behind a column.

"Illumination," Finch responded. "Watch."

Weatherby finished reloading and aimed for a space above the end of the hallway. He fired—and a streak of blinding white light erupted from his pistol, arcing through the hallway before embedding itself above another set of double doors and illuminating six people armed with muskets.

"The sanctum doors!" St. Germain said. "He is inside there!"

Shaila darted out from her cover and took aim with her zapper, downing two of the assailants with two rapid shots. Diaz hit a third before they finished reloading and took aim again. Their shots echoed through the hallway, and were followed quickly by a cry from Finch, who slumped to the floor.

"Doctor!" Weatherby cried. Having reloaded, he took aim and managed to hit a fourth, leaving two riflemen left, before turning and rushing back to his shipmate.

"Just the arm," Finch said through gritted teeth. "I believe it passed through."

"Tell me what to do, Finch," Weatherby said. "Where is your bag?"

"No time," he said. "Give me your kerchief. Go and finish them." Weatherby tossed his kerchief at Finch, then wheeled around and, crouching, dashed back to his column opposite Shaila.

"I'm low on charges," Shaila said.

"Your weapon?" Weatherby asked.

"Yeah. I need to conserve in case there are more inside. Got a spare pistol?" Shaila figured Diaz' self-defense caveat was now in full effect.

Weatherby pulled a pistol from his belt and tossed it to Shaila. She looked at it for a few moments, then held it out, aiming, before she squeezed the trigger. "Dammit. Missed. How the hell do you fight with these things?"

"Practice, milady," he replied, taking aim once more. He too missed. "I admit, they're horribly inaccurate at this range."

Two more shots whizzed down the hallway toward the group, but neither hit. "Now!" Weatherby said suddenly. He dashed up the hallway, sword drawn.

"Shit," Shaila muttered. She chugged off after him as fast as her suit would allow. She could see the riflemen fumbling with their muskets, trying desperately to reload before the charging officers could reach them.

They were too late. One of the riflemen tried to parry Weatherby's sword with his musket, only to find it cleanly sliced in half, along with his left forearm. He fell, shrieking, while his compatriot hit Weatherby in the ribcage with the stock of his rifle. The *Daedalus* officer stumbled to the side, leaving himself open to the rifleman's bayonet.

Shaila arrived just in time to grab the rifleman's arm, using his forward motion to spin him around, where her other fist met his face. She then used a jujitsu move to throw him over onto his back and take the rifle from him, then thrusting the weapon's butt into the hapless man's face to finish the job.

"Hand-to-hand training, I take it," Weatherby said as Shaila helped him up. To his credit, he didn't hesitate in taking the proffered hand. "Quite impressive, Lieutenant."

"Thank you, Lieutenant," she said cooly. *Take that, Neanderthal.* She turned around, expecting the rest of their combined force to be right behind them. Instead, they were back down the hall, huddled together over one of the McAuliffe astronauts.

Shaila took off at a run back down the hall, only to find Diaz prone on the floor, her pressure suit blotched with a growing pool of red blood on the left side of her abdomen.

"Report," Shaila said curtly, worry on her face.

Finch didn't bother to look up as he cut open the pressure suit with his good arm. "Musket shot," he said. "The round appears to be still inside."

Diaz was still awake, grimacing through the pain. "Jain, get everyone in there and figure out what's going on. I'll be fine right here."

Weatherby knelt beside her. "No, madam, you must be treated. Dr. Finch, are you well enough?"

"It is not me I am worried about," he said as he stripped off his waistcoat and used it to put pressure on the wound. "I must create more curatives. And I need more light!"

Shaila and Weatherby glanced at each other a moment, asking and answering the same question wordlessly. "Stephane," Shaila said, "help Finch get her back outside. Take her to the side of the temple, out of sight as best you can."

"Yes," Stephane replied. "Colonel, we must get you standing up."

"Negative, dammit. Just leave me here and go!" Diaz hissed. But her protest went unanswered as the two men slowly pulled her up, supporting either side of her.

"Sorry, Colonel," Shaila said gently. "You're too exposed here, and you're bleeding out." She paused and smiled. "I'm sure there's a reg somewhere that lets me countermand your orders."

Diaz tried to laugh, but grimaced in pain instead. "Ow, dammit. OK. Let's go, guys. Yuna, take my zapper and put it on wide-arc."

Yuna carefully took the weapon from Diaz' belt. "Yes, ma'am," she said softly, adjusting the zapper's setting. "Get better."

Shaila watched the doctors take Diaz haltingly back down the hallway, then turned to the rest. "OK, move out. Let's get a look at those doors."

A moment later, they were assessing the large double-doors that apparently led to the building's central space. They were seemingly made of metal, not stone. Each door had an image of the Tree of Life in relief upon its surface, and was otherwise covered in patterns of sigils. There were no handles, and it appeared the hinges were on the other side, meaning that they swung inward.

Weatherby put his shoulder to the door and felt it give slightly. "I believe it is merely barred from the inside," he said, taking his sword in hand. He slid the blade in the crack between the two doors, and swung downward. A crunch indicated the blade hit true, and the doors rattled as voices could be heard shouting from the other side.

"Well done," St. Germain said. "Now, let us see what my errant student is up to."

Before they could go forward, Shaila's comm buzzed. "McAuliffe to Diaz, come in, over."

"Jain here," Shaila said. "The colonel's been wounded and we're all pretty busy right now."

"Sorry, ma'am, but I have the results of the search Col. Diaz asked me to do."

Shaila held her hand up, motioning for the others to stop. "Talk to me, Adams."

"Well, I had to go back quite a ways, and I had to account for the access roads that cross through that area," Adams said. "There really wasn't much regular activity going on until about eight years ago."

"Get to the end," Shaila snapped.

"Right, sorry, ma'am," Adams said. "The only person who repeatedly visited the area in question was Dr. Hiyashi, and she's been through that area regularly every few weeks since she got here, until about six months ago. Then it was a bunch of Billiton people taking over. There's a handful of those radio signals in those same areas as well."

Shaila whipped around to look at Yuna and saw that she had Diaz' zapper pointed at the rest of the group. Any other reaction was cut off as every cell in Shaila's body erupted in pain, with only the blackness of unconsciousness giving her any reprieve.

Waking up from a microwave-emitter shot was something akin to a horrible hangover after a night of epic binge drinking. The first thing Shaila felt was her head, which ached and pounded ferociously. The nausea came next, and it was all she could do not to cough up breakfast on the ground next to her.

Then she realized she was indeed lying on the ground. A stone floor, to be exact. That brought her mind back to the present and, along with it, a furious urge to punch Yuna Hiyashi in the face.

"Eleven minutes," she heard a voice say. "That's impressive, Shaila. I'm so sorry I had to do that."

Shaila opened her eyes to see Yuna crouched over her. The older woman's face remained kindly, but there was something else to it as well. It held contained excitement and muted rapture, the zeal of a true believer kept in check by a lifetime of self-discipline.

"Not as sorry as you will be," Shaila muttered. She tried to move her hands, but found they were tied behind her back. Same with her feet. "So what's going on, Yuna?" she asked crossly.

"The preparations are complete. Althotas will be here soon. And we're going to welcome the first alien life form mankind has ever encountered. First contact, Shaila! It's a historic moment," Yuna said, eyes shining.

Shaila's mind cleared a bit more. Looking around, she saw a few more pirate goons with muskets standing around, their weapons casually pointed down at her and...the others. Looking over her shoulder, she saw Weatherby, Greene and St. Germain lying next to her, still out cold. They were, by all appearances, beyond the doors and inside the pyramid's central chamber, but Shaila could see little of it behind Yuna.

"Right," Shaila said, turning back to Yuna. "So if this is all so lovely, why turn on us?"

"Because these primitives," Yuna said, nodding at Weatherby and St. Germain, "were completely misinformed about Althotas' intentions."

"And you weren't?"

Yuna smiled again, which only pissed off Shaila more. "It started as these recurring dreams, about fifteen years ago, right after the Europa landing. They seemed silly, really. But I remembered enough of the symbolism within them that I started to do some research. That led me to the pieces of evidence I found, scattered throughout the scientific data, the history, archeology. Thousands of years of it. I tracked down the clues, broke the codes, and understood how to create the gateway necessary to bring him here. So I transferred to Mars, even though I knew it meant never returning to Earth again."

"And you planted your little EM boxes and got 'em up and running," Shaila said, her voice rising. "Screwed around with the suit beacons to cover your tracks. You tried to hide the Cherenkov radiation signature in the database. You put me in medical and you killed that miner!"

Michael J. Martinez

Yuna looked down, seeming chastened. "This was not how I wanted it to go. I never expected Billiton would survey that lava tube. I had filed reports years ago saying it wouldn't be a good site. But Kaczynski had to go out there, and you followed him. I knew the time was getting short. I'm sorry. I didn't mean to hurt anyone."

"Doesn't bring Jack Heath back," Shaila spat.

"You don't understand, Shaila. Althotas will be the first alien humans will ever encounter," Yuna said. "I know that he comes in peace. He will help us. The knowledge he possesses will put us light-years ahead of where we are today in terms of technology, exploration...."

"Dr. Hiyashi?" a deep voice boomed from the heart of the room.

Yuna turned and rose. Behind her, Shaila saw a man approaching. He was short, somewhat rotund, with graying hair pulled back into a Beethoven-style ponytail. His face was round, and his eyes bulged out from his face slightly, making him look as though he were always slightly alarmed. He was wearing a long white robe, adorned with sigils and pictures similar to the ones in the pathway and hallway walls. Shaila could see his buckled shoes and stockings peeking out from under it.

"Yes, Count Cagliostro?" Yuna said.

"We are about to begin," he replied in a slight Italian accent, before looking down at Shaila. "Ah, awake already? I do hope you aren't entirely uncomfortable, milady. This is an unfortunate but necessary measure. I assure you, you will be freed when our great working is complete." He fixed Shaila with a gentle smile.

He doesn't look like a murderer or a nutcase, Shaila thought. *I suppose they never do, do they?* She wracked her brain for anything she might say that could try to disrupt things, but came up with next to nothing. "You look ridiculous, you know that?" she told the alchemist.

Cagliostro frowned a moment, then allowed a smirk to play across his face. "Those who do not understand have always mocked those who do," he said, as though to an errant child.

"I should think a good mocking would do you some good, Alessandro," said a voice next to Shaila. It appeared St. Germain was awake as well. "You are naught but a fool. The Xan imprisoned Althotas for a reason. Freeing him is madness."

Cagliostro turned to his old mentor with a wicked grin. "My dear Francis,

352

I am glad you are awake. We can, of course, debate the matter later, if you like, but for the moment, I shall only ask you a question. Did Althotas' forces destroy Phaeton, turning it into that which is called the Rocky Main? Did Althotas raze Mars and reduce it to a waste? No, of course not. It was the Xan. The same race which has written the history of Althotas for your unquestioning consumption."

"And I suppose Althotas himself has told you something quite different?" St. Germain said.

"Do not be jealous, Francis. It is woefully unbecoming of such a great mind as yours. Wait but a while, and soon you may debate me freely in the presence of the Ascended Master himself."

Cagliostro turned to go back into the center of the chamber, with Yuna following, but Shaila shouted after them. "If this Althotas is such a nice guy, why are you running around killing people? You think he'd like that?"

Yuna hesitated, but kept walking, while Cagliostro turned, a sad look on his face, to address Shaila. "Milady, rest assured, I regret the harm I have inflicted. My instruments in this quest have been too blunt, I agree," he said, nodding toward the surly-looking pirates nearby. "Time was of the essence, and a handful of lives cannot be justly weighed against the paradise this working will usher in upon both our universes." With that, he walked off.

"Idiocy!" St. Germain grumbled.

"Men often do the worst evil whilst believing in their own righteousness," Weatherby said quietly, shaking his head to fight off the after-effects of the zapper.

Shaila looked around. Weatherby and St. Germain were both fully awake, glaring after Cagliostro. Greene was just coming to, his head lolling on the ground. "I've never been hit with one of those before," Greene said. "That was awful."

"All right, everyone," Shaila said quietly. "First rule, assess the situation. Take a hard look around for a minute. Think strategically."

All four captives began looking around as best they could, though they were all lying on their sides, wrists and ankles bound tightly. They were in a large square room, perhaps twenty meters per side, with walls made from massive red-stone blocks, rough-hewn and aged. There were carvings here, too—four figures, some thirty meters high, adorned each wall. Each figure was vaguely humanoid, with elongated bodies and massive eyes taking up the upper half of their heads. One held a bowl, a second held a sword, while a third held a long staff in its hand. The fourth, opposite the door, seemed to be cupping a planet, perhaps even Mars, in its hands. Each figure was framed by a series of Martian sigils. The whole place was lit by torches, though the ceiling, some forty meters above, remained shrouded in shadow. There was red dust everywhere.

The center of the room held a raised platform, about a meter and a half above the floor and about four square meters wide, with steps leading up to it so that someone could enter the double doors and walk right up. Upon the platform stood an altar of red stone with white veins throughout, polished to absolute smoothness. There seemed to be a number of items on the altar, but Shaila couldn't see what they were. Yuna stood to one side, using Greene's holocam to record the proceedings.

Cagliostro was climbing the stairs to the altar, which faced away from the entry doors and toward the figure carrying the planet. He stopped briefly to converse in French with one of the guards—most likely the one who just inherited command from whoever was in charge in the hallway.

Whispering amongst themselves, the captives quickly took stock of their situation. There were still half a dozen armed guards—two at the door and four standing over them, but they were paying more attention to the altar than the prisoners. There was only one door, but a lever near the altar seemed to pull on a rope that led off to one of the walls, and from there up toward the ceiling—a trap door, perhaps.

"Cagliostro seems to have completed his preliminaries," St. Germain said, peering at his one-time student. "This is a highly occult ritual. It stretches the very bounds between alchemy and the darker sciences of sorcery."

"You guys have sorcery?" Shaila asked.

St. Germain blinked. "Alchemy is a refinement of ancient occult practices and primitive science and medicine, milady," he explained, as if it were the most obvious thing in the world.

"Du calme!" one of the guards growled, motioning with his bayonet-tipped musket. Shaila didn't speak French, but a translation was utterly unnecessary. The guards quickly descended upon the captives, grabbing them by their shirts or suits and shoving them up to a seated position against the wall, just out of reach of one another. The one who moved Shaila caressed her face with a filthy, calloused hand. She thought about biting him, but decided to choose her battles. So she simply glared. He laughed before turning to watch the altar once more.

Their new seated positions allowed them to look around a bit better. Shaila spotted their weapons—pistols, swords and her zapper—in a pile next to the raised platform. Thankfully, she didn't see any more guards.

"Let us begin this Great Work," Cagliostro intoned from atop the dais. He spread his arms wide. "Mighty Althotas! Ascended Master! You who have been unjustly imprisoned for defending your people! Your humble student has gathered the keys to your release!"

Shaila shook her head in disbelief. "He can't be serious," she said quietly.

To her left, St. Germain chuckled ruefully. "My student was always a bit grandiose," he whispered.

Cagliostro continued: "I call upon the great Ascended Masters of the past to aid in this working. To the east, I call upon the keeper of air, she who is called Nut, Enlil, Hou Tu." Cagliostro bowed toward the carved figure on the wall carrying a staff before continuing. "To the south, I call on the bringer of fire, he who is called Utu, Ra, Zhu Rong." That was followed by a bow to the figure with the sword.

"To the west, I call on the master of the waters, she who is called Naunet, Ki, Mazu." Another bow, this one toward the figure with the cup. "And finally, to the north, I call upon the protector of the lands, he who is called Geb, Nunurta, Tu Di Going." Cagliostro bowed lastly to the figure holding a planet in his hands.

"Those names sound familiar," Greene whispered. "Ancient gods?"

St. Germain nodded. "From what we learned from the Xan on Callisto, it's quite possible the Martians appeared to early humans as such. I imagine the names are but symbols for the figures you see upon the walls. All that should be needed for this particular ritual is the acknowledgement, not their actual Martian names, which are likely lost to history."

Cagliostro was walking around the altar, sprinkling a powder on the floor and then flinging the rest toward the wall opposite the doors before taking his place at the altar once more. "This circle is cast. Althotas! The time of your freedom is nigh! Come forth to the bars of your prison, so that you may be released! I call upon thee to take your place in the tree, in the sphere of Malkuth!"

The floor of the place rumbled for several seconds, sending fine red dust floating down from the walls. Yuna looked around excitedly, panning across the room with the holocam before refocusing it on Cagliostro, who stood quietly, head bowed.

"I guess he's here," Shaila said, turning to St. Germain. "How long do you think we have?"

"Cagliostro likely distilled the essences he needed whilst en route from Jupiter," St. Germain responded. "With the pyramid in such pristine condition, I would venture to suggest he may only need but a few minutes to complete the working now."

"That's it?" Shaila asked, incredulous.

"It would be less but for his penchant for theatrics," St. Germain grumbled. "The difficulty is not in enacting the ritual, but in finding and distilling the appropriate elements."

Shaila strained against the bindings on her hands. They were hempen rope, about a half-inch thick and tied tightly. She started rubbing her wrists up against the wall behind her in hopes of loosening the rope, and saw that Weatherby was doing the same. Already she could tell the knots were expertly tied; it would take several minutes before her hands were free. Of course, after that, there was the little matter of the guards.

Cagliostro spread his arms wide again and continued his intonations. "The tree progresses. We come to great Xanath, your oppressors of old, mighty Althotas. Here, in the sphere of Yesop lies the foundation of your woes, the root of your imprisonment. I cast the mighty Sword of Xanthir to the stone, breaking it in twain, ruining the foundations of tyranny!" With that, the alchemist raised the Xan blade over his head and swung it down upon the altar. The ancient, diamond blade shattered on the stone, producing a crack that resounded through the chamber. The larger pieces slowly rose above the altar, coming together to form a rough-hewn sphere, the smaller pieces forming minute rings.

All four captives began struggling against their bindings as unobtrusively as they could. Thankfully, Cagliostro's guards were too busy looking at the ritual than their charges. "How many of these spheres are there?" Greene whispered.

"Ten," the count responded. "Yet each step is a working in and of itself. There may come a point in his ritual where the harm he has inflicted on the space between spaces becomes irreparable."

Cagliostro placed the broken sword upon the altar carefully; Shaila assumed that the placement would mirror the drawing of the Tree of Life Weatherby had scribed in his journal. The alchemist bowed again, and the floor rumbled a second time.

"Come forth, Althotas, to the sphere of Nod! Splendorous Jupiter awaits!" Cagliostro shouted. "The grand sphere of the star-to-be brings forth her children. Fire, air, earth and water combine to bring forth life once more. Bask in the glory of this simple grandeur, and see the patterns of the elements in which you may take form!"

Cagliostro took a bowl from the side of the altar and poured a vial of water in it. "Europa! Cradle of life," he cried. Next came a small vial of glittering dust, also poured into the bowl. "Ganymede! Bounty of the earth," he said. A light mist began rising from the bowl as Cagliostro took a small bellows and, placing the tip into the bowl, squeezed it. "Callisto! The air of freedom." Finally, he took a small block of charred rock and dropped it into the bowl, quickly standing back as it burst into flame. "Io! Fires of heaven!" he said.

Shaila could see the bowl erupt into flames. Seconds later, a salmon-colored sphere rose out of the bowl, hovering a few inches above it. "The essence of Jupiter awaits, Althotas!" Cagliostro shouted. "The building blocks of form and matter! See how they are made! Take their form as you prepare to rejoin us!"

The room rumbled once more, this time louder and more violently than before, sending a fresh rain of red dust down from the ceiling. Cagliostro bowed his head; Shaila could see the ghost of a smile on the man's face. Yuna continued to record the ritual, scanning around the room now and again with a euphoric look on her face.

The alchemist raised his hands once more. "Mighty Althotas! Your time of victory is nigh! Come to the sphere of Netzach, where your greatest defeat will become your finest hour! Mourn the loss of your sister world, Phaeton, but use the power that destroyed her to break the walls of your prison now!"

Cagliostro placed four rocks in another bowl. "Pallas. Ceres. Juno. Vesta. Come together once more and let your power break through to our Ascended Master!" The rocks suddenly jumped up out the bowl, swirled around each other and collided with a loud crunch and a flash of light. Shaila saw another sphere rise out of the bowl, this one a smooth, perfectly round rock.

As Cagliostro bowed his head, an ear-splitting crack reverberated through the chamber. On the wall facing the altar, the planet in the hands of the Martian god cracked—and a white light seeped through behind it, casting a thin beam down onto the altar.

"That can't be good," Shaila muttered. Her shoulders were starting to ache from the effort against her ropes.

"He has created a breach!" St. Germain said as the floor rumbled once more.

Shaila suddenly felt a pair of hands on her ropes behind her, and felt breath in her ear.

"Sorry I am late," Stephane whispered as he began untying her.

Weatherby glanced over and smiled. "I should never have thought I'd be happy to see a Frenchman."

CHAPTER 27

June 19, 1779
July 28, 2132

"What the hell are you doing here?" Shaila whispered as Stephane struggled against the knots of her bindings.

"We heard the noises from outside," he replied softly. "The colonel ordered us to check on you."

"Us?" Weatherby asked.

"Yes. Finch is preparing some sort of distraction. He says it is something he does best. And we have reinforcements."

Shaila shushed Stephane as she felt the ropes against her hands loosen and slip. She looked toward the guards, but they were all focused squarely on Cagliostro and the ritual, and most had taken several steps forward toward the altar; Stephane must have been able to sneak right in behind them. She quickly moved to untie her legs while Stephane went to work on Weatherby's ropes.

"Keep still," she hissed. "Wait until we're all untied before we make a move."

"If we have time," St. Germain muttered, looking toward Cagliostro, who was on his way to the next sphere on the Tree.

"The beauty that was once Mars shall be again," Cagliostro shouted, once again raising his arms. "In the sphere of Tiphereth lies your home world, mighty Althotas, where your servant awaits you. It has been laid waste to by the cowardly Xan, but hew to the memories of old and see the glories that you may yet again achieve!" Cagliostro took a small metal globe from one side of the altar, holding it within the beam of light. The globe was that of an Earth-like world, with oceans and continents upon it. Shaila could see vestiges of the Martian geography she knew well.

Cagliostro let go of the globe, which hung suspended in mid-air. The floor rumbled once more as he bowed his head.

"That's everyone," Stephane whispered. He looked over toward the door, where Shaila could see Finch peeking around the corner.

"What's your plan?" she whispered.

Stephane turned to her and smiled wanly. "You think there is a plan?"

Suddenly, Finch stepped out into the middle of the entryway, a pistol in one hand and something else in the other that Shaila couldn't see. His arm sported a bloody bandage from his pistol wound, and he looked pale. Nonetheless, he stood tall—and right out in the open. "Cagliostro!" he shouted.

The guards all spun around toward the door, while Cagliostro whipped around, surprised.

And in that moment, Finch fired the pistol.

Cagliostro jumped, then looked down at his robes…and smiled. The shot plowed into the stone behind and to the left of the villain.

"Damn his aim," Weatherby muttered.

Finch was prepared, however. The young alchemist held up the other object—a brass wand about a meter long, attached by various lines and tubes to a small box on his belt. He pressed a button on the wand, and immediately bolts of lightning poured out of it randomly, cracking across the room and striking two of the guards. It also nearly sent a bolt directly into St. Germain, who swore as he rolled away. Soon, the room was filled with prodigious amounts of black smoke, and the lightning stopped as abruptly as it started.

"Capture him!" Cagliostro shouted. Three of his men quickly advanced toward the door, which was fully obscured by smoke.

That's when the rumbling began again—but this time, from the hallway.

Weatherby started to get up, but Shaila held up her hand to keep him there. With the noise from the hall now echoing louder from the chamber, she figured Finch's play wasn't finished yet.

She was right.

More lightning spewed forth into the chamber from the hall as the rumbling grew louder. A roaring crescendo of shouting accompanied the rumbling and seemed now to pursue the *Chance* men back into the ritual chamber, prompting Cagliostro to look up from his preparations in consternation…then shock.

Right upon the heels of the pirates, a wooden spar appeared, attached to the front of what appeared to be a cart…with a squat mast in the middle of it holding up a sail. Finch was at the front of the contraption, frantically turning a wheel attached to his pack that would, by all appearances, get his lightning wand going again. Behind the cart, four men from the *Daedalus* were pushing it at a rapid clip, shouting at the top of their lungs.

And jogging behind them… "Anne?" Weatherby whispered.

"Now!" Finch yelled. With a final shout, the *Daedalans* gave a great heave, sending the wheeled cart flying into the chamber and straight for the altar and Cagliostro. Finch fired his device once more, sending deadly lightning and bilious smoke coursing throughout the chamber—so much, in fact, that Finch toppled over in the cart from the shock as it careened toward Cagliostro.

"Attack!" cried Anne, drawing her sword. The men of the *Daedalus* responded as if Captain Morrow himself had given the order, throwing themselves against their adversaries with naught but dirks and fists. Barely seen through the smoke, the cart—with an unconscious Finch aboard—crashed into the altar pedestal with a massive crunch of wood against stone.

Good a time as any, Shaila thought. "Now!"

She sprung up onto her feet and lunged at the guard two meters in front of her, just as he was turning around and bringing his pistol to bear in response to her shout. Shaila grabbed his wrist and, using the momentum of his turn, swung his arm over her head so that he fired into the wall above. She kept going, twisting his arm further as she crouched and swung her leg out, catching him behind his knees and sending him crashing to the floor. A heavy boot to the face finished the job quickly.

Shaila looked up to see Weatherby awkwardly punching another guard in the face. His form was atrocious, but the hit sent his opponent sprawling to the ground. Weatherby grabbed the man's sword and ran to help St. Germain and Greene, who were struggling with yet another guard. It seemed more pirates had entered the fray behind the sail-cart; pickets from outside the pyramid or stragglers from within, maybe. It was all swordplay now—even Anne was dueling with a couple of unwashed Frenchmen. Shaila looked down at her unconscious opponent again and, cursing inwardly, grabbed the man's sword, hoping she wouldn't stab herself with it if she tried to use it.

As she tested the blade in her hands, she heard Cagliostro's voice once again. "Gebhurah, sphere of strength!" he cried hurriedly, eyeing the battle below him. "The dreams of Althotas' strength will be reality once again. Luna, keeper of dreams, restore the dream of victory to our Ascended Master!" Cagliostro quickly emptied a small pouch of dust onto the altar; the dust motes rose into the air quickly, like a reverse hourglass, until they too formed a sphere that hovered above the altar.

Shaila turned back to her allies. "Weatherby, Stephane, with me," she snapped as she headed toward the altar. "Count, you and Greene figure out a way to disrupt this thing for good." She started for the altar, only to find Yuna rushing down the steps, zapper in hand.

"Down!" Shaila yelled.

Shaila hit the deck as Yuna fired. She heard Greene scream as the wide-array blast hit him and felt his body land on top of hers. As she struggled to get out from under his twitching, unconscious body, she saw Yuna rushing toward her, the older woman's lips forming a thin, frustrated frown as she dodged the numerous hand-to-hand skirmishes that now filled the room.

Yuna raised her zapper once more, just as Shaila had managed to roll Greene off her. She flinched as she saw Yuna pull the trigger…but nothing happened.

Shaila smiled broadly. "Those wide-area shots drain charges pretty fast," she said, getting to her feet in the heavy pressure suit, testing the weight of the cutlass in her hand. "Get out of my way, Yuna."

The older woman looked dismayed, but stood her ground. "I can't," she said. "You're wrong about this, Shaila."

Another rumble filled the room, and Cagliostro started shouting again. "Our Earth is in the sphere of Chesed, and we ask, Althotas, that you show your mercy to our world, knowing that its children are the ones freeing you this day! May all your actions be tempered with mercy, allowing the life embedded in the Philosopher's Stone to thrive!" With that, he pulled a fist-shaped rock out of a bag on the altar.

"The stone!" cried St. Germain from behind Shaila. The alchemist rushed toward his former student, but was tackled before he could get there; one of the guards was not as unconscious as they had thought. Cagliostro took the Philosopher's Stone, placed it into the light, and soon it hovered along with the other spheres above the altar.

Shaila, who had been watching the whole thing, turned back to Yuna and swore to herself for getting distracted; Yuna wasn't there. Shaila swung around, trying to spot her again.

And that's when the wall of the temple exploded, knocking Shaila and everybody else in the chamber to the floor and sending a torrent of pebbles and dust spewing into the room.

"MERCY?"

Shaila shook her head as she tried unsuccessfully to pry herself off the floor, her head pounding in the spot where a brick or rock struck her. The voice she heard—a deep rasp that sounded like an earthquake made of bees—reverberated through her body.

"WHO HAS SHOWN ME MERCY?"

As she struggled to stand, Shaila looked up at the wall facing the altar. The thin beam of light was gone, along with a section of the wall itself. In its place was a swirling vortex of darkness, about three meters wide. The inky depths were so black, Shaila's eyes began to water looking at it.

A cry and a gurgling sound tore her attention from the wall to a spot a few feet to her left, where she saw Weatherby take advantage of the confusion to dispatch another one of the pirates—permanently, this time. His sword withdrew from the man's belly covered in blood.

"CONTINUE THE RITUAL," the voice rasped. "EARN MY MERCY."

Cagliostro dragged himself off the floor, using the altar itself for support. He stared wide-eyed into the void above and in front of him. "My Lord Althotas!" he cried. "I will continue!" With trembling hands, the alchemist snatched up a flower from the altar—the va'hakla plant, Shaila surmised. "Divine mother Venus, housed in the sphere of Binah, source of verdant life! Bring forth the knowledge of life itself, so that matter may take breath and life may flow to you, mighty Althotas!"

Cagliostro released the flower into the air, where it hovered over the altar and, improbably, grew new shoots and blooms even as it too became spherical. The ground trembled once more, the most violent tremor yet, and the hole in the wall grew by at least another meter.

"Lt. Jain!" Weatherby shouted as he staggered over to her. "We must press on!"

Shaila looked around anxiously. "Where's Stephane?"

"I do not know," Weatherby said, taking her arm. "Follow me to the steps. I will clear the way."

The two Royal Navy officers made for the stairs leading to the altar, but were intercepted by the three pirates that had gone after Finch. The ruffians drew their swords and charged. Weatherby rushed forward, attempting to fight them all at once, but one of the three shoved past him and made his way straight for Shaila, sword back and ready to strike.

Reflexively, she raised her own cutlass and managed to parry the blow, sweeping the pirate's blade to her right. She lunged forward in attempt to skewer him, but he sidestepped the blow; she felt his blade crunch into her pressure suit on her right side, felt a sharp line of fire on her skin just below her rib cage. She dropped her blade in pain as a wave of terror swept over her. It was the greatest fear she had ever felt, greater than when *Atlantis* was struck over Jupiter. She knew what she had to do back then, but not now. Not here.

She staggered backward from the pain. Her hands fluttered at her sides, looking for a weapon. They found her helmet instead. She grasped it and, with a scream, lashed out at the man.

The helmet connected with her assailant's head, dazing him and forcing his attempted coup de grace off target. His blade caught more of her pressure suit, but that was all. He stumbled backwards, his sword limp in his hand.

A moment later, he looked down to see a foot of steel protruding from his chest. With a gurgle, he fell to his knees. Behind him, Anne Baker withdrew her sword from his body with efficient prowess and a grim look on her face.

"Miss Baker," Shaila said hoarsely, giving the younger woman—Christ, she was just a girl, really—a nod of gratitude.

Anne nodded back and raised her bloody blade in salute. "Lieutenant," she said, the ghost of a smile approaching her lips for a moment.

"Divine Father Mercury!" they heard Cagliostro cry out. "Come now into the sphere of Chaknah, and show our Ascended Master Althotas your wisdom, so that he may bridge the gap between worlds and slip into the spaces between space!"

Cagliostro opened another vial and a silvery liquid snaked up out of it, forming a swirling globe above the altar. The room rumbled violently.

"Go!" Weatherby shouted. Shaila turned to see him dueling desperately with one of the pirates. The other was dead at his feet. "Go! Stop him!"

With Anne at her side, Shaila ran for the stairs, taking two at a time despite the pain from her wound. The cut wasn't deep, but it was deep enough for her to feel her own blood trickling down her side. She knew she wouldn't have very long before the blood loss countered her own adrenaline.

They reached the top…and froze.

Inside the shattered wall and inky abyss, a face was visible, one that was vaguely human but undeniably beautiful. Long blond hair fell straight from the top of its head, while its alabaster features were both elongated and rounded. The face grew closer with a smile of serenity, and white light began to fill the ritual chamber.

"Althotas!" Cagliostro shouted, ethereal joy spread across his face. "Come toward the portal, my master! Come into a world that welcomes you!"

The angel reached up a robed arm, its hand opened, palm downward, seemingly seeking to grasp the edge of the wall from the inside.

"It's coming through," Anne said quietly, seemingly in awe. All Shaila could do was stare, enraptured, awash in feelings of wonder and peace. What if Yuna was right? What if this…

As the alabaster human hand reached the edge of the portal, it began to change, becoming a sickly shade of green. The fingers—now four instead of five—grew elongated and now sported a wicked barb upon the tips of each. The arm followed, also growing longer and more heavily muscled, covered in a thin sheen of viscousness. Next, a leg began to jut out of the portal, insectoid in movement, covered in the same alien slime. Shaila stared in horror as the four-toed foot—three in front, one jutting right out the back heel—hit the ground.

"YOU HAVE DONE WELL," bellowed the voice from beyond the portal. "I SHALL COMPLETE THIS WORK NOW."

Shaila and Anne turned to Cagliostro, whose furrowed, sweaty brow and open mouth spoke of confusion and terror. "My lord Althotas," he said quietly. "You are not as you once appeared to me."

"YOU SAW THAT WHICH I WISHED YOU TO SEE, AND THAT

WHICH YOU WANTED TO SEE FOR YOUR OWN ENDS," the voice said, a hint of mockery flavoring the gravelly hiss. "I AM AS I ONCE WAS. AND YOUR WORLDS WILL BE MINE ONCE MORE."

Anne didn't bother to wait for Cagliostro's response; she grabbed the alchemist by the arm and, using all her strength, shoved him away. He lost his footing and tumbled down the steps with a scream.

That left Yuna, who had made it to the top of the platform and was staring into the vortex, fear etched on her face.

"How do we close it?" Shaila demanded.

"I don't know," she said softly.

"He told you nothing?" Anne asked incredulously.

Yuna could merely shake her head as Weatherby quickly mounted the steps behind them, having finally dispatched his opponent. However, his left arm was now hanging limply at his side, rendered useless by a pirate blade. He, too, stopped short at the sight before him.

Within the swirling darkness, the face of the angel entered the chamber—and transformed into a monster from Hell.

Its eyes were huge black oval pools, framed by green, slimy skin. Its nose was nothing but two nostrils flat upon its face, its head bare. And its small mouth was open, gaping, full of teeth and dripping ichor.

"STAND ASIDE," the creature said. "MY REBIRTH IS NIGH."

Another arm reached out, gripping the edge of the portal, while the other leg stamped down onto the ground. The rest of the creature unfolded itself from the portal, its torso bony and yet still sinewy. Finally, it stood before them, more than three meters tall.

It smiled. Horribly.

"I AM ALTHOTAS, WARLORD OF MARS," it rasped. "I RULED YOUR WORLDS IN AGES PAST. I WILL DO SO ONCE MORE."

Shaila stopped staring long enough to look down at the altar. The globes hovered there in the shape of the Tree of Life, with only the topmost remaining. "What's left?" she asked. "All the planets, the moons…"

"The sun," Yuna said dully, still staring at Althotas.

Althotas stepped forward to the altar, leaning over it so that he was nearly face to face with Shaila. "KETHER, SOURCE OF LIGHT AND LIGHT. I HARNESS YOUR POWER ONCE MORE. SHINE UPON ME AND ALL SHALL BE AS IT ONCE WAS."

Althotas reached out toward the altar, toward the lever in the floor Greene had spotted earlier. Shaila had no idea what it would do, but it couldn't be good. She rushed forward and swung her blade at the creature's arm.

And missed.

Althotas moved impossibly fast, dodging under her blow to strike her squarely in the chest, sending her sprawling backward into the altar. He then pushed Weatherby backwards with a second lightning strike, sending him sprawling to the ground. Grinning with all its horrible teeth, Althotas grabbed the lever...and pulled.

"NOW!" he rasped, looking up.

Nothing happened.

He yanked at it again.

Nothing.

With an inhuman, ear-splitting shriek, Althotas yanked the lever completely out of the floor, pulling the rope along with it, then looked up expectantly.

A loud crack rang out through the chamber—and a dark green spot appeared over Althotas' left eye. He staggered back with another shriek, clutching his face.

Shaila looked up toward the sound, where she saw Stephane, dangling upside down five meters off the ground, yet with a smoking flintlock in hand. His leg was tangled up in a rope hanging from the ceiling, the unexpected result of his sabotage of the trap door.

"Nice shot," Shaila whispered with a smile. She rolled off the altar, barely managing to stay on her feet and mentally adding broken ribs to her growing list of injuries.

A second shot rang out from behind her. She spun to see Anne with a pistol in hand—where she got it, Shaila couldn't say. The shot managed to hit Althotas squarely in the chest, and the Martian let out a second shriek as it staggered back, clawed hands flailing.

"It's strong," Weatherby said, clawing his way back to his feet. "Pistol shot will not do."

Anne dropped her pistol in frustration. "Where is St. Germain?" she asked.

"He fell in the explosion. Alive, but unconscious," Weatherby said. "It falls to us, now."

Weatherby, Anne and Shaila turned to look at the altar for a moment, keeping one wary eye on Althotas as the creature clutched at its head and chest. There was something that was gnawing at Weatherby's mind, the solution upon his lips but failing to come out.

Anne got it first: "To everything there is an opposite," she said, as if from rote. "What can be done…"

And Finch's words came rushing back to Weatherby. "…can also be un-done by working in reverse!"

Weatherby reached out and quickly took the Mercurium sphere in his hand, feeling it nestle fluidly in his palm. He weighed his options for a moment….

…and then threw it right into the open portal.

A blinding flash of light erupted from the vortex, punctuated by another shriek from Althotas. "NO!" it screamed as the swirling black increased in intensity and speed. "YOU CANNOT!"

Anne picked up the va'hakla flower and threw that as well. It was quite light, so much so that it did not appear the sphere would make the portal. Yet it nonetheless flew directly into the vortex, as if drawn there.

Seizing upon their idea, Shaila grabbed the Philosopher's Stone and like-wise hurled it into the portal. "All of them!" she shouted. "Throw 'em all in!"

But they didn't need to do any more. One by one, the alchemical essences of the Solar System began rising off the altar into the vortex, which grew brighter and swirled even faster, choked with new energy.

As they watched, Althotas too began to be drawn into the portal, his clawed feet scratching at the floor. He reached out and grabbed the altar, a look of terror on his nightmarish face. "YOU CANNOT!" he rasped. "I WILL NOT GO BACK!"

Yuna, who had been watching with disbelief and horror, seemed to find herself in that moment. Grimly she stepped in front of Shaila and Weath-erby. "You will go back," she said quietly. "You tricked us. You had us mur-der for you. Go back there and stay there." And with that, she took a piece of the broken Xan blade from mid-air, just as it was about to rise toward the portal, and drove it into the top of Althotas' head.

Shaila gasped as the creature cried out, a sickly gurgle that echoed in the chamber. It lashed out with its claws, catching Yuna across the face and chest—but in doing so, it lost its grip on the altar and started rising toward the vortex.

Shaila caught Yuna as she crumpled. The older woman's face bore three claw marks that bubbled and oozed with blood and a green, viscous substance; the front of her pressure suit was in tatters. Yuna gasped, eyes like saucers, and began to tremble violently.

Shaila turned to look at Althotas with anger, but the creature was quickly being drawn back into its prison. He was suspended above the floor now, his body entering the vortex as his arms and legs flailed uselessly around him.

"TRAITORS!" he shouted. "ANIMALS! WHEN I RETURN, YOUR PEOPLE WILL BE DESTROYED! I PROMISE YOU! I—"

Althotas was cut off as his head re-entered the portal, leaving only his limbs visible. A few moments after that, only one claw remained, and that too was inexorably drawn back in.

Cradling Yuna's body, Shaila looked up at Weatherby and Anne. "I think we did it," she said, slightly dazed.

The Royal Navy officer nodded, with the bare hint of a smile. "Well done, Lieutenant."

Another blinding flash erupted from the wall, bathing the entire chamber in impossibly bright light. Shaila saw Weatherby turn and shelter Anne in his arms before the light blinded her. A roar of sound flowed into Shaila's ears, followed by silence.

Not quite silence, actually. There was a slight breeze, a very, very cold one. Shaila tried to chase the spots from her eyes and took a deep breath.

Her lungs erupted in protest. And in that moment, she knew she was screwed. The Mars she had known all her life had returned to this place.

Unfortunately, she had no idea where her helmet was.

She clambered slowly to her knees and looked around. There—about 10 meters away, a dented helmet lay upon the rocky surface. She took a step, but immense pain in her side forced her back down to all fours. She looked to see a red mist seeping from the hole in the side of her pressure suit.

Her blood was literally evaporating in the low-pressure Martian atmosphere.

Gasping, Shaila started crawling toward her helmet, scrabbling across the red dust and rock. She felt her eyeballs freezing, becoming sticky against her eyelids, and fresh spots began to appear before her eyes. Her lungs burned as she huffed and puffed, desperate for life-giving oxygen and warmth.

The last thing she saw was her helmet, just a meter out of reach, before everything went black.

CHAPTER 28

August 3, 2132

Shaila's first sensation after falling unconscious was sound, specifically a regular cadence of soft chirps and beeps. The sound faded in and out for what seemed like a very long time as she slept, edging toward consciousness but only to fall away again. A small part of her subconscious grew frustrated with the whole thing.

The next sensation was light. Behind her closed eyelids, she began to discern light and darkness. This prompted her to try to wake up more, but sleep was persistent. She floated in a hazy, beep-strewn state of semi-wakefulness for another unknown span of time.

Finally, she managed to open her eyes, even though her lashes felt crusty and the light hurt like hell. When she was finally able to focus, she saw a face smiling down on her.

"Welcome back," Stephane said softly.

She smiled weakly. The beeps and chirps would be from the medical sensors. She was nice and comfortable and, most importantly, alive.

"What...?" her voice trailed off.

"What happened?" Stephane said, finishing the sentence. "I finally got you into bed." His grin grew wider.

"Asshole," she said weakly, her own smile showing.

Stephane didn't say much more for the next few minutes, stepping back to allow Doug Levin to check her vitals and give her a few doses of something or another. After a moment, she felt more awake and, with a bit of surprise, recognized she was feeling really hungry.

"Can I get something to eat?" she asked quietly.

"Sorry, girlie," Levin said. "You're on a diet until tomorrow at the earliest. You've been through a lot."

"What exactly have I been through?" she asked.

Levin cocked his head toward Stephane. "Damned if I know. It's classified to hell and back. Ask him."

Stephane sat down on the edge of the bed. "To start with, you saved two universes from something really, really disgusting and awful. Yuna's holocam caught everything, even though she had set it down on the altar at some point."

"Wow…I would love to see that holo," Shaila said.

"Not right now. You need rest," Levin said.

"Soon," Stephane added. "It is enough to say that as soon as that Martian thing got sucked back into where it came from, the overlap between our universe and theirs came undone almost instantly."

"And that left me without my helmet," Shaila said.

"It left us all without helmets, my dear. Mine was still attached to my suit, so I was able to get it on quickly. The colonel was some distance away, but I could see she was conscious and able to get her helmet on as well. She managed to keep a finger in the hole in her suit until we could reach her. And that left you and Greene."

"And Yuna."

Stephane bowed his head. "Yuna is dead, Shay," he said quietly. "The wounds were not that severe, but the substance on that creature's claws was poisonous, I am told. We are still analyzing it, but it seems to be something completely new and different."

Shaila paused a moment to take that in. "Greene?" she finally asked.

"He is fine. His suit was intact. He only spent a day in here. Col. Diaz was released yesterday."

"Yesterday…how long have I been out?" Shaila asked.

"Four days." He picked up a chart off the table. "If I am reading this right, you had three broken ribs, four cracked ribs, a slightly punctured lung, a lacerated kidney—lacerated is cut, yes?—a nasty 15-centimeter slash on your side, blood loss, shock, some lung damage due to the cold atmosphere and severe dehydration."

Her eyebrows rose. "And I suppose you're the one who found my helmet and saved me?"

"Of course," he grinned.

"God, you're going to be insufferable now," she said. "How'd you manage the suit rupture?"

"The newbie, as you say, learns well. Duct tape."

"You duct taped the suit?" she asked.

"Actually, Shay, I duct taped your wound, then the suit."

Levin laughed. "Damnedest thing I ever saw, too." Shaila and Stephane turned to look at him, and he quickly decided that he had errands to run elsewhere.

Shaila laid quietly for a moment, absorbing. She thought about complimenting Stephane's ingenuity, but he seemed to be feeling pretty full of himself. "So," she said finally. "What's been going on around here?"

Stephane stood up. "You should hear of that from the colonel," he said. "Things are interesting, but better than you might think." He reached out to hand her a printout. "Your Royal Navy friend left you a note."

It was a letter from Thomas Weatherby.

She frowned. "How'd we get this?" she asked.

"It was the last page of the journal, recorded by the sensors in the containment lab before the book just disappeared. No Cherenkov radiation, no nothing. Just gone."

"How's that even possible?" Shaila said as she looked upon the neat penmanship. "Didn't we seal the gateway?"

"Dr. Greene has his theories," Stephane said. "He believes that there may be some lingering link between our two universes. He went on about sympathetic quantum patterns in space-time and things like that. He lost me quickly. Anyway, it was addressed to you. Of course, we all read it."

"Of course," she smiled. She began to read. "Christ, he spelled my name wrong."

June 21, 1779

To Lieut. Sheila Jane, Royal Navy

I write in the hopes of reaching out one last time to you to apprise you of events that have unfolded after your heroic acts of two days ago. I hope you will be pleased to know that, for the most part, all is well here. Where "here" is in relation to your location, I dare not venture to say. I have heard much from the Count St. Germain on the topic, and my head has yet to stop swimming.

Yes, the Count has recovered from his injuries, which were minor. Dr. Finch was wounded again in the wake of his ill-advised but wholly brave surprise, having been shocked by his own overloaded device, but he is coming along well, it seems. Miss Baker is likewise well, and has managed to salvage her sail-cart, which brought her to our rescue so expediently. She has christened it Second Chance, *and I find the name wholly fitting. We all hope that you, your commander and your fellows are similarly recovering from these extraordinary events.*

We have signaled the Badger *successfully, and now merely await our rescue, though this will likely take at least a month. Our stores should be sufficient, and the men tell me that certain Martian beasts make good eating. Though you have not met him in person, you should also know that Captain Morrow is up and about, and has asked me to send his sincerest compliments.*

Cagliostro now sits in our makeshift brig, salvaged from the remnants of the Daedalus *and* Chance. *Dr. Franklin and St. Germain pepper him with questions constantly, to which he responds most dully, though with exactitude, I am told. He is a broken man. Like your colleague, I dare say he was duped by the creature we saw. We are trying to piece together all that has occurred, as well as the repercussions thereof. For now, however, we do feel Althotas has been duly thwarted.*

I do not know if you will ever read this. Nonetheless, the Count and Dr. Franklin both believe that you may receive this missive through careful place-ment and the good offices of their alchemy. I pray you do. If so, know that for your heroism and bravery, you have my deepest gratitude, and that of my crew and compatriots as well. We are of very different times and worlds, it would seem, but if His Majesty's Royal Navy produces officers of your caliber in 350 years, I will sleep soundly to-night, with great confidence in the future of any world in which you may play a part.

With respect and admiration,

Lieut. Thomas Weatherby, HMS Daedalus

August 4, 2132

"Way to score one for the ladies, Commander," Diaz said as she entered the medical berth.

Shaila was reading Weatherby's letter again. In fact, the printout was starting to look a little weathered from all the handling it had received.

"Thanks, ma'am," Shaila said with a small grin. She then paused. "Commander?" she added with some confusion.

"Yep," Diaz replied, wincing as she pulled a datapad out of her pocket. "Still a bit sore from that bullet. Anyway: 'By order of the Admiralty, Lt. Shaila Jain is hereby promoted to the rank of lieutenant commander, with all the duties and privileges thereof.' Signed Admiral Sir So-and-So, First Sea Lord, bunch of initials after that, whatever." She tossed the datapad on the table next to the bed. "Congratulations, Commander. I'd salute, but my side's killing me."

Shaila smiled, but said nothing. Her first instinct was to say something pithy and self-deprecating, but the words sounded hollow before she even said them. She did, however, have to fight back a tear or two.

"Nice to know you have a future ahead of you, isn't it," Diaz said quietly as she sat on the bed.

"Aye, ma'am," Shaila replied, finding her composure once more. She looked up and saw a star on Diaz' coverall. "You got new jewelry too?"

It was Diaz' turn to grin big. "Brigadier general. Saving the multiverse has its privileges," she said. "Besides, I didn't want you catching up to me so damn fast."

"Couldn't have that," Shaila said. "You've been busy."

"We all have. You're lucky. You got to sleep through it," Diaz responded. "Reactor's back online thankfully, and I've had teams out with sensors since I woke up. Houston's having kittens. Their experts are still nearly three weeks out, so it's up to us to give them answers."

"And do we have any?"

"Just more questions," Diaz said. "The affected area still has traces of Cherenkov radiation here and there, but far less than before. The atmospheric and gravitational anomalies are just plain gone. You see the holovid yet?"

Shaila frowned. "No, Levin won't let me."

"Probably smart. That was some scary shit out there, Jain. And if it weren't so crazy, I'd say Houston was over-reacting. But it *is* crazy, so I'd say they're handling it well. And Harry's actually been pretty forthcoming with resources and data, for a change. Oh, and he's dropped the assault charges against you.

"And with that cleared up, you might be happy to know that you've been offered a couple of new assignments," Diaz added.

"Oh? Already?" Shaila said. "Like what?"

"One, JSC is starting up a brand new task force to study the phenomena here and on Earth. Codenamed DAEDALUS, of course. They even convinced Greene to quit his show and come on as the science lead for it."

Shaila smiled. "He must be thrilled."

"Like a pig in shit. I don't think he's slept in days. Anyway, DAEDALUS is ultimately tasked with the study of extradimensional science, such as it is, along with extradimensional defense, should that ugly son of a bitch try to come back. Maybe even extradimensional travel, if we can pull it off. Greene thinks we can."

"Which would make us...dimensanauts?"

"Cute. Anyway, you can sign up with us if you want," Diaz said. "I'm heading up the military side of it and I need an XO."

Shaila blinked in surprise. "Really? Thanks."

"Well, you haven't heard the other offer," Diaz said. "They've re-tasked the *Armstrong*. No more Jupiter. After everything we've read about the Xan, they're sending her to Saturn. Major mission, multiple landings, you name it. Well funded this time, too. And they need an experienced pilot and EVA specialist."

Shaila exhaled. "Wow. Saturn."

"The next final frontier," Diaz smiled. "It's a long-ass trip, but the ship's top notch." The general looked over her shoulder for a moment. "And the planetary scientist they got going with them is pretty cute, too."

It took a moment for Shaila to realize what Diaz was saying. "Stephane's going?"

The general grinned and arched an eyebrow. "Yep."

Shaila's face turned a deep shade of red. "Huh. Well. Um...I guess I'll have to think about it."

Diaz stood up. "Oh, bullshit. Go to Saturn. Be the first pilot to surf the rings or something. Nice thing is, it isn't leaving for another year. You can come play with DAEDALUS for a while and join up again when you get back."

"Thanks," Shaila said, looking down at her hands, again at a loss for words.

Diaz put a hand on her shoulder. "You know, Shaila, this whole thing is already being covered up huge. Very few people will ever know what you did out there. But those who *do* know are pretty high up there, and they're really proud of you. You did *so* good."

Shaila nodded and tried to smile, but could not help but think that she hadn't told anyone about the voices or visions she experienced in the cave. Doing so now could screw her chances of flying again. She wasn't going to let that happen—in fact, the tears started coming as she contemplated losing out on that.

Another voice clamored in from the corridor. "*Now* can I see her again?"

Diaz winked at Shaila, who snuffled a bit and put a smile back on her face. "Sorry, Steve," Diaz called out. "Debriefing, you know." The colonel turned back to Shaila, whispering, "I've had to order him three times not to loiter around in here."

"She is fine, is she not?" Stephane protested.

Diaz raised her good hand. "OK, OK, I'm going, I'm going. Geez." She looked back down at Shaila with a wink. "But if you're in bed any longer than necessary, I'm writing you both up for dereliction of duty." Diaz turned and headed for the door. "You behave yourself, Steve." She gave him a clap on the arm.

"Shoo!" Stephane said. "I mean, *please* shoo, General."

When Diaz left, Shaila gave Stephane an amused look. "Hear you're taking a trip."

"A little one," he allowed as he took a seat on her bed. "I hear the view is fabulous. And they say the pilot is pretty good."

"I haven't said whether I'm going," Shaila said.

Stephane looked at her incredulously. "Please. You are an explorer. And you made me one, too."

"Yeah?"

"Yeah. How can I go to a teaching job after this? You and I are the only living humans in the universe—well, this universe—to see a real live alien."

Shaila thought about that for a moment. "I guess we are. Too bad he was such a bastard."

"Well, yes. Anyway, I think the people in Houston would be quite happy to see us both off on a journey for a few years. Fewer people to talk to about what we saw."

"Good point," Shaila said. "Of course, I could go to work for Diaz' task force instead. Maybe even go back and see Weatherby again."

"Trying to make me jealous?" Stephane asked.

"Maybe."

"It is working," he said with a lopsided grin. "I never thought I would say this to a woman, but why not." His face grew serious as he leaned in toward her, his eyes meeting hers. "Come to Saturn with me."

A shiver ran up her spine and a smile crept across her face. "That's absolutely the hottest thing I've ever heard," she said quietly.

"Is that a yes?"

"Yes."

They looked at each other for a few moments, both grinning like idiots, until Shaila couldn't take it any longer. "So is this the part where you kiss me or something?"

Stephane raised an eyebrow and looked up at the monitor above her head. "If I am reading this right, your heart rate and temperature are increasing," he said with a smirk. "I would hate to tell Levin you are not behaving."

Shaila laughed. "You wouldn't."

"No, I wouldn't," he said gently. "But you still need rest, and I want you well again. Once you have been freed from here, I will ravish you then."

"Ravish?" Shaila said, parroting his outrageous pronunciation of the word. "You looked that up, didn't you."

Stephane grinned as he headed for the door. "Of course. And a lot of other interesting words. It is a long trip to Saturn."

Shaila watched him leave, then laid back on the bed with a smile—and a wince. Her side hurt, her lungs felt charred inside and she could barely lift the datapad in front of her.

In all her life, she never felt better. Yeah, she still had some questions about the voices she heard in her head through all this, but with a Saturn mission to think about—not to mention the company on the trip—she was able to put it out of her mind. It was probably just some kind of quantum overlap. Maybe one day she'd ask Greene about it, when she was far enough away for him not to want to dissect her brain.

EPILOGUE

June 22, 1779

Lt. Thomas Weatherby stood at the helm of the broken frigate *Daedalus*, his hand upon the weathered wheel. Somehow, the damage was far worse than he remembered. She had been a beautiful ship. For all the lives lost in the pursuit of Cagliostro, he mourned the loss of the *Daedalus* nearly as much.

And the questions in his mind continued to spin. Yes, the Mercurium was restored to England with the capture of Cagliostro. And more importantly, Althotas was once again imprisoned in his inscrutable prison-realm. But even that seemed small, somehow. The Xan remained out there, and Franklin had voiced his concern, more than once, that some among their number may have aided Cagliostro somehow. Were they also in contact with Althotas? Or did the warlike faction among them, no matter how greatly in the minority, seize upon the opportunity that Cagliostro presented to them? What would become of Earth, especially when mankind was far from united and far from enlightened, despite the Xan's comment to the contrary?

And what of the other realm he had glimpsed? An entire universe, held away from his own, behind an inscrutable veil that he couldn't even begin to comprehend, much less describe.

Shouts and applause distracted him from his gloomy reverie. He looked out over the Martian terrain, now strewn with various tables, chairs and tents on the lee side of the vessel, shaded in the afternoon Martian sun, the crew's new home while they awaited rescue. Beyond that, a number of the men had started up a cricket game, with O'Brian refereeing the affair, and apparently someone had just scored. He felt a twinge of jealousy that they could enjoy such simple pursuits, and wondered if he could ever lose himself so easily in simple camaraderie any more.

Watching from the sidelines at a table set for tea—grounded or not, they remained Englishmen, after all—were the Count, Franklin and...Anne. He watched as the three talked animatedly, seeming more distracted by the game than watching it. Weatherby looked off toward the bow of the ship, where *Second Chance* stood in proudly in the light. Over the past few days, the little sail-cart had aided foraging, hunting and scouting immensely. It was a little wonder, but far less so than its creator. Weatherby watched Anne laugh with Franklin, and noticed that she debated the Count St. Germain more freely than ever. She was, in so many ways, a woman coming into her own.

"Sad to see her this way," said a voice from behind him.

Weatherby turned and saluted Capt. Morrow. "Ummm...excuse me, sir?"

"The ship, Mr. Weatherby," Morrow said, taking in the battered vessel with a glance. "She was a good ship.

"The finest," Weatherby said. "As bold and true as her captain and crew, I would say."

"Thank you, Mr. Weatherby," Morrow said quietly. The two stood on the quarterdeck for a few minutes, looking over the wreckage, until Morrow spoke once more. "How is Miss Baker faring?"

Weatherby cleared his throat. "Well, sir. She has been spending much time with St. Germain. I am told he may even take her on as an apprentice."

Morrow smiled. "You are told?"

"Aye, sir. I...I'm afraid I may have misspoke to her at one point."

"And misjudged her, I should think," Morrow said gently.

"Aye, sir," he admitted.

Morrow sighed. "And now?"

"I have always believed, sir, that he who is without sin should be the first to cast stones. It took Dr. Finch, of all people, to remind me of that." The two officers smirked at this before Weatherby continued. "And yet the sin of pride led me to cast my own. What she may have done in the past is not whom she is today. I do not blame her for not wishing to speak with me,"

Weatherby said sadly. "She will do well with the Count, I believe. A woman who sets her mind to something can be quite formidable."

Morrow smiled at that. "So it seems. Was our little alchemical society able to send off your letter to Lt. Jain?"

"The journal disappeared briefly, sir," Weatherby said. "They said that would be enough."

"Well, then," Morrow said. "Mr. Weatherby, I would like to make you an offer."

"Sir?"

"Our orders were to make for Ganymede, of course. What I failed to disclose at the time was that, once there, I was to take command of *Invincible*, leaving *Daedalus* under the command of Mr. Plumb."

Weatherby smiled. The *Invincible* was an impressive 74-gun vessel, a third-rate ship of the line and one of the most powerful 'round Jupiter. "Congratulations, sir! That is wonderful news."

"Yes, yes," Morrow said, "I suppose it is. I assume that, despite the loss of the *Daedalus*, we have comported ourselves well enough for me to assume that command regardless, especially now that Cagliostro has surrendered the Mercurium formula." Morrow turned to address Weatherby directly. "If that be the case, I should very much like it if you would agree to join me as first lieutenant."

The younger man blinked several times. "Why, um…of course! Yes, gladly!" he blurted out before regaining his composure. "I mean, it would be an honor, sir. Thank you."

Morrow extended his hand, which Weatherby took firmly. "No need to thank me, Mr. Weatherby. You've performed admirably here on Mars. In fact, admirably does not even begin to describe it." Morrow nodded down to the shady side of the ship, where Dr. Finch had already joined the other alchemists at table. "Shall we join our learned colleagues and see what new discoveries they've made over tea?"

Weatherby smiled as he assisted the still-healing captain down the stairs. They made their way through the wreckage of the main deck and down into what was once the hold; by ducking, they could wend their way to a hole in the hull large enough for them to leave the ship.

"I tell you, Franklin, I find the whole matter extremely troublesome," they heard St. Germain state loudly. "I would never have recommended such an impetuous ploy!"

"Now, now, my lord, what's all this?" Morrow said as he approached. Dr. Finch hastily rose and grabbed chairs for the two newcomers.

"My apologies, Captain," St. Germain responded, still scowling. "We were discussing the implications of the method used to close the portal between and betwixt the two universes involved in Althotas' plottings."

Weatherby frowned. "Am I to take it that there may be some issue with our conduct?"

St. Germain turned beet red, enough so that Franklin reached out and laid a hand on his arm. "Now, Lieutenant, let us say up front that you and your compatriots from the other realm, for want of a better word, acted most bravely and with great insight," Franklin said with a smile and a side-long glance at St. Germain. "The actions that you and Lt. Jain—it was Jain, was it?—the actions you took were exceedingly intuitive and most valiant."

"But?" Morrow said, watching as the ship's steward poured his tea.

"But," Finch said, "there is some question as to what might have become of those alchemical essences. If I may translate for my shipmates, gentlemen?" Franklin nodded, while St. Germain still seethed. "You see, by disposing of the alchemical essences in the reverse order of the ritual, you rightly assumed the ritual would be undone, and that Althotas would be returned to his prison."

"Indeed. All well and good," Morrow said as he poured his tea. "So?"

It was Anne who continued Finch's thought. "We all believe, sir, each of us, that it was unnecessary to actually hurl the essences back into the portal. Simply removing them from the altar might have been enough. If not that, destroying them might have sufficed."

"Very well then, but the deed is done," Weatherby said, trying not to sound put off, though Anne found reason to frown slightly at him anyway. "I am sorry, Count, if the Philosopher's Stone is lost to you, and the other essences besides. It served a greater good."

St. Germain slammed his cup down upon the table. "But now *he* has them!" the count roared.

Morrow looked over at the count. "Who, exactly, has them?"

Franklin spoke up instead. "Well, Captain, if my colleague's fears are correct—"

"They are," St. Germain snapped.

"*If* his fears are correct," Franklin continued, "it would appear that Althotas might now possess these items. Now, granted, we know not how large or small his prison realm may be, nor the extent of the wounds he suffered. It could take him years, even centuries, before he can gather the essences to himself, if he is even still alive. And it's quite unknown whether he could actually employ them to any use whilst still imprisoned."

"But you're worried," Weatherby said, feeling the pit of his stomach lurch slightly.

"Yes, my boy, I'm worried," Franklin replied. "We all are. Perhaps nothing shall come of it, but I do believe it falls to us to be vigilant for signs of future mishaps." Franklin took a sip of tea before continuing. "And really, someone needs to tell the Xan what happened. I dare say there is far more to their stories of Althotas than they have told us."

"In that, I agree," Morrow said. "A diplomatic mission to Callisto, at the very least, is in order, if not to Xanath itself. They imprisoned this monster, and by all appearances, they didn't do a good enough job of it."

"I should very much like to accompany that mission," Franklin said. "I hope the hostilities between the Crown and Ganymede can be resolved amicably for that to take place. For if St. Germain is correct, we shall need to stand together against this threat, should Althotas return."

"In terms of the current disagreement, we will of course do our duty," Morrow said. "But if it's in any way possible to bring you to Xanath, Dr. Franklin, I promise you I shall."

Franklin smiled. "That's all I can ask, Captain."

St. Germain scowled. "He will return, gentlemen. Of that, I have no doubt."

Morrow turned on him. "Then, damn it all, we will face him again!" the captain growled. "Weatherby here did not risk life and limb for you to tell him he did it wrong, man! Your alchemy and your secrets do far too much to imperil people already. I am quite content knowing that, should the time come, we shall stand firm together once more."

As St. Germain looked on, stunned at Morrow's eruption, Franklin smiled and raised his teacup to Morrow. "Well said, captain. We'll stand together, and we'll be ready."

They all raised their teacups in salute. Weatherby tried to catch Anne's eye once more, but she instead nudged the Count, who reluctantly lifted his cup a few inches from the table. That drew a very charming smile, one Weatherby wished had been favored toward himself instead.

May 31, 1785

The young man rushed through the halls of the Ecole des Cadets-gentilshommes, his uniform chafing around his neck as he hurried on to his appointment, brushing past his classmates, some of whom sneered as he sped past. "Le petit general," they whispered after him. *The little general…* Perhaps they had little else to do, but this young man's sights were set much higher.

He jogged the last few yards, stopping to adjust his uniform before knocking. "Come in," came the voice from inside.

The student entered to find his favorite professor, Pierre-Simon Laplace, writing at a desk inside the small but well-furnished room. "Ah, there you are," Laplace said. "You're late."

"I'm sorry," the cadet said, coming to attention before his professor. "Our drills ran late, monsieur le professeur."

Laplace placed his quill back in its inkwell and regarded the young man closely. He was stocky but strong, with a swarthy look to his face and eyes that, even at the age of sixteen, seemed to bore into people. He burned with energy, having completed the two-year course at the school in just one year due to his father's untimely passing—and the resulting lack of tuition.

Laplace was a mathematician, astronomer and alchemist, charged with teaching young men how to aim a cannon properly—child's play, really, for a man of his talents. The school, on the outskirts of Paris, was a playground for the idle privileged, those who would join the ranks of the officer corps for a few years before riding off to their estates.

But this cadet was different. He came from more modest means, but wanted so very much from life. He would suffice.

"Come, sit," Laplace said, motioning his charge toward a chair. "You are, perhaps, not the best student in my classes, but one of the most driven, and I am appreciative of that."

"Thank you, monsieur," the young man said.

"Are you familiar with the art of alchemy, the Great Work?"

At this, the student's brow furrowed under his dark hair. "I have not taken up a full course of study, monsieur. Do you think it necessary?"

"No, no, I merely ask because you may find use for alchemists in your career. The English, as you well know, certainly do."

The young man nodded. "I am familiar with the effects to which alchemy may be employed in battle, and for my chosen vocation, I had hoped it to be enough."

Laplace smiled. "It will be. There is an alchemist, a true master of the Great Work, who has need of a young officer of superior talent and drive. I have recommended you to him."

The cadet's eyes widened. "You are most kind!"

Laplace leaned back in his chair. "Not at all. It is he whom you should thank. He sees the decadence of the current times, sees the empire the English have built, even with their recent losses on Ganymede. He sees France in decline, but would not have it this way."

"Pray, monsieur le professeur, what is his name?"

"He wishes to remain anonymous," Laplace said. "In time, you may meet him. But for now, he seeks to sponsor young men such as yourself, in the hopes that your efforts may work to bring France back to its former glory, and more."

"I am honored, truly," the cadet said. "What is it that he would have me do?"

"For now, nothing," Laplace said. "Finish your schooling. Join the army, as you have planned. Rise through its ranks as you are able, and your new mentor shall pave your way according to your ability. And when the time is right, you might truly make a difference in this world, and others."

The young man nodded, his smile carefully hiding his concerns. There was no true generosity amongst men, and he doubted any man was such a patriot as to sponsor officers for the mere love of king and country. But the cadet was no fool, either. He would accept the aid, rise through the ranks as he had been told, and use this patronage to his own ends.

And one day, he thought, with or without the help of this mysterious alchemist, France will know the name Napoleone di Buonaparte.

ACKNOWLEDGEMENTS

It would be impossible to list everyone who had a hand in the genesis of this novel, but I'll do my best with the space I have. If you're not listed here, I assure you the omission isn't intentional!

My mother always encouraged a love of books and writing, and bought me my first copy of the *Advanced Dungeons & Dragons* books before I even turned 10. And my late grandfather always told me that hard work and determination would pay off. Thank you, Mom and Pop.

More than 20 years in journalism and communications has left me with a ton of people to thank for making me the writer I am today. If you ever edited anything I wrote, know that I was listening—even when it seemed I wasn't—and that you helped me get to the point where I could write this book.

My fantastic agent, Sara Megibow, believed in this book before it was even any good, and taught me so much about the art and business of writing. She is an outstanding agent and a better human being. Never has there been a more determined advocate, and I firmly believe you would not be reading this without her efforts.

I must also thank my old friend Andrew Montgomery, a fantastic writer in his own right, for his ideas and critiques of this book over the past decade. Likewise, Jason M. Hough has been very generous with his time and thoughts on this project, even while working on his own novels. And John LeMaire not only lent his name to a pirate, but used his art to plant amazing visuals in my head so many years ago.

Michael J. Martinez

Jeremy Lassen of Night Shade Books continues to take chances on debut writers, and for that I am most grateful. I learned so much from my editor, Ross E. Lockhart, about what works and doesn't work in fiction writing, and his patience and encouragement were amazing. Thank you to both of you, and to everyone at NSB.

Then there are the two people who make everything in my life worthwhile. My amazing daughter Anna is the soul of kindness, encouragement and love. I hope this book shows her the power of following your dreams and working hard, just like my grandfather's example showed me. You can do it, kid, whatever "it" is.

My wife, Kate, has truly helped make me the person I am to today. Without her patience, support, faith and love, I wouldn't be anywhere near the man I want to be, and this book just wouldn't be here. I love you, Kate.

Finally, to whomever is reading this book, thanks for giving it a shot. I hope you like it!

Michael J. Martinez